JENNIFER ESTEP

D0030397

*Her love life
is killer.*

SPiDER'S BITE

AN ELEMENTAL ASSASSIN BOOK

"JENNIFER ESTEP'S EXCITING
NEW VOICE WILL LEAP INTO READERS'
HEARTS IN A SINGLE BOUND."
—Rachel Gibson, *New York Times* bestselling author

"You're coming with me," he said.

With his free hand, Caine reached inside his jacket pocket and drew out a pair of silverstone handcuffs. He tossed them on the balcony between us. The metal clinked to a stop at my booted feet.

"Put those on."

"Handcuffs. Kinky. But I prefer to have a bit more freedom during sex. Don't you?"

Caine jerked as though I'd yanked the gun out of his hands and shot him. His eyes flicked down my body, going to my breasts and thighs, before coming back to my face. Yeah, he was thinking about it. All the distraction I needed.

"There's no need to bother with those because you aren't taking me in, detective."

"Where are you going to go?" Caine asked. "You're trapped up here."

I smiled. "Me? Trapped? Never."

I turned, leaped up onto the balcony wall, and launched myself over the side into the darkness below.

More praise for *SPIDER'S BITE*

"*Spider's Bite* is a raw, gritty and compelling walk on the wild side, one that had me hooked from the first page. Jennifer Estep has created a fascinating heroine in the morally ambiguous Gin Blanco—I can't wait to read the next chapter of Gin's story."

—Nalini Singh, *New York Times* bestselling author
of *Blaze of Memory*

This title is also available as an eBook.

"I love rooting for the bad guy—especially when she's also the heroine. *Spider's Bite* is a sizzling combination of mystery, magic and murder. Kudos to Jennifer Estep!"

—Jackie Kessler, author of *Hotter Than Hell*

"Jennifer Estep is a dark, lyrical, and fresh voice in urban fantasy. Brimming with high octane-fueled action, labyrinthine conspiracies, and characters who will steal your heart, *Spider's Bite* is an original, fast-paced, tense, and sexy read. Gin is an assassin to die for."

—Adrian Phoenix, author of *In the Blood*

"A sexy and edgy thriller that keeps you turning the pages. In *Spider's Bite,* Jennifer Estep turns up the heat and suspense with Gin Blanco, an assassin whose wit is as sharp as her silverstone knives. . . . She'll leave no stone unturned and no enemy breathing in her quest for revenge. *Spider's Bite* leaves you dying for more."

—Lisa Shearin, national bestselling author of the Raine Benares fantasy series

KARMA GIRL

"Chick lit meets comics lit in Estep's fresh debut. . . . A zippy prose style helps lift this zany caper far above the usual run of paranormal romances." —*Publishers Weekly*

"Secret identities and superpowers take on a delightful and humorous twist in Estep's exciting debut. Fun and sexy. . . . Here's hoping for more Bigtime adventures from this impressive talent." —*Romantic Times*

"Karma Girl is hilarious and, an even better trick, real. We all know these people, but who among us can say we'd seize our destiny the way brokenhearted Carmen does? *Karma Girl* kicks ass!"

—MaryJanice Davidson, *New York Times* bestselling author of *Undead and Unwelcome*

"Jennifer Estep's action-packed world of radioactive goo, alliterative aliases, and very hot-looking leather tights is outrageously entertaining. Jennifer Estep's exciting new voice will leap into readers' hearts in a single bound."

—Rachel Gibson, *New York Times* bestselling author of *True Love and Other Disasters*

"A big thumbs-up. *Karma Girl* had me laughing and cheering to the end! Engrossing, sexy, laugh-out-loud fun. I want to be a superhero!"

—Candace Havens, author of *Dragons Prefer Blondes*

"A fresh, hilarious new voice. *Karma Girl* will have you rooting for the good girls."

—Erin McCarthy, *USA Today* bestselling author of *Bled Dry*

HOT MAMA

"Snappy and diverting." —*Entertainment Weekly*

"Smokin'. . . . Feverishly clever plotting fuels Estep's over-the-top romance." —*Publishers Weekly*

"It's back to Bigtime, NY, for more sexy, sizzling and off-beat adventures with those zany superheroes. Estep's twist on the world of superheroes is kick-ass fun!"

—*Romantic Times*

Spider's BITE

AN ELEMENTAL ASSASSIN BOOK

JENNIFER ESTEP

POCKET BOOKS

New York   London   Toronto   Sydney

Pocket Books
A Division of Simon & Schuster, Inc.
1230 Avenue of the Americas
New York, NY 10020

This book is a work of fiction. Names, characters, places, and incidents either are products of the author's imagination or are used fictitiously. Any resemblance to actual events or locales or persons, living or dead, is entirely coincidental.

First Pocket Books paperback edition February 2010

POCKET and colophon are registered trademarks of Simon & Schuster, Inc.

For information about special discounts for bulk purchases, please contact Simon & Schuster Special Sales at 1-866-506-1949 or business@simonandschuster.com.

The Simon & Schuster Speakers Bureau can bring authors to your live event. For more information or to book an event contact the Simon & Schuster Speakers Bureau at 1-866-248-3049 or visit our website at www.simonspeakers.com.

Cover design and illustration by Tony Mauro

Manufactured in the United States of America

10 9 8 7 6 5 4 3 2 1

ISBN 978-1-4391-4797-9
ISBN 978-1-4391-5543-1 (ebook)

As always, to my mom, for all those trips to the library.

To my grandma, who hates wearing socks.

To Andre, a.k.a. Wheezley Blighter, because I said I would.

And to me, because I always wanted to write an assassin book.

Acknowledgments

Any author will tell you that her book would not be possible without the help and hard work of many, many people. Here are some of the folks who helped bring Gin Blanco and the city of Ashland to life:

Thanks to Kelly Wimmer, for encouraging me to write the book, and to Annelise Robey, for taking me on and being so enthusiastic about the series.

Thanks to Lauren McKenna, for all her editorial advice in the early stages, and to Megan McKeever, for her sharp editorial eye and ready answers to all of my many questions.

You all helped make the book the best it can be, and it's been a pleasure working with you.

And finally, thanks to all the readers out there. Entertaining you is why I write books, and it's always an honor and privilege.

Happy reading!

Spider's BITE

✹ 1 ✹

"My name is Gin, and I kill people."

Normally, my confession would have elicited gasps of surprise. Pale faces. Nervous sweat. Stifled screams. An overturned chair or two as people scrambled to get away before I buried a knife in their heart—or back. A sucking wound was a sucking wound. I wasn't picky about where I caused it.

"Hi, Gin," four people chorused back to me in perfect, dull, monotone unison.

But not in this place. Within the walled confines of Ashland Asylum, my confession, true though it might be, didn't even merit a raised eyebrow, much less shock and frightened awe. I was relatively normal compared to the freaks of nature and magic who populated the grounds. Like Jackson, the seven-foot-tall albino giant seated to my left who drooled worse than a mastiff and gurgled like a three-month-old child.

A long string of clear, glistening spittle dripped out of his oversize lips, but Jackson was too busy cooing nonsense to the crude daisy tattooed on the back of his hand to pay attention. Or do something sane and hygienic, like wipe his mouth. I shifted away from him so I wouldn't come in contact with the oozing mucus.

Disgusting. But Jackson was typical of the sorts of folks in the asylum. *Asylum.* The word always made me smile. Such a pretty name for a hellhole.

It was bad enough I'd been stuck here for almost a week. But what really set me on edge was the noise—and having to listen to the building around me. The screams of the damned and deranged had long ago sunk into the granite walls and floors of the asylum, the way all emotions and actions do over time. Being a Stone elemental, I could feel the vibrations in the rock and hear the constant, insane chatter even through the industrial carpet and my white, cotton socks.

When I'd first gotten here, I'd tried to reach out to the stone, to use my own magic to bring it a bit of comfort. Or at least quiet the screams so I could get some sleep at night. But it had been no use. The stones were too far gone to listen or respond to my magic. Just like the poor souls who shuffled along on top of them.

Now, I just blocked out the damn noise—the way I did so many other things.

A woman at the head of the circle of plastic chairs leaned forward. She was directly across from me, so it was easy for her light eyes to find mine. "Now, Gin, you've made this claim before. We've discussed this.

You only *think* you're an assassin. You are most certainly not one."

Evelyn Edwards. The shrink who was supposed to cure all the crazies in this magical nuthouse. She radiated professional cool and confidence in her tight black pantsuit, ivory blouse, and kitten heels. Square black glasses hung on the end of her pointed nose, highlighting her greenish eyes, and her sandy hair was cropped into a short, tousled bob. Evelyn was pretty enough, but a hungry look pinched her pasty face—a look I recognized. The hard gaze of a sly predator.

The reason I was here today.

"I most certainly am not a mere assassin," I countered. "I'm the Spider. Surely, you've heard of me."

Evelyn rolled her eyes and looked at the tall orderly standing just beyond the ring of chairs. He snickered, then raised his finger to his temple and made a circle.

"Of course I've heard of the Spider," Evelyn said, attempting to be patient. "Everybody's heard of the Spider. But you are certainly not him."

"Her," I corrected.

The orderly snickered again. I raised an eyebrow in displeasure. The joke was on him because that laugh had just cost him his life. I didn't care to be mocked, even if I'd spent the last few days masquerading as a loon.

In order to kill people, you have to get close to them. Put yourself in their world. Make their likes your likes. Their habits your habits. Their thoughts your thoughts.

For this job, putting myself in Evelyn Edwards's world

had meant getting tossed into Ashland Asylum. To Evelyn and her orderly underlings, I was just another schizo dragged off the streets, driven crazy by elemental magic, drugs, or a combination of the two. Another poor, lost ward of the state who wasn't worth their time, attention, consideration, or sympathy.

I'd spent the last few days locked up in the asylum convincing Evelyn and the others I was just as June-bug crazy as the rest of the babbling psychos. Spouting nonsense about being an assassin. Drooling. Finger-painting with the moldy peas they served for lunch. I'd even hacked off gobs of my long, bleached blond hair during craft time to keep up the pretense. The orderlies on call had taken the scissors away from me, but not before I'd used them to pry a screw loose from the rec room table.

The same screw I'd sharpened to a two-inch-long, dartlike point. The same screw I had palmed in my hand. The same screw I was going to shove into Evelyn's throat. The weapon rested on my palm, and the steel felt rough against my scarred skin. Hard. Substantial. Cold. Comforting.

Of course, I didn't really need a weapon to kill the shrink. I could have offed Evelyn with my Stone magic. Could have reached for the elemental power flowing through my veins. Could have tapped into the acres of granite the asylum was constructed out of and made the whole building come crashing down on her head. Using my Stone magic was easier than breathing.

Call it professional pride, but I didn't use my elemental power to kill unless I absolutely had to, unless there was no other way to get the job done. Just too easy otherwise. But even more important, magic got you noticed in these parts. Especially elemental magic. If I started collapsing buildings on people or braining them with bricks, the police and other, more unsavory characters would be sure to take note—and an unhealthy interest in me. I'd made more than my share of enemies over the years, and the only reason I'd stayed alive this long was by keeping to the shadows. By creeping in and out of places completely unnoticed, just the way my namesake did.

Besides, there were plenty of ways to make someone quit breathing. I didn't need my magic to help me with that.

"The Spider." Evelyn's scarlet lips twitched, and she allowed herself a small titter. "As if someone like *you* could be someone like *that*. The most feared assassin in the South."

"East of the Mississippi," I corrected her again. "And I most certainly am the Spider. In fact, I'm going to kill you, Evelyn. T-minus three minutes and counting."

Maybe it was the calm way I stared at her, my gray eyes steady and level. Or perhaps it was the complete lack of emotion in my tone. But the laughter caught and died in Evelyn's throat like an animal in a trap. She wouldn't be too far behind.

I got to my feet and stretched my arms over my head, moving the screw into a better position in my hand. The long-sleeved, white T-shirt I wore rode up over my matching pajama pants, exposing my flat stomach. The tall orderly licked his lips, his eyes locked on my crotch. Dead man walking.

"But enough about me," I said, dropping into my chair once more. "Let's talk about *you,* Evelyn."

She shook her head. "Now, Gin, you know that's against the rules. Therapists aren't allowed to talk to patients about themselves."

"Why not? You've been asking me questions for days now. Trying to get me to open up about my past. To talk about my feelings. To come to grips with the fact I'm cold and emotionally unavailable. Turnabout, you know. Besides, you did plenty of talking to Ricky Jordan."

Her eyes widened behind her glasses. "Where—where did you hear that name?"

I ignored her question. "Ricky Robert Jordan. Age seventeen. An Air elemental with a serious bipolar disorder. A sweet but confused kid, from all accounts. You really shouldn't have gotten involved with him, Evelyn."

The shrink's hand tightened around her long, gold pen until her knuckles cracked from the pressure. The orderly frowned, and his eyes flicked back and forth between us, as though Evelyn and I were playing a game of verbal tennis. Jackson and the three other patients sitting around me kept drooling, gurgling, and murmuring nonsense, locked in their own twisted worlds.

"Correction," I continued. "You shouldn't have used him as your psycho ward boy toy. Did you panic when he realized you weren't really leaving your husband for him? Did he threaten to tell his parents how you seduced him the way you do all the handsome young men put into your care? Is that why you pumped him full of hallucinogens and sent him home to his family?"

Evelyn's breath puffed out of her mouth in short gasps.

The pulse in her throat fluttered like a hummingbird's delicate wings.

I leaned forward, capturing her panicked gaze. "Mommy and Daddy Jordan didn't appreciate it when Ricky had a psychotic break and hung himself in his own closet, Evelyn. But before he died, he wrote them a letter, telling them how he just couldn't go on without *you*."

Normally, I wouldn't have bothered with the whole assassin's exposition. Such a cliché. I would have infiltrated the asylum, killed Evelyn, and escaped before anyone knew she was dead. But letting Evelyn Edwards know exactly why she was dying had been part of the job requirement. And was netting me an extra half million dollars.

"That's why I'm here, Evelyn. That's why you're going to die. You fucked with the wrong boy."

"Guard!" Evelyn screamed.

Last word she ever said. I flicked my wrist, and the sharp point of the screw zipped across the room and sank into her throat, puncturing her windpipe. Ace. Evelyn's scream turned into a whistling wheeze. She slid from her plastic chair and hit the floor. Her hand wrapped around the screw, and she pulled it free. Blood spattered onto the carpet, looking like an abstract Rorschach pattern. Stupid of her. She might have lived another minute if she'd left it in her throat.

The orderly cursed and raced forward, but I was faster. I snatched the shrink's gold pen from the floor where it had fallen, stood up, and rammed it into his heart.

"And you," I murmured in his ear as he jerked and flailed against me, "I'm not getting paid for you. But considering how you get your kicks by raping female patients, I'll consider it a public service. Pro-fucking-bono."

I yanked the pen out of his chest and stabbed him twice more. Once in the stomach, and once in the balls. The flickering, lecherous light in the orderly's eyes dimmed and died. I let go, and he thumped to the floor.

In less than thirty seconds, it was over. Game, set, match. Too easy. I wasn't even winded.

My gray eyes flicked to the four other people in the room. Jackson still drooled at nothing. The other two men stared at the floor as if something was wrong, but they weren't sure what it was. The fourth person, a woman, had already gotten down on her hands and knees. She dipped her fingers into Evelyn's blackening blood, then licked it off like it was the sweetest honey. Vampires. They really would eat anything.

The granite floor's insane murmurs intensified, fueled by the fresh coat of blood seeping through the loose weave in the carpet and dripping onto the stone. The harsh discord made me grind my teeth together. I would be glad to leave this place and that noise behind. Far, far behind.

I yanked the pen out of the orderly's groin and picked up my screw. Witnesses were bad, especially in my line of work, and I considered killing Jackson and the others. But I wasn't here for them. And I didn't slaughter innocents, not even these pathetic souls who would be better off dead and free of their cracked mortal shells.

So I pocketed my still bloody weapons and headed toward the door. Before I stepped out into the hallway, I glanced over my shoulder at Evelyn Edwards's lifeless body. Her face and eyes were wide open in a look of shocked surprise. An expression I'd seen more than once over the years. No matter how bad people were, no matter what evil they committed, or who they fucked over, nobody ever really believed death was coming for them, courtesy of an assassin like me.

Until it was too late.

✵ 2 ✵

Now came the trickier part—getting out of the asylum. Because while all it had taken to get thrown in here was a faked psychotic episode and a few greased palms, several obstacles lay between me and the outside world, namely two dozen orderlies, a couple of security guards, a variety of locks, and twelve-foot-high walls topped with razor wire.

I crept to the end of the hall and peered down the next passageway. Deserted. It was after seven, and most of the patients had already been put back into their padded cells to scream away the night. With any luck, Evelyn and the orderly wouldn't be discovered until morning. But I was going to be long gone before then. Never count on luck to get you through anything. A lesson I'd learned the hard way long ago.

Using the route I'd memorized and keeping in mind the orderlies' timed circular sweeps, it was easy enough to make my way through the dim corridors to the right wing of the asylum. Thanks to the piece of tape I'd put over the lock, the door to one of the supply closets was already open. I slipped inside. Industrial supplies were crammed into the dark area. Mops. Brooms. Toilet paper. Cleaning solvents.

I walked to the back corner, where the builders had been too cheap to cover the granite wall with paint, and pressed my hand to the rough stone. Listening. As a Stone elemental, I had the power, the magic, the ability, to listen to the element wherever it was, in whatever form it took. Whether it was gravel under my feet, a rocky mountain outcropping soaring above my head, or just a simple wall, like the one I had my hand on now, I could hear the stone's vibrations. Since people's emotions and actions sink into their surroundings, especially stone, over time, tuning into those vibrations could tell me a number of things, from the temperament of a person living in a house to whether a murder had taken place on the premises.

But the stone wall underneath my hand only babbled its usual insanity. There were no sharp notes of alarm. No clashing and clanging vibrations of hurried activity. No sudden disturbances rippling through the rock. The bodies hadn't been discovered yet, and my fellow crazies were probably still drooling on each other. Excellent.

I climbed up on a metal shelf set against the wall, pushed aside a loose ceiling tile, and grabbed the plastic-wrapped bundle of clothes I'd hidden there. I stripped off my blood-spattered, white inmate pajamas and shimmied into the new garments. One of the first things I'd done when I'd been committed had been to break into the patients' repository and liberate the clothes I was wearing when the cops had brought me here. In addition to my blue jeans, long-sleeved navy T-shirt, boots, and navy hooded fleece jacket, I'd also had a couple of pocketknives on me, along with a silver watch that had a long spool of garrote wire coiled inside the back. Small, flimsy weapons, but I'd learned long ago to make do with what I had.

In addition to the repository, I'd also paid a visit to the records room, grabbed my fake Jane Doe files, and destroyed those, as well as erased any mention of my stay here from the computer system. Now, there was no trace I'd ever been in the asylum at all. Besides Evelyn Edwards's cooling body, of course.

I snapped the watch around my wrist. A bit of moonlight streaming in the window hit my hand, highlighting a scar embedded deep in my palm. A small circle with eight thin lines radiating out of it. A matching scar decorated my other palm. Spider runes—the symbol for patience.

I uncurled my hands and stared at the lines. At the tender age of thirteen, I'd been beaten, blindfolded, and tortured—forced to hold onto a piece of silverstone metal, a medallion shaped like the spider rune. My hands had been duct-taped around the rune, which had then been superheated by a Fire elemental. The magical metal had melted and burned into my palms, hence the scars. Back then, seventeen years ago, the marks had been fresh, ugly, red—like my screams and the laughter of the bitch who'd tortured me. The scars had faded with time. Now, they were just silvery lines crisscrossing the swirls of my pale skin. I wished my memories of that night were as dull.

Moonlight highlighted the silverstone metal still in my flesh and made the marks more visible than they were during the day. Or maybe that was because I did most of my work at night, when the dark things, the dark emotions, came out to play. Sometimes I almost forgot the runes were there until moments like these, when they showed themselves.

And reminded me of the night my family had been murdered.

I ignored the painful tug of memories and continued with my work. The job was only half-done, and I had no intention of getting caught because I'd become misty-eyed and maudlin over things best forgotten. Emotions were for those too weak to turn them off.

And I hadn't been weak in a very long time.

I stuffed the bloody pajamas and the empty plastic wrap into the bottom of one of the buckets the janitors used to mop the floors. Then I grabbed a can of bleach off the metal shelf, opened it, and dumped the liquid into the bucket. Using my jacket sleeve to hold one of the mop handles, I gave the whole thing a good stir. There'd be no DNA to be had from these clothes. Assuming the police even bothered to check for any. Murders, especially stabbings, weren't exactly uncommon in the asylum, which is why I'd decided to take out the shrink here instead of at her home.

When that was done, I reached into my coat pocket and pulled out a pair of silver glasses with oval frames. The bluish lenses went on my face, obscuring my gray eyes. The other pocket held a baseball hat, to hide my dyed blond hair and cast my features in shadow. Simple tools really did work best, especially when it came to changing your appearance. A bit of glass here, some baggy clothes there, and most people couldn't tell what color your skin was, much less what you actually looked like.

My disguise complete, I palmed one of the pocketknives, opened the door, and stepped out into the hallway.

Wearing my regular clothes and a big ole, friendly, southern smile, I left. Nobody gave me a second look, not even the so-called security guards who were paid for their stellar vigilance and exceptional attention to detail. Five minutes later, I scrawled a fake name across the visitors' sign-out sheet at the front desk. Another orderly, female this time, scowled at me from behind the glass partition.

"Visiting hours were over thirty minutes ago," she sniped, her face drawn tight with disapproval. I'd interrupted her nightly appointment with her romance novel and chocolate bar.

"Oh, I know, sugar," I cooed in my best Scarlett O'Hara voice. "But I had a delivery to make to one of the kitchen folks, and Big Bertha told me to take my sweet time."

Lies, of course. But I put a concerned look on my face to keep up the act.

"I hope that was all right with y'all? Big Bertha said it was fine."

The orderly blanched. Big Bertha was the wizened

woman who ran the kitchen—and just about everything else in the asylum—with an iron fist. Nobody wanted to mess with Big Bertha and risk getting whacked with the cast-iron skillet she always carried. Especially not for twelve bucks an hour.

"Whatever," the orderly snapped. "Just don't let it happen again."

It wouldn't happen again because I had no intention of ever coming back to this horrid place. I turned up the wattage on my fake smile. "Don't worry, sugar, I sure won't."

The orderly buzzed open the door, and I stepped outside. After the asylum's overpowering stench of drool, urine, and bleach, the night air smelled as clean, crisp, and fresh as line-dried sheets. If I hadn't just killed two people, I might have dawdled, enjoying the sound of the frogs croaking in the trees and the soft, answering hoots of the owls in the distance.

Instead, I walked toward the front gate with sure, purposeful steps. The metal rattled back at my approach, and I gave the guard in his bulletproof booth a cheerful wave. He nodded sleepily and went back to the sports section of the newspaper.

I stepped back into the real world. My feet crunched on the gravel scattered outside the gate, and the stone whispered in my ears. Low and steady, like the cars that rumbled over it day in and day out. A far happier sound than the constant, insane shriek of the granite of the asylum.

A large parking lot flanked by a row of dense pine trees greeted me. The far end of the smooth pavement led out to a four-lane road. No headlights could be seen coming or going in either direction. Not surprising.

Ashland Asylum was situated on the edge of Ashland, the southern metropolis that bordered Tennessee, North Carolina, and Virginia. The metropolitan city wasn't as big as Atlanta, but it was close, and one of the jewels of the South. Ashland sprawled over the Appalachian Mountains like a dog splayed out on a cool cement floor in the summertime. The surrounding forests, rolling hills, and lazy rivers gave the city the illusion of being a peaceful, tranquil, pristine place—

A siren blared out, cutting through the still night, overpowering everything else. Illusion shattered once again.

"Lockdown! Lockdown!" someone squawked over the intercom.

So the bodies had been discovered. I picked up my pace, slipped past several cars, and checked my watch. Twenty minutes. Quicker than I'd expected. Luck hadn't smiled on me tonight. Capricious bitch.

"Hey, you there! Stop!"

Ah, the usual cry of dismay after the fox had already raided the henhouse. Or in this case, killed the rabid dog that lurked inside. The gate hadn't slid shut yet, and I heard it creak to a stop. Footsteps scuffled on the gravel behind me.

I might have been concerned, if I hadn't already melted into the surrounding forest.

Although I would have liked to have gone straight home and washed the stench of insanity out of my hair, I had a dinner date to keep. And Fletcher hated to be kept waiting, especially when there was money to collect and wire transfers to check on.

I jogged about a mile, keeping inside the row of pines that lined the highway, before stepping out onto the main road. A half mile farther down, I reached a small café called the End of the Line, the sort of dingy, stagnate place that stays open all night and serves three-day-old pie and coffee. After the asylum's moldy peas and pureed carrots, the stale, crumbly strawberry shortcake tasted like heaven. I wolfed down a piece while I waited for a cab to come pick me up.

The driver dropped me off in one of Ashland's seedier downtown neighborhoods, ten blocks from my actual destination. Storefronts advertising cheap liquor and cheaper peep shows lined the cracked sidewalk. Groups of young black, white, and Hispanic men wearing baggy clothes eyed each other from opposite sides and ends of the block, forming a triangle of potential trouble.

An Air elemental begged on the corner and promised to make it rain for whoever would give him enough money to buy a bottle of whiskey. Another sad example of the fact that elementals weren't immune to social problems like homelessness, alcoholism, and addiction. We all had our weaknesses and caught bad breaks in life, even the magic users. It was what folks did afterward that determined whether or not they ended up on the street like this poor bum. I gave him a twenty and walked on by.

Hookers also ambled down the street like worn-out soldiers forced into another tour of duty by their general pimps. Most of the prostitutes were vampires, and their yellow teeth gleamed like dull bits of topaz underneath the flickering streetlights. Sex was just as stimulating to some vamps as drinking blood. It gave them a great high and let them fuel their bodies just as well as a nice, cold glass of A-positive, which is why so many of them were hookers. Besides, it was the world's oldest profession. Barring your normal traumatic, life-threatening injuries, vamps could live a long time—several hundred years. It was always good to have a skill that would never go out of style.

A few of the vampire whores called out to me, but one look at the hard set of my mouth sent them scurrying on in search of easier, more profitable prospects.

I walked two blocks before ditching the glasses in a Dumpster next to a Chinese restaurant. The metal container reeked of soy sauce and week-old fried rice. The baseball hat and fleece jacket got left on top of a homeless woman's shopping cart. From the threadbare condition of her own green army jacket, she could use it. If she came out of her rambling, drunken binge long enough to notice they were even there.

The neighborhood got a little better the more blocks I walked, going from drug-using, gang-banging, white trash to blue-collar redneck and working poor. Tattoo parlors and check-cashing joints replaced the liquor stores and peep shows. The few prostitutes who trolled these streets looked cleaner and better fed than their tired, gaunt brothers and sisters to the south. More of them were human, too.

With the pieces of my disguise disposed of, I slowed my pace and strolled the rest of the way, enjoying the crisp fall air. I couldn't get enough of it, even if it was tinged with burned tobacco. Several good ole boys chain-smoked and knocked back beers on their front stoops, while inside, their wives hurried to put dinner on the table in time to avoid getting a fresh shiner.

Thirty minutes later I reached my destination—the Pork Pit.

The Pit, as locals called it, was nothing more than a hole-in-the-wall, but it had the best barbecue in Ashland. Hell, the whole South. The outline of a multicolored, neon pig holding a full platter of food burned over the faded blue awning. I trailed my fingers over the battered brick that outlined the front door. The stone vibrated with muted, clogged contentment, like the stomachs and arteries of so many after eating here.

The sign in the front window read Closed, but I pushed the door open and stepped inside. Old-fashioned, pink and blue vinyl booths crouched in front of the windows. A counter with matching stools ran along the back wall, where patrons could sit and watch cooks on the far side dish up plates of barbecue beef and pork. Even though the grill had been closed for at least an hour, the smell of charred meat, smoke, and spices hung heavy in the air, a cloud of aroma almost thick enough to eat. Pink and blue pig tracks done in peeling paint covered the floor, leading, respectively, to the women's and men's restrooms.

My gray eyes focused on the cash register perched on the right side of the counter. A lone man sat next to it, reading a tattered paperback copy of *Where the Red Fern Grows* and sipping a cup of chicory coffee. An old man, late seventies, with a wispy thatch of white hair that covered his mottled, brown scalp. A grease-stained apron hung off his thin neck and trailed down his blue work shirt and pants.

The bell over the door chimed when I entered, but the man didn't look up from his paperback.

"You're late, Gin," he said.

"Sorry. I was busy talking about my feelings and killing people."

"You were supposed to be here an hour ago."

"Why, Fletcher, it almost sounds like you were worried about me."

Fletcher glanced up from his book. His rheumy eyes resembled the dull green glass of a soda pop bottle. "Me? Worry? Don't be silly."

"Never."

Fletcher Lane was my go-between. The cutout who made the appointments with potential clients, took the money, and set up my assignments. The middleman who got his hands dirty—for a substantial fee. He'd taken me in off the streets seventeen years ago and had taught me everything I knew about being an assassin. The good, the bad, the ugly. He was also one of only a few people I trusted—another being his son, Finnegan, who was just as greedy as the old man was and not afraid to show it.

Fletcher set his book aside. "Hungry?"

"I've been pushing peas around a plastic plate for the better part of a week. What do you think?"

I settled myself at the counter, while Fletcher went to work behind it. The old man clunked down a glass of tart lemonade filled with blackberries in front of me.

I tasted it and grimaced. "It's lukewarm."

"All the ice is in the freezer for the night. Cool it yourself."

In addition to being a Stone elemental, I also had the rare gift of being able to control another element—Ice, though my magic in that area was far weaker. I put my hand on the glass and concentrated, reaching for the cool power that lay deep inside me. Snowflake-shaped Ice crystals spread out from my palm and fingertips. They frosted up the side of the glass, arced over the lip, and ran down into the beverage below. I held my hand palm up over the glass and reached for my magic again. A cold, silver light flickered there, centered in the spider rune scar. I concentrated, and the light coalesced into a square Ice cube. I tipped it into the yellow liquid, then formed a few more and dropped them in as well.

I tasted the lemonade again. "Much better."

The next thing Fletcher set on the counter was a half pound hamburger dripping with mayonnaise and piled high with smoked Swiss cheese, sweet butter-leaf lettuce, a juicy tomato slice, and a thick slab of red onion. A bowl of spicy baked beans followed, along with a saucer of carrot-laced coleslaw.

I dug into the food, relishing the play of sweet and spice, salt and vinegar, on my tongue. I swallowed a spoonful of the warm beans and focused on the sauce that coated them, trying to isolate the many flavors.

The Pork Pit was famous for its barbecue sauce, which Fletcher whipped up in secret in the back of the restaurant. People bought gallons of it at a time. Over the years, I'd tried to discover Fletcher's secret recipe. But no matter what I attempted, no matter how many batches of the stuff I made, my sauce just never tasted the same as his. Fletcher claimed there was one secret ingredient that gave the sauce its spicy kick. But the gruff old man wouldn't tell me what it was or how much of it he used.

"Are you ever going to tell me what's in the barbecue sauce?" I asked.

"No," he said. "Are you ever going to quit trying to find out?"

"No."

"Then I guess we're locked in a stalemate."

"I could fix that," I muttered.

An amused grin flashed across Fletcher's face. "Then you'd never get the recipe."

I shook my head and concentrated on my food. While I ate, Fletcher picked up his book and read a few more pages. He didn't ask me about the job. Didn't have to. He knew I wouldn't have come back unless it was done.

I always missed the Pit's food when I was working. Missed the smell of spices and grease tickling my nose. Missed the loud clatter of plates and the cheerful scrape of silverware. Missed cooking in the kitchen and bitching about demanding customers and lousy tips. But mostly, I missed shooting the breeze with Fletcher late at night, when the front door was locked and everything was quiet, except for the two of us. The Pork Pit was more than just a restaurant to me. It was home—or at least the closest to one I'd had the last seventeen years. The only one I was likely to ever have again. The life of an assassin wasn't exactly conducive to puppies and picket fences.

"How's Finn?" I asked after I'd eaten enough to take the edge off.

Fletcher shrugged. "He's fine. Making his deals. Taking control of other people's money. My son, the investment banker and computer genius. He should have taken up an honest job, like thieving."

I hid my grin behind my glass of lemonade. Finnegan Lane's gloss of legitimate civility never failed to amuse his father. Or me.

I'd just popped the last bite of the heart-stoppingly good hamburger into my mouth when Fletcher reached below the counter. He came up with a manila folder and placed it beside my empty plate. His speckled brown hands rested on the folder a moment before sliding away.

"What's this?" I asked. "I told you I was taking a vacation after the shrink."

"You've been on vacation for days now." Fletcher took a long slurp of his cooling coffee.

"Spending six days locked away in an insane asylum isn't my idea of a good time."

Fletcher didn't respond. The folder lay between us, a silent question. I couldn't help but wonder what secrets it contained. And who had pissed someone off enough to wind up in my line of sight. My expertise didn't come cheap. Especially when you added Fletcher's handling fee on top of it.

"Who's the target?" I asked, giving in to the inevitable.

Damn curiosity. One emotion I couldn't quite squash, no matter how hard I tried. Something I'd picked up from the old man over the years. He was even more inquisitive than me.

Fletcher grinned and flipped open the folder. "Target's name is Gordon Giles."

He pushed the file over to me, and I skimmed the contents. Gordon Giles. Fifty-four. The chief financial officer of Halo Industries. A glorified accountant and paper pusher, in other words. Divorced. No kids. Enjoys fly fishing. Likes to visit hookers at least twice a week. An Air elemental.

That last piece of information was unfortunate. Elementals were folks who could create, control, and manipulate the four elements—Ice, Stone, Air, and Fire. Some people also had talents for using offshoots of those, like water, metal, and electricity. But you weren't considered a true elemental unless you could tap into one of the big four.

My Stone magic was strong and let me do just about anything I wanted to with the element, from crumbling bricks to cracking concrete to making my own skin as hard as marble. I couldn't do as much with my weaker Ice magic, other than create cubes, icicles, the occasional knife, and other small shapes. The miniature animal Ice sculptures made me popular at parties, though.

Since Gordon Giles was an Air elemental, he could control currents, sense the wind, feel vibrations in the air the same way I could in stone. And he could manipulate them too, just like me. Depending on what sort of innate talents he had and how strong his power was, Giles could use his Air magic to try to suffocate me before I killed him. Force oxygen bubbles into my veins. Pummel me with the wind. Or a hundred other nasty things.

I studied the photo clipped on top of the information. Gordon Giles's salt-and-pepper hair flopped over his forehead, just brushing the tops of his gold glasses. His eyes were like puddles of powder-blue ink behind the lenses. His face reminded me of a ferret's—long and thin. Pinched lips. Pointed chin. A sharp triangle of a nose.

Gordon's eyes held a look of nervous anticipation. The gaze of a man who knew monsters walked the streets and expected them to leap out and grab him any second. Twitchy men were far more difficult to kill than oblivious ones. I'd have to be careful with him.

"And what's Giles done to merit my particular brand of attention?"

"Seems the chief financial officer has been cooking the books at Halo Industries," Fletcher said. "Somebody found out and wants to address the situation."

"Protection?" I asked.

Fletcher shrugged. "None that I know of, but the rumor is Giles is getting nervous and thinking about turning himself over to the cops, as if they would even bother to keep him safe."

Cops. I snorted. What a joke. Most of Ashland's finest were more crooked than the mountain roads that crisscrossed the city. If you went to the po-po for protection, you might as well hang yourself and save your cellmate the trouble of tearing up his perfectly good bed sheets.

"Halo Industries," I murmured. "Isn't that one of Mab Monroe's companies?"

"She's the major stockholder," Fletcher said. "But one

of her flunkies, Haley James, and James's sister, Alexis, actually front the business. Halo Industries was started by their father, Lawrence. Him and the sisters kept it in the family for years, until Mab decided she wanted a piece of the action and muscled in on them. The father died of a heart attack two weeks after Mab took over. At least, that's what the official word was."

"And unofficially?" I asked.

Fletcher shrugged. "Rumor has it the father was making lots of problems. Wouldn't surprise me if his heart attack was more of an unfortunate accident arranged by Mab herself."

"A heart attack? That's not really her style," I said. "Usually, she just incinerates people with her magic, burns their house to the ground, that sort of thing."

"True," Fletcher agreed. "Which meant she probably passed the job on to one of her boys and asked them to make it look like natural causes. Either way, Lawrence James ended up dead."

Ashland might have a working police force and government, but the city was really run by one woman. Mab Monroe. Mab was a Fire elemental—strong, powerful, deadly. All that was bad enough, but she wasn't just your run-of-the-mill elemental. Mab Monroe had more magic, more raw power, than any elemental had had in five hundred years. At least, that's what the rumor mill churned out. Given the fact that anyone who went up against her got dead sooner rather than later, I tended to believe the hype.

A respectable, multitiered business front hid Mab's moblike empire. Intimidation. Bribes. Drugs. Kidnappings. Murder. None of it bothered Mab. She reveled in the blood like a hog in slop. She had her spies everywhere. Police department. City council. Mayor's office. Cops, district attorneys, judges, and other assorted good guys didn't last long in this city, unless they went over to the dark side—and into Mab's hip pocket.

Like all savvy businesswomen, Mab Monroe hid her true nature behind a veneer of cultured sophistication. Donating money to charity. Spearheading fund-raisers. Giving back to the community. All of it designed to distance her from the ugly things she ordered done on a daily basis. Mab kept her eye on the big picture, which is why she had two lieutenants, for lack of a better word, who ran the day-to-day operations. Her lawyer, Jonah McAllister, and Elliot Slater.

McAllister handled the people who challenged Mab through legal means. The slick lawyer buried the poor folks in so much paperwork and red tape that most of them went bankrupt just trying to pay their own attorneys. Slater claimed to be a security consultant, but the giant was really nothing more than an enforcer in a nice suit. He handled Mab's minions and dealt with those who crossed the Fire elemental in a swift, brutal, permanent manner—when Mab didn't deign to do it herself.

To most folks, Mab Monroe was a paragon of elemental virtue, a perfect marriage of money and magic. But those of us who dealt in the shady side of life knew Mab for what she really was—ruthless. The Fire elemental had a stranglehold on Ashland, her fingers in every worthwhile, lucrative, or helpful operation in the city, but it just didn't seem to be enough for her. Mab just kept reaching for, and accumulating, more and more and more, as though money, power, and influence were the vital oxygen she needed to fuel herself. Simply put, she was a bully, albeit one with enough magic to back up any claim she made and get her anything she wanted.

I'd never liked bullies.

But Mab's magic didn't keep folks from quietly plotting against her. Several times a year, Fletcher got inquiries about hiring me to take out Mab Monroe. We'd done some recon on her over the years and had decided it was too close to being a suicide mission to bother with. Even if I could get through her layers of security and giant bodyguards, Mab could always kill me herself. She wasn't afraid to use her own Fire elemental magic. That's how she'd clawed her way to the top in the first place—by killing anyone who challenged her meteoric rise through the ranks of Ashland's underworld.

Still, Fletcher kept an open file on the Fire elemental, tracking her security, her movements, looking for any signs of weakness. For some reason, the old man wanted Mab dead. He just hadn't found a way to get it done yet. At least, not one that didn't involve him going out in a blaze of glory with her.

"You're telling me Gordon Giles was stupid enough to embezzle money from one of Mab Monroe's companies?" I asked.

Fletcher shrugged. "It appears that way. Client didn't give any more details, and I didn't ask. If you'll flip to the back page, you'll see there's a time limit on this one."

I turned to the appropriate sheet and read the info. "They want the job done by tomorrow night? You want me to do a job on less than twenty-four hours' notice? That's not like you, Fletcher."

"Read the payment."

My eyes skimmed farther down the paper. Five million. Question asked and answered. Fletcher might have loved me like a daughter, but he also loved getting his fifteen percent. I wasn't adverse to my cut, either.

"It's not a bad chunk of change," I admitted.

"Not bad? It's twice your going rate." A mixture of pride and anticipation colored Fletcher's rough voice. "The client's already made the fifty percent deposit. Do this job, and you can retire."

Retirement. Something that had been on Fletcher's mind ever since I'd come back with a broken arm and a bruised spleen from a botched job six months ago in St. Augustine. The old man kept talking about me retiring in a dreamy tone, as if there were a world of options that would magically open up to me the second I put down my knives. Instead of the dull boredom of reality.

"I'm thirty, Fletcher. A highly effective, well-paid, sought-after professional in my area of expertise. I'm good at my job, the blood doesn't bother me, and the people I kill have it coming. Why would I want to retire?"

More importantly, what would I do with myself? I had a very particular skill set, one that didn't lend itself to a lot of options.

"Because there's more to life than killing people and counting money, no matter how much one might enjoy them." His green eyes locked with mine. "Because you shouldn't have to look over your shoulder for the rest of your life. Don't you want to live in the daylight a little, kid?"

Live in the daylight. Fletcher's catchphrase for having a normal life. Seventeen years ago, I'd wanted nothing more. I'd prayed for the world to right itself, for time to rewind so I could go back to the safe, sheltered existence I'd once had. But I'd given up that fairy tale long ago. Nothing but wistful pain would ever come of wanting something I couldn't have. That gilded dream, that soft hope, that sentimental part of me was dead, burned away and crumbled to ash— just like my family had been.

People like me didn't retire. They just kept going until they got dead—which was usually sooner, rather than later. But I was going to roll the dice as long as I could. Even if it was a sucker's bet in the end.

But I didn't want to fight with the old man. Not tonight. Like it or not, he was one of the few people left in this world that I loved. So I distracted him by waving the folder in the air. "You really think this is a good idea? This assignment?"

"For five million dollars, I do."

"But there's no time to do prep work with this job," I protested. "No time to plan, to go over exit points, nothing."

"Come on, Gin," Fletcher wheedled. "It's an easy job. You can do something like this in your sleep. The client even suggested a place for you to do the hit."

I read some more. "The opera house?"

"The opera house," Fletcher repeated. "There's going to be a big shindig tomorrow night. They're dedicating a new wing to Mab Monroe."

"Another one?" I asked. "Aren't enough buildings in this city named after her already?"

"Apparently not. My point is there will be lots of people there. Lots of press. Lots of opportunity to get lost in the crowd. It should be easy enough for you to slip in, do Giles, and slip out. You are the Spider after all, known far and wide for your skill and prowess."

I grimaced at his grandiose tone. Sometimes Fletcher reminded me of a circus ringmaster making the sad elephants, browbeaten horses, and two-bit acts seem more thrilling than they actually were.

"The Spider was your idea, not mine. You're the one who thought you could charge more for my services if I had a catchy name, Tin Man," I said, referring to the old man by his assumed assassin name.

Fletcher grinned. "I was right, too. Every assassin has a name. Yours just happens to have a better ring than most, thanks to me."

I crossed my arms over my chest and glared at him.

"C'mon, Gin. It's easy money. Pop the accountant tomorrow night, and then you can take a vacation," Fletcher promised. "A real vacation. Somewhere warm, with oily cabana boys and boat drinks."

I raised an eyebrow. "And what would you know about oily cabana boys?"

"Finnegan might have pointed them out when he took me to Key West last year," Fletcher said. "Although our attention quickly wandered to the lovely ladies sunning topless by the pool."

Of course it had.

"Fine," I said, closing the folder. "I'll do it. But only because I love you, even if you are a greedy bastard who works me too hard."

Fletcher raised his coffee mug. "I'll drink to that."

✴ 3 ✴

I finished my lemonade, took the folder, said good night to Fletcher, and went home.

My apartment was located in the building across the street, five stories up on the top floor, but I never went straight home from the restaurant—or anywhere else. I circled around three blocks and cut through two alleys, making sure I wasn't being followed, before coming back and slipping into the building. Everything was quiet, given the late hour, except the squeak of my shoes on the granite floor in the lobby.

I rode the elevator up to my floor. Before I slid my key in the lock, I pressed my hand against the stone around the door frame. Nothing of note. Just the stone's usual low, muted voice. I wasn't home enough for my presence to sink into the gray-colored brick. Or perhaps I just didn't care to listen to my own innate vibrations.

I'd chosen this particular apartment because it was the

one closest to the stairwell, with access to the roof and a sturdy drainpipe that ran down the outside of the building. My escape routes, along with a few others. I tested them at least once a month, played possible scenarios of capture and evasion in my mind. My own mantra for survival. You could never be too careful, especially in my line of work, when even a small fuckup could mean death. My death.

I flipped on the lights. The front room was an oversize kitchen and den, with the master bedroom and bathroom off to the left, and a spare set of matching rooms off to the right. A couch, a love seat, a couple of recliners, appliances. A plasma-screen TV, with DVDs and CDs piled around it. Piles and piles of well-worn books stacked three feet high in some places. A nice set of copper pots and pans hanging from a rack in the kitchen. A butcher block full of high-end, silverstone knives sitting on the counter.

There was nothing in here I couldn't walk away from on a moment's notice. Always a possibility in my profession. I was careful on my jobs, and Fletcher was extremely selective when choosing clients. But there was always a chance of discovery, exposure, torture, death. More reasons Fletcher wanted me to give up the business.

Still, to placate the old man, I tried to lead a somewhat normal life, except for my nighttime activities. My main cover ID was as Gin Blanco, a part-time cook and waitress at the Pork Pit and perpetual student at Ashland Community College. Architecture, sculpture, the role of women in fantasy fiction. I took any class that appealed to me, no matter how eclectic.

But the literature and cooking classes were my favorites, and I signed up for at least one every semester. Cooking was a passion of mine—the only real one I had besides reading. I enjoyed the smell of sugar and spices. The endless combinations of sweet and salty. The simple and complex formulas that let you turn separate ingredients into cohesive, edible works of art. Plus, cooking gave me an excuse to have plenty of knives lying around. Another necessity in my line of work.

Seeing everything was in order, I moved farther into the apartment. I should have gone on into the bathroom, taken a shower, then curled up in bed, studying the Gordon Giles file. Planning the hit. Writing down the supplies I'd need. Visualizing my escape. And dreaming about the oily cabana boys Fletcher had promised were waiting for me in Key West.

But I lingered in the den, staring at a series of framed drawings on the mantel over the television. An art class I'd just finished. For our final project, the instructor had asked us to do a series. Three drawings in all, each one different, but with a connected theme.

I'd drawn the runes of my dead family.

Instead of a crest or coat of arms, magic users identified themselves through runes. Vampires, giants, dwarves, elementals. Runes were everywhere you looked. Tattoos, necklaces, rings, T-shirts. Even some humans used them, especially for business logos.

Some of the magic users sniffed at that, claiming that runes should only be used by those with power. Most of those same folks also harbored crackpot dreams of a magic-controlled society run by elementals and the like, instead of the current balance of power between all the races. The reason no one race had taken over was simple: guns were great equalizers. So were knives, baseball bats, chain saws, and wood chippers. And most folks in Ashland had at least one of each. Magic was great, but three bullets in the back of the head was enough to put almost anyone's lights out for good. So the humans used runes, the magic users scoffed at them, and the city kept on turning.

But the humans using runes had no real impact on anything. Only elementals could imbue runes with magic; make the symbols come to life and perform some specific function. And really, a Fire elemental tracing a sunburst rune into a wooden log to start a campfire was just a flashy way of showing off. Especially when he could just snap his fingers and do it outright. But magical runes were good for some things—trip wires, alarms, timed or delayed bursts of magic. That last one had obvious appeal to certain assassins. Trace an explosive Fire rune on a package, mail it to your mark, and you could be sipping margaritas in the Caribbean when the poor idiot opened the box and it went *boom*.

Most runes had no power in and of themselves, but were simply ways to announce your lineage, show your alliances, and say something about your temperament, business, occupation, or hobbies. The rune of my family, the Snow family, had been a snowflake—the symbol for icy calm. My mother, Eira, had the rune fashioned into a silverstone medallion she'd worn on a chain around her neck. My mother had taken the tradition a step further and had a rune necklace created for each of us, with the symbol revealing something about our personalities.

The snowflake rune was the first piece on the mantel, followed by a curling ivy vine—representing elegance—my older sister, Annabella's, rune and necklace. And finally, there was a primrose, symbolizing beauty, which had been given to my younger sister, Bria.

There wasn't a picture of my rune—the spider rune—on the mantel. The small circle surrounded by eight equidistant lines hadn't been intricate or interesting enough to merit a drawing for my class. Of course, I didn't actually have the spider rune medallion anymore, but if I wanted to see the damn thing, all I had to do was look at the scars on my palms.

I shook myself out of my trance. The memories were always worse during the fall. That's when my mother and Annabella had been killed by the Fire elemental, their bodies reduced to ash. Bria had escaped that fate, only to be buried alive by the crumbling remains of our house. All I'd found of my baby sister had been a splash of blood on the stone foundation.

The clear, crisp tang in the air. The bright, cerulean blue of the sky. The rich, damp smell of the earth turning. The way the approaching winter chill slowed the murmur of the stones underfoot. It all reminded me of them, even now, seventeen years later.

But the runes on my mantel weren't going to bring my family back. Nothing could do that. I didn't know why I'd done the damn drawings in the first place. I really did need a vacation. Or perhaps Fletcher's talk of retirement had unsettled me more than I'd realized.

My fingers tightened around the folder in my hand. I pulled my eyes away from the drawings, went into the bedroom, and closed the door, cutting off my view of the runes.

Out of sight, almost out of mind.

At eight o'clock the next evening, I stood outside on the topmost balcony of the Ashland Opera House, a massive building constructed of gray granite and glistening white marble. An old-fashioned architectural gem, the opera house spread over three downtown blocks. A slender turret marked each one of the building's three wings, which always made it seem like an elaborate dollhouse to me. Black flags embossed with silver music notes—the opera's rune—fluttered on top of each turret in the listless September breeze.

Twenty minutes ago, I'd walked through the front door of the opera house. With my white shirt, black pants, low-heeled boots, and cello case, I looked like any one of the dozens of musicians here for tonight's performance. No one had glanced twice at me as I'd strolled through the lobby, walked up the grand staircase, and climbed up several more flights. I'd used my Ice magic to create a pair of long, slender lock picks, which I'd used to jimmy the door that led out to the balcony. I might have come in through the front, but after the job was done, I was making my escape out the back. So to speak.

While the front of the opera house faced one of Ashland's busy downtown streets, the back side of the building squatted on top of a series of jagged cliffs, which fell away to the Aneirin River. Cliffs I was going to rappel down in another hour or so.

Staying in the shadows, I opened my cello case and pulled out the plastic shell that resembled the classical instrument. Hidden beneath was a secret compartment with my supplies for the evening, including two hundred feet of climbing rope. I anchored the rope to a brass flagpole planted in the low balcony wall and threw the length of it down the side of the cliffs. The gray rope blended into the uneven stones below, and you wouldn't spot it unless you knew it was there. Still, I grabbed a few crumpled brown leaves from the balcony floor and spread them over the base of the flagpole, obscuring the rope. It was unlikely anyone would venture out here, given the activity and excitement inside the building, but you never knew who might wander this way for a quick cigarette or a quicker fuck. Better not to take unnecessary chances.

As I worked, my hands brushed the stone of the building. The granite sang under my fingertips. The music from the orchestra's performances had long ago permeated the rock and now ran through it like a vein of ore. I closed my eyes and flattened both hands against the rough stone. The sound was so rich, so pure, so beautiful, after the insane discord of the asylum, that I reached for my magic.

I sent a trickle of my power through the stone, giving it a subtle command. The separate seams of the granite dipped and rose in a small wave, one after another, as though I were running my fingers up and down a piano keyboard. The seams settled back into place, and I allowed myself a small smile. Elemental magic could be amusing as well as deadly.

My work here done, I grabbed my cello case, opened the balcony door, and slid back inside.

The balcony was an extension of the topmost floor of the opera house, a gray, featureless space where the executive and administrative offices were located. The area was deserted, with only the low house lights on for illumination. I slipped into the emergency stairwell and walked down several flights of stairs, before emerging onto the second floor of the building.

It was like stepping into another world. The second floor was circular, with a large entrance room several thousand feet wide. A grand staircase led down to the ground floor, topped by a dazzling crystal chandelier that resembled an elegant cluster of icicles. The carpet was a warm burgundy, swirled throughout with a delicate gold paisley pattern. The walls featured heavy, matching soundproof drapes, along with an occasional mirror and glossy painting. White marble set with squares of black and burgundy gleamed in the lobby below.

A couple of blocks over, a vampire hooker would do you in your car for fifty bucks, while the homeless guys dug through trash cans looking for enough garbage to eat for the night. But here, the darkest, dirtiest things were the lipstick stains on the champagne glasses—and the souls of the people indulging in the bubbly.

People milled around the entrance room, with some trailing down either side of the wide staircase. As befitting any elite arts function in Ashland, the attendees wore designer gowns in jewel tones, resplendent black tuxedos, and other appropriate finery that was just as sophisticated as the furnishings. Gems small, medium, and large flashed, winked, and glittered on throats, wrists, and fingers. The stones whispered proudly of their own beauty and elegance. Some people sipped champagne and mixed drinks, while others took chicken skewers, spring rolls, and other dainty, bite-size hors d'oeuvres from passing waiters. Conversation trilled through the air, punctuated with bass rumbles of laughter and sudden, sharp guffaws.

Since I looked like all the other musicians, the glitterati paid me about as much attention as they did the carpet, and I moved through the crush of people with ease, looking for my quarry.

Gasps surged through the crowd, and I searched for the source of the sudden disturbance. My gaze locked onto Mab Monroe. The Fire elemental swept through the lobby and walked up the grand staircase. Every eye turned to her, and conversation stopped, like a song cut off in mid-chorus. Mab had that effect on most people. Her softly curled red hair gleamed like a new penny, and she wore a gown of the darkest scarlet imaginable, cut low in the front to show off her creamy décolletage. Her eyes were black pools in her face. Fire and brimstone. That's what I thought about every time I saw Mab.

A flat gold necklace ringed the Fire elemental's delicate neck. My eyes caught on the centerpiece of the design: a circular ruby surrounded by several dozen wavy rays. The intricate diamond cutting on the gold made it seem as though the rays actually flickered. A sunburst. The symbol for fire. Mab's personal rune, used by her and her alone. Even across the room, I could hear the gemstone's vibrations. Instead of beauty and elegance, it whispered of raw, fiery power. The sound made my stomach clench.

Mab Monroe strolled through the crowd, laughing, talking, smiling, shaking hands. I eyed the elemental, once again thinking about how much money I'd turned down over the years to kill her. A shame, really. I didn't consider myself to be any sort of hero, but I wouldn't have minded giving the good citizens of Ashland a fighting chance by removing Mab's fist from around their throats. Bullies always made me eager to see how tough they really were—and knock them down a few pegs.

My gaze skipped over to her entourage. A burly man wearing a tuxedo stayed close to Mab, while two more circulated through the room at large. Elliot Slater wasn't among them tonight, but they were all giants like him, with thick necks, oversize fists, and big, buglike eyes. Perfect meat shields. Not that Mab really needed them. Her Fire elemental magic was more than enough to deal with any threat. The giants were for show, more than anything else.

Mab Monroe's current path was going to take her close to me, and I melted back into the shadows. But she and her guards swept by without a glance in my direction, and I continued searching for my prey for the evening—and any other players who might impact the drama about to unfold.

Haley James entered the lobby a few minutes later and headed for the stairs. Her skin was the color of fresh cream, and her strawberry-blonde hair was curled into ringlets piled on top of her head. She wore a short cocktail sheath dress done in sage green, which showed off her lush, curvy body. The emeralds in her chandelier earrings sparked and flashed like smoldering embers. The gems matched the blue-green of her eyes.

Alexis James followed her sister inside. Alexis was several inches taller, with the same light coloring, although her hair was cropped short. She wore a simple black cocktail dress. A string of pearls ringed her throat, while black gloves crawled up to her elbows. A pearl bracelet hung off her right wrist. Understated class, compared to Haley's emerald flash.

Haley James called out to Mab, and the two women paused to exchange meaningless pleasantries. Alexis stood off to one side, her face expressionless.

According to Fletcher's file, Haley James was the chief executive officer of Halo Industries, with Alexis serving as the head of marketing and public relations. The company had been in their family for years and dealt in a variety of areas, but the main focus was magical speculation, specifically harnessing Air elemental magic for a variety of medical and cosmetic products. The James sisters employed a whole staff of the elementals, but they weren't known to be magic types themselves.

I wondered if Haley James was the one who'd discovered Gordon Giles cooking the books. If she'd put the contract out on him to cover it up. To make an example of him. Or to keep Mab Monroe from finding out she was getting bilked out of millions and avoid the Fire elemental's wrath. If Mab discovered Giles's embezzlement, she'd not only take her ire out on the accountant, but on the James sisters as well for letting themselves get bamboozled. There were any number of reasons Haley James could have decided to eliminate Giles.

But I put the conjecture out of my mind. It didn't matter to me who had put the hit out on Giles, as long as the rest of the money appeared in a timely fashion after the fact. If it didn't, well, then I'd get interested in who wanted Gordon Giles dead. But not before.

Speaking of Mr. Giles, he'd finally arrived. He shuffled through the lobby and up the grand staircase, just as Mab Monroe had done, although with far less fanfare.

Gordon Giles wore a tuxedo that was just a bit too large for his small frame. He was so thin, his shoulder bones poked up through the fabric of his suit. His face was tight and pinched, as though the very act of breathing pained him. He continually dry-washed his hands, and his eyes flicked back and forth over the lobby, moving from Haley James to Alexis to Mab Monroe, through their sea of onlookers, and back again. Trying to see which direction the danger would come from. What shadow the bullet would whiz out of. But he wouldn't see it, wouldn't see me, until it was too late.

But really, it had been too late as soon as the client had contacted Fletcher. Because I was the Spider. I always followed through.

And I never, ever missed.

✴ 4 ✴

People started drifting into their boxes to watch the performance. Gordon Giles slipped into a box marked A3, the one I'd been told was his.

I climbed back up to the top floor, created another pair of lock picks with my Ice magic, then used them to open the door to the stairs that led to the catwalk. I paused inside the door and stripped off my thick white shirt, revealing a long-sleeved black T-shirt underneath. The white garment got stuffed inside the cello case, and I pulled out a snug-fitting, black vest filled with my usual supplies: cash, disposable cell phone, credit cards, a couple of fake IDs. A black toboggan I'd had folded in my pocket went on my head, hiding my bleached blond hair.

I made my way up the steps and strode out onto the catwalk. It wasn't a true metal catwalk but a carpeted balcony, a narrow, walled strip ringing the entire opera house in a giant circle, just as the floors below did. The houselights had already gone down, and several spotlights focused on the stage, highlighting the gleaming instruments of the orchestra. The musicians sat silent on the wide, semicircular stage, waiting for the cue from the maestro.

I crept down the catwalk. From this high vantage point, I could look down over the entire complex—and straight into the second-floor VIP boxes, including the one that belonged to Gordon Giles.

Giles was already seated. He must not have found the program for the evening very interesting, because he'd rolled it up. Giles shook his hand, and the paper baton slapped against his knee in a rapid, staccato pattern. The nervous twitch of a man who knows he's in trouble.

The maestro cleared his throat and tapped his baton. The crowd sputtered, stilled, and hushed. The metal baton came down again, and the orchestra burst into song. Energy. Emotion. Joy. I closed my eyes, listening to the swell of the orchestra, the perfect harmony the instruments created as they enunciated their complex patterns of notes and chords. All blending and melting together into a cacophony of supreme beauty.

I listened a few seconds more, reveling in the harmony. Then I tuned out the music and got to work. According to the timetable in Fletcher's file, the job had to be done before intermission. The client wanted to make a spectacle of Gordon Giles's untimely demise by having his body discovered then.

I opened my cello case and pulled out the plastic shell once more. Hidden in the compartment underneath was my weapon of choice for the evening—a crossbow.

The weapon looked like your typical crossbow, except for the powerful rifle scope mounted above the trigger and the barbed metal bolt already in firing position. The bow was the perfect weapon for mid-range jobs like this one. Since I didn't want to take a chance on Gordon Giles using his elemental Air magic against me, I'd decided to do this one from a distance. Pull the trigger and walk away. No muss, no fuss, no blood spattered on my clothes, for a change. The only real downside of my job.

I could have used a rifle, of course. Easier to get, cheaper to buy, same result in the end. But guns jammed too much for my liking. With a bow, you didn't run that risk. The same reason I used silverstone knives on most of my jobs. Along with the crossbow, I had several knives secreted on my person tonight. Two tucked up my sleeves. One against the small of my back. Two stuffed inside my boots. My usual five-point arsenal. Just in case things didn't go exactly as planned, and I had to get up close and personal with someone.

The great thing about using silverstone knives was the fact that the magical metal was almost unbreakable, and the only jamming a blade ever did was when I shoved it too far into someone's chest and had trouble yanking it out again. By that time, well, it didn't much matter.

I grabbed the crossbow and placed it on the edge of the balcony wall. It was dark up here, and no one looked in my direction, but I'd still chosen to launch my attack from the deepest shadow. Same reason I'd ditched the white shirt. I didn't want some bored kid staring up and asking Mommy what the black figure with the scary weapon was doing way, way up in the rafters. I might be here to kill somebody, but there was no need to frighten the other people in attendance and ruin their evening out. And one scream could shatter my moment of opportunity. Given Gordon Giles's jumpy nature, I doubted I'd get another shot at him anytime soon. I was surprised he'd appeared at such a public function. If I'd been an accountant stealing millions from Mab Monroe, I would have been having my face lifted on a deserted island. Not taking in a performance at the local opera house.

The scope's magnification gave me an eagle-eyed view into the box. Which is why I was able to see a sliver of light as the door in the back cracked open. My gray eye widened in the scope, trying to determine the identity of the newcomer—and how much he was going to fuck up my plans.

Donovan Caine stepped into the box.

I knew Caine by sight—and reputation. Donovan Caine was one of the few honest cops in the city, raised to be so by his dearly departed detective daddy. According to Fletcher, Caine was the sort of man who didn't look the other way, no matter who was putting on the pressure. Didn't take bribes. Didn't do drugs. Hell, he didn't even smoke, according to Fletcher.

The detective had been assigned to investigate some of my previous Ashland jobs, although with little success. Unlike some of my fellow assassins, I wasn't stupid enough to sign my work. Some contract guys, especially the magic users, actually took the time to carve their own personal runes into the flesh of their victims or on the surrounding walls or floor. I'd even heard rumors of a certain vampire who liked to draw the rune with his victim's blood—after mixing it with his own. Idiots. Leaving a rune behind was as bad as leaving a fingerprint. Showing off with them was a one-way ticket to the electric chair. Folks in the South weren't shy about executing people, especially when such demonstrations were sanctioned by the government.

But Caine knew I existed, mainly because of my last assignment in the city a couple months ago—when I'd killed his partner.

Cliff Ingles hadn't been a bad cop—except for his off-duty tendency to beat up and rape hookers. In Ashland, that wasn't even enough to get him thrown off the force, much less warrant my particular brand of attention. Until Ingles had turned his forcible ways to the thirteen-year-old daughter of one of the hookers. The vampire knew enough to send a message asking for help in Fletcher's general direction. The old man didn't like rapists, especially those who targeted kids. I didn't either, so I'd done the job pro bono. Another public service. The mayor should give me a medal.

Caine had known his partner wasn't the cleanest guy around, but evidently he didn't realize the extent of Ingles's depravity. Because after I'd put a knife in Ingles's oversize gut and sliced off his balls, Donovan Caine had publicly vowed to bring his partner's killer to justice. Swore up one side and down the other to find the assassin responsible for his partner's painful, untimely demise and make her pay every which way he could. The investigation had stalled, but Caine hadn't given up. Every week or so, he sent out a new public service announcement to the local media outlets, pleading for info on the Ingles murder.

Oh, Caine didn't know it was specifically me, Gin Blanco, the Spider, who had killed his partner. All the detective knew was that an assassin had hit Cliff Ingles. If it had been a gangbanger or some other lowlife, he might have been stupid enough to brag about it, somebody would have snitched, and Caine probably would have found him by now. Either way, the detective wanted to hit back at whomever had murdered Ingles and get revenge for his dead partner.

Since then I'd taken an interest in the detective. His dogged determination amused me, however fruitless and misguided it was, and I had Fletcher compile a file on him.

I tracked Caine through the scope as he approached Giles. Thirty-two. Six foot one. Cropped black hair. Hazel eyes. Strong chin. Square jaw. Bumpy, crooked nose. Lean body. Bronze skin that showed his Hispanic heritage.

He was handsome enough, although not as pretty as some of the other men I'd seen in the lobby. But Caine moved with the loose, easy confidence of a man who knows what he's doing—and knows he can handle anything that comes his way.

Was there anything sexier than confidence and the skill to back it up? I didn't think so. A hot awareness coursed through my body. My breasts tightened, and a small, pleasant ache settled between my thighs. I wondered if Donovan Caine would be that smooth and sure in bed. Bet he would.

For a moment, I let myself fantasize about the detective. Naked. Writhing under me. His mouth teasing my pebbled nipple. His calloused fingers kneading my breasts. I pictured myself sinking onto his throbbing length. Riding him with quickening strokes until he screamed out my name. Draining every ounce of pleasure I could out of his lean body, until we were both spent and sweaty and satiated. Mmm.

Too bad he played for the opposition and wanted to put a bullet in my head. My daydream would remain just that.

Fletcher had said Gordon Giles might go to the police for protection. That must be why Caine was here. To meet with Giles. Placate him with the usual assurances of safety, immunity, whatever.

A smile tugged at my lips. I wondered what Donovan Caine would do when I put an arrow in Gordon Giles's heart. Would he try to administer some sort of medical attention, even though it was already too late? Would he call for help? Or would he race out of the box, gun drawn, determined to find the assassin?

All I had to do was pull the trigger and I'd find out.

But instead of finishing the job, I watched the detective. Caine took a seat to Giles's right. The two of them bent their heads together and started whispering. Well, Caine did most of the whispering. Gordon just shook his ferret-like face in a definite *no-no-no* pattern. Whatever Caine wanted him to do, Gordon wasn't giving in just yet.

I was so preoccupied with Donovan Caine that the telltale *click* didn't register until it was too late. But the cold gun pressed against the back of my neck definitely got my attention.

"Drop the weapon," a voice hissed in my ear.

❋ 5 ❋

"Drop the weapon," the voice hissed again.

The barrel pressed against my spine at the base of my skull. If he shot me there, I'd be dead before I hit the floor, especially if he was using silverstone bullets.

For a moment, I thought about reaching for my Stone magic, using it to harden my skin to an impenetrable shell. But if the bastard was faster than me, just half a second, he might be able to pull the trigger before I brought enough magic to bear. Besides, using that much power would zap my strength. Judging from my current situation, I was going to need every bit of my energy this evening. Better to save that trick for when I was really desperate. This was only a mild annoyance so far.

"Drop it right fucking *now*."

"Sure," I replied in a calm, easy voice. "I'll drop it. But you're going to have to give me some room. I can't pull back with you right on top of me."

A blatant lie, of course. But he'd gotten the drop on me, and right now I was in no position to outmaneuver him—or the gun on my spine.

"Fine. But don't try anything stupid."

The gun lifted from my neck, and I felt him take five steps back. Perfect. I let go of the bow's trigger, eased the weapon off the balcony wall, and set it down, with the bolt pointing back at him.

"Now, stand up and turn around—slowly. Hands up where I can see them."

I did as he asked and turned to face him. A short, stocky, Asian man with thick, powerful muscles stood behind me. He wore his black hair in a low ponytail, and a white scar slashed across his right cheek, going from the corner of his brown eye down past his jaw line. Like me, he was dressed in black. Assassins didn't really wear any other color when they were working.

"Hello, Brutus."

He tipped his head. "Gin."

Every assassin had a name, a code word that identified him or her, and perhaps gave a hint about his specialty. If you wanted someone poisoned, you were probably going to reach out to Hemlock. Death by fire? Look up Phoenix. Gutted entrails? Hooke was your girl. Fletcher Lane had been known as the Tin Man because he never let emotion get in the way of a job.

Brutus's moniker was Viper, and a rune tattoo of the fanged snake curled up the side of his neck. Brutus called himself Viper because he was the kind of guy who crept around in the underbrush. The one you didn't see until you stepped on him or he decided to strike. Like now.

Since there are a limited number of people who specialize in our profession, at least at our level, we'd run into each other more than once over the years. Three times now, our respective clients hired us to kill the other person. I'd put a knife in Brutus's back in Savannah the last time we'd met. He'd returned the favor by shooting me in the stomach. All six of our clients had died.

I might have been stone-cold efficient when it came to my assignments, but Brutus was a machine. He never showed any sort of emotion. Not pleasure, not pain, not even a glimmer of satisfaction at a job well done, nothing. He showed up, killed his target, and moved on.

I stood there with my hands up. A silencer capped the gun in his hand. The weapon was level with my heart. Brutus wouldn't miss. Unless I made him.

"You know, I'm actually sorry about this, Gin." Despite his apology, Brutus's voice was flat. Emotionless. "But the money was just too good to pass up."

My eyes flicked to the box seats. Donovan Caine and Gordon Giles whispered to each other, oblivious to the drama taking place above their heads. Caine seemed to be demanding something from Giles, who was still shaking his head *no no no*. My mind spun, trying to make sense of the situation.

"What is this?" I asked. "A setup? I kill Giles, then you kill me?"

"That was the plan, but since you were taking your sweet time, I decided to do you first."

My gray eyes narrowed. "Why? I was going to finish the job. Going to kill Giles. I'm a pro. I don't take jobs unless I plan to follow through with them."

Brutus shrugged. "The accountant's death will raise some tricky questions, so my employer decided it would be better if his assassin was caught. Immediately."

"So you're going to make me the fall guy to protect your client." My voice was as flat as his.

Brutus nodded. "This way, there's no manhunt, no drawn-out trial, no awkward questions. But there will be a shootout with one of the opera house's security guards. When the smoke clears, you'll be the only one not breathing. The trail starts and ends with you."

"So you've got someone on the inside then. Someone helping you."

Brutus didn't say anything, but I didn't need him to confirm my suspicion. My gaze went back to the box, but no one had joined Donovan Caine and Gordon Giles. Brutus must have someone stationed outside the door, standing by in case Giles got jumpy and tried to leave.

"What's my motivation?" I asked, shifting my weight onto my right foot.

"Nothing too elaborate. Just a poor, no-class hooker pissed at Giles for promising to marry her and make her an honest woman. A deranged woman enraged by love and jealousy who decided to take matters into her own hands."

"A hooker killing for love? In this city?" I sneered. "You couldn't come up with something more creative than that?"

Brutus shrugged. "Not my call."

I nodded. "Of course not. Well, I have to admit it's a solid plan, Brutus. Your client should give you a bonus. By the way, who is your client?"

Brutus shook his head. "You should know better than to ask me something like that, Gin."

I did know better, but asking gave me the opportunity to move my left foot closer toward the crossbow.

"I'd love to keep chatting, but I have a schedule to keep." Brutus's grip tightened on the gun. "You're a decent assassin, Gin. Almost as good as me. I really am sorry—"

I kicked out with my left foot, jiggling the trigger on the crossbow. The bolt shot out, catching Brutus above his right ankle. The other assassin grunted and fired a shot as I threw myself to the right. The bullet from his gun just clipped my shoulder, spinning me around. I hissed as a ribbon of hot fire erupted in my muscles. But that was better than the projectile piercing my heart.

I pushed the pain away, hit the ground rolling, grabbed my pseudo cello case, and got back up on my feet. I brought the case up over my chest. Two more bullets *thunk-thunked* into it. I shook my left arm, and a silverstone knife fell down my sleeve and into my hand. Another bullet slammed into the case, and I staggered back as though I'd been hit. Then I pivoted, slung the case to one side, and threw the knife at Brutus. The blade caught the assassin in his right shoulder. The gun slid from his twitching fingers and plopped onto the floor.

"You and those fucking knives," Brutus muttered and yanked the blade out of his shoulder socket. "Get a real weapon. Get a gun."

"Guns are for people who don't have the guts or skill to use a blade."

I threw down the bullet-laden cello case and palmed

the knife hidden up my right sleeve. Brutus shifted his weapon to his right hand.

And then we danced.

We circled round and round on the narrow catwalk, kicking, punching, slashing with our knives. Brutus sliced my left bicep, adding to the hot fire on that side of my body. I slammed my elbow into his mouth. He punched me in the kidneys. I kneed him in the groin.

We were evenly matched professionals. Trained, skilled, efficient, deadly. But the bolt in Brutus's ankle hindered him more than the bullet graze in my shoulder did me. He stepped back to get out of the way of my slashing dagger, and his ankle went out from under him. He stumbled to the floor. All the opening I needed.

Before Brutus could recover, I yanked the crossbow bolt out of his ankle and threw myself on top of him. This time, Brutus couldn't stop the whimper of pain that escaped his lips. He tried to grapple with me, but I shoved my knife against his neck. The blade just cut through his skin. He froze.

"Now," I said, raising the bolt up and pressing the bloody tip close to his left eye. "You're going to tell me exactly who hired you and why he wants Gordon Giles dead so badly. Or I'm going to put this bolt through your fucking eye and into your brain."

Brutus smiled, his teeth red with his own blood. "You've got two options, Gin. You can kill me or save yourself—or try to."

I touched the top of the bolt against his eye. Brutus might be as cold as stone, but even he shuddered at that. "What do you mean?"

"I told my client you were good, that you might get away. So we devised a backup plan. Even if you kill me, you're still going to get blamed for Giles's murder. I've got another man standing by ready to take him out. The paper trail leading back to you has already been set up. Threatening letters and the like. It's all in place—"

I raised my knife up and slammed it into Brutus's heart. The first time, he gasped in surprise and pain. The second time, his brown eyes bulged, and more blood trickled out of his mouth. By the third time I stabbed him, he was dead.

"Arrogant prick," I muttered, climbing to my feet. "You should have just shot me. Not talked yourself to death."

Brutus's body spasmed a final time in agreement.

I was already stepping over him and gathering up the weapons. Because Brutus was right about one thing. I had to save Gordon Giles's life instead of taking it—if I had any hope of saving my own.

I stuffed the crossbow back into the cello case, sprinted down the catwalk stairs, and shoved through the exit door. My wounded shoulder hit the doorjamb, and I hissed. Being shot, even just grazed, always felt like someone had shoved a red-hot metal poker into my flesh. Like a Fire elemental had put her hands on me and let loose with her incendiary magic. But I ignored the discomfort. Compartmentalizing pain, learning how to block it out and keep going no matter what, had been one of the first things Fletcher had taught me.

Fletcher. My thoughts turned to him. He was in this, too. If Brutus's client wanted me to take the fall for Gordon Giles's death, killing Fletcher would be next on the to-do list. They couldn't afford to leave him alive. Finnegan Lane either. I had to get to them. Soon.

I hurried through the executive floor, dropped the cello case by the unlocked balcony door, and went on into the stairwell. I pounded down the stairs to the second floor. Intermission was still several minutes away. No one crowded into the hallway yet, and I had a clear path to Gordon Giles's VIP box. I didn't need people to start screaming when they realized a woman dressed in black was holding a bloody knife in one hand and an even bloodier barbed bolt in the other.

Up ahead, a man pulled open the door to the box seats and stepped inside. Brutus's backup. And I realized he wasn't just going to kill Giles. A dead-end trail and no witnesses meant he'd have to take out Donovan Caine, too. Killing Giles and blaming me was one thing, but I didn't need the heat of a dead cop on top of that. Especially an honest one like Caine, who was something of a folk hero in Ashland. The cops, even the crooked ones, would lean on everyone they knew to get Caine's killer. The insatiable appetite of the press and public pressure would force them to. Donovan Caine and Gordon Giles definitely needed to keep breathing tonight.

I quickened my pace and charged through the door. Gordon Giles squatted half in, half out of his seat, his blue eyes wide with panic and fear. Donovan Caine stood tall and erect. He just looked furious.

The man with the gun turned at the sound of the

door opening. I stepped forward and sucker-punched him. His nose crunched under my tight fist, and blood spattered onto the curtain-covered walls. The man cursed and stumbled back. I used his own momentum to spin him around, pull him toward me, and hook my right arm around his shoulder. My knife pressed into his throat.

"Nobody moves or he dies!" I hissed.

He was going to die anyway, but they didn't need to know that. Gordon Giles didn't move. Donovan Caine's hand fluttered over the gun in the holster on his hip. Cowboy.

The would-be assassin jerked against me, trying to break my hold. More hot pain blossomed in my shoulder, but I ground my teeth together and shut it out. I jabbed the knife tip into his throat to dissuade him from further movement.

"Who are you working for?" I snarled in his ear.

"I don't know what you're talking about." Sweat trickled down the back of his neck, mixing with my own. He stank of garlic.

"Bullshit. You were assigned to kill Giles if I didn't."

Giles gasped, and his ferretlike face paled. Donovan Caine's hazel eyes narrowed, and his mouth flattened into a hard line.

"Tell me who you're working for, or I am going to cut your throat right here, right now. Brutus isn't coming to help you."

The man stiffened at the mention of the other assassin's name. For a moment, I thought he might tell me, might give me the information I needed, but he arched his back, and I knew he'd made the wrong decision.

"Go to hell, bitch," he spat out the words, along with a mouthful of blood.

"You first."

I cut his throat. Hot, sticky blood spurted out onto my hands. The man gurgled and clutched at the open wound. Gordon Giles screamed once, a high-pitched, girlish sound better suited for an enthusiastic cheerleader than a middle-aged man. He swayed back and forth. His eyes rolled up in the back of his head, and the accountant toppled over in a dead faint. Donovan Caine had a stronger stomach. The detective went for his gun.

Before Caine could get his weapon free of his holster, I shoved the dying man forward, sending him into the detective. Then I turned and sprinted out of the box.

I ran back the way I'd come, pounding up the stairs to the executive floor, grabbing the cello case, bursting through the doors, and running out on the balcony. As soon as I stepped onto the stone patio, I hurled the cello case over the side into the river and rushed toward the hidden rope.

I'd heard Donovan Caine's heavy footsteps in the stairwell below me. No time to be cautious, to be safe. I'd have to climb down the side of the cliffs and hope Caine was a lousy shot or didn't cut the rope before I reached the bottom—

"Stop right there!" a male voice boomed.

I froze and looked over my shoulder. Donovan Caine advanced on me, his gun leveled at my chest with the steadiness of a man who knows he's an excellent shot. I turned and raised my hands, even as I took a step back toward the balcony.

"Who are you?" he snarled. "Who are you working for?"

"I honestly don't know," I said in an even voice. "Things have gotten a little complicated this evening."

His eyes glinted like smoky topaz. "Complicated how?"

He wasn't shooting me on the spot. Good for me, sloppy on his part.

"Somebody set me up," I said. "I was supposed to kill Giles and walk away, but somebody had other ideas. They wanted to kill me before I did the job, then blame me for his murder. If you check up on the catwalk, you'll find a dead man. His name is Brutus. He's an assassin. Goes by the nickname Viper."

Caine took another step forward. "I don't believe you."

"I don't care what you believe. The point is Gordon Giles is still in danger. I'd be more worried about him than me."

The detective thought about it, his black jacket struggling to contain the strength of his coiled muscles. His features were rough and rugged in the shadows. Patches of darkness painted his cheekbones, but the moonlight frosted his dark hair and outlined his thick lips.

Despite the seriousness of the situation, I thought about those lips against mine. His heavy tongue stroking my own, then moving down my body one sweet, slow inch at a time, before plunging into the curls at the junction of my thighs. Mmm.

"You're coming with me," he said.

With his free hand, Caine reached inside his jacket pocket and drew out a pair of silverstone handcuffs. He tossed them on the balcony between us. The metal clinked to a stop at my booted feet.

"Put those on."

"Handcuffs. Kinky. But I prefer to have a bit more freedom during sex. Don't you?"

Caine jerked as though I'd yanked the gun out of his hands and shot him. His eyes flicked down my body, going to my breasts and thighs, before coming back to my face. Yeah, he was thinking about it. All the distraction I needed.

"There's no need to bother with those because you aren't taking me in, detective."

"Where are you going to go?" Caine asked. "You're trapped up here."

I smiled. "Me? Trapped? Never."

Using my legs, I turned, leaped up onto the balcony wall, and launched myself over the side into the darkness below.

✳ 6 ✳

I managed to propel myself far enough out from the balcony so that I missed the sharp, jagged rocks of the cliffs
below. The wind screeched in my ears before my body
plunged into the murky depths of the Aneirin River.

I flipped over during my descent and hit the water
feetfirst. The force of my fall ripped the weapons from
my hands and knifed me down to the rocky riverbed, fifty
feet below the surface. The black water was so cold I felt
like I'd been flash-frozen. The icy, cruel shock of it stole
precious air from my lungs. But I didn't flail or try to
struggle to the surface. Instead I let the current catch me
in its rough embrace and drag me downriver. I started
counting the seconds in my head. Ten, twenty, thirty . . .

When I reached forty-five, I kicked up. My water-
logged clothes and boots weighed me down, but I broke
free of the water. I gasped in a breath and sank back under
the surface. Ten, twenty, thirty . . .

When I reached forty-five, I kicked up again. This time, I stayed up. I treaded water and looked back at the opera house. Lights blazed on the balcony, from which I'd jumped. Figures moved back and forth on the ledge, but I was too far away to see who they were. I wondered if Donovan Caine was still on the balcony. Or if he'd gone back to Gordon Giles to hustle the accountant to safety.

But I couldn't think about them right now. I had to reach Fletcher. Even though Brutus was dead, news of the botched assassination attempt would start leaking out—along with the fact Giles was still alive. Whoever had hired Brutus would start cleaning house, killing everyone who might be able to point the finger of guilt at him, including Fletcher.

I turned my head and swam for shore.

It took me twenty minutes to reach the opposite side of the river. By the time I plodded up the sloping, muddy bank, I'd drifted half a mile downstream from the opera house. Blue and red police lights flashed in the distance, and a bloodhound bayed at the moon. His brothers and sisters joined him in a low, throaty chorus. The sound echoed across the river to me, then bounced back. They weren't assuming I'd drowned. Too bad.

Despite the Ice magic in my veins, the frigid water had taken its toll. My teeth chattered, and my short fingernails had blued out from the cold. The groove in my shoulder where the bullet had grazed me felt tight and numb, and my kidneys ached from Brutus's blows. So did my left arm where he'd sliced it with the knife. And worst of all, I smelled rotten, like catfish.

But I forced myself to keep moving, to put one foot in front of the other. I increased my puttering pace to a swift walk, then a jog. I had to move. Had to keep warm until I could get some dry clothes.

While I jogged, I unzipped a pocket on my vest and fished out my cell phone. Thanks to my waterproof case, I still had a signal. I dialed the number for the Pork Pit. The phone rang and rang and rang. Fletcher should have been there. He always waited for me at the barbecue restaurant after a job. He should have answered.

I tried Finnegan's number. No answer. Dread flooded my body, adding to my misery, making my chest hurt, weighing me down. But I pushed it aside and forced my feet to move. Faster. I had to go faster. Water squished out of my boots with every quick step.

I ran two miles in the dark, stumbling most of the way. I stayed just inside the dense row of shrubbery and fir trees that lined the highway. Cars whizzed by on the four-lane, but I didn't dare try to stop one of them or hail a cab. A wet possum looked more appealing than me right now. Smelled better too.

Up ahead, I spotted a sign for one of the Sell-Everything superstores that dotted the city like cavernous zits on a teenager's face. One of Mab Monroe's many business interests. For once, I was grateful to see such a blatant symbol of southern corporate America. Because all of my knives had gotten ripped away from me when I'd hit the river, and I'd need new weapons to save Fletcher and Finn. Dry clothes and shoes too, or I ran the risk of hypothermia. Despite my jog, my teeth still chattered and my hands shook from the cold water. Hard to cut somebody if your fingers were too numb to wrap around the hilt of your knife. As much as I hated a second's delay in getting to Fletcher and Finn, I needed some supplies before I went after them.

Or we'd all be dead.

I trudged into the parking lot and headed for the fall garden section, deserted except for the day's fading pansies and bags of mulch that hadn't sold. I slipped past the low wall of cinder blocks that separated the flowers from the parking lot. Rows of rakes and leaf blowers hung on the makeshift peg-board walls, and the whole area reeked of fertilizer. The door to the store itself was still open, and I headed inside. All around me, the cheap concrete of the building beeped and chimed like a cash register.

An empty cart, abandoned by some wayward shopper, stood by the entrance. I pushed the squeaking metal contraption to the women's section and grabbed the first clothes that looked like they might fit. Jeans. A bra. Panties. Long-sleeved black T-shirt. Matching fleece jacket. Socks. Boots. A black baseball cap with a red primrose rune stitched on it. The symbol for beauty. Because baseball caps were so beautiful in and of themselves.

My next stop was the pharmacy, where I grabbed antibiotic ointment, gauze, superstrength aspirin, and more medical supplies. I did a drive-by in the beauty section, picking up deodorant and body freshener to try to smother my catfish perfume. Then I went to the outdoors aisle and dumped several packs of chemical hand warmers into the cart. My final stop was the kitchen section. Several large knives went on top of my pile of goods.

I pushed the full cart to the self-checkout lane in the front of the store. I fished a credit card with a fake name out of my soggy vest and paid for the items. A clerk stationed by the registers gave me a bored look, then went back to her magazine. Since I was merely wet and cold, and not strung out and jonesing for blood like the vampire hookers who shopped late at night, I didn't merit her attention.

I took my items to the bathroom in the back of the store. I locked the door behind me and stripped off my wet clothes, shivering all the while. Using the supplies I'd just bought, I cleaned the wound in my shoulder and the one on my bicep, glued them together with liquid skin, and covered both with gauze bandages. The injuries still throbbed and pulsed with heat, but they weren't deep enough to need stitches. The bullet had just grazed my shoulder, instead of punching through it.

Of course, I could have gone to Jo-Jo's and had her take care of me. A few minutes with the Air elemental healer, and I would have felt like I'd spent a week being pampered at a ritzy spa. But I didn't have that kind of time.

Not if I wanted to get to Fletcher and Finn before they got dead.

I tried calling the father and son again as I hosed myself down with the deodorant and body freshener, changed into the dry clothes, and cracked aspirin between my teeth. No answer.

I ripped open the hand warmers and stuffed them into

the pockets of the jacket and jeans, and down into the space between my boots and socks. The bloody clothes got tossed into the trash. No point in hiding them. They were generic clothes you could find in any store. It wasn't like I'd stitched my name inside them: Property of Gin Blanco.

Besides, if Donovan Caine was smart, he'd check every store, gas station, and cab company in a five-mile radius of the opera house. Sooner or later, he'd get the surveillance footage from Sell-Everything. He would know I'd come in here to get cleaned up.

But that was all he'd know.

I ripped open the plastic covering the knives and tested one with my thumb. Not as sharp as I liked; the balance was off, and the wooden handle was slick as hot shit in the summertime, but it would do the job. Just about anything would, if you put enough force behind it. I tucked two knives up my jacket sleeves. One went against the small of my back, and two more slid into my boots, nestled next to the hand warmers.

Brutus had already paid for double-crossing me. Now it was his mysterious employer's turn and anyone else who got between me and Fletcher and Finnegan. I hoped Donovan Caine and the rest of the police force were stocked up on coffee and doughnuts and approved for overtime. Because the body count in Ashland was about to go up tonight—way up.

Hidden in the shadows, I stared at the front door of the Pork Pit. The neon pig glowed in the dark night, its pink lights taking on a blood-red tinge. Or perhaps that was just my thoughts darkening at what I might find inside the innocent-looking storefront.

I checked my watch. After ten. More than two hours since the botched assassination attempt at the opera house. I'd been crouching here three minutes, hoping for a sign of life inside. Nothing. Using my cell phone, I'd called the restaurant again, but Fletcher still hadn't answered. I'd tried Finn again, too. No response.

They were both probably dead already.

Brutus's employer would want to know about me—where I'd go, what I'd do, who I'd talk to. Fletcher and Finnegan could give him that information. Two hours was a long time to be in the hands of the enemy. Two minutes was enough to break most people. Even without magic.

The smart thing to do would have been to walk away. To melt into the shadows. To disappear the way Fletcher had taught me. The way we'd always planned if something went wrong. I had enough fake IDs and credit cards in my vest to get me started, and more than enough cash hidden in various overseas accounts to live a life of anonymous luxury. It would have been easier than eating peach pie.

But I couldn't do that. I couldn't push Fletcher and Finn out of my mind. Couldn't turn my back on them. Couldn't disregard them and walk away like they would have wanted me to. Not when there might be a chance of saving one or both of them. I owed them that. They'd taken me in off the streets when I'd had nowhere else to go. I owed them everything. And they would have done the same for me. The father and son would have come for me as soon as they could, despite their own vows to the contrary. No, I wasn't walking away from them. Not now, not ever.

Besides, I'd never been one to take the easy path in life. Easy was for people too weak to suck it up and do what needed to be done.

And I wasn't weak. Not anymore.

I approached the Pork Pit from the back, slipping into the alley that ran behind the building. My eyes caught on a black crack across from the back of the restaurant, a narrow space just big enough for a child to squeeze into.

A hard smile curved my lips. An old hiding spot of mine, back when I'd been living on the streets. Empty and much too small for me now. Besides, I didn't need to hide. I'd become what I was so I'd never have to run and hide again.

But that didn't mean I still shouldn't be cautious. So I hunkered down beside one of the metal Dumpsters. Looking. Listening. Waiting.

Nothing. Not even a rat digging in the container beside me. Something very, very bad must have happened to scare the rats away.

I put my hand on the building, listening to the stone. The clogged contentment of yesterday had taken on a harsh, strident note. Something had upset the brick, intruded on its usual peace. Something sudden. Unexpected. Bloody. Violent. The low, sharp, vibrating rasp pounded in my skull like a dirge for the dead.

Fletcher.

My hand reached for the back door of the restaurant.

I stopped. The door stood ajar just a tiny crack, hardly enough to be noticeable, but I'd spent the last seventeen years noticing everything and everyone around me. The kitchen knives slid into my hands. I backed away from the door and peered at it. A thin, black wire wrapped around the doorknob and led inside, hence the crack. Using one of the knives, I sliced the wire, careful not to jiggle it. Then I stood to one side of the door and pulled it open.

A shotgun had been erected inside the back room, rigged to fire when the door was opened. Turn the knob, step inside, and get two barrels to the chest. A crude but effective trap.

I waited and listened. Silence. Cold, cold silence.

Fletcher should have been puttering about the kitchen or doing inventory in the stockroom. Should have been brewing his chicory coffee and reading his latest book. The quiet chilled me far more than the river had, soaking into my bones like an icy rain, despite the chemical hand warmers in my pockets.

I eased into the restaurant, checking the floor and ceiling around the door for more traps. Nothing. I paused after every step. Waiting, looking, searching. Nothing moved, not even the granddaddy long-leg spiders in their cubbyholes in the corners.

Finally, in front of the counter in the storefront, I found him.

Fletcher Lane sprawled across a crimson pool of blood on the floor. Several jagged stab wounds and spatters of blood marred his ripped, torn, blue work apron, almost like a bottle of ketchup had exploded on him. His clothes lay in tatters around him, defensive cuts blackened his hands, and his knuckles were swollen and bruised, as though he'd hit someone repeatedly. Money spilled out of the busted cash register, sticking to the tacky, bloody floor, along with the battered copy of *Where the Red Fern Grows* he'd been reading. Pieces of a broken cup dotted the floor beside him, along with the dregs of his chicory coffee. Caffeine fumes lingered in the air. The faint aroma made my heart twist.

Fletcher had also been tortured—by an Air elemental.

Long pieces of skin were missing from his face, arms, hands. The stomach-turning stench of raw meat over-powered the pancake pools of copper-scented blood on the floor. The Air elemental had used his fingers like they were fucking sandblasters, forcing oxygen under Fletcher's skin. Making it blister and burn and bubble up before he ripped it off, muscles, tendons, and all. A small strip here, a thumbprint-size indentation there, a fist-shaped mark right over his heart. None of the wounds immediately lethal, but all of them excruciatingly painful. The wounds were so deep I could see Fletcher's bones in places. Sticks of dirty ivory floating in a red, soupy mess of ripped flesh.

Fletcher had been flayed alive by magic.

And the Air elemental had kept right on torturing Fletcher, even after he was dead. That was the only way to explain all the missing skin. All the gruesome blisters and horrid bubbles of flesh. There were so, so many of them. All causing more pain than most folks experienced in a lifetime.

It turned my stomach.

I might have killed people, but I usually ended their lives quickly. A single wound. Two at the most. Quick, sure, accurate. This . . . somebody had taken extreme pleasure in this. Glee. Joy, even.

My vision blurred. Something burned in my eyes. Crying. I was crying. Something I hadn't done in seventeen years. I drew in a breath and exhaled a sob. My body shook. My lips trembled. A curious lightness filled my head. I couldn't look at Fletcher. Not now. Not when I was so close to losing control. To giving in to this emotional weakness.

I hunkered down on my ankles and forced myself to take deep breaths. To focus on drawing the air deep into my lungs and down into the pit of my roiling stomach. As though that was the most important thing in the world. As though Fletcher wasn't lying a foot in front of me. Dead.

When I'd come back to myself, I opened my gray eyes and stared at the repulsive wounds. Not as a person who'd just discovered a horrific murder. Not as the woman who'd just lost her mentor, the old man she'd loved. And definitely not as Gin, whose shredded heart had just been sliced up and dumped onto a plate like shoestring french fries.

No, I examined the wounds as an assassin, as the Spider. Cold. Clinical. Detached. Determined to learn what I could from them.

And I found something. The elemental who'd burned Fletcher was a woman, someone with slender, delicate hands, judging from the dainty size of the fist over Fletcher's heart. I balled up my own hand in comparison. Hers was smaller.

The fact that a woman had tortured Fletcher didn't surprise me. I'd learned long ago the fairer sex was much more vicious than men—and much more patient. This one, this sadistic bitch . . . she'd reveled in torturing Fletcher. In using her magic to hurt him. In slowly flaying him alive. In hearing him scream for mercy until his throat was as red as his raw skin.

And she was going to pay for it. More than she'd ever fucking imagined.

Whatever else happened tonight, whether Finn was dead or alive, I wasn't running. Not from this. Not from her. I wasn't skipping town and lying low in some foreign country for a while. Ashland might not be the most pleasant place, but it was home. More importantly, the Pork Pit was home, as crazy as that sounded. I wasn't leaving it behind. Not like this. Not with Fletcher's blood covering the floor like a fresh coat of wax.

I held my breath, waiting for Fletcher to turn his head, open his dull green eyes, and grouse at me for keeping him waiting. But he didn't do that. And he never would again.

The bitch who'd done this was going to pay for that.

I needed to go. Needed to move. Needed to get to Finn, if it wasn't already too late. But I couldn't tear myself away from Fletcher's body.

He was the one who'd taken me in off the streets when I'd had nowhere else to go. Who'd rescued me from fighting the rats for garbage to eat. Saved me from selling my body to the vampire pimps. Taught me how to be strong. Showed me how to survive—and live with what I had to do to stay that way.

As I crouched there over Fletcher's bloody body, a faint scuffle sounded. A slight, scraping noise that intruded upon my grief. More than enough to snap my cold, calm control back into place. A shadow fell over the pools of Fletcher's drying blood, turning the crimson puddles an inky black.

Sloppy, sloppy, sloppy.

My fingers tightened around the knife in my hand. I turned and whirled it at the man behind me. The metal flashed through the air and sank into his right arm. He howled in pain and lunged at me, slashing with a switch-blade. I sidestepped his clumsy, awkward blow. Using his own momentum, I shoved the man forward. He crashed into the counter and fell to the floor. I leaped on him and knocked the blade out of his hand. I straddled the man, crushing his ribs between my knees.

I didn't care about the wound throbbing in my shoulder or the burning nick on my arm. Didn't think about the cold that just wouldn't leave my body or the exhaustion slowing my movements. I just hit him—over and over and over, smashing my tight knuckles into his face until the skin on my hands broke and bled.

It felt good to hurt him. So fucking *good*.

The man moaned and mumbled with pain. I forced myself to stop before I killed him. Not yet. I drew in a ragged breath. The metallic scent of his blood pooled in my mouth like saliva, making me hunger for more. I yanked my knife out of the man's arm. He snarled. I leaned forward and pressed my forearm against his throat, cutting off his oxygen.

I brought the bloody tip up where he could see it. "You

will tell me everything that happened in this room to-night. You will tell me who you're working for, what her plans are. You will tell me anything I want to know and be glad to do it."

"And why . . . is that . . . bitch?" the man spat out.

I leaned forward until my gray eyes were directly over his.

"Because the first cut won't kill you," I said in a calm, dead voice. "Nor the second, nor the third, nor even the tenth. But you will wish to all the spirits you pray to that they had."

❖ 7 ❖

I didn't get a specific name or much useful information out of him. I was too angry and in too much of a hurry to use the finesse needed for those sorts of things. Besides, he was just the help, dispatched to do one final check to see if I'd show up at the restaurant. He'd seen the open back door and followed me inside. But the man confirmed my suspicion—Finnegan was next. Which meant I had to move if I had any hope of saving him.

As much as it hurt, I left Fletcher's body where it was behind the counter. Sophia Deveraux, the dwarven cook who came in early every morning to bake the sourdough bread for the day's sandwiches, would find Fletcher. She'd call the cops. Given the debris and overturned cash register, the police would think it was a robbery gone wrong. That's what they thought every crime was in Ashland. Fletcher would be just another statistic, another case file, another unsolved murder among hundreds every year.

Before I left the restaurant, I washed the blood off my hands and face, along with my tears. I also dragged the dead man's body to the cold storage room and dumped him in one of the empty freezers. I taped a pink sticky note to the top of the appliance to catch Sophia's eye. She'd know what to do with the body. The dwarf was Fletcher's go-to gal for disposal work.

I reached behind a different freezer and pulled out a black duffel bag, one of several I had stashed in various spots throughout the city. Money, cell phones, credit cards, weapons, fake IDs, makeup, a few clothes. Everything I needed to make a quick getaway, change my appearance, or do an unexpected, dirty job.

I stepped back into the front of the restaurant and crouched beside Fletcher. A few more tears gathered in my eyes as I looked at his still, brutalized form. I let the stinging, salty wetness trickle down my face. There wasn't time to properly mourn Fletcher, to let myself grieve. The time to do that would come later—when the bitch who'd killed him was as dead as he was.

Cold comfort. Because no matter what I did to her, no matter how much I tortured her, no matter how slowly I killed her, it wouldn't bring Fletcher back. Nothing would do that.

"Good-bye, Fletcher." My voice cracked on the words.

A tear dripped off my cheek and mixed with the blood and burns on his face. I straightened and wiped the rest of the moisture away, composing myself once more. Then

I smashed the glass and lock on the front door, stepped outside, and walked away.

It took me twenty minutes to reach Finnegan Lane's place. Like me, Finn lived in an apartment building near the restaurant. Except his place made mine look like a hobo's wet cardboard box. The metal behemoth towered twelve stories into the air, topped by an elegant spire, like it was a real skyscraper instead of a piss-poor southern substitute.

I headed around to the side entrance for the tenants, tastefully hidden behind two tall magnolia trees. A minute and two Ice picks later, the door opened, and I slid inside. Despite the late hour, folks still prowled the halls, as the businesspeople who lived in the building brought their nightly conquests back for a few more drinks and some alcohol-fueled fumbling and fucking in the dark.

I got into one of the elevators on its way up. A man in his eighties wearing a rumpled tux and a shaggy toupee slobbered on the ear of a blond hooker, while another rubbed his burgeoning crotch. A third girl, a brunette, stood off to the side, not involved or not caring to become so in the ménage à trois. Four really was a crowd.

The two hookers gave me a hard stare. Their red lips drew back, and they flashed their fangs at me. Vampires. Upscale ones, from the pearl white color of their pointed teeth. But when they realized I wasn't horning in on their action, they went back to telling the old guy how much they were going to enjoy getting screwed by him. My lips twitched. Funniest damn thing I'd heard all night.

The man got off on the sixth floor with his two friends for the evening, leaving me alone with the third woman. I stared at her outfit. Bright color, flashy enough, not too tight, around a size six. It would work.

I hit the stop button in the elevator and turned to the other woman. Her hand drifted down to her purse, and she eyed me with the wary look of a high-priced call girl who knows strangers can be dangerous, especially in the nice part of town. Her fangs poked through her lips. Another vampire.

"I'll give you two thousand dollars for your clothes, shoes, and that purse," I said.

"The clothes?" she asked, her brown gaze even more uncertain now. "That's it? Nothing weird? Nothing extra?"

I flashed her a wad of bills. "Nothing weird *or* extra."

Five minutes later, the hooker got off on the ninth floor wearing my cheap jacket, jeans, and boots. A minute after that, I stepped out onto the eleventh floor. I went into the emergency stairwell and opened my duffel bag. Hairbrush, lipstick, compact. It didn't take long for me to paint my face, tease out my bleached hair, and otherwise transform myself into Gin, the ditsy call girl. I also grabbed three silverstone knives out of the bag, sticking the first against the small of my back and palming the second in my right hand. The third got stuffed inside the hooker's minuscule purse.

Girded for battle, I left the bag in the stairwell, got back in the elevator, and rode up to the twelfth floor—Finn's floor.

Investment banker, computer expert, and all-around

shady character Finnegan Lane had done well for himself, which is why his apartment took up the entire floor instead of several thousand spacious feet, like the building's other housing units. Finn didn't believe in hiding one's wealth, and he didn't care that his gauche, nouveau riche ways upset his older, more genteel clients. Those folks, especially the vampires who'd been around since before the Civil War, despised his flashy ways, but Finn made them enough money to get them to choke on their antiquated southern standards.

Still, I was always extra cautious when I visited Finn's place. He might not be as deep into the assassin business as I was, but he still made plenty of enemies with his banking and stockbroker schemes—legal and otherwise. People were more vicious about money than any other thing, even sex. Add Finn's rampant womanizing to the mix, and it was a wonder somebody hadn't hired me to kill him years ago.

The elevator opened, and I stepped out into the glossy antechamber that fronted Finn's apartment. Low walnut table. Two chairs. Gilded mirror on the wall. A couple of fake pecan trees planted on either side of the front door. Southern decor at its finest.

A guard stationed outside jerked his head in my direction at the sound of the elevator opening. A big man, tall and wide with a beefy neck that would have been a perfect fit on an NFL linebacker. Probably some giant blood in his family tree. Still, he was only one guy. I would have had at least three men out here. Maybe more, since I knew exactly what I was capable of—and how very determined I was to get to Finnegan before he quit breathing.

The guard frowned, but he didn't go for his gun or knock on the door behind him to alert whoever might be inside. Mistake number one. I ambled toward him, swinging my hips and letting my short, zebra-striped skirt ride up and show off my long, toned, fishnet-clad legs. I'd already undone most of the buttons on my scarlet silk blouse to let my five-dollar black bra peep through.

The floor of the antechamber was made of fine marble, and the stone's delicate murmur rang in time to my heels tapping across it. For the first time tonight, my spirits crept up. The vibrations would have been different if Finn had been dead already. Darker, lower, somber. Like the stones at the Pork Pit. A sound I'd never, ever forget.

Fletcher.

I pushed all thought of my mentor, all weak, devastating emotion aside, and focused on the man in front of me. On what I was here to do. I stopped about three feet away from the guard, struck a model pose, dropped my head, batted my lashes, and gave him my most flirtatious look. If there was one thing all southern women instinctively know how to do, it's flirt. It's encoded in our DNA, along with a fondness for grease, sugar, and oversize hats.

"Hi there, handsome," I said in a soft, breathy voice. "I'm Candy. I'm here to see Finny."

"Mr. Lane is otherwise engaged this evening. Important meeting." The guard's tone was gruff, but his pale eyes scorched a path from my breasts down my legs and back up.

I giggled. "Yeah, with me, silly."

The guard let himself look a second longer, then shook

his head. "Sorry. This is another meeting. You're going to have to leave."

I pouted. "But Finny and I *always* have a date on Sunday nights. I'm his after-hours girl."

The guard didn't say anything, but his gaze kept flicking between my breasts and legs. If he did that any faster, he'd give himself vertigo. I pouted a moment longer, then widened my gray eyes and smiled, as though the most amazing thought in the world had just occurred to me.

I stepped forward. The guard stiffened, but he didn't back away. I looked at him through my lashes and trailed my fingers down his broad chest. He wasn't wearing anything underneath his blue pinstriped shirt. No vest, no protective gear. Bad for him, good for me.

"Well, what about you, sugar? Can I interest you in sampling some sweet, sweet Candy tonight? A girl's gotta pay her rent, if you know what I mean."

The guard opened his mouth, but he never got a chance to respond. Because I brought my right hand up and shoved the knife I had palmed there into his chest. His eyes bulged with surprise. I clamped my hand over his mouth to keep him from screaming, wrenched the knife out, and stabbed him again.

The guard should have shot me the second I stepped out of the elevator. Never mind the mistake of letting me within arm's reach. Sloppy, sloppy, sloppy. But a pretty girl is a pretty girl, and men always want to look at and talk to and fuck those. Even if his boss had warned him to watch out for any woman who came near him tonight.

The guard's eyes glazed over, and he quit struggling. I eased his large, heavy body to the floor and retrieved my knife. I also rifled through his pockets, pulling out his wallet and cell phone, and putting them on the walnut table for pickup later. He wasn't wearing any jewelry, not even a watch.

Underneath my feet, the light, dainty murmur of the marble floor took on a harsher note as puddles of blood sluiced on top of it. Another sound I was familiar with.

Once I had the guard taken care of, I turned my attention to the apartment door. Since the walls themselves were constructed of metal and wood instead of stone, I couldn't use my elemental magic to sense what waited behind the barrier. But I wasn't leaving without discovering what was happening, or had happened, to Finn. I'd just have to take my chances.

I turned the knob and opened the door a crack. Voices drifted out to me, faint, low, indistinct murmurs. They must be in the living room.

I slid inside the door and paused. Finn's apartment was shaped like a large F. The elevator led to the narrow antechamber, which in turn led to the hallway where I stood. The hall flowed all the way to the back of the apartment before taking a right turn and opening up into a wide living room. The master bedroom and bath were located at the far end of the living room. Halfway between here and there was another right turn, which led into the kitchen.

I tiptoed forward, knives in both hands now, and eased into the kitchen. Appliances, marble countertops, a couple of sinks. I passed them all, hugging the wall and moving farther into the room.

I paused when I came to the cutout that connected the kitchen to the living room. A mirror glinted on the back wall of the other room. The pane of glass gave me a clear, if backwards reflection of that area.

They had him tied to a straight-backed chair. Finnegan Lane was very much his father's son, with ruddy skin, a thick, muscular body, and dark, walnut-colored hair. Sturdy Scots-Irish stock, just like me and so many other folks in the Appalachian Mountains. His eyes would have been a merry green, if they hadn't been mostly swelled shut. Cuts and bruises showed on his face, and blood dribbled down his chin, spattering on his white dress shirt, black pants, and polished shoes.

Anger filled me at the sight of Finn's battered face, but I pushed it aside and kept staring at his body, looking for missing pieces of skin and other signs of torture. I didn't see any, and the stench of ripped flesh didn't contaminate the air. The Air elemental who'd tortured Fletcher wasn't here—yet.

Finn looked like he'd been out on the town before he'd been tied up. He might have even been at the opera to-night. Finn enjoyed those sorts of social functions, mixing with rich people who had even more secrets than he did and would do anything to keep them.

If Finn had been at the opera house, it would have been easy enough to grab him in the confusion and bring him back to the apartment for a more private conversation. It would also explain the delay in having tortured and killed him by now.

I studied the guards. The first guy was almost seven feet tall, with wide, powerful shoulders, pale, milky skin, and oversize, buglike eyes. A giant, and definitely the muscle, which is why I didn't see any bulges under his loose-fitting suit. Who needed a gun when your fists were the size of bowling balls?

The other guy was shorter, a human. His skin was dark, like polished ebony, and he wore a set of square, gold-frame glasses. He carried a gun—one under either shoulder.

As I watched, Shortie stepped forward.

"Just tell us where she is, and this can all be over with," he said in a pleasant voice. "I promise we'll make the end quick. Three in the back of your head. You won't feel a thing."

Finnegan raised his head and stared at the guy through his bruised, swollen face. "Here's what I think of you and your fucking promises."

Finn spat blood into Shortie's face. The scarlet spittle hit his glasses, spewing over the lenses like windshield washer fluid. Shortie straightened and removed his glasses. He jerked his head at Tall Guy, who slammed his fist into Finn's face. His nose popped and crunched like cereal. Despite the beating, I had to smile. Finnegan Lane never lacked for defiance or style.

Tall Guy finished his latest round of punishment, and Finn sat there coughing up blood. Shortie drew a hand-kerchief out of his pocket and cleaned his glasses. Once the lenses were back on his face, Shortie circled Finn, try-ing his tactic again.

"Surely you see how pointless this is. Your father is already dead."

Fletcher. Hearing the words out loud was a bitch slap to my heart. I gritted my teeth against the pain and fo-cused on what was important now—Finn.

"No one is coming to save you," Shortie continued. "Certainly not the assassin. She jumped off a two-hundred-foot balcony at the opera house. If the fall didn't kill her, she's probably on her way out of town—if the police don't catch up with her first."

I frowned. Police? I didn't like the sound of that. Especially the way Shortie referred to them as if they were his own personal force. This had morphed from a mere setup into a full-blown conspiracy. I wondered how long Brutus, Shortie, and their compatriots had been planning this—and how Fletcher, Finn, and I had been so sloppy as to get caught in the middle of this sticky spiderweb.

"Come on," Shortie wheedled. "Make it easy on yourself. Tell us where she might go. That's all we want. Some places to start looking for her—if she's not already dead."

Finn laughed, though the effort made him cough up more blood.

"What's so funny?" Shortie asked. "I would think a man in your situation would be incapable of something as foolish as laughter."

Finn raised his head. A twinkle of green could be seen through the red and purple bruises that marred his face. "She's not dead, and you haven't caught her because she's smarter than you are. Better. Stronger. But she'll be coming for you soon, asshole. You and whoever you work for. You might as well start planning your own funeral."

"She's only one woman," Shortie pointed out.

Finn laughed again, a deep, throaty chuckle that tugged at me. I'd never realized before how much his laugh sounded like Fletcher's.

"She's not one woman—she's the fucking Spider. That's why you hired her, remember? Because she's the best. So you can take your questions and promises and screw yourself six ways from Sunday. Because I'm not saying another word, and I'll be seeing you in hell real soon."

I made sure the knives were properly positioned in my hands. I'd only get one shot at them before they killed Finn. I wasn't losing Finn. Not now, not ever.

"He's not going to talk. This is pointless. Finish him," Shortie snapped.

Tall Guy stepped forward and drew back his fist for the killing blow. Finn looked up at his approaching death and smiled. I skirted around the wall and stepped into the room.

Tall Guy was too focused on Finn to notice me. My first knife went into his left eye, one of the few soft spots on a giant's head. Tall Guy jerked, a puppet whose strings had been snapped. His other buglike eye widened, and for a moment, I thought it might spring from his head like a toy. He went down on his knees, then pitched forward. His head ended up in Finnegan's lap. He never made a sound.

Shortie was more observant. Faster, too. He managed to get a gun out from under his suit jacket. But I crossed the room in quick steps and knocked the weapon away before he could bring it up. Shortie swung at me, but I ducked his wide blow, came up inside his meager defense, and plunged the second knife into his heart. He spasmed against me, whimpering and struggling to get free, even as his blood coated my hand.

"You really should have listened to Finn," I hissed in his face, forcing the weapon deeper into his chest.

He died with a sputter.

Shortie slackened against me, and I shoved him away. The body thumped onto the floor. Lovely sound.

"It's about time you got here." Finn's voice came out in a low, pain-filled rasp.

I pulled the knife out of Shortie, then yanked the other one out of Tall Guy's eye. I used the bloody weapons to slice through Finn's bonds, then shoved the giant's body off him.

"And the man outside? Or do I even have to ask?" Finn said.

I looked at him.

"Right. Dumb question."

I stared at the bodies on the floor. Blood oozed out of their wounds, ruining the pristine white of the fluffy shag carpet. Still more gobs of blood covered me, as though a bucket of paint had been upended over my head.

But all I could see was Fletcher's body, beaten and flayed and tortured inside the Pork Pit. Broken and dead. My eyes flicked to Finn. His handsome face, reduced to mushy pulp. I didn't often feel rage, but a cold, hard knot of it pulsed in my chest, right where my heart would be.

My thumb traced over the hilt of my knife. Too quick. This had all been too damn quick. These men hadn't suffered like Fletcher had. They'd barely felt a thing. A ribbon of fire, the world fading away, and they were gone. Easy. Fast. Relatively painless.

The knot of rage in my chest twitched, and I wanted to leap onto the guards' bodies, to hack and slash and mutilate them until no one would be sure what part was which or went with whom. To send a message to their boss, just the way she'd sent one to me by brutalizing Fletcher.

But Finn was hurt and needed a healer. Besides, something could always go wrong. I'd had enough adrenaline for this, but now I could feel the crash coming. My hands and legs twitched from fatigue, stress, overuse. And I still felt cold and clammy from my swan dive into the icy river.

Revenge, justice, retribution, karma, whatever the fuck you wanted to call it, could wait. Keeping Finn safe and breathing, that was my priority now. My mission. That's what Fletcher would have asked me to do.

For once in my life, I was going to do exactly what the old man wanted.

I turned my back on the bodies. Finn lowered himself to his hands and knees, rifling through the dead men's pockets, pulling out their wallets and cell phones. He also ripped off their watches and a gold chain from Shortie's neck. Finn started to open one of the wallets, but I took it away from him.

"Later," I said. "We need to get you over to Jo-Jo's. You look like shit warmed over."

Finn grimaced. "That bad, huh?"

"Trust me. You don't want to look in the mirror right now. Your ego couldn't take it."

Finn snorted. "Please. My ego can take anything." He jerked his head at the bodies. "What about them?"

"Sophia, of course. You know how she loves this sort of work." I picked up the cordless phone resting on a table and hit the number 7. Like me, Finn had the dwarf programmed into his speed dial. The phone rang twice before she picked up.

"Hmph?" The low grunt was Sophia Deveraux's usual greeting. The dwarf wasn't big on conversation.

"It's Gin," I said. "I've made a mess over at Finn's apartment. Need you to come clean it up."

"Hmm." A little more interest in this grunt than the first one.

"Two inside, one before you get to the elevator. Small, medium, and large." Our code for a human, a half giant, and a giant.

"Damage?" Her voice rasped worse than a whiskey-drinking, hard-living chain smoker's would have. When she did deign to speak, Sophia liked to limit herself to small spurts of syllables. Nothing too strenuous. Then again, her dwarven sister, Jo-Jo, talked enough for both of them.

I eyed the blood-soaked carpet. Finn might have thought he was hip having that white shag installed, but now it resembled spaghetti covering the floor—with a couple of meatballs on top. "Let's just say the marble floor outside the apartment will be considerably easier to clean than the carpet inside. You coming?"

"Um-mmm." Sophia's grunt for yes.

"Good. And be careful. Small, medium, and large might have some friends come check on them later. We're heading to Jo-Jo's. See you there." I hung up the phone and turned back to Finn. "She's on her way. Go get whatever you need for the next few days. Clothes, your computer, whatever. You're staying with me until this is over."

Finn nodded, got to his feet, and took a step. One of his legs crumpled. He stumbled, swayed, and almost fell over the chair he'd been tied to. I hurried to Finn's side, put my shoulder under his, and helped him into the bedroom. Finn sat on the bed while I threw some suits, his laptop, and a few more requested items into a duffel bag, along with the wallets and jewelry we'd taken off the dead guys.

Ten minutes later, the doors on the elevator slid open, revealing the dim parking garage attached to the back of Finn's building. I helped Finn limp out of the elevator. Dark, dirty concrete rolled out in every direction. Late-model luxury sedans sat waiting in their assigned slips in front of a narrow ramp that angled and turned up to the next level. Fluorescent lights flickered over the vehicles, and a bug zapper hung in one corner. A moth flapping around the zapper decided to land on the glowing, tempting blue surface. The resulting *crack* and *sizzle* sounded like a grenade exploding in the enclosed space.

Finn pointed to a set of stairs that ran between the levels, and we tiptoed down them. The smell of motor oil and trapped exhaust thickened the air. I skimmed the fingers of my free hand against the concrete wall. Sharp notes of worry punctuated the stone's mutter. Not unusual. Everybody got a little paranoid and claustrophobic in parking garages, even me.

The low, growling sound didn't ease my mind. Not after the long, bloody night I'd had. But we made our way down to the second level without incident. I dragged Finn toward the closest car I saw that was his—a flashy silver Aston Martin that would have looked right at home in a James Bond movie. Finn collected cars like other people did knickknacks.

"No," Finn groaned. "Not the Aston. Anything but the Aston. I just got it a month ago. The blood will never come out of the leather seats. Even Sophia won't be able to get it out."

"What do you suggest then, your highness?" I snapped.

He pointed. "Get my Benz. At least it's burgundy inside."

I rolled my eyes but did as he asked. Finnegan Lane might not have been my blood brother, but he annoyed me just like a sibling would. Teasing, nagging, provoking, until I wanted to cut out his tongue and fry it up in a skillet for dinner. Still, I'd do anything for him. Even smear his clotting blood inside the vehicle of his choosing.

I opened the door on the black Benz, dumped Finn in the front, threw our stuff in the back, and sank into the driver's seat. The leather felt as soft as a warm mattress, cupping my ass, straightening my spine, supporting my neck and shoulders. Mmm. It felt so good to just sit still for a minute and not worry about my next move—or who might be waiting around the corner to try and take me out. I could have put my head back on the seat and been asleep in under a minute.

Too bad my night was far from over.

Two minutes later, we exited the parking garage. I turned onto the appropriate street and headed north to Jo-Jo's. My route took us past the Pork Pit. The neon pig gleamed like a beacon in the darkness. I tried not to think of Fletcher, lying in a pool of his own blood in the storefront, but the image of his flayed body, his ruined flesh, filled my mind. For the second time tonight, hot tears pricked my eyes. Damn. I hadn't cried this much since I was a kid.

Finn saw the sheen of moisture. "Hey, hey. He wouldn't want you to do that. You know how he felt about crying."

"A waste of time, energy, and resources."

The words came automatically, the way so many of Fletcher's teachings do. The tears were harder to force back, but I managed.

I always managed.

We rode in silence. I coasted to a stop at a red light and drew in a breath. Time to get on with things. Finn and I needed to talk before we got to Jo-Jo's.

"Tell me about it. Where you were, how they jumped you, why they brought you back to your apartment."

"Sure." Finn moved his beaten body to one side so he could look at me without turning his head. "Dad had told me about the job, of course, so I decided to attend the grand opening of the new wing at the opera house. For moral support."

I raised an eyebrow.

"All right, so my lady friend wanted to go too, and I had some clients to schmooze with," Finn admitted. "Several birds, one stone. Know what I mean?"

"Sure," I said in a wry tone.

Finn continued his story. "So I'm at the opera house, private box, wonderful seats, when I hear a man scream. At least, I think it was a man. Rather light in his loafers if you ask me."

Gordon Giles, after I'd cut the other assassin's throat.

"And I figured you'd done your thing and were on your way out of the building. So me and the lady friend go outside with everyone else to see what the commotion's about. And I spot a guy holding a gun chasing after a slim black figure."

Donovan Caine pounding down the hallway after me.

"The news leaks out there's been a murder in one of the private boxes. My lady friend is very, very upset, so I suggest we go somewhere a little quieter where she can calm down."

I rolled my eyes again. "You mean where you can get her alone and have *I'm-so-happy-I didn't-get-my-throat-cut* sex."

A faint grin pulled up Finn's fat, split lips. "We go downstairs to one of the private salons and become otherwise engaged. The door bangs open just as things are getting interesting."

"So they caught you with your pants down."

Finn sighed. "The bastards could have at least let us finish. But they pulled me away, told my lady friend to scram, and drove me to my apartment. I suppose they were hoping you'd show up to save me."

"Did they say anything? Any mention of who they were working for? Why they wanted Gordon Giles dead? Anything?"

"Nothing." Finn shook his head. "They just started hitting me and demanded to know where you were."

I kept driving, stopping at red lights, making the appropriate turns, keeping the car just under the speed limit. The last thing I needed was to get stopped by the police, especially considering the fact Finn and I were both covered in blood. We were almost to Jo-Jo's when Finn asked me the question I'd been dreading ever since I'd stormed into his apartment.

"What—what about Dad?" he asked in a low voice. "What did they do to him?"

My heart lurched, but I kept my gray eyes on the road, avoiding Finn's bright, searching gaze. My hands strangled the steering wheel. I wished it was the Air elemental's neck instead.

"Stabbed him to death. I found him in the Pork Pit. He was already dead when I got there."

I left out the part about the Air elemental and the gruesome torture. Finn didn't need to hear about that. Despite his shady deals and occasional need for violence, Finnegan Lane really was a gentle soul. Suits, cars, women, cash, those were the things he enjoyed. Finn was perfectly happy to fuck and drink his way through life, counting his money and scheming to get more. Harmless, by Ashland standards. And the reason Fletcher had trained me to be the assassin and not his son, even though at thirty-two, Finn was two years older than me. I was stronger than Finn. Harder. Colder. I'd had to be just to survive my childhood.

Finn kept staring at me, wanting to know the rest of the story. I gave him the short, edited version. The fight with Brutus at the opera house. Being chased by Donovan Caine. Swan dive into the river. Making my way first to the Pork Pit, then to his apartment.

"They also sent a guy back to the restaurant in case I showed up," I added.

"And what did you do to him?"

I gave Finn a flat look.

"What you do best," he murmured. "Thank you for that, Gin."

I shrugged. "Fletcher was like a father to me. It was the least I could do. I only wish I'd had more time with the bastard."

More time to slash and wound and kill—more time to act and less time to think about what I'd lost tonight.

And how much it fucking hurt.

❉ 9 ❉

Despite the darkness, a noticeable change swept over the city streets as I drove farther away from the Pork Pit. The Civil War might have been over, but a battle of another kind still raged in Ashland—between Northtown and Southtown.

The two sections of the city took their names from their respective geographic locations and were joined together by the sprawling, circular confines of the downtown area. But that was where the similarity ended. Southtown was the rough, raw part of town, where the working poor and blue-collar folks lived in run-down public housing units among the vampire hookers, junkies, and other white trash. The Pork Pit and my apartment were located downtown, close to the Southtown border.

Northtown was a dewy debutante in comparison, home to the city's white-collar yuppies and monetary, social, and magical elite. The area featured themed subdivisions with cutesy names like Tara Heights and Lee's Lament, along with sprawling, plantation-style mansions and estates. But the old-fashioned, antebellum elegance didn't make that side of town any better. In Northtown people called you sugar to your face while they stabbed you in the back. At least in Southtown the decor matched the danger.

Jo-Jo made her home in Northtown, as befitting an Air elemental of her power, wealth, status, and social connections. I made the turn into the Tara Heights subdivision, coasted onto a street marked Magnolia Lane, and steered the Benz up a circular driveway paved with white cobblestones. They gleamed like bleached bones under the pale moonlight.

A three-story plantation house resplendent with rows of white columns perched at the top of a grassy knoll, a diamond queen on her emerald throne. Three steps led up to the wraparound porch, partially obscured by a trellis covered with curled kudzu vines and bare rose bushes. A lone bulb burned on the porch, making the shadows around the house seem a little less sinister.

I helped Finn out of the car and up the steps to the porch. A flimsy screen door fronted a heavier wooden one. I pulled the screen open, then reached forward and banged the knocker against the interior door. The knocker was shaped like a puffy cloud—Jo-Jo's personal Air elemental rune.

A dog barked once somewhere inside the house. Rosco, Jo-Jo's fat, lazy basset hound. Heavy, familiar footsteps sounded, and I could smell her Chantilly perfume even out here. The door opened, and a woman stuck her face outside.

"What do y'all want this late?"

Even though it was close to midnight, Jolene "Jo-Jo" Deveraux looked like she was ready to go to Sunday church. A flowered dress covered her stocky, muscular figure, and a string of pearls hung from her short neck. Her feet were bare, although flirty pink polish covered her stubby toenails. The color matched her lipstick and eye shadow. Jo-Jo's bleached blond-white hair was coiffed into its usual, helmetlike tower of ever-tightening curls, although her black roots were starting to show. At an even five feet, she was tall for a dwarf, and her hair only added to her height. But I still had a good seven inches on her.

"Hey, Jo-Jo." I dragged Finn forward into the light. "It's Gin. My boy here could use some help."

The dwarf's eyes were almost colorless, except for the pinprick of black at their center. Her pale gaze flicked over Finn's battered face, and the blood spatters that coated both of us like strips of wet wallpaper. The crow's feet and laugh lines that grooved her middle-aged face deepened with worry.

"Hell's bells and panther trails," Jo-Jo drawled in a voice as light and sweet as apricot syrup. "Come in, come in. Take him in the back. You know where."

I half-dragged Finn inside and through a long, narrow hallway that opened up into a large room that took up the back half of the house. It looked like your typical southern beauty salon. Padded swivel chairs. Old-fashioned hair dryers. A couple of counters covered with hairspray, nail polish, scissors, rollers, and gap-toothed combs. Pictures of models with hairstyles twenty years old covered the walls, while beauty and fashion magazines stood six inches deep on every available surface. A door to one side led to a room filled with tanning beds.

Jo-Jo Deveraux made her living as what she called a "drama mama," using her Air elemental magic on the beauty pageant, debutante ball, and society circuits in Ashland and beyond. If it could be purified, plucked, smoothed, tweezed, waxed, cut, curled, dyed, tanned, or exfoliated, Jo-Jo did it in her beauty shop. Air magic was great for smoothing out unwanted wrinkles and lifting someone's breasts back to the way they had looked five years and two kids ago.

Only a few select friends knew about the dwarf's side business as a healer. But Jo-Jo and Fletcher went way back, and I'd made generous use of her services over the years.

I hauled Finn over to one of the cherry-red chairs, put him down, and plopped myself in the next seat over. Jo-Jo scuttled in behind us. She went over to one of the sinks that lined the wall and washed her hands. Rosco, the basset hound who'd howled earlier, sat in his usual spot in a wicker basket by the door. The hound looked up at me, snuffled once, then dropped his brown and black head down on top of his tubby stomach. The only time Rosco moved out of his basket was when there was food involved.

Jo-Jo pulled a free-standing chair over to Finn. She clicked on a bright halogen light and angled it so that it spotlighted his beaten face. "What the hell happened, Finn? When I saw you earlier tonight, you were smooching some sweet young thing at the opera house."

Jo-Jo Deveraux was a social butterfly of the highest order. Nothing she loved better than curling her hair, putting on a nice dress, some nicer shoes, and going out to a party, ball, or benefit. And she got invited to every single one. You knew a lot of people when you were two hundred fifty-seven and counting.

Finn winced. "Unfortunately, we got interrupted."

Jo-Jo opened her mouth to ask another question, but I cut her off.

"Fletcher's dead." Somehow I forced out the words, even though they burned my throat like acid.

Jo-Jo's pale gaze shifted to me. A shadow passed over her face, but she didn't seem overly surprised. In addition to being a healer, Jo-Jo also had a bit of precognition. Most Air elementals did, given the fact they could listen and tap into vibrations and emotions in the air. Or perhaps the dwarf just realized we wouldn't have come here at this time of night if something bad hadn't happened. "Fletcher's dead? How?"

For the second time I told my story. Opera house. River. Fletcher dead on the floor of the Pork Pit.

"I'm so sorry, Gin, Finn," Jo-Jo said in a soft voice. "Fletcher was a hell of a man. Sophia and I loved him, just as much as you two did."

"Yes, he was," I replied. "And I know you did."

Each one of us fell silent, overwhelmed by thoughts and memories of the old man. We didn't speak for a long while. I was grateful for the silence.

Jo-Jo examined Finn's face another minute before she went to work. She held her hand in front of his face, her palm not quite touching his bloody, bruised flesh. The dwarf's eyes began to glow an opaque, buttermilk white, as though thick clouds drifted through her gaze.

A similar glow coated her palm. Power crackled through the room, and I shifted in my chair. Air was an opposing element of Stone, and I always felt unsettled whenever so much of that sort of magic was being used. It just seemed wrong. Then again, my Stone and Ice magic would feel the same way to Jo-Jo or any other Air or Fire elemental.

Finn closed his eyes and leaned his head back against the chair, as though he were getting a facial. In a way, he was. Jo-Jo passed her palm over his face, forcing oxygen into his open wounds, making it circulate under his skin, using the molecules to heal and meld everything back together. It was like watching a time-lapse photo. The puffy swelling on Finn's face reduced. The purple bruises ringing his eyes faded. The cut on his forehead and the ones on his fat lips zipped up.

It took Jo-Jo a few minutes to fix all the damage, and when she finally dropped her palm, Finn looked like his usual, carefree self, right down to the devilish glint in his green eyes. I couldn't help but think of Fletcher, and how differently another elemental had used her Air magic on him. To flail and bruise and peel his flesh away one slow inch at a time.

Jo-Jo nodded, pleased with her work. "Now strip. And let's get a look at the rest of you."

Finn grinned. "Why, darling, I thought you'd never ask."

Finn was all too happy to ditch the remains of his bloody, ruined tuxedo. Underneath, he wore a pair of navy blue boxers made out of high-end silk dotted here and there with white sailboats. Preppy. The boxers hung low on Finn's hips, bringing out the ruddy tones in his skin. His chest was broad and solid, and a generous dash of brown, curly hair led down below the waistband of the fabric. But ugly bruises marred his figure. The fist-shaped marks painted his body in pansy purples and garden greens.

Still, most women would have found Finn extremely sexy and highly fuckable, especially when you added the boyish charm of his face to the rest of the toned, slick package. But I'd seen it and done it all before, during my younger, more foolish years.

Jo-Jo held her palm out over Finn's chest and started healing the bruises on his torso and whatever damage lay inside his chest.

"You know, there's something wrong when a guy wears more expensive underwear than I do," I murmured.

"You're just jealous more people see me in mine than they do you in yours," Finn said. "Still having those boring one-night stands with the young studs down at the community college?"

"Still sleeping with anything that will hold still long enough?" I countered.

"Touché."

Jo-Jo smiled at our banter, and, for a moment, the darkness of Fletcher's death receded. I half expected him to come through the salon door, a cup of chicory coffee in one hand and a wide grin stretching across his face. But the old man wasn't here. And he never would be again. We all knew it. We were just dealing with it the only way we knew how. By going on with business as usual. It's what Fletcher would have wanted us to do.

After she finished with Finn, the dwarf turned to me. "Your turn, Gin," she said.

I raised an eyebrow. "What makes you think I need healing?"

"Because you're you—too ballsy and stubborn to back down from anyone."

Jo-Jo knew me too well. Even as Finn got dressed, I took off the vampire hooker's blood-spattered shirt, leaned back in my chair, and let the Air elemental work her magic. Jo-Jo removed my bandages and put her palm next to my wounded shoulder. A tingle sizzled to life in the muscle under my skin and spread outward. Then another, then another. Hot, warm, insistent, until my whole shoulder throbbed with them.

I gritted my teeth, trying to ignore the odd sensation that was nothing at all like the cool caress of my Ice and Stone magic. The forced influx of magic also made the spider rune scars on my palms itch and burn, as the silverstone metal reacted to the Air power. Silverstone absorbed all kinds of magic, and many elementals used it to store bits and pieces of their own power, sort of like batteries they could draw on later when they needed a little boost. Even through my scarred skin, the metal hungered for the Air magic being forced into my body.

"You know you could have prevented this," Jo-Jo murmured, her eyes white in her face. "All you had to do was use your Stone magic to harden your skin. Ain't nothing can penetrate your magic."

The image of my mother, Eira, then my older sister, Annabella, disappearing into balls of fire flashed through my mind. For a moment, the air smelled like charred flesh. My stomach clenched.

"You know I don't use my magic like that unless I absolutely have to," I said. "It's okay for small things, but I'm not going to let myself depend on it. Not in my line of work. Because the moment I do is when it fails me. And then I die."

Jo-Jo moved her hand to my kidneys, where Brutus had punched me. More tingles spread through my torso. "You're going to have to rely on it one day, Gin. Magic is just as strong as the person wielding it. You're strong. It's not going to let you down because you never let yourself down."

I didn't know if Jo-Jo was speaking in vague generalities or because she'd seen some smoky glimpse of the future. Either way, I wasn't buying it. "That's all well and good— until the person I'm fighting is stronger than me."

Flinging raw power, raw magic, at each other was how elementals fought. Testing their strength against the other person's. Sometimes, the duels took seconds. Sometimes, hours. But eventually, someone's magic always prevailed, always overpowered the other person's. And when that happened, the unlucky elemental was overwhelmed and fell under the onslaught of the other's power. Suffocated by Air, frozen by Ice, hammered by Stone.

Burned alive by Fire, like my mother and older sister.

I shook my head, banishing the ugly memories. "No thanks. All I need to get the job done is my silverstone knives. Nothing else. Magic is too easy. Makes you take stupid chances, makes you think you're invincible, makes you sloppy. I'll use it when I have to, but I'm not going to depend on it."

I didn't mention the fact I'd already done enough horrid things with my magic to last a lifetime. That I'd killed with it long before Fletcher had taken me in off the streets. That I'd lashed out with it without thinking, and used my power to crumble the stones of my own house so I could escape from my torturers. That the combination of fires the elemental had started and my magic made the whole structure come tumbling down. That Bria, my younger sister, had died because of what I'd done, been buried alive just like everyone else.

Some of the many reasons I didn't use my power like that now, unless there was no other option. It only reminded me of that darker time, when everything I'd known had been lost in one fiery night.

Jo-Jo finished her work and dropped her hand, but her pale eyes stayed on my face. "We'll see."

The front door banged open, and heavy footsteps smacked against the hallway floor. A few seconds later, Sophia Deveraux stepped into the salon.

Sophia was an inch taller than her older sister, and her body was thicker, with an extra layer of hard muscle. Where Jo-Jo was light, Sophia was dark—as in Goth. Short, straight black hair clung to her head, matching her eye shadow, eyeliner, and lipstick. Her eyes were also a flat black. Instead of a dress, Sophia wore black jeans, black boots, and a black T-shirt embossed with hot-pink skulls. The skulls matched the plastic ones hanging off the spiked, black leather collar that ringed her thick throat. Even though she was a hundred and thirteen, Sophia had the moody adolescent look down pat.

Sophia flopped into one of the salon chairs and examined the pink glitter polish on her nails. Jo-Jo leaned over and patted her sister's hand. Despite their obvious differences, the sisters were close. Living together for more than a hundred years would do that to you. Sophia gave Jo-Jo a half smile, her most animated and pleasant expression.

"Any problems getting rid of the bodies?" I asked.

Sophia's black eyes met my gray ones. "Nuh-uh." The Goth dwarf's version of no.

Like Jo-Jo's healing, I'd also inherited Sophia's expertise when Fletcher retired from the assassin business. I didn't know exactly how Sophia disposed of the bodies I sent her way. What she did with them, where she put them, why she even liked doing that sort of dirty work in the first place. But the Goth dwarf could clean up like nobody's business. Sophia left every site pristine. No blood, no fibers, no hairs, no DNA, or evidence of any sort. The fact she baked the best sourdough bread in Ashland was an added bonus.

"Good. I'm going to need you to run the Pork Pit the next few days." I swallowed the acid that once again coated my throat. "And call the cops in the morning."

I told Sophia about everything that had happened tonight. The dwarf didn't say anything. But for a moment, something dark and soulful sparked in her gaze. It might have been sorrow. Hard to tell with Sophia. She was even colder than I was.

Once I made the arrangements with Sophia, I thanked Jo-Jo for her hospitality and skills, and promised to have Finn wire her the usual amount. Then I stood up, put the hooker's bloody shirt back on, and roused Finn, who was taking a catnap in the salon chair.

"Come on," I said. "We've still got things to do tonight."

"Like what?" Jo-Jo asked.

I ran a hand through my hair. My fingers caught on a clump of blood. "We took some things off the guys at Finn's apartment. I want to go through them. I also want to see what's on the news and what's been leaked to the press. Gordon Giles's attempted murder is going to be a big story, and we need to stay on top of it."

Jo-Jo nodded, her blond curls bobbing. "Well, y'all be careful. Fletcher Lane was one of my oldest, dearest friends. If you need anything, anything at all, just give me or Sophia a holler."

A grim smile tightened my face. "Thanks. But I don't think we'll need you again, especially not Sophia. Because once I get my hands on the person responsible for all this, there won't be enough left of her to put under a microscope, much less dispose of."

Across the room, Sophia Deveraux grunted her disappointment.

* 10 *

Before we left, Jo-Jo promised to take care of Fletcher's funeral arrangements. I was happy to cede that task to her. I needed to focus on finding his killer, not the raw emotions the old man's death had infected me with. Jo-Jo also gave me some tubs of her magically infused healing ointment in case Finn and I had any lingering issues in the morning.

Thirty minutes later, after stashing his Benz in an anonymous parking garage a few blocks away, Finn and I were in my apartment. I'd checked the building and the stone around the door before we'd entered, but the vibrations had been low and steady as usual. Whoever had hired Brutus didn't know where I lived. Otherwise, she would have been camped outside by now. Despite Jo-Jo's ministrations, I was glad for the respite. I really didn't want to deal with any more blood or bodies tonight. Even I had limits.

But I still took the precaution of using my magic to trace runes into the stone outside the door. Small, tight, spiral curls—the symbol for protection. The runes shimmered with a silver color before sinking into the stone. If someone tried to get into the apartment tonight, my magic would trigger the runes and echo through the stone—rising to a shrill shriek that would wake me from the deepest, deadest sleep.

Finn and I sat at the kitchen table rifling through the wallets and other items we'd taken from the men at his apartment. I flipped open Shortie's wallet and stared at the driver's license inside.

"Fake," Finn pronounced.

I stared at the laminated card. "How can you tell?"

"The Ashland city seal's on the wrong side. It should be on the right, away from the photo, not on the left on top of it."

In addition to handling other people's money, Finn was also rather good with documents. He'd done all my fake IDs and could lay out a paper trail so thick and elaborate it would fool the most studious forensic accountant.

Something gold glinted underneath the pile of wallets. I snagged my fingers on the metal and pulled out the chain Finn had torn off Shortie's neck. A small medallion hung off the end—a triangular-shaped tooth with sharp, jagged, sawlike edges done in polished jet.

"What does this look like to you?" I asked.

"A tacky piece of man jewelry."

"Come on. Be serious. Look at it again."

He peered at it. "A tooth. No, wait, that could be a

rune. A tooth . . . the symbol for strength and prosperity. You think an elemental is involved in this?"

Finn's gaze flicked to the three drawings on my mantle. The snowflake, the ivy vine, the primrose. The symbols of my dead family. His green eyes dropped to my hand and the spider runes burned into my palms. Finn knew I was a Stone and Ice elemental, although I'd never told him anything about my family. But I was sure Finn had researched the runes I'd drawn and found out who they belonged to. Information was like an aphrodisiac to Finn. Uncovering people's secrets an amusing game. Fletcher had been the same way. But neither one of them had ever asked me about the runes or my past.

Don't ask, don't tell. The only rule the three of us had had.

"Yeah, an elemental's involved in this."

"How do you know?" Finn asked.

"There was some damage at the Pork Pit. Overturned tables, broken chairs, busted windows, like a tornado had ripped through the storefront. Looked like Air elemental damage to me." A smooth, easy lie. "But I've never seen this exact symbol before, and I know the runes of all the major elemental families in Ashland."

The extremely rich elementals, anyway. They were the only ones who could afford my services. Their feuds alone could have kept me busy the rest of my life. Members of opposing elemental families, like Stone and Air or Fire and Ice, rarely mixed unless forced to by business or the occasional ill-fated Romeo and Juliet love affair. Those elementals were always jockeying for position, money, power, along with the wealthy humans, vampires, giants, and dwarves who comprised the city's upper crust. If the elementals couldn't get what they wanted with money, they used their magic, often with vicious results. The others did too. Duels at dawn were not uncommon in the city. When that failed, well, that's when they hired someone like me to clean up the mess.

The weaker elementals and other magic users of more modest means led simpler lives. They worked jobs and put their kids through school. Lived out in the cleaner suburbs and drove minivans to ballet class. Some of them rarely used their power at all.

In contrast, the poor and the downtrodden elementals used their magic the most. They performed parlor tricks on the street corner for the amusement of passersby and spare change to feed whatever habit they had. Drugs, booze, sex, blood. The constant struggle to survive and use of their magic burned them out—or drove them crazy. I'd seen more than one psychotic elemental during my stay in Ashland Asylum. Magic had that affect on some people, some elementals. Using their power gave them a high better than alcohol, better than drugs, until they were hooked on it. But elementals were much more dangerous than your common junkies, because they'd lost control but still had all that raw magic running through their veins.

"Well, it's not a sunburst, so it's not Mab Monroe's symbol," Finn said.

I thought of the rune I'd seen on Mab's necklace earlier tonight. A sunburst. A ruby surrounded by gold, curled, wavy lines. So much like my own spider rune, but so different.

"I don't know," I murmured. "She could be involved in this. Gordon Giles did work for one of her companies. Maybe Mab found out he was doing something she didn't approve of. Rumor has it she killed the previous head of the company, the James sisters' father, for making too many waves when she took over."

"And so Mab did what?" Finn scoffed. "Hired you to take care of it, then decided to take care of you? Doesn't make sense. You just said it yourself. Mab's never been afraid of getting her hands dirty. Everybody knows she killed that federal judge three months ago because he was merely *thinking* about trying to indict her. If Mab didn't like whatever Gordon Giles was up to, she would have taken care of it herself. Not set you up to take the fall."

Finn was right. Mab Monroe ran this town. She wouldn't have cared about getting caught. She would have killed Gordon Giles, stood over his body, and blown off her smoking fingers in front of everyone at the opera house. No, Mab Monroe hadn't gotten to where she was by being sneaky. This was someone else's handiwork. Someone who didn't have the guts to accept the consequences of her actions. Cowardly bitch.

"We can't rule Mab out completely. But she's probably not the one pulling the strings."

"Who does that leave us with?" Finn asked.

I shrugged. "Most of our clients are motivated by sex, money, or revenge. According to Fletcher's file, Gordon Giles didn't have a wife or steady girlfriend. He preferred to buy and pay for his sexual entertainment."

"Hookers?"

I nodded. "Hookers. Lots of them. But no hooker in her right mind would promise to pay me five mil to kill Giles. Only a few would even be able to put their hands on enough money for the down payment, much less the back end. So that pretty much rules out sex as a motive. Fletcher said Giles was stealing money, so I'd have to go with Haley James."

"His boss at Halo Industries?"

I nodded again. "She could have found out about the embezzling and decided to kill Giles rather than let the info go public. It wouldn't be good for her company if word got out she was being bilked by her top paper pusher."

"Maybe. But Giles dying any sort of way isn't going to look good for Halo Industries. And embezzling is down the list as far as crimes go. We need more information." Finn looked at the jet tooth again. "A tooth rune . . . that could be any elemental. Stone, Air, Fire, Ice. Or even someone with a minor talent for metal or water or something else. It's not specific enough."

Most elementals chose runes that represented their magic. Like my mother's snowflake for her Ice magic, or Mab Monroe's sunburst for her Fire power. A tooth would be better suited for a vampire, for obvious reasons. Finn was right. There was no way to tell which kind of elemental it belonged to. The rune didn't mean anything in and of itself, just like they had no real power unless you created or imbued them with magic.

I might have dismissed the tooth rune as a mere trinket, if not for the gruesome way Fletcher had been tortured. I'd seen just about all the bad things people could do to each other, and I knew the signs of Air elemental magic when I saw them. Shortie had been working for someone. It made sense he would wear his employer's symbol, whoever she might be.

"We'll figure it out," I promised. "Let's see what else is here."

We went through the rest of the items. More fake IDs, a few credit cards, and several hundred bucks in cash. Nothing useful. The television droned on in the background while we worked. At five in the morning, the early news program blared on. The top story was the incident at the opera house. Finn and I sat on the couch and watched the spectacle.

A reporter stood outside the opera house. Red lights flickered in the background. "A tragedy occurred last night at the Ashland Opera House, as a deranged woman attempted to kill one of the attendees. The target was believed to be Gordon Giles, a wealthy Ashland businessman and the chief financial officer of Halo Industries."

The same headshot of Giles that was in Fletcher's file popped up on the screen. The reporter recounted the events of the evening, albeit with a great deal of spin. Now, instead of busting into the box seats, detective Donovan Caine had prevented me from entering, with an innocent bystander tragically losing his life in the process. Media bullshit. I wondered how they would explain the bloodstains being inside the box instead of out in the hallway.

"Even though Giles was not harmed in the initial incident, he was involved in a traffic accident on his way home. A large SUV hit his limo. Police say the impact ignited the gas tank, and the vehicle exploded. Giles and his driver were pronounced dead at the scene."

The television cut to a shot of a limo engulfed by flames. Killing Giles, torturing Fletcher. Busy girl, our mysterious Air elemental.

"They killed Giles anyway," Finn murmured. "They really must have wanted him dead."

The reporter appeared on the screen again. "Giles was attacked by this woman, believed to be the businessman's disgruntled former lover and a possible prostitute. She is also believed to have been behind the car accident that led to his death. Police are not releasing her name, but a detective on the scene provided officials with this sketch."

I snorted. They weren't releasing my name because they didn't know it. But a moment later, my face appeared on the monitor. Or at least, what might have passed for my face if you tilted your head just right and squinted real hard. It wasn't a completely inaccurate rendering. Donovan Caine had at least gotten my eyes and the hard set of my mouth right, even if the black toboggan had hidden my bleached blond hair. Still, I wasn't worried about someone recognizing me from the sketch. It was too rough for that. Besides, people never really looked at those things anyway or remembered them after the fact. Not in a city like Ashland where everyone could be a potential threat.

Speaking of Caine, his was the next face to flicker onto the screen. He stood behind one of the Ashland Police Department's senior captains, who was speaking into a microphone. More cops flanked the two men.

". . . and although she did not succeed in harming Mr. Giles initially, she is still wanted for his murder."

That was the captain speaking. Stephenson was his name, according to the ID on the screen. Wayne Stephenson. A giant with pale eyes and stubby, salt-and-pepper hair, whose once trim physique was going to fat. Perhaps it was the media spotlight, but Stephenson looked stressed. A greenish hue tinged his pasty skin, and he blotted a sheen of sweat off his forehead with a white handkerchief.

A reporter waved her hand, shouting Donovan Caine's name and trying to get him to answer a question. The detective scowled and opened his mouth to respond, but the captain stepped in front of Caine, blocking him from view.

"Nice defensive maneuver," Finn said.

"Somebody doesn't want Caine talking about what really happened."

Finn shook his head. "Honesty will get you killed in this city."

All the reporters started speaking at once, a flock of cawing crows shouting questions at Caine and the other officials. Captain Stephenson held out his arms for silence.

"We want to send a message to the woman who killed Mr. Giles. Whoever you are, wherever you are, if you're out there watching us, know this—we're going to do everything in our power to find you."

Finn elbowed me. "Looks like somebody's got the hots for you, Gin."

The captain, Stephenson, kept talking. "Mr. Giles was

a respected businessman and upstanding member of the community. Mr. Giles's employer, Halo Industries, has authorized me to announce a reward for information leading to the capture and arrest of his murderer."

The captain gestured to his right, and Alexis James stepped forward. Sometime during the night she'd traded her little black cocktail dress for a severe black pantsuit. The pearls still wringed her throat and wrist. Why would she be at the press conference instead of her sister, Haley? Then I remembered. Alexis was the head of marketing and public relations. The company mouthpiece.

The sight of Alexis James added to the reporters' frenzy.

"Alexis! Alexis! How much are you offering?" one of them screamed over the din.

Alexis put her lips close to the microphone. "One million dollars."

Finn and I sat there in stunned silence.

But Alexis James wasn't finished. She talked about what a great guy Gordon Giles was and how she hoped the reward money would help the police catch me, the evil bitch who'd killed him.

The press conference finally ended, but the reporters weren't ready to let their sources slip away. They tried to ask the police captain and Donovan Caine a few more questions. But Stephenson waved them off, and he and Caine left the podium and disappeared from sight, along with Alexis James.

"A million bucks? Fuck," Finn said.

That summed up my feelings perfectly.

✣ 11 ✣

Nothing more to do or say. Not tonight. Finn shuffled into the spare bedroom, while I took a shower to wash the matted blood out of my hair. The vampire hooker's ruined clothes went into the trash. I'd take them down to the incinerator in the basement and burn them later.

Thanks to Jo-Jo and her healing magic, my left shoulder and arm no longer throbbed where Brutus had shot and knifed me. But my chest still burned with cold rage from losing Fletcher. At what had been done to him. At the desecration of the Pork Pit. The sadistic glee the Air elemental had taken in accomplishing both. And for what? So I could be blamed for a murder I didn't even commit? Pointless. All of it.

I couldn't believe Fletcher was gone. Dead. That I hadn't gotten to him in time. That I hadn't been able to save him, like he'd saved me so long ago.

My troubled thoughts turned to the last conversation

I'd had with Fletcher. *Do this job, and you can retire.* His gruff voice whispered the words in my mind. I'd scoffed at his suggestion, sneered, dismissed it, the way I had for six months now, ever since the old man had first brought up the subject of me quitting the business.

Maybe—just maybe—if I'd listened to him the first time he'd asked me to retire all those months ago, Fletcher would still be alive. Maybe if I'd quit killing people back then, the Gordon Giles hit would have never come his way at all. Maybe if I'd just given in to his wishes, to his hopes of a more normal life for me, the old man would be over at the Pork Pit right now, reading a book and drinking coffee, instead of staring up at the ceiling with dull, sightless eyes. Maybe if I'd retired when he'd first asked me to, Fletcher might still be alive.

My fault. Everything was my fucking fault.

Guilt and grief welled up in my chest, cracking the walls around my heart, crumbling the cold stone to dust. My throat closed up, and tears, hotter than the water cascading around me, scalded my eyes. I sank to my knees in the shower, huddling against the slick tile.

And for the first time in seventeen years, I truly, deeply wept.

Ten minutes passed, maybe fifteen. I wasn't sure. But the cooling water cut through my grief, and I shivered against the shower wall. Some might have called me a hypocrite for my grief at Fletcher's death and my rage at the Air elemental who'd killed him. I had buckets of blood on my hands, and my actions had left plenty of folks crying for their loved ones. But there were lines, rules, codes, no matter how twisted they might appear. No kids, no pets, no torture, no framing someone else for what I did. The way the elemental had tortured Fletcher . . . she deserved to be punished for that alone. Put down like a rabid dog before she did it to someone else.

Fletcher was gone, but I was still here. So was Finn. And I was going to do everything in my power to keep it that way. The old man had drilled survival into my head above all else—emotions, conscience, fear, regrets. If that made me a hypocrite, so be it. Worse things to be. Like dead.

I forced myself to go through the motions of my late-night rituals. Washing my body, shampooing my hair, drying off, slipping into my softest flannel pajamas, the ones Jo-Jo had given me with the puffy blue clouds on them. Guilt, tears, and emotional breakdown aside, I'd need to be at my best tomorrow. And for the foreseeable future. Oh, I wasn't worried about the bounty. Fletcher had taught me how to be careful, how to be invisible, a skill I'd perfected these last seventeen years. Which made it all the stranger that someone had been able to target us. I still didn't understand how or when we'd been that careless, that sloppy. But somebody, somewhere, sometime had talked about what the three of us did. When I got up close and personal with the Air elemental, I was going to ask how she'd found Fletcher—and I wasn't going to ask nicely.

Before I went to bed, I shuffled around the apartment and pressed my hand to the stone around the door frame and all the windows one more time, checking my protection runes. The stone murmured in response before falling back down to its usual, low hum.

As added insurance, I tucked a silverstone knife under both my pillows and put a few more on the nightstand within easy reach. Then I curled into a tight ball underneath the soft sheets. The tension in my body slowly unknotted, and I dreamed . . .

Great, heaving, breath-stealing sobs wracked my body, shaking me from head to toe. Tears rushed down my chapped face in an endless torrent, mixing with the dirt on my hands. I drew in a ragged breath and licked my cracked lips, tasting my own salt.

"That's not doing you any good," a low voice cut through my misery.

Footsteps sounded on the blacktop, and I glanced up, sniffling. A man stood in front of me, middle-aged and tall, with dark brown hair. A greasy apron hid his blue work shirt and pants. Brown boots covered his feet, and a black trash bag dangled from his right hand.

"Tears are a waste of time, energy, and resources," he said in a serious tone, as though imparting some great, mystical secret to me.

My mother and sisters were dead. People wanted to kill me. I was alone and living on the streets. Cold. Tired. Hungry. So hungry. I had plenty to cry about.

The man looked at me, his green gaze taking in my dirty face, matted hair, and ripped clothes. He sighed, then reached into the black trash bag.

I tensed, reaching for the magic flowing through my veins. If he pulled out a knife and came at me, I would use my power on him. Make the bricks fly out of the alley wall and smash him in the face. Form an Ice dagger with my bare hands and stab him with it. Whatever it took. Even if it meant using my magic to kill—again.

The man pulled out a crumpled, white paper bag. I was sitting down, my knees drawn tight to my chest. My eyes were just level with the pig logo printed on the side of the bag.

"Here." The man held out the bag. "There's a burger in here. Takeout somebody didn't pick up. Baked beans, too. You can have them, if you want."

My stomach screamed yes, but I shook my head no. Nobody gave you anything for free on the streets of Ashland. He'd probably want me to blow him here in the alley. I wasn't desperate enough to do that. Not yet. I didn't have much to offer at thirteen, besides barely developed breasts and thin hips, but I'd realized most men looking to get laid didn't care, as long as they got off.

The man shrugged. "Suit yourself, kid."

He opened the Dumpster and threw away the black bag. The white one followed. Whistling, he opened the back door to the restaurant and disappeared inside. I counted the seconds in my head. Ten, twenty, thirty . . . When I reached forty-five, I got to my feet, ran to the Dumpster, and plucked the white bag out of the smelly, shadowy depths.

I darted back across the alley and slipped into a black hole. The crack was big enough for me to worm into, but not so large that anyone could come in after me. I ripped open the bag, tore into the sandwich, and chewed. So good, I wanted to cry. I couldn't remember the last time I'd had meat, especially this much. Hands shaking, I popped the top off the Styrofoam cup, tilted back the container, and let the lukewarm baked beans slide into my mouth. The sauce on

*them was sweet, but with a spicy kick. After the garbage I'd
been eating, it tasted like heaven—*

"Son of a bitch!"

The cursing woke me. I cracked open my gray eyes, my hand already around the hilt of the silverstone knife under my pillow.

"Son of a bitch!"

The exasperated voice came again. Finn. Just Finn. I relaxed my grip, slid out of bed, and padded into the den. Finn stood in the kitchen, flipping a toaster pastry from one hand to the other to keep from getting burned.

"What time is it?" I asked, my voice thick with sleep and dreamlike memories I couldn't quite banish.

"Five in the afternoon." Finn took a bite of the pastry and almost spit it back out because it was so hot.

"Twelve hours? Why did you let me sleep so long?"

"Because you needed the rest. We both did."

He was right. Jo-Jo might be the best, but being healed by an Air elemental still took a toll, as your body tried to adjust from being severely injured to suddenly being well again. Despite my day of sleep, I still felt tired, my arms and legs moving slower than usual. Or perhaps that was because I'd used my body so strenuously for so long last night. But magic always had a cost, which was another reason I didn't like to use my power to kill. I didn't like paying the price afterward. It always drained me, made me weak. I couldn't afford to be weak. Ever.

The toaster burped up another pastry. Finn grabbed it and tossed it to me. I clutched the thin wafer in my right hand. The heat didn't bother me. Then again, Finn wasn't the one with scars on his hands. Wasn't the one who'd felt the spider rune burn into his flesh. Silverstone metal could contain only so much magic. The Fire elemental who'd been torturing me had had more than enough to turn my rune into superheated liquid, mark me forever, and laugh all the while. The memory made my head ache, and I massaged my temple.

The television was on, although the sound was muted. Some incomprehensible game show with what looked like screaming contestants flickered on the screen. I changed the channel to the Food Network.

"Any more news about my botched hit last night?"

"Nothing much," Finn said. "More press conferences at lunchtime with the police, namely Captain Wayne Stephenson vowing to catch you no matter what. Another one with Alexis James talking about what a great guy Gordon Giles was and how she hopes the reward will help bring his killer to justice. Do you know they've gotten more than a thousand tips since she offered that money last night?"

"A million dollars." I shook my head. "Every nut job in Ashland, elemental and otherwise, will be after me. Or at least chasing my ghost."

"Hell, for that much, I'm tempted to turn you in myself."

I stared at him.

"Not that I ever would," Finn amended. "Friendship is much more important than money."

I arched an eyebrow. Finn's lips started to twitch, and he let out a low chuckle.

I snorted. "I can't believe you said that with a straight face."

"Me either," he confessed.

I threw one of the sofa pillows at him. Finn ducked out of the way.

His smile faded, and he jerked his head at one of the windows that fronted the street. "Sophia called the cops to the Pork Pit. They arrived around three this afternoon."

I got up and stared through a crack in the curtains at the street below. Yellow crime-scene tape hung across the front door of the restaurant. The afternoon sun flashed on the slick tape, creating a bright spot that burned my eyes. No one moved inside the storefront. Normally, at five on a weekday afternoon, folks would be waiting to get in and be seated. But people passing by only slowed their steps and shot curious but knowing looks at the restaurant. In Ashland, crime-scene tape was better than an obit in the newspaper.

I usually worked in the afternoons, since the restaurant was so slammed, and I missed the noise and rush of the supper crowd, along with just knowing that Fletcher was leaning against the cash register, sipping his chicory coffee and reading a few pages of his latest book the way he had for so many years now.

Things that the old man would never do again.

The grief and guilt threatened to overwhelm me again, but I focused on the cold rage in my chest, letting it freeze out the other, softer emotions. I'd had my crying fit last night. Now was the time to be strong. For me, for Fletcher, and especially for Finn. I'd let Fletcher down. I wasn't going to do the same to his son.

"The cops are gone already?" I murmured.

"Yeah," Finn said. "Bastards weren't even there an hour.

The coroner arrived before they did. The cops looked around a few minutes, loaded up his body, and left."

We stood there a minute, watching the world turn. A world Fletcher wasn't part of any more. The cold rage beat in my chest, a slow, steady drum.

Finn spoke first. "I hate to be demanding, but we need some sort of plan, Gin. Because this little conspiracy we've gotten caught up in isn't going to go away until we're both dead. I know Dad always told us to leave town. To get away if anything happened to him or one of us. But I—I can't do that, Gin. I just can't. Not until whoever is behind this pays for what he did to Dad. I understand if you want to leave town—"

"Shut up," I snarled. "I'm not going anywhere. I'm not running, and I'm not leaving town."

Finn blinked. "You're not?"

Fletcher's flayed face flickered in front of me. His ruined flesh. His blood on the floor of the Pork Pit. The icy knot in my chest tightened. "No, I'm not going anywhere."

"Are you sure?"

"Positive. Double-crossing us is one thing. If this had been about not paying us the rest of our fee, well, I could have understood that. It's happened before. But they killed Fletcher. They hurt you. They set me up. And that is unacceptable."

Finn pulled his green eyes away from the Pork Pit and looked at me. "So what's the plan? How do we find out who's behind this?"

"One body at a time."

Finn blinked at the vehemence in my voice, but I'd already moved on to more practical matters.

"What about work? What are you telling the money men at the bank?" I asked.

"Already taken care of. I told my boss I'm sick with grief over the murder of my father and taking a week off," he said. "Not a lie, really."

"What we need to do first is figure out what Gordon Giles was really up to."

"You think the client lied to Dad? That would *never* happen." Finn's voice dripped with sarcasm like grease off a piece of bacon. "How do you propose we decipher the motives and activities of a dead man? Because Gordon Giles certainly isn't going to tell us anything."

I rolled my eyes. "Simple. All we have to do is meet with Donovan Caine."

Silence. Finn squinted at me for a few seconds. Then he stuck one finger in his ear, wiggled it around, and pulled it out, as if clearing wax out of the passageway.

"Sorry, Gin, but I think you stayed in the insane asylum a little too long. Because that's the craziest idea you've ever had. Meet with *Donovan Caine*? Are you out of your fucking mind?"

I ignored Finn's rising tone. Sometimes he screeched worse than a five-year-old.

"It makes perfect sense. Donovan Caine was at the opera house to see Gordon Giles. Somebody went to a lot of trouble to kill Giles, blame me, and tie the whole thing off with my corpse. That tells me this is about more than just embezzled funds. I want to talk with Caine and see what he knows. See why he was meeting with Giles."

Finn scratched his chest and leaned against the wall. The muscles in his shoulders rolled and bulged with the movement. "And how do you propose to get Caine to tell you all that?"

"Because we know something he doesn't."

"And that would be . . ."

"That somebody in the police department is in on this."

"This is Ashland, Gin. The police are usually in on it. They make careers out of that sort of thing."

I stared at Finn.

He sighed. "Fine. Tell me what you're thinking."

"Before he died, Brutus told me a paper trail had already been set up, linking me to Gordon Giles. The guy at your apartment said the cops were looking high and low for me. A couple hours later, my distorted sketch is all over the news, along with my supposed relationship with Gordon Giles. How could all that happen without an inside guy in the police department?"

"Something Donovan Caine could figure out himself, if he was smart enough," Finn said. "I still don't see how this will get the detective to help you."

"He might be smart, but Caine has a blind eye and soft spot for his fellow boys in blue. He's loyal to them and the idea cops are good people. That they really do serve and protect and all that. You saw how hot and bothered he was to find his partner's killer. How do you think he'll react if I tell him somebody in the department is helping Giles's murderer? And that he was okay with taking Caine out too just for being there?"

Finn thought about it. "He'd probably be pissed."

"Exactly. So I'll offer to trade information with him. He helps me find the person who set up Giles. I help him root out corruption in the police department. You know what a do-gooder Caine is. I'll appeal to his sense of justice."

More silence. Then Finn snorted. "I can't believe *you* said that with a straight face."

I grinned.

Finn shook his head. "That elemental magic in your veins has finally driven you nuts, Gin. Insanity. Complete insanity. Did you see that press conference? Donovan Caine isn't exactly running the police department. His captain shuffled him to the background for a reason—to keep him quiet. The cops want you dead because they're being paid to look the other way or just don't care enough to find out what really happened. Probably both."

"Which is all the more reason to go to Caine. He was trying to protect Gordon Giles, and he can tell me what Giles was up to. Plus, he's probably the only cop in the city who won't shoot me on sight. Or try to."

"Maybe, maybe not. You know my thoughts on honest men."

"That there aren't any."

Finn shot his forefinger at me. "Precisely."

I went over to the sofa, sat down, and put my feet up on the coffee table. "Do you have a better idea? Because if you do, tell me. I'm the one wanted for a murder. Normally, that wouldn't bother me, except this time I didn't even do it."

"But how do you know Donovan Caine will even listen to you?" Finn asked. "You killed his partner, Gin. He might not have known that before, had any clue who you were or what you looked like, but after your performance at the opera house last night, I'm willing to bet he's put two and two together. Or is at least thinking real hard about it."

I thought of Caine's hesitation on the balcony. He could have shot me, and the case would have been closed. Could have put a bullet in my heart as easy as I could slam a knife into his. But he hadn't.

"Donovan Caine wants to figure out who's behind this, too. His sense of honor, of duty, won't let him leave it alone. Especially when he realizes he would have been just as dead as Gordon Giles if I hadn't mucked up everything."

"All right," Finn said. "Say the good detective does want to see truth and justice and all those other platitudes prevail. How do you propose we make contact with Caine? Without getting shot or otherwise immediately killed? Somebody's sure to be keeping tabs on him."

"Simple," I replied. "We're going to do the thing the Air elemental and the cops will least expect us to do."

Finn shook his head. "Don't say it. Please don't say it."

"We're going to pay Donovan Caine a visit—in broad daylight," I finished.

Finn just groaned.

Finn tried to talk me out of it, of course. Listed all the reasons why meeting with Donovan Caine was tricky at best, lethal at worst. Finn talked and pleaded and begged until his face was just as blue and purple and green as it had been before Jo-Jo healed him.

But he didn't change my mind.

Despite all my training, despite all the times I'd walked away from botched jobs, I wasn't going to run. Not this time. Assassins weren't supposed to take anything personally, weren't supposed to give in to their emotions or indulge their feelings. Get paid. Do the job. Walk away. Don't look back. That was the way the game was played.

But I couldn't ignore the cold, hard knot of rage in my chest. I didn't mind being shot at or thought of as a monster. I had too much blood on my hands to think of myself as anything else. But I'd be damned if I was going to let somebody double-cross me because she was too much of a coward to accept the consequences of her own actions. Fletcher had died, been hideously tortured, because of this scheme, and Finn had almost been beaten to death. Somebody was going to pay for that—all of it. With her fucking life.

After Finn realized I wasn't budging, we got to work. Finn reached out to a few people willing to give him information on Donovan Caine—for a price. Meanwhile, I went back through the file Fletcher had given me on Gordon Giles.

I didn't know when Fletcher had been approached to do the job or by whom, but he'd compiled a substantial amount of information on Giles. Net worth. Business deals. Real estate holdings. Hobbies. Habits. Charitable causes. Favorite restaurants. Fifty-four years of life reduced to a single folder's worth of paper. Kind of sad.

But the more I reviewed the information, the less convinced I became that Gordon Giles was a devious embezzler who'd stolen millions. For one thing, he didn't need the money. Giles had several million tucked away in various accounts and annuities, and pulled down even more as the chief financial officer of Halo Industries. And he didn't spend money like it was going out of style. Other than expensive suits, nice meals, deep-sea fishing trips every few months, and weekly visits to hookers, Giles tucked most of his money away. He even gave more than a million dollars to breast cancer research every year, in honor of his dead mother. What a prince.

Sure, lots of people hid their true natures behind fundraisers and winning smiles, Mab Monroe being the prime example. But I was good at reading people, even on paper, and there was nothing in the file to suggest Giles needed or had the desire to steal. He just didn't seem greedy or desperate enough.

I flipped back to the part that detailed Giles's spending habits. You could tell a lot about a man from his vices, and they'd helped me get close to more than a few of my targets. Hookers seemed to be Giles's main expenditure. At least once a week, he dropped several thousand bucks on the girls at Northern Aggression, an upscale nightclub that would service any need, desire, or addiction you had. Sex, drugs, blood, a combination of all three. Hmm. Finn and I might have to pay Roslyn Phillips a visit at the club and see what she knew.

It was a long shot, but maybe Giles had told one of Roslyn's hookers something, had whispered some sweet bit of nothing into her ear that might lead me to his killer.

Information was power, and more importantly, leverage. I didn't like blackmail, thought of it as the basest form of arm-twisting, but I'd stoop to it if it got us out of this mess. And then, in a couple of days or weeks or months, when the Air elemental thought our agreement was holding and everything was kosher, I'd kill her.

There was a reason my mother had given me a spider rune. Even as a child, I'd been patient. Able to wait for my turn, for the right moment to speak, hell, even for Christmas to come every year. Somehow I'd always had that sort of internal restraint. I might feel cold rage over Fletcher's death, but I could control it—no matter how long I had to wait to avenge his murder.

An hour later, Finn leaned back in his chair and laced his fingers behind his head. He sat at the kitchen table, a mug of chicory coffee by his laptop. "According to one of my sources and his credit card receipts, Donovan Caine likes to have lunch every day at the Cake Walk."

"That greasy dive over on St. Charles Avenue?" I asked.

"The one and the same."

The Cake Walk was a lot like the Pork Pit—a hole-in-the-wall gin joint that served better food than Ashland's five-star restaurants. The Cake Walk specialized in desserts, along with soups, sandwiches, and iced tea so sweet you could grit the sugar in it between your teeth. It was close to the community college, and I'd eaten there several times. Too much mayo in the chicken salad for my taste.

Using my own laptop, I googled the restaurant, pulling up all the information I could find. The Cake Walk sat across from one of the quads that ringed the edge of the community college and fronted a busy four-lane street that cut through downtown. My eyes studied an online map showing the restaurant and other landmarks.

"Get me the blueprints of the restaurant and some better maps of the area," I told Finn.

He nodded, dialed a number on one of my disposable cell phones, and spoke to someone in low tones. A few minutes later, Finn flashed me a thumbs-up sign and hung up.

"Being e-mailed to me straight from the city planner's office," he said.

I raised an eyebrow. "City planner's office? Not your usual crowd. Which one of the secretaries did you fuck over there?"

Finn grinned. "Bethany. Older lady. Husband left her for a younger woman. I helped her realize exactly what she had to offer the fine men of Ashland."

"And that would be?"

"The best pair of legs I've ever seen." Finn sighed. "Gorgeous gams that seemed to go on forever, especially when we were in bed—"

"Spare me the details and just show me the file."

I walked to the kitchen table and leaned over his shoulder. Finn's hands slid over the keyboard as he pulled up one of his fake e-mail accounts. Forget penicillin. The Internet was the best thing that had ever been invented. It made exchanging information while staying anonymous so much easier.

The computer pinged, and Finn opened a new e-mail. The schematics and maps popped up on the screen, along with some street-level shots. Bethany really had enjoyed her time with Finn to give him this much information so quickly. I compared the squiggles to the online map I'd just seen.

"It looks doable," Finn said, voicing my thoughts. "A couple of exits, lots of lunchtime foot traffic, several side streets and buildings to get lost in, not to mention the college campus. But you're still taking a big risk. Caine is a detective, after all. Whoever hired Brutus will probably have people watching him, just to make sure he stays in line."

"I know. But I need to talk to Caine. Meeting with him is the only way we're going to get to the bottom of this and find out who set us up—and why."

"When do you want to do it?" Finn asked.

"Tomorrow," I said. "We make first contact tomorrow."

* 12 *

"Let me go in with you," Finn said.

We sat in a black Cadillac Escalade down the street from the grimy storefront that housed the Cake Walk. Last night, Finn had borrowed the luxury SUV from one of the downtown parking garages. He might be a glorified banker, but Finn was also rather handy at changing ownership of certain items, like cars.

Normally, we would have driven his Benz or one of Finn's other half-dozen cars. But since the Air elemental knew exactly who Finn was and had someone in the police department working for her, we'd decided to steal whatever transportation we might need over the next few days instead of using his vehicles. Just in case someone in the department had put out an APB on Finn's wheels. Besides, swiping someone's car was pretty low on the list as far as crimes went in Ashland. Even if someone reported her car stolen, it would be a couple of days before the paperwork went through to report it. This thing would be long over with by then.

Once we'd gotten the vehicle, we'd worked late into the night on how I was going to approach Donovan Caine. What to say, reveal, promise, threaten. Finally, around three in the morning, we'd crashed in my apartment to rest up for my big lunch date.

"You're going to need some backup," Finn added. "Just in case Caine decides he wants to take you in, no matter how much collateral damage there might be."

"Guys like Caine try to avoid collateral damage. That doesn't mean things couldn't go wrong, but it's better if you stay out here. I don't need to worry about you while I'm talking with the detective." I grinned. "Besides, somebody has to drive the getaway car."

Finn snorted. "This isn't *Driving Miss Daisy*. And you certainly don't look like Jessica Tandy."

Blending in with your surroundings was another essential skill assassins had to master. Sometimes I used flashy clothes to do it. Wigs, makeup, glasses, jewelry. Sometimes I used my body. Affecting an accent, walking a certain way, being loud and loquacious.

But what I excelled at most was being invisible. In looking and acting so completely normal and so ordinary that I grayed out, just like wallpaper. Slow movements, quiet voice, neutral expression. You saw me, but you didn't really register the fact I was there. A skill I'd perfected while living on the streets as a kid. None of the dirty, disenfranchised, and downtrodden ever wanted to draw attention to themselves, except for the vampire hookers.

The last approach was the one I'd decided to use today. Just being myself. Jeans, boots, T-shirt, fleece jacket. Casual comfort. My only concession to today's meeting was my white T-shirt, which featured a mound of blackberries. The shirt dipped into a deep V in the front that cut through the blackberries and showed off my cleavage and the edge of my white lace bra. Every man liked to look at breasts, no matter who they were attached to. If it gave me a momentary advantage or the detective a cheap thrill, all the better. I wasn't above using what I had.

But I wasn't going in without my silverstone knives. One up either sleeve, two tucked in my boots, and another hidden against the small of my back. My usual five-point arsenal. And Jo-Jo was right. I had my Ice and Stone magic to tap into, if things got really desperate.

But that wouldn't happen. Because I was smarter than that. Stronger. And Donovan Caine wasn't the lecherous, rapist bastard his dead partner had been.

I stared out the tinted windows at the Cake Walk. An enormous chocolate cake topped with chipped whipped cream and a faded cherry covered most of the front window. People relaxed at small tables inside. It was almost one o'clock, and a steady stream of folks entered and exited the restaurant, as though eating lunch on an assembly line.

Finn and I had been sitting in the same spot for the last hour. Finn kept his eye on the flirty coeds who sashayed in and out of the diner, while I watched for Donovan Caine.

"Where do you think Caine is? It's almost one. He should have been here by now."

Finn shrugged. "My source said he was usually in the restaurant by twelve thirty. Most of his credit card receipts have him leaving around one fifteen, one thirty. Maybe he caught a case."

I'd just turned back to the window when I spotted Caine rounding the corner. He strolled down the street, once again moving with that loose, easy confidence I found so attractive. He wore a wrinkled blue suit and a white shirt that made his skin gleam like polished bronze. A silver striped tie hung loose around his neck. Caine's black hair was rumpled, as though he'd been running his fingers through it in frustration, and his face was set into a scowl. I could see the hard glint of his hazel eyes even from this distance. The detective reminded me of a Hispanic Dirty Harry, ready to plug anybody who got in his way. Somebody hadn't had a good morning. I wondered if it was because he'd been told to back off the Gordon Giles murder.

Caine yanked open the door to the Cake Walk and stepped inside. I stayed where I was, watching the flow of people and cars. About thirty seconds after Caine entered the restaurant, two guys wearing dark suits appeared at the end of the block.

They had the corporate look down pat and blended in well with the crush of businessmen, except for a couple things. First of all, they weren't in a hurry to get back to the office like everyone else was. Second, their faces were harder, colder than those of the corporate raiders around them. Third and most telling, they held their arms slightly out to their sides in a manner that suggested each one had a gun stuffed inside his suit jacket. Maybe two.

One of them bought a newspaper from a vendor on the corner, while the other lit a cigarette.

"The good detective's got a tail," Finn said.

"I expected as much," I murmured. "The question is does he know about it or not? Are they part of the Air elemental's team? Are they cops?"

"Definitely not cops," Finn said. "Even the dirtiest detectives know better than to sport five-thousand-dollar suits. Those guys are wearing the latest designs from Fiona Fine's fall menswear collection."

I shook my head. "You and your clothes. Worse than a woman. The next thing I know, you'll be talking about wingtips."

"Nah," Finn said. "It's all about the suit. Nobody ever looks at a man's shoes."

I stared at the two men. One man seemed content to read his newspaper while Caine ate lunch. The smoker was more adventurous. He wandered over to three women leaning against the building, sipping iced mochas and eyeing all the businessmen who walked by. Coeds, from the looks of their tight shirts, glittering belly button rings, and backpacks. On the prowl for their Mrs. degrees. The man struck up a conversation with the girls, then pulled a piece of paper out of his pocket and passed it to one of them. Hmm. That could be useful.

"Keep an eye on those girls. Make sure they don't wander away while I'm inside."

"Gladly," Finn replied.

I waited a few more minutes, but Caine's watchers made no move toward the restaurant, except to glance up whenever anyone stepped inside. I didn't like the fact someone was watching Caine, but this was the best chance I had to get close to the detective. To find out why he'd been so interested in Gordon Giles and what Giles had really been up to. I had to risk it. And if I had to lullaby the two men following the detective, well, I'd be more pissed about getting blood on my T-shirt than dropping their bodies on the pavement.

"All right," I said. "I'm going in. If I'm not back in twenty minutes—"

"I'm supposed to leave you behind," Finn finished. "I know the drill, Gin. I was doing this for my dad long before you were around."

The mention of Fletcher cast a dark shadow in the car. Finn's face tightened, and he turned away. Even through the dark lenses of his sunglasses, I could tell he was blinking back tears. The same sort of sadness filled me, although I'd cried all my tears the other night in the shower.

But the thought of my murdered mentor motivated me to get on with this. Finding out who set us up and why was the only way I could keep Finn safe—and make sure Fletcher hadn't died for nothing.

I reached over and squeezed Finn's hand. He didn't look at me, but his fingers tightened on mine.

"Wish me luck," I whispered and got out of the car.

I walked at an angle toward the front of the restaurant, as though I were coming in from the grassy quad of the community college several hundred feet away. I put my right hand next to my hip and palmed one of my knives so that the tip barely protruded out of the sleeve of my jacket. My thumb caressed the hilt.

Out of the corner of my eye, I could see the guy with the newspaper peering over the top of it at me. But he didn't recognize me from my poor police sketch because he didn't move in my direction, gesture to his buddy, or whip out a cell phone and call for backup. Still, I added a flirty shimmy to my long stride to give him something else to focus on besides my face.

I waited for a couple of guys carrying briefcases to move away from the front door and stepped inside the Cake Walk. The restaurant was dark and cool after the heat of the midday sun, and I slowed, letting my eyes adjust to the dimmer light. My fingers brushed against the wall by the door, and I listened to the stone's vibrations. Loud, cheery, and brassy, just like the bellows of the restaurant's workers as they shouted orders to each other. The only thing to be concerned about in here was how many calories the triple chocolate cake had—and how fast they'd go straight to your ass.

A counter, not unlike the one at the Pork Pit, ran along the back wall. Behind the glass partition, workers made chicken salad sandwiches on sourdough bread, ladled up bowls of potato soup, and cut slices of bright blackberry pies and moist, golden Mountain Dew cakes. The smell of sugar, cinnamon, and nutmeg flavored the air, and I could almost feel the grease on the walls. The red booths, metal tables, and iron chairs were clean, but faded and shiny from wear.

Donovan Caine sat by himself at a booth in the corner, overlooking the street. He'd taken off his jacket and rolled up his white shirtsleeves. A sprinkling of black hair covered his corded, brown forearms. Caine munched on a ham sandwich. A bag of chips, a side of coleslaw, and two pieces of blackberry pie decorated his tabletop, along with a glass of iced tea. A man with a hearty appetite.

I went down the assembly line, opting for a piece of the Mountain Dew cake and a lemonade I wasn't going to get a chance to eat or drink. I kept one eye on Caine, but the detective focused on his food. He didn't look up, not even once. The two watchers outside made no move to come into the Cake Walk, so I decided to go ahead with my plan.

I paid for my dessert, walked over, and plopped my tray on the table.

"That seat's taken," Caine growled, without even looking up.

"Don't worry, sugar, I won't stay long." I slid in across from him.

He recognized my soft voice. I could tell by the way his broad shoulders stiffened underneath the fabric of his white shirt. The way his whole body tensed. The way he gathered his strength down into the pit of his stomach, getting ready to strike.

Donovan Caine put his half-eaten sandwich down onto his plastic plate with slow, careful, calm movements. He laid his hands flat on the tabletop, then raised his hard gaze to mine.

I smiled. "Care if I join you?"

Donovan Caine didn't panic. Didn't sputter, scream, pull his gun, or do anything stupid that would get him dead.

Instead, his hazel eyes narrowed, and he regarded me with a cool expression.

"You're either the most daring assassin I've ever met or the stupidest." His voice, a low, rich baritone, rumbled out of the deepest part of his chest.

My smile widened "You have to be both in my line of work."

My quip was met with another flat stare. Donovan Caine needed to work on his sense of humor.

"Why are you here?" he asked. "To finish what you started the other night?"

"No," I said. "I'm not here to kill you, detective. I just want to talk."

Another hard look. Then his eyes dropped to the gun holstered on his belt. A brief flicker, a quick glance down and nothing more, but I saw it.

"If I were you, detective, I wouldn't do anything stupid, like attempt to pull your gun."

His body tensed, a coiled spring wound that much tighter. "Why not?"

I jerked my head toward the window. "See that black Caddy out there? The SUV?"

He nodded.

"One of my associates is in that vehicle. He happens to have several guns with him. If I don't leave the restaurant in fifteen minutes, he's going to start shooting the coeds over in the college quad. If I am impeded or followed, he's going to start shooting coeds. If he gets bored or his nose itches, he's going to start shooting coeds. Your choice, detective."

I didn't mention the fact I also had a knife palmed in

my hand and that I could sever his femoral artery under the table quicker than he could draw his weapon. I hoped it wouldn't come to that, though. I needed the detective, and right now he needed me as well, if he wasn't too stubborn to see it.

Caine didn't respond. Instead, he kept staring at me, as if he could discern the secrets to my character just by peering into my eyes. After a few moments, his gaze moved away from mine. Caine studied my face, hair, clothes, committing them to memory for later use. He'd probably have a new, better sketch of me circulating to the media in time for the six o'clock news. But the good detective wasn't above checking out my breasts. A brief flicker, a quick glance down and nothing more, but I saw it.

"Fine," he muttered. "Talk."

I took a sip of my lemonade. Not nearly tart enough. "I have a proposition for you."

Caine snorted. "Really? What would that be? Letting me choose my own death?"

"No," I replied. "But I thought you might be interested in learning who paid me to kill Gordon Giles."

His gaze sharpened. "You know who that is?"

"Not yet, but I'm going to find out."

"Why?"

"Because they double-crossed me. They sent someone to take me out after I killed Giles."

Caine laughed—a harsh, bitter sound that could have peeled paint off the walls. Several people stared at the detective. He waited until they turned their attention back to their half-eaten pieces of pie before he spoke again.

"Does that surprise you?" he asked. "The lack of honor among murderers?"

"No. But that they tried it with me does. I have a reputation. One that's been tarnished by this incident. I'm going to correct that."

"So you have a name," Caine said in a flat tone. "Some stupid moniker that doesn't mean anything to anyone but you."

The name *the Spider* did mean something to me, but not in the way Donovan Caine thought. It had been Fletcher's idea, and I'd gone along with it. He'd called me that because of the rune scars on my palms. He also said I'd reminded him of a spider when we'd first met—all thin arms and long legs hiding in a dark corner. The memory tugged at me, wanting to blossom into something more. But I curled my free hand into a tight fist and willed the unwanted emotions away. Now was not the time to show any sort of weakness.

"Care to tell me what that name is?" Caine asked.

"Some people call me the Spider."

Assassins don't exactly advertise, but lots of folks who dealt in the shady side of life knew my moniker, if nothing else. Donovan Caine was no exception. But the slight bulge of his eyes and the flare of his nostrils told me exactly who and what he was thinking about: Cliff Ingles. And whether or not I was the one who'd murdered him.

"If you're wondering if I'm the one who killed your partner, the answer is yes."

No reason to hide the information since Caine was considering the possibility already. Better to have it out in the open rather than have him be distracted by speculating about it. Especially when I needed Caine to focus on the matter at hand, which was finding the Air elemental so I could kill her. If the detective got all indignant and righteous about his slain partner, if he did something stupid, like go for his gun, I'd do him right here—no matter how much he might be able to help me. No matter how weary I might be of blood and death right now.

Caine leaned forward. Disgust and hate burned like hot coals in his eyes. "You killed Cliff Ingles, my partner, a cop, and you come in here with a proposition for me? Are you crazy or just stupid?"

"Neither. I hope you're not too stupid to hear me out." I also leaned forward, my eyes meeting his. The detective wasn't the only one who could do the hard stare. "These people tried to kill me. That, I can understand. Being a target, being hit yourself, is a job hazard. But they weren't content with just me. They killed my handler. Another one of my associates was almost beaten to death. In short, they framed me and then tried to tie up the loose ends. They crossed the line, even among murderers."

Caine snorted again. "Am I supposed to feel sorry for you?"

"No," I replied. "I don't want or need your sympathy. What I'm offering you is my help, detective."

He leaned back in the booth, studying me, trying to read my eyes and face. But I'd learned a long time ago to keep my expression as blank as a piece of slate. Say nothing, do nothing, give nothing away you didn't want or have to.

"Even if I were able to overlook the fact you murdered

my partner and consider your offer, what would I get in return? Besides a knife in the back?"

I ignored his snide comment. "I have some information that might be useful in tracking down who's behind the Gordon Giles hit. It's not much, but it's a place to start. Agree to work with me, feed me any leads or theories you have, and I'll give my information to you—along with my other services. For free. A tit-for-tat situation."

His eyes flicked to my breasts again before coming back to my face. "Other services?"

"You're going to need help tracking down the people who did this—and dealing with them."

Another snort. "Lady, I'm a cop. I can deal with these people on my own."

My turn to scoff. "Really? Is that why Captain Stephenson did all the talking at the press conference outside the opera house? Is that why he stopped you from answering any questions? Is that why I'm being blamed for Gordon Giles's murder, even though we both know I was fishing myself out of the Aneirin River when he was killed in that fake car accident? Face it, Caine, the whole Ashland police department is as dirty as a pair of three-week-old gym socks. Present company excluded, of course."

He didn't say anything.

I drew in a breath. "I had the chance to question some folks I ran into last night. Some of the people involved in this conspiracy. They all said the same thing. That somebody, some cop in the department, was helping them. Think about it. How quickly things happened. How fast my supposed connection to Giles was discovered, and my sketch plastered on television. And then there's you, detective. That guy outside of the box wasn't just going to pop Giles. He was going to do you, too. You have to know that. And now you know somebody in your precious police department was in on it. That he was okay with you getting dead. Somebody doesn't like you very much, detective."

Silence. Donovan Caine shifted in the booth. His index finger tapped out a pattern on the tabletop. A muscle twitched in his right cheek. He wanted to go for his gun. The desire to do it tightened his face, his whole body. His gaze flicked to the SUV outside, and he forced himself to keep his emotions in check. To relax an inch. I'd been right. Caine wasn't the sort of cop who was okay with collateral damage. No matter how much he wanted to kill me right now.

"Do you really think these people are going to stop whatever they're doing just because I get arrested, put in jail, or killed? Not in this city. Not with Mab Monroe running things. She could be the one who wanted Gordon Giles dead in the first place, although I'll admit it's doubtful at best."

"Why?" he asked.

"Because Mab Monroe tends to deal with these sorts of situations herself. It's the only fucking thing I admire about her."

The corner of Caine's mouth lifted, and he grunted. He wasn't going to argue that point.

"Think about my offer." I cut off a sliver of my cake to keep up appearances, even though I had no intention of eating it. Too bad. The golden Mountain Dew cake looked scrumptious. "You were talking to Gordon Giles for a reason. Somebody didn't like what they thought he might say to you and what you might do with the information. That's why they killed him. Everything else is just decoration."

He grimaced. "And what guarantee do I have you're telling the truth? That this all isn't some elaborate scheme to kill me?"

My lips drew back in a toothy grin. "Because if I wanted you dead, detective, I would have just stabbed you at the opera house—or I could put my knife in your throat right now."

He tightened up again.

I gave him a cool stare. "But I'm not going to do that. I want to get to the bottom of this, and you're the only person who can help me. Face it, Caine. We need each other—whether we like it or not."

My time was up. I slid out of the booth and got to my feet. "You have a few hours to think it over. If you agree to my proposal, turn your front porch light on at six o'clock tonight. I'll bring the evidence I have, and we can work out further terms. Double-cross me, and you'll end up like Gordon Giles—naked, burned to a crisp, and lying on a cold steel slab at the morgue."

"And if I don't agree? Don't want to work with you?" he asked.

I shrugged. "Then don't. Just stay the hell out of my way."

"Is that a threat?"

"No," I said, backing toward the front door. "Just the way things are. Someone was very determined to kill Gordon Giles without implicating herself, and so far, she's pulled it off. In my experience, determined people have a way of succeeding. And this time, I'm the one who's determined. I'm going to find who's responsible for this, detective. You can work with me, and I'll let you have the dirty cop. Or you can wade through the blood and bodies after I'm done. Your choice."

Caine stared at me, his face unreadable. I nodded at him, then turned and walked out into the blazing sunlight.

13

Finn saw me exit the Cake Walk and eased the black SUV in my direction. I listened for the sound of the bell over the front door. Even though I'd admitted to killing his partner, Donovan Caine wasn't charging after me, gun drawn and screaming—yet.

Neither of the two men tailing him looked in my direction. The first man was deep into the sports section of the newspaper, while his buddy had stopped hitting on the coeds long enough to buy a pretzel from a vendor. I eyed the second man, committing his features to memory. A short guy, with thinning black hair, a thick neck, and a strong, stocky body. He grinned at the pretzel vendor, showing off a set of fangs. A vampire. One who wasn't very big on personal hygiene, judging from the yellow tint to his teeth.

My gaze cut to the coeds. Still slurping on their mochas. They wouldn't go anywhere for a few minutes. Good.

Finn pulled the black SUV up to the curb beside me. I opened the passenger's side door and hopped inside. Finn pulled away from the sidewalk, not so fast as to make the tires squeal, but quick enough to mean business. He cut in front of a trophy wife with TBH—Tennessee big hair—in a red Lexus, and she beeped her horn in displeasure. Finn stuck his finger out the window.

"Classy," I murmured. "Very classy."

We reached the stoplight at the end of the block, and I glanced in the side mirror. Donovan Caine stood on the sidewalk. His head swiveled around to the two men, who were busy pretending to eat and read the newspaper. He frowned, looked at our SUV, and scribbled down something on a notepad. Then Caine turned and walked in the opposite direction, probably heading back toward the police station. After about thirty seconds, his watchers followed him.

Finn saw the detective too. "Good thing I boosted this last night. Because unless I'm mistaken, the good detective just copied down our license plate number. He's probably on his way to headquarters right now to turn it in."

I snorted. "Typical. Try to do somebody a favor, and he sics the traffic cops on you."

"You do kill people," Finn pointed out. "It's only natural he'd be cautious."

"Let's hope he's not too cautious to take my deal. Now, go down a couple of blocks, then circle back around to the Cake Walk."

"Want to tell me why?"

"You'll see."

Finn did as I asked, and five minutes later, he parked in

the same spot he'd started from. Once I made sure Donovan Caine and his watchers were gone, I got out of the car and walked over to the trio of coeds the vampire had been chatting up. I dug into my jeans pocket and pulled out all the cash I had on me—three hundred bucks and change. Should be more than enough for what I had in mind.

I stopped in front of the girls and flashed the money at them. "Ladies, can I have a moment of your time? I'll make it worth your while."

The girls looked at each other, then at me.

"Sorry," said one of them, a petite black woman in her early twenties. "We're not hookers."

"I'm not looking for a hooker," I said. "That guy who was talking to you earlier. The vampire with the receding hairline. He gave you something. I'm thinking a business card?"

The second girl, a pretty brunette, snorted. "Yeah, he gave us his card. Said he was a talent scout and asked us if we'd ever done any modeling. Like we all haven't heard that line before."

The three women shared a harsh, knowing laugh. So young and already so jaded. I liked them.

I fanned the money at them. "Well, there's a hundred here for each of you if you give me that card."

The third woman, a chubby blonde, frowned. "Why would you want that creep's number? We were going to toss it with our coffee cups."

I gave her a wide smile. "I'm tailing the bastard for his wife. She thinks he's cheating on her. Every little thing I can get him for is another nail in his coffin, and more alimony in her pocket. Want to help a sister out?"

The three women glanced at each other, then at the money in my hand.

The brunette shrugged, reached into her jeans pocket, and plucked out a crumpled slip of paper. "For three hundred bucks, it's yours."

I swapped my C-notes for the card and gave them another winning smile. "Pleasure doing business with you, ladies."

I left the coeds to their mochas and jogged back to Finn.

"You looking for some girl-on-girl action or something?" Finn asked after I'd slipped into the passenger's seat.

"Only in your dreams, Finn."

I glanced at the wrinkled card in my hand. Charles Carlyle. A cell phone number squatted underneath the blocky script, but my eyes settled on the symbol printed on the card—a triangular shaped tooth with sawlike edges done in black ink. The mysterious Air elemental's rune.

"So what was this little detour all about then?" Finn asked.

My thumb rubbed over the rune. "Putting a name with a face. Now, let's get out of here, before Donovan Caine sends the po-po back this way."

Finn dumped the SUV in the first parking garage we came to and liberated a similar one—another late-model Cadillac. He drove through the streets, circling around the downtown district twice before taking a swing through the suburbs to make sure we were clear of anyone who might have an unhealthy interest in us.

Since the Appalachian Mountains cut through most of Ashland, the surrounding suburbs were greener and cleaner than what you'd find in most metropolitan areas. The city planners worked hard to keep it that way, especially in Northtown. Trees and copses of dense woods crept into the landscape here and there, thieves staking their claims amid new subdivisions and cobblestone-fronted shopping malls. Ashland also had its share of industrial complexes, but careful plantings of maples and walnut trees hid the dilapidated buildings and acres of concrete from sight. Rows of pine trees and twisting, grassy knolls obscured the tall towers of the city's paper mills. Irony at its finest.

I stared out the window. Everything looked so normal, so innocent in the burbs. Soccer moms hauling around vans full of unruly kids. People power-walking with their dogs. Shoppers ambling down the nicer streets, arms full of bags. A Fire elemental letting flames dance over his fingers and doing a few other magic tricks for spare change in one of the parks. An Ice elemental performing a similar show for kids at a playground a mile away.

I couldn't help but imagine what this day might have been like, if I'd listened to Fletcher's advice about retiring and quit the business six months ago. Or if I hadn't let him talk me into doing the Gordon Giles's hit. If we'd both had just paid more attention to the job and what might be wrong with it, and less to the hefty payday. Greed would get you every single time, just like luck.

I might have been over at the Pork Pit, waiting tables during the lunch hour rush, helping back in the kitchen, or trying to make yet another batch of Fletcher's secret sauce. Or I could have been over at the library at the community college, working on my latest assignment for whatever class I'd decided to audit. Could have even been dozing on a flight to Key West to take my long-awaited vacation.

Instead, I was on the run from the law and some mysterious figure who wanted me dead. Rock and a hard place. Story of my life.

"I made a couple calls while you were schmoozing with the detective," Finn said. "Sophia disposed of the body you left in the freezer at the Pit. She said to tell you nice work."

I grimaced. For whatever reason, the bloodier and more mutilated the body, the more the Goth dwarf enjoyed her disposal work. I didn't know why. Didn't *want* to know why. Fletcher had trusted Sophia, and that was good enough for me. Her methods, predilections, and possible fetishes were her own business.

"Sophia finished the disposal this morning. She said she thought it would be better to wait until today, since the cops had already removed Dad's body." Finn's voice cracked on the last word.

"I'm sorry, Finn."

He cleared his throat and shrugged. "We all knew it would probably happen like this one day. Dad understood and accepted the risks, just like we do."

"Fletcher might have been an assassin, but he always kept his word. He didn't deserve to be double-crossed like that. It won't go unpunished."

Finn nodded. "Sophia says the cops are treating it as

a robbery gone wrong, yet another one in a borderline Southtown neighborhood that's going downhill."

I snorted. "In other words, they've already closed the case and moved on to the next one."

"Way of the world, Gin. Way of the world." He gave me a sidelong glance. "Before she called the cops yesterday, Sophia took a picture of Dad's body. She thought I might want to see him for myself."

I tensed. Damn that dwarven Goth girl. Damn and double damn her.

"She e-mailed the photo to me while you were inside the Cake Walk." Finn turned his head to stare at me. "Why didn't you tell me he'd been tortured to death by an Air elemental?"

I couldn't see Finn's green eyes behind his black sunglasses, but raw grief roughened his voice, as though someone had scraped a cheese grater over his vocal chords.

"Because dead is dead. You can't come back from it, so it doesn't particularly matter how you get there." My voice was as rough as his.

Finn's hands tightened around the steering wheel. "You still should have told me."

"I was trying to spare you the details."

Emotion sharpened my voice, making it harsher than I would have liked. I'd seen a lot of bodies in my time, but none as bad as Fletcher's. The image of his flayed, ruined face, the malicious glee someone had taken in doing that to him, would always haunt me. Another ghost of the past I'd never be able to banish, no matter how hard I tried.

Because I might have stopped it. Should have stopped

it. Should have gotten to the Pork Pit sooner. Should have been stronger, faster, better, smarter. Should have been everything Fletcher taught me to be, instead of just a bitter disappointment.

The memories of two more bodies flashed through my mind—the smoking, burned-out shell that had been my mother, Eira. The smaller one that had been my older sister, Annabella. A splash of blood on the rocks where Bria had been hiding. The smell of charred flesh filled my nose. Shrieks of fury and pain rang in my ears, along with my own choked sobs—

The SUV bumped over a pothole, breaking the morbid spell. But the tight knot of rage in my chest beat on, keeping perfect time with my heart.

Once I got control of myself, I leaned over, put my hand on top of Finn's, and squeezed. He didn't pull away, but he didn't look at me, either. I let go and sat back in my seat. We didn't speak for several minutes.

"Did Sophia tell you anything else? She is keeping her promise to watch over the restaurant, isn't she?" I asked.

"Yeah, Sophia said she could take care of the Pork Pit. Not a big deal. She's done it before."

"What are you going to do with the restaurant?" I asked. "Once this is over? It's yours now."

Finn shrugged. "I don't know. I haven't gotten that far yet. I suppose it depends on what we find out—and whether or not we get killed in the process."

I nodded. The thought of dying didn't scare me. I'd seen too much of it, dealt out too much of it, to fear it. It was the torture that could be inflicted before the kill that worried me. That's where the real pain was. And if you got unlucky and didn't die, the memories needled you that much more, each one a fresh set of pins pricking your heart.

Death was a release, in so many ways. An end to suffering. An escape to something else. What that something else was, I didn't know. Maybe heaven. Maybe hell. Maybe nothing at all. But I doubted it could be any worse than some of the things I'd seen and done in my lifetime.

Or the ones I was going to have to do to make sure Finn and I survived the next few days.

When he was certain no one was following us, Finn headed back to my apartment. He left the stolen SUV six blocks out. Using a circuitous route, we walked the rest of the way, arm in arm, heads close together, like a couple of lovers oblivious to the rest of the world.

Our route took us past the Pork Pit. The tattered awning looked the same, but the neon pig was dark, sad, broken. Just like Fletcher. Guilt and grief filled me, and I concentrated on my breathing, trying to squash the feelings. But instead of frying grease and spices, tobacco smoke filled the air, adding to my discomfort. A cigarette dangled from the thin lips of the man standing in front of the restaurant. He held a tape measure in one hand and took a swig from the Dr. Enuf soda pop he had clenched in the other. A toolbox sat on the cracked sidewalk next to his booted feet. A bored glazier, fixing the pane I'd smashed.

My eyes flicked past the man, and I spotted Sophia Deveraux inside the storefront. The Goth dwarf wore her usual black jeans and boots, although today, her T-shirt of choice was white with a giant black skull and crossbones on the front. A collar set with silver spikes ringed her neck. Her black lipstick was a dark slash in her pale face.

Sophia was too busy cleaning to notice me. She pushed a mop back and forth across the floor. The thick muscles in her arms tightened and relaxed with every movement. Sophia gazed at the floor as though she could clean it with the force of her mind, if not her powerful strokes. I'd never seen the dwarf do any magic, but Sophia's steadfast black stare made me wonder if she'd gotten any of the Air elemental power her sister Jo-Jo had—and what she might be able to do with it.

Each of the four elements lent themselves to various things. Some Airs could control the weather. Others became healers. Stones often worked in construction or the coal mines that lay north of the city. Most of the Ices were fond of artistic leanings, like sculpture. Some of the Fires were also artists, using their heat to forge pottery and other things. Elementals could do too many things to name, and this wasn't even counting the folks with aptitudes for offshoots of the elements like metal, water, and electricity. I looked at Sophia, and I wondered.

Finn spotted Sophia too. It took him a few seconds to realize what she was doing—and exactly what she was cleaning up. Impossible to miss. Fletcher's blood had long ago turned the thick, white mop strings a rusty pink. The rhythmic *slop* and *swish* of the mop splatting against the floor was like a knife in my heart. Twisting and turning until there was nothing inside me that hadn't been ripped to ribbons.

Finn's steps slowed and faltered. I tightened my grip on his arm and dragged him across the street, before he could do something stupid, like stop. Or worse, try to go inside the restaurant. The Air elemental might not have men watching the restaurant since Fletcher was dead, but it was a chance I wasn't going to take.

"Soon," I whispered in his ear. "Soon."

Finn nodded, and we strolled on.

We took the elevator up to my floor and approached my door. I pressed my hand against the stone, letting the rough texture dig into my palm. No notes of alarm, no sudden bursts of distress. The stone murmured in a low voice, like usual. No one had been near the place all day.

"Clean," I said.

Finn shivered and put his key in the lock. "You know how creepy that is, right? You listening to a pile of rocks? It's just not natural."

"What's not natural is the fact you spend more on hair-care products than I do," I said, trying to lighten the mood. I reached over and rubbed his head, messing up his walnut locks.

"Hey! Hey!" Finn protested. "Anything but the hair."

I almost managed a grin.

We stepped inside. Finn settled himself at the kitchen table and fired up his laptop. He clicked through his various e-mail accounts and messages, seeing what his sources had been able to dig up on Gordon Giles and anyone who might have wanted him dead.

"Here." I reached into my hip pocket and passed him the business card I'd gotten from the coeds outside the Cake Walk. "See what you can find out about this guy, too. Who is he, where he works, where he hangs out at."

Finn waved the card at me. "Do you really think this will lead us anywhere? The IDs we got off the other men were all fakes."

I shrugged. "Dumbass was stupid enough to hand it out to those coeds while he was tailing a guy. I bet he was stupid enough to give them one with his real name on it. If we strike out with Donovan Caine, we can always go pay Mr. Smooth a visit. Worth a shot."

While Finn tested the silky threads of his information web, I moved into the kitchen.

"On to more important matters—any special requests for lunch?"

"Sandwich," Finn murmured, never taking his eyes off the flickering screen. "You make the best sandwiches."

Truer words had never been spoken. I opened the refrigerator and scanned the sandwich fixings inside. Five minutes later, I had two turkey-and-Gouda sandwiches on chewy pumpernickel bread. I added a kosher pickle and a couple of baby carrots to each plate, along with some double chocolate chip cookies. Color and presentation were key when it came to food preparation. At least, that's what my culinary professor had claimed last semester, when he'd showed us how to turn tomatoes into roses with our paring knives. I'd aced that final.

I put a plate in front of Finn and took the chair on the other side of the table.

"Anything on Mr. Smooth yet?" I asked.

Finn gnawed off a bite of his sandwich. "Working on it. You were right. Dumbass was stupid enough to give you his real name, which is Carlyle, by the way. Charles Carlyle, although his friends probably call him Chuck. Guess where he works?"

I didn't even have to think about it. "Halo Industries."

Finn shot his finger at me. "Bingo. He's an executive vice president."

I frowned. Carlyle hadn't struck me as a true corporate type. More like a bouncer dressed up in a suit. "Executive vice president? That's a nice way of saying he's someone's corporate bitch."

Finn kept his green eyes on his computer. "Haley James's corporate bitch. Looks like he reports directly to her. A new hire. Just started a couple months ago."

Haley James's name kept popping up everywhere we looked. Not enough to prove her guilty of being the Air elemental or behind the hit on Giles, but definitely enough to make her a person of serious interest.

"I'll put out more requests for info on Carlyle," Finn promised. "By tonight, I should have a record of everything he's ever done."

"Good," I said. "What about the tooth necklace? Any leads?"

"The rune? Nothing so far. It's not used by anyone I or my considerable friends know. I've put out more feelers to my contacts. Maybe something will turn up."

I frowned again. Runes were important, especially to magic users. They transmitted information, showed allegiances, inspired awe—and fear. Hell, I hated the damn things, but I still had three of them on my mantel. And two more on my palms, whether I wanted them there or not.

A tooth represented prosperity. Power. Using that as your symbol meant you were trying to send a message you were strong. Someone to be reckoned with. If we found who used the rune, we'd find who had set this whole thing up. Or at least some of her underlings. I had no qualms about killing my way up the food chain until I got to the Air elemental herself. Charles Carlyle would be as good a guy as any to start with.

"What about Caine? Think he'll take you up on your offer to trade information?" Finn crunched a carrot between his teeth.

I shrugged. "I don't know. It depends on what he wants more—me dead for killing his partner or to find out who really murdered Giles and which one of his fellow esteemed boys in blue is helping her. My money's on the second one. Caine already thinks I'm a monster. He'll want to go after the other two—the ones he doesn't know."

Finn glanced at his watch. "It's almost three. He's only got a few hours to make up his mind."

"I know. And I hope he makes the right decision. For everyone's sake."

Finn snorted. "You're just saying that because you want to fuck him."

I started. "What makes you say that?"

"Come on, Gin, don't play games with me. You've got a thing for Donovan Caine. You have ever since you killed Ingles, his partner, and he went all dogged and determined on you. Fletcher told me about the file he compiled on the good detective."

My fingers smushed into my sandwich, leaving grooves in the pumpernickel bread. Damn Fletcher. Damn and double damn him. That file was just supposed to be between the two of us. But I should have known he would have told Finn about it. The old man had shared everything with his son—including my curious interest in the detective.

Maybe it was his dark good looks or the air of confidence that radiated off Donovan Caine. Maybe it was the perpetual scowl that tightened his face. Or the strain of being an honest man that sat on his shoulders like he was Atlas bearing the weight of the world. Or perhaps it was the simple fact he still clung to ideals I'd given up long ago. But something about him fascinated me.

"Maybe I find him . . . interesting," I admitted. "Attractive in an uptight sort of way. But that won't keep me from killing him if he does something stupid—like try to double-cross us. That is something that's nonnegotiable, no matter how much fuck potential Donovan Caine might have."

Finn raised his coffee mug to me. "That's my girl. A bitch to the bitter end."

I saluted him with my sandwich. "Always."

❖ 14 ❖

"Exactly how long are we going to sit out here?" Finn asked. "It's been *hours* already."

Finnegan Lane might be an expert when it came to computers, international banking laws, and getting women to take off their clothes, but patience was not one of his virtues. Another reason Fletcher had trained me instead of him. Assassins who didn't like to wait did stupid things—and then they got dead.

"Long enough for him to think we're not coming tonight and relax his guard," I said. "Now quit your bitching. You whine worse than a toddler."

I peered through a pair of night-vision goggles. Donovan Caine lived in a modest cabin home in Towering Pines, one of Ashland's rustic-themed subdivisions. The two-story, wooden structure was located at the end of a cul-de-sac and squatted about two hundred feet up on a hill. Stunted pine trees lined the curving driveway that led up to the house, not quite matching the subdivision's boastful name.

Finn and I had gotten a fresh car and slipped into the suburban neighborhood just before six. Lucky for us, one of Caine's college-age neighbors had decided to throw a raucous party. Two dozen cars lined the streets, three deep in some places, while at least a hundred people, most in their early twenties, milled in and around the ranch-style house that was the closest one to the detective's abode. One particularly drunk frat boy had stumbled by, turned, and thrown up all over the hood of our stolen SUV. I had to stop Finn from getting out and rubbing the guy's nose in his own vomit.

"It's not even your car," I pointed out. "You lifted it out of a mall parking lot."

"It's the principle of the thing," Finn sniffed. "This is a Mercedes. You don't puke on a Mercedes."

We sat about two hundred feet away from the cabin, out of range of any surveillance cameras or equipment that might be on or around the structure. Besides the party shack, there hadn't been much activity on the street. A few folks coming in from work and going back out to get dinner. Some kids wearing football uniforms piling out of a truck. People lugging groceries inside. The usual suburban routines.

At exactly six o'clock, the light on Donovan Caine's front porch had clicked on. The detective appeared to have accepted my terms. Or at least wanted me to think he had. I hadn't spotted any scurry of activity around the house. No cops hidden in the bushes, no plainclothes detectives masquerading as put-upon suburbanites, no

SWAT team parked in an unmarked van. But that didn't mean Caine wasn't waiting inside with a dozen of Ashland's most corrupt.

After the light had appeared, Finn and I had driven out of the subdivision. We'd killed time by eating some spicy fajitas, salty corn chips, and chunky salsa at Pepe's, one of the local Mexican restaurants. We'd returned just after eight and had spent the last three hours watching Caine's house.

"I still can't believe he turned on his porch light," Finn said, shifting in the driver's seat. "He must be as crazy and desperate as we are."

"Or he knows there's more to this than meets the eye and wants to get to the bottom of it," I replied.

"You know you could be walking into a trap. Caine could be waiting in there with a shotgun, ready to blast you to hell and back."

"He could, but I don't think he will," I said. "By turning on that light, he gave me his word. That means something to a man like Donovan Caine."

Finn snorted. "Yeah, it means you'll realize he's an exceptionally good liar when you're clutching your intestines and choking on your own blood on his living room floor."

I leaned forward and stared through the goggles at the house. It was after eleven now, and day had long ago given way to night. Darkness would have shrouded the street, covered in a blanket of silence, if every single light over at Party Central hadn't been turned on and cranked up full blast, along with an impressive sound system. Somebody over there was on a Lynyrd Skynyrd kick. They'd played

"Sweet Home, Alabama" so many times I wanted to crash the party, kill the radio, and knife whoever was selecting the music.

But the blaring southern rock, warm glow, and beer buzz didn't reach up the hill to Caine's place. Shadows pooled around the cabin like puddles of ever-expanding blood, encroaching on the cheer from the party.

A light snapped on in one of the second-story windows, and a tall, lean figure moved in front of it. Donovan Caine. I adjusted the goggles, but I couldn't make out his features through the thick curtains. He appeared agitated, pacing from one side of the room to the other. His hand was held to his head, as though he was talking on a cell phone. He seemed to be arguing with someone.

A pair of headlights popped up in the rearview mirror, ruining my night vision. Cursing, I blinked away the spots that exploded in my eyes. But instead of stopping at Party Central and spewing out more college kids, the black sedan glided by. Its headlights snapped off, and the vehicle coasted to a stop at the end of the cul-de-sac, blocking the entrance to Caine's driveway.

"What do you see?" Finn whispered.

I blinked away the rest of the spots and squinted through the goggles. "Five men. Suits. All armed with guns. All headed toward the house. Four going up to the front. One headed around the back of the cabin."

"Fuck."

"Fuck is right," I muttered, pulling off the goggles. "There's only one reason you send five guys to a cop's house in the middle of the night."

The same scenario had played out when my family

had been murdered. The sneak attack late at night. The old memories tugged at me, the hoarse screams echoed in my ears, but I blocked them out. Now was not the time to dwell on the past.

"Somebody's decided the good detective is more of a liability than an asset," Finn finished my thought. "He's probably been asking too many questions about the Giles murder."

"Justice will get you every single time. Now, you take the rear guard and keep him from coming up behind me. I'll surprise the others."

Finn sighed. "So we're going to go help him then?"

I didn't answer. I was already outside, running toward the cabin.

Several low hedges and growing pines dotted the landscape between the street and the cabin. Stiff needles clutched at my clothes, and the tangy scent of pine sap tickled my nose. But it was easy enough for me to hopscotch my way from bush to bush, tree to tree, shadow to shadow. I paused about fifty feet away from the steps leading up to the front porch. Listening. Watching. Waiting. A lone man stood outside the front door. His three friends must have slipped inside while I'd been approaching the house. I'd seen the fifth guy go around the cabin, probably to keep Donovan Caine from bolting out a back door. No worries. Finn would take care of him.

I shook my sleeves, and my silverstone knives fell into my hands. Cold and comforting, as always.

I picked my way up the hill, coming at the porch from

an angle. The end of the wooden, wraparound porch stood about four feet off the ground, supported by a couple of low beams. I squatted down and peered over the edge, my gray eyes just above the porch line. The guy still stood by the front door, but his body was turned away from me, facing inside. He wasn't expecting trouble, at least not from this direction. Sloppy, sloppy, sloppy.

I hooked one of my legs onto the porch and pulled myself up. The wooden slats felt cold against my warm stomach, and the nail heads pressed into my chest like icy, round brands. I slithered over to the corner, where the shadows were the deepest, and crouched behind an antique rocking chair. The guard kept looking inside the house.

I got to my feet and repositioned my knives. Hugging the wall, I slid toward the front door.

Another light flared to life on the second story, brightening the yard beyond the porch. Shouts rang out from the interior above my head. A gun burped once, then twice more. The guard cursed and rocked back and forth on his feet, unsure whether he should charge in or not. He clutched his gun close to his chest, right over his heart.

It didn't do him a damn bit of good.

My knife slid into his back, through his ribs, and up into his heart. His blood spurted out onto my hand. Hot. Wet. Sticky. The sensation was the same, yet different every time.

He jerked, and I clamped my hand over his mouth to keep him from crying out. Shouldn't have bothered. Something crashed deeper inside the house. Loud, vicious curses drifted out onto the night breeze, drowning out whatever noise the dying man might have made.

I pulled the knife out, eased the dead guard to the porch, stepped over him, and slipped inside. A couple of dim overhead lights cast out a bit of weak illumination. The front hallway branched off in three directions—up, right, left. A den lay to the right, with a big-screen TV, a brown leather couch, and a couple of recliners. A small dining area was off to the left. A dirty plate and glass littered the rectangular table, along with a crumpled newspaper. Cozy.

The stairs lay in front of me, and I headed up them. Again, I hugged the wall, wincing at the inevitable *crack* that sounded as my weight shifted on the slick wood. I peered over the lip of the landing. Another hallway with rooms branching off either side. To my right was what looked like a never-used guest bedroom and an office with a computer half-buried by stacks of sports magazines. In front of me was a bathroom, with a heap of towels twisted together on the tile floor. Another room lay beyond that one down the hallway, probably the master bedroom.

Lights blazed in the last room, the one I'd seen Donovan Caine pacing back and forth in. Several hard *slap-slap-slap*s rang out, followed by a low, throaty groan. The detective was getting the shit beat out of him.

I eased onto the landing, wincing as the stairs let out a final, unwanted creak. But the men inside the bedroom were too intent on hitting Caine to worry about possible intruders. Besides, they'd left two guards stationed downstairs, one in the front and one in the back. Nothing could possibly go wrong when you left a couple of guys alone and in the dark to watch your back.

A knife in either hand, I tiptoed down the hallway toward the bedroom. The indistinct voices sharpened into meaningful conversation.

"Tell us where it is," a man said. "Surely you can see how pointless this is. No one's coming to save you, detective."

Déjà vu all over again.

"All we want is the flash drive and the information Gordon Giles gave to you at the opera house. That's it."

"Yeah," another male voice chimed in. "Give it to us quick enough, and we might even let you live."

I rolled my eyes. Liar. The only way Donovan Caine was leaving this house was in a black body bag.

A low cough rumbled out, followed by the sound of someone spitting. Caine, hacking up his own blood.

"I told you Giles didn't give me anything. No flash drive, no files, nothing," Caine said in a raspy voice. "He didn't have time to before your assassin came into the box."

"But you were there to get it, to convince him to turn the information over to you," a third man's voice sounded. "He must have told you something, given you *something*."

Another series of *slap-slap-slap*s sounded, punctuated by the solid *thwack* of fists hitting flesh. Caine groaned again.

"Where's the boss lady?" Number One asked. "She'll get him to talk. Right quick, too."

"Really? Like she made the old guy at the restaurant talk?" Number Two said. "Creepiest thing I've ever seen, the way she kept ripping off his skin, and the way he kept laughing at her. Even gave Carlyle the willies, and you know what a cold bastard he is."

Fletcher. They'd been there in the Pork Pit that night. This guy and Charles Carlyle had seen Fletcher die, probably held him down while the Air elemental did her worst to him. My hands tightened on my knives, and the cold knot of rage in my chest throbbed with anticipation.

Fletcher.

"The geezer was tough. The detective here isn't that strong, are you, Caine?" Number Three said.

"The elemental's on her way," Number Two cut in. "Shouldn't be too much longer. Ten minutes, tops. Just keep hitting him. No reason not to soften him up for her. It'll make his skin peel off easier."

They all shared a good chuckle at that. The laughter faded away, and more *slap-slap-slap*s rang out, steady and insistent. Someone enjoyed being the muscle. I blew out a soft breath and readied myself.

"Speaking of the elemental, go downstairs and check on Phil and Jimmy, will ya? I don't want those two slacking off and her seeing it."

Number Two talking again, although I had no idea if he was addressing One or Three. Didn't much matter. They'd all be dead in another minute. Two, tops.

I crept closer to the bedroom, my back skimming the wall, until I was just next to the doorjamb. Footsteps whispered on the carpet, headed in my direction. I waited, gathering my strength. A shadow fell over me, and a man stepped into the hallway.

I rammed my knife into his chest.

The man screamed and stumbled back. I used his own

momentum to shove him deeper into the bedroom. My eyes flicked over the area, taking in everything in a second's time. Donovan Caine handcuffed to a chair. Two men dressed in suits standing over him. One guy holding a gun by his side.

The guy I'd stabbed hit an end table, knocked over a lamp, and did a header onto the carpet. Dead on arrival.

I hurled my other knife at the man with the gun. He jerked to one side, and the blade caught him in the shoulder instead of in the throat. He raised his weapon and fired. I threw myself forward and onto the floor, the rough carpet burning my knees and stomach through my jeans and long-sleeved T-shirt. The shot went over my head and shattered a lamp. Glass rained down on me, nicking my hands.

But I was already moving. I rolled over and came up onto my hands and knees. My foot lashed out, and my sharp kick caught the third guy in the knee. He yelped and bent forward, putting himself between me and his friend. I plucked a knife from my boot and cut his throat with it. Blood spattered in my eyes and onto my face, but I ignored the uncomfortable, wet, stinging sensation and grabbed hold of the dying man.

One guy left.

He raised his gun and fired three more times. But his friend was in the way, and the bullets slammed into his back instead of my chest. I pulled myself up and shoved the dead guy at the last man. The body flopped against his wounded arm, and the gun slipped from his hand.

I threw myself at the last guy, but he saw me coming. His fists slammed into my chest. Hard, solid blows. I jerked back, my foot caught on something, and I fell to the carpet. He leaped on top of me, wrapping his hands around my throat. I tried to break his grip, but he was stronger. My hands scrabbled on the floor, looking for one of my knives, his gun, anything I could hurt him with.

A leg moved in my peripheral vision, and a foot slammed into the guy's head. The man grunted, and his grip loosened. I shoved him back and rolled out from under him, my eyes flicking over the bloody carpet. There. I grabbed the base of one of the broken lamps. The curved glass had shattered, leaving a sharp, serrated edge about five inches long. Perfect.

The guy clamped a hand on my shoulder and yanked me up, determined to finish choking me.

I spun around and slashed his throat.

The glass dug into his flesh, instead of slicing deep and clean the way my knife would have. The edges caught and snagged on his stubbled skin. Nothing easy and pain-less about it. The man shrieked an ear-splitting sound of keening pain. He tried to jerk away, move away. I thought of Fletcher and followed him. I pulled the glass out, tak-ing chunks of flesh with it, then shoved it right back in. Hard. What had been a trickle of blood increased to a crimson torrent, spattering down my torso and onto my T-shirt, jacket, and jeans.

The man's hand clamped down on my shoulder like a vise, making me wince. Blood and mucus bubbled out of his trembling lips. We stood there. Me driving the glass in deeper and deeper, his hand tightening that much more with every millimeter. His eyes glazed, and after about thirty seconds, his grip slackened. I shoved him away, and he joined his two dead buddies on the floor.

My eyes went to Donovan Caine. To my surprise, he had his leg up, ready to kick out with his foot again. The detective stared at me, then the men on the floor. He lowered his boot.

"Sorry about the mess," I said.

✸ 15 ✸

The corner of Donovan Caine's mouth lifted up into a faint smile—or grimace. Hard to tell since red welts and shallow cuts dotted his features like lumpy, ugly freckles. The beginnings of a shiner rimmed his right eye, and a bruise had already darkened his left cheekbone. I'd saved Caine from being beaten as bad as Finn, but the detective had still taken several good licks.

"You're the one who's a mess," Donovan Caine said.

I glanced at my reflection in the mirror over the dresser. Blood coated my face like some sort of mud mask Jo-Jo might use at her salon. More blood covered my jacket and T-shirt, blackening the fabric, and drips and drops painted my jeans and boots in gobby, Jackson Pollock patterns. Distinct fingertip bruises ringed my throat, a macabre necklace of purple jewels. I probably had a matching set on my shoulder from the guy's death grip. When you added the blood and bruises together, I looked like I was dressed up for Halloween—as a murder victim.

Not exactly the face I wanted to present to the detective, but I'd looked worse. Much worse. But tonight, something about the blood made me feel old. Tired. Used up. Just once, it might be nice to go out at night and not have to incinerate my clothes when I got home. Just once.

I dropped my eyes from the mirror. "Job hazard."

Caine couldn't go anywhere, since he was still strapped down. I walked behind him. The detective's hands were cuffed, with the chain threaded through the back of the chair. Silverstone handcuffs. Looked like Caine never went anywhere without a set. Kinky.

"Key?"

Caine jerked his head. "On the dresser."

I retrieved the metal key and bent down behind the detective. His rigid muscles coiled, and he drew in a sharp breath. He smelled faintly of soap, and I could feel the strength of his body, even though he was shackled to the chair. Caine probably thought this was just a ruse. That I was going to slit his throat instead of freeing him. I might have considered it, if I hadn't already offered to work with the detective. My word still meant something to me, too.

The handcuffs clinked open, and Donovan Caine got to his feet. He turned to face me and massaged his wrists, rubbing the feeling back into his hands. His gaze skimmed over the mess of blood, bodies, and broken furniture. He spotted the discarded gun, half-hidden under the remains of one of the crystal lamps, near his feet.

"You have a decision to make," I said in a quiet voice. "You can pick up that gun. Turn it on me. Try to avenge your partner's death."

I didn't add he'd die where he stood when my knife ripped through his heart. Caine had seen what I was capable of. Witnessed my skills firsthand. I just hoped it was enough to temper his dogged determination to make me pay for Cliff Ingles's death.

"Or?" The detective kept rubbing his wrists, but his hazel eyes never left the weapon at his feet.

"Or we can call a truce, and you can come with me. Work with me to get to the bottom of this. They want you dead now, too. They want us all dead."

Donovan Caine stared at the gun. A second ticked by. Five more. Ten. Fifteen. Thirty. He flexed his fingers, an Old West sheriff about to draw down on the mangy, good-for-nothin' gunfighter threatening his town, his peace of mind, his way of life. I tensed, ready to strike.

The detective lifted his eyes to mine. His gaze was the color of smoky topaz, or perhaps a fine whiskey, oscillating from pure gold to burnished brown and back again. Emotions flickered in the amber depths, one after another, like lightning bugs winking on and off. Disgust. Anger. Mistrust. Suspicion. Curiosity.

"Why did you come here?" he asked. "You could have let them kill me."

I shrugged again. "Like I said before, I need you. Need to know what you know about Gordon Giles. I believe I heard something about files and a flash drive?"

Caine rubbed a hand through his black hair. "Yeah. They seem to be missing. My friends here were under the assumption I had them."

"But you don't?"

He didn't respond. Caine knew how to keep his face blank too.

I moved around the room, picking up my knives and slipping them back into their various slots. I also rifled through the dead guys' pockets, digging out their wallets, cell phones, and jewelry. Nobody was wearing a chain with the triangular tooth rune on it, but one of the men had the shape tattooed on the back of his left wrist. I spotted it when I took off his watch.

I frowned. That damn symbol again. I was getting real tired of seeing it without knowing who the fuck it belonged to.

Caine saw me staring and crouched down to get a better look. He took care not to get within arm's or knife's reach of me. Smart man.

"Is that a rune?" he asked.

"Yeah. One I've been seeing a lot of lately." I pulled my cell phone out of my back jean pocket, used it to snap a picture of the rune, then stuffed the device into my jeans once more.

Caine didn't say anything else, but he grabbed the guy's wrist, held it up to the light, and stared at the crude symbol, committing it to memory.

I straightened. "All right, detective. Time to decide. Are you in? Or out?"

He glanced up. "What happens if I'm out?"

"You go your way, and I'll go mine. I'll look for your fellow boys in blue to fish your body out of the Aneirin River in a couple of days."

He shook his head. "That won't happen."

"Really?" I asked. "I was watching the house. I noticed you arguing with someone on the phone right before these guys showed up. I'm willing to bet it was someone on the force. Care to tell me who you were talking to?"

Caine's eyes dropped to the floor, and I spotted another cell phone swimming in a puddle of blood. Must be his.

"Stephenson," he muttered. "I was talking to Wayne Stephenson, my captain."

The overweight giant who'd given the press conference. The one who'd kept a muzzle on Caine the whole time. I made a mental note to get Finn to start digging into the police captain. If the Air elemental had paid him off, maybe she'd left a trail back to herself.

"And what did Stephenson want? To make sure you were home before he sent the dogs in?"

"He wanted to talk to me about the Giles case," Caine said. "That's all. It doesn't prove anything."

"No," I said. "It doesn't prove anything. But it's a pretty damning coincidence."

Silence. Donovan Caine stared at me. Emotions continued to flash in his eyes. Faster now. Like lightning striking the earth again and again on a hot summer night. Although he didn't look at it, I knew the detective was still thinking about the gun lying just a few tempting feet away. About how he could take care of one of his problems right here, right now. I hoped he'd realize how stupid that would be. Or I'd be wearing even more blood in another minute. Two, tops.

But some of my reasoning must have resonated with him. The detective exhaled. He let go of the dead man's wrist and got to his feet.

"I'm in," he said.

"But . . ."

He shook his head. "But not without serious reservations and some rules. This truce you're offering only goes so far. I won't cover up anything you've done. Not one damn thing. I won't kill for you, and I won't let you hurt any innocent people."

I laughed. The harsh sound smacked against the bedroom walls like the kiss of death. "Innocent people? Like the gentlemen who came to see you tonight? The ones who were going to hold you down while their boss tortured you? I don't think you have to worry about stumbling over many *innocent* people on this case, detective."

"Maybe not. But that's how it's going to be."

I'd expected nothing less from him, and I could live with those terms. It was Caine's personal vendetta against me, that hot, seething, unreasonable rage, that could be his undoing. "Say the rest of it. You know you want to."

"The second this is over, I'm coming for you. Getting justice for Cliff Ingles, my partner, no matter what I have to do, even if that means killing you. Do you understand me?"

Caine's harsh, angry promise blazed like a bonfire in his eyes. His mouth was a flat line in his face, his hands bunched into fists, his whole body tight and tense. I'd pushed him as far as I could.

"Understood." I said. "Now, grab whatever gear you can get your hands on in three minutes. Clothes, money, whatever. We need to move. Now."

He stared at me. I met his hard gaze with one of my own. The detective nodded, and I knew he'd stick to his word. We were on the same side—for now.

"We need to leave because the Air elemental's on her way?" Caine skirted around me, still keeping out of arm's reach, and headed toward the closet. He didn't completely turn his back to me.

"Yeah. So hurry up."

Donovan Caine pulled a duffel bag out of the closet. He hooked his finger under a jagged strip of carpet inside the small space, rolled it up, then moved a loose floorboard underneath. He stuffed a couple of bricks of cash into the bag, along with two guns and several boxes of ammunition. Perhaps the detective wasn't the paragon of virtue I'd thought. Or perhaps he just realized the value of being prepared for anything in this city. Either way, my respect for him grew a little more. Despite his outdated ideals about justice, the detective was smart. A trait I'd always admired.

Caine moved over to the dresser and grabbed some clothes. Jeans, socks, boxers. I focused on the last item. Black boxers. Made from a nice silk, although not nearly as high-end as Finn's. I thought of that silk rubbing against me, followed by the thick, hard length of him. Mmm. Too bad he hated me, and I looked like an extra from a slasher movie right now. Otherwise, I might have considered seducing Donovan Caine.

"I would think someone like you would relish the

challenge of taking on an elemental." Caine continued to stuff clothes into the bag.

I pushed my fantasy aside. "I might be an assassin, detective, but I don't particularly enjoy killing people."

"Then why do it?"

The inevitable question. I decided to give him my standard, pat answer. Donovan Caine didn't need to know about my murdered family or time living on the streets. He didn't need to know I'd been tired of being weak and afraid and hunted. That I'd chosen to become an assassin so I'd never feel that way again. So I would be strong.

And he especially didn't need to know how none of my skills were helping me cope with Fletcher's death or this sudden, nagging weariness I felt.

"Because I'm good at it, the blood doesn't bother me, and it pays very, very well. Not because I get some sick, twisted thrill out of watching the light leak out of people's eyes," I said in a glib tone. "As for elementals, they die, just like everybody else. Magic doesn't make you invincible. Gordon Giles was an Air elemental, but his power didn't save him from being burned to death in that fake car accident. That being said, I don't want to take on an Air elemental when I've already been knocked around and saddled with an injured man. Besides, I don't know how many more men she might be bringing with her. She'll probably have a couple guys, maybe more. Not the kind of odds I like. As you can guess, I prefer more one-on-one action."

"Point taken."

The corner of his mouth lifted. This time, I was sure I

hadn't imagined it. Whether it was a grimace or smile, I still couldn't tell.

Caine zipped up the bag and slung it over his shoulder. "Lead on, Macduff."

"Quoting Shakespeare? I never would have guessed, detective."

"I never guessed I'd be working with an assassin either. Stranger things."

"Touché." I flashed one of my silverstone knives at him. "Stay behind me and keep quiet. There was one more guard who went around the back of the cabin. My associate should have taken care of him, but you can never be too careful."

He raised a black eyebrow. "Associate?"

"Associate. Now, follow me."

I turned and strode over to the bedroom door. My hand tightened on the knife hilt, and I waited a beat, listening. But Caine didn't go for his third gun, the one I'd seen him slip out of the dresser and against the small of his back, the one he thought I didn't know about. The detective was honoring his agreement. He wasn't going to shoot me in the back—yet.

I tiptoed into the hallway. Everything was quiet, and no scurries of movement sounded. No hoarse whispers. No ragged gasps. Nothing.

Donovan Caine stayed close to me. His clean, soapy scent washed over me again. The warmth from his body enveloped my own, and his breath puffed against the back of my neck, almost like a kiss. We reached the part of the hall that overlooked the first floor. I made a motion with my hand for Caine to stay put. Then I dropped to my knees, slid down the wall, and peeked through the railing.

Finn leaned against the front door, reading a newspaper. The dead guard lay where I'd placed him. Finn had a foot propped up on the guy's bloody back, which meant he'd already gone around the house and killed the last man. He wouldn't have been standing there otherwise. I shook my head and straightened.

"Come on," I told Caine. "The coast is clear."

We went downstairs. Finn didn't look up as the wood creaked and cracked under our weight. I snatched the newspaper out of his hands and tossed it aside.

"Hey," he protested. "I was reading that."

"Now you're not."

I stepped back so Finn and Caine could have a clear view of each other.

"Donovan Caine, this is my associate, Finnegan Lane. And vice versa."

The two men stared at each other. Caine looked at Finn's supple leather jacket, designer khakis, and custom-made polo shirt. Finn eyed the detective's ratty duffel bag, the threadbare patches on his jeans, and the stains on his faded boots. Assumptions were made, judgments rendered, dicks measured.

After about twenty seconds of intense scrutiny, Finn stuck out his hand. Caine just looked at it, with his flat, deadpan, cop stare.

"Not a hand shaker, eh? Too bad." Finn dropped his hand.

"The rear guard?" I asked.

"Dispatched, of course."

Finn didn't have much use for knives, but whenever he backed me up on jobs, he always carried a couple of guns with him. Usually a silencer as well, which is probably why I hadn't heard him take out the rear guard. Among his many character quirks, Finnegan Lane happened to be an excellent shot.

He gestured at the dead man at his feet. "I take it all the others wound up like this one, Gin?"

"Of course."

Finn grinned at me. "Touché."

Donovan Caine stared at me. "Gin? Is that your real name?"

I realized I'd never told the detective my name, just my assassin moniker, the Spider. But he was going to have to call me something, since we were going to be working together, and it was too late now to concoct some sort of alias. "More or less."

"Gin?" Caine asked again.

"Yeah, like the liquor."

"Gin." Caine said the word carefully this time, as though it were a fine wine he was tasting on his tongue, instead of a bastardized version of my real name. "It suits you."

Despite the situation, I found his slow drawl low, warm, and inviting. "Glad you think so. Now let's go."

We skulked down the hill through the yard. The party next door was still going strong, although the radio now blared out "Free Bird." A few more frat boys had stumbled outside and were sleeping off their drunken stupors on the lawn. Nobody appeared to have heard the gunshots or the sound of five men dying in and around Donovan

Caine's cabin. The southern rock music was so loud and twangy, I doubted anyone on the whole street could hear themselves think. Noisy neighbors. A blessing in disguise sometimes.

We reached the SUV. Finn got into the driver's seat, while I slid into the passenger's side. Donovan Caine paused, staring into the dark depths of the vehicle. He pulled in a breath, opened the door, and climbed into the backseat. He hesitated again and let out the same breath before he shut the door. *No going back.* That's what he had to be thinking right now. Also short for *what the fuck am I doing getting into an assassin's car?*

But the detective seemed to be sticking with his decision. With our truce. He pushed his bag down onto the floorboard and buckled his seat belt. The sharp snap reminded me of handcuffs clinking together.

"Now what?" Caine asked.

I turned to answer him and saw a pair of headlights headed down the street toward us. "Duck. Here they come."

We scooted down in our seats until the vehicle passed. Another luxury sedan. It stopped next to the one parked at the bottom of Donovan Caine's driveway.

"Are those more of our new friends?" Finn mocked. "They're a little late for the party. I hate how we just keep missing them."

"Let's find out," I said.

I picked up the night-vision goggles and peered through them. The driver's side door opened, and the interior light winked on, showing me three guys. Sloppy, sloppy, sloppy, not disabling that. I recognized two of the men. Charles Carlyle, the vampire who'd hit on coeds outside the Cake Walk today, and his friend who'd been reading the newspaper. Didn't know the third guy, but he was dressed in a suit just like the other two.

"Three more goons," I murmured.

The men got out of the sedan and talked to each other over the broad hood. A fourth figure remained shrouded in darkness in the backseat. My eyes narrowed, and the cold knot of rage in my chest tightened into a noose.

Get out, I thought. *Get out and show yourself, you sadistic bitch.*

"What about the Air elemental?" Donovan Caine asked. His breath brushed against my cheek.

"She's sitting in the backseat," I replied.

The leather-bound steering wheel creaked under Finn's hands. "The one who—"

"Yes."

I cut Finn off before he could say anything about Fletcher. Finn glared at me, but he pressed his lips together.

I kept watching. Carlyle went around to the back of the vehicle and opened the door. He held out his hand, and the woman took it and stepped up and away from the sedan, as though she were some debutante exiting her limo at her coming-out party. Pretentious bitch.

"Damn it," I cursed. "She's on the far side of the car with her back to me, and she's wearing a long, black cloak. Who the fuck wears a cloak? This isn't Dungeons & Dragons. The hood's up. I can't see a thing. Not her face, not her hair, not even her clothes. Nothing."

The steering wheel creaked again. "We could take her

out, right here, right now," Finn said. "They won't be expecting us. They won't be expecting *you*."

"No. I'm not taking on the elemental. Not tonight. She'd kill us all. And I'm not letting that happen to you."

"But—"

"No, Finn," I snapped. "Listen to me. You might think you know what an elemental can do, but you don't. No matter what picture you saw. You don't have a clue how vicious their magic can be. But I do."

The image of Fletcher's body flashed through my mind, followed by the burned, smoldering remains of my mother and older sister. The familiar grief pressed down on my lungs, trying to smother me. The spider runes on my hands itched, as though they were the real creatures wiggling underneath my scarred flesh, instead of just ghastly memories.

Donovan Caine's hazel eyes flicked back and forth between us.

"But—"

Finn never got to finish his sentence. A gust of wind ripped out from the cabin, whistling like the swing of a death scythe. The blast of air flattened all the stunted pine trees in the yard before sweeping down the hill and rushing down the street like a miniature tornado. Trash cans overturned. Mailboxes ripped up out of the ground. One poor cat got picked up by the wind and tossed against the side of a pickup truck. It didn't get back up.

The Air elemental had found the first body crumpled by the front door, and she wasn't happy about it.

I squinted into the goggles, trying to get a glimpse

of her face. The hood cast her face in shadow, but she'd pushed back the sleeves of her cloak. The ends of her fingers burned milky white with magic, as if each digit were an individual welder's torch. The sort of concentrated power that would cause excruciating pain. The sort of magic that could strip flesh from bone. The sort of torture Fletcher had endured.

Fletcher.

The grief and guilt mixed with the rage in my chest, each one smashing into the other, until I wasn't sure what I was feeling—besides pain. But I forced myself to think, to let my cold judgment temper my emotions. If it had just been me, I might have snuck back up to the cabin and had a go at the elemental and her crew. But I had Finn to think about. Donovan Caine, too.

Besides, Fletcher had called me the Spider for a reason. I was at my cautious best when I was creeping in and out of the shadows. Spinning my own webs, making my own plans. Not being stupid and going out in a blaze of glory.

I pointed. "See that light? That glow? That's her magic. Do you want that to be us, Finn? Because I'm sure the Air elemental would be happy to show you exactly how pissed she is right now."

Finn thought about it. Weighing his desire to avenge his father's death against what he knew would be a disastrous plan at best, deadly at worse.

In the backseat, Donovan Caine kept looking back and forth between the two of us.

After about thirty seconds, Finn sighed and let go of the steering wheel. "No. I don't want that to be us."

I reached over and squeezed his hand. "Smart man. Don't worry. We'll take care of her, Finn. I'll take care of her. Just not tonight."

"Promise?" His voice dropped to a whisper.

I squeezed his hand again. "Promise. Now, let's go. Before the bitch realizes we're still here and watching her."

❊ 16 ❊

Finn waited until the wind died down and the Air elemental had swept into the cabin before he started the engine and did a U-turn in the middle of the wide street. Headlights off, Finn eased the vehicle toward the end of the block. He coasted over another street before he flipped on the lights and picked up speed.

"Where to?" Finn asked.

He gave me a sidelong glance. Such a simple question, but I knew what he was really asking—if I was going to take Donovan Caine back to my apartment. No other choice. Finn's place was out, and I needed to keep the detective close to make sure he wouldn't do something stupid—like go off on a righteous mission and get us all killed.

"Home," I said.

"Home?" Donovan Caine echoed. "You live in Ashland?"

"Born and bred, detective."

The light turned red. Finn stopped and used the pause to stare in the rearview mirror at the detective's bruised features.

"We're not going to the, ah, salon first?" Finn asked. "To take care of some things?"

I knew what he was asking. If we were going to swing by Jo-Jo's, so the dwarf could slap Donovan Caine with some of her healing Air elemental magic. Taking the detective back to my anonymous apartment was one thing. I could always move after this was over with. Planned on it already.

But I wasn't going to haul the detective over to Jo-Jo's and ask her to heal him, especially since his injuries weren't life-threatening. The dwarf had been entrenched in her house since before the Civil War. She wouldn't move or disappear no matter what happened. Donovan Caine didn't need to know about my connection to Jo-Jo Deveraux and her body-disposing sister, Sophia. Besides, if things went all to hell, Jo-Jo's was one of our safe houses, a place where Finn and I could crash for a few hours or days. I wasn't risking that.

"No," I replied. "I got some supplies at the salon last night. We're good, so it's straight to the apartment."

Finn nodded and made the appropriate turn. In the backseat, Donovan Caine said nothing. I clicked on the radio, and the soft strains of music filled the car. "Margaritaville" by Jimmy Buffett. The cheery song made me think of the easy, breezy Key West vacation I'd told Fletcher I was taking after the Gordon Giles hit. Fletcher would never get the chance to see the sun set over Mallory Square again. I wondered if I would share his fate.

"Well, you've rounded up your band of merry men and saved them from the wicked witch. Now what?" Finn asked, cutting into my dark thoughts.

The detective snorted at the illusion.

"You're mixing up your stories. Besides, aren't you too old to be talking in fairy tales?" I sniped.

"Maybe. But we still need a plan, Gin. We can't keep skirting around the elemental and her men. One time she'll get lucky instead of us. Be there ahead of us. Out-think us."

"I know. Believe me, I know." I rubbed my head. Dried blood flaked off my hands and face, dotting the front of my clothes like crimson snowflakes. Making me that much dirtier. For the second time tonight, I felt old and tired and used up.

"We'll go to my apartment." I leaned my head back against the seat. "Get settled for the night. Tomorrow, we'll start getting to the bottom of this."

"Original," Finn said.

Donovan Caine remained silent in the backseat.

"Do you have a better idea?" I asked.

Finn lifted his shoulders. "No. I'm just the driver, remember, Miss Daisy? I don't know nothing 'bout coming up with no plans."

"Then shut up, Mamie," I snapped. "Before I throw you out of the car."

After taking the usual circuitous route, we reached my building thirty minutes later. Finn waited in the emergency stairwell with Donovan Caine while I made sure no one was hiding inside my apartment. I brushed my fingers over the rough stone around the door frame. The same low hum as always murmured back to me. No visitors today. Good.

I slid the key in the lock and went inside. The first thing I did was go over to the mantel, grab the three rune drawings, and hide them under my bed. Donovan Caine didn't need to see those. Hell, I wasn't even sure I wanted to look at them tonight. My eyes scanned the rest of the den and kitchen, looking for anything that might tell the detective more about me than I wanted to reveal. But there was nothing. The space was empty, remote, spartan.

I stuck my head into the stairwell. "We're clear. Come on in."

Finn went to the kitchen table to fire up his laptop and check his e-mail. The man couldn't go two hours without some form of electronic check-in. Computer junkie.

Donovan Caine stalked from one side of the den to the other, staring at my furniture, my many books, even the DVDs around the television. His hazel eyes flicked over everything, but I couldn't read what conclusions he'd drawn.

I went into the kitchen, unzipped my bloody jacket, and threw it in the trash on top of the vampire hooker's ruined clothes from two nights ago. Might as well wait another day or two. The way things were going, I'd have more items to toss inside for a late-night trip down to the basement incinerator.

"I'm going to take a shower. Make yourself comfortable, detective. Watch television. Raid the fridge. Whatever." I might be an assassin, but never let it be said I wasn't as gracious a hostess as the next gal.

"You." I pointed at Finn. "Keep an eye on him. When I'm done, we'll talk."

The two men eyed each other. Assessing strengths. Looking for weaknesses. Measuring dicks once again.

Shaking my head, I slipped into the bathroom and closed the door. I stripped off the rest of my bloody clothes and stepped into the shower. The water hissed on, and I turned it as hot as it would go and not scald my skin. Then I leaned my head against the slick tile and exhaled.

What a fucking night. Running all over town, making deals, trying to save people before they got dead. A new experience for me. When I'd woken up this morning, I hadn't expected any of this. Certainly not rescuing Donovan Caine.

Oh, I didn't have any regrets about killing the Air elemental's men. Them or me. I'd choose me every single time. But more than that, I'd come to terms with what I did long ago. The bodies, the blood, the tears of those left behind. Even the fact I was probably going to burn in hell didn't bother me. Much.

But for some reason, the disgust and anger in Donovan Caine's eyes had annoyed me. I'd seen those same emotions shimmering in many people's gazes—usually right before I killed them. When people realized you were an assassin, they automatically judged you. Thought you were cold and sadistic and crazy, no matter what sins they'd committed themselves. But coming from Donovan Caine, that judgment irked me. Perhaps because of my curious attraction to the detective. I'd much rather he see me as Gin Blanco than as the Spider.

I snorted. Wanting something I couldn't have. Thinking about Fletcher's plea to retire. Dreaming about a vacation. Feeling old, tired, run-down. I was turning into a fucking cliché. Next thing you'd know I'd be in therapy—or back in Ashland Asylum with the rest of the crazies.

Ten minutes later, I stepped out of the shower and pulled on a pair of navy sweatpants, a matching long-sleeved T-shirt, and thick socks. A wide-tooth comb smoothed the snarls out of my wet hair. I leaned forward and dropped my chin, staring into the mirror. Jo-Jo's roots weren't the only ones that were showing. Maybe this time I'd just let my hair go back to its natural color.

The thought surprised me, and the comb caught in a tangle hidden deep in my damp locks. I couldn't remember the last time my hair had just been my hair, and not teased, dyed, or cut short for some job, some persona, some role I was playing. I wasn't entirely sure I remembered the exact color it really was. For some reason that bothered me.

I dropped my eyes from the mirror, finished with the comb, opened the bathroom door, and padded out into the den. Finn still sat at the kitchen table, typing on his laptop. He probably hadn't moved the whole time I'd been in the shower, except to drag his computer closer.

Donovan Caine had made himself comfortable. He leaned back against one of the thick cushions on the sofa. A dish towel filled with ice covered his right eye, and an old black-and-white movie flickered on the television in front of him. *Jezebel* with Bette Davis. Caine moved the ice to the other eye and winced.

"Want me to look at your face?" I asked the detective. "I'm pretty good at patching people up."

"Yeah," Finn agreed. "When she's not killing them."

Donovan Caine grimaced at his bad joke. But evidently the detective wasn't afraid of me and what I could do to him, because he got to his feet.

"Sure," he said. "It can't feel much worse than it does right now."

He could be dead and not feeling anything at all, but I let the matter slide.

Caine followed me into the spare bathroom, and I directed him to sit on the closed toilet lid while I fetched one of the tubs of healing ointment Jo-Jo Deveraux had given me.

"Spread your legs," I said.

"Excuse me?"

I gestured to his legs. "Open your legs, so I can shimmy in between them. I can get to your face easier that way."

"Oh. Right."

The detective spread his legs wide, and I got down on my knees in front of him. Once again, the warmth of his body washed over me. Despite all the blood he'd come into contact with, the detective still smelled of soap. Squeaky clean to the bitter end. I'd never thought such a simple aroma could be so intoxicating. But Donovan Caine smelled so good I wanted to bury my face against his neck and just breathe in his scent. Mmm.

I grabbed the tub off the counter. The only marking

on the white container was Jo-Jo's cloud rune painted in a vivid blue on top of the lid. I unscrewed it, and the soothing smell of vanilla wafted up out of the tub. In addition to healing with their hands, Air elementals like Jo-Jo could also infuse their magic into other products, like this ointment, and give them a little extra kick.

I dipped my hand into the ointment. It felt warm and slick against my fingers, and tingles spread up into my hands and arms, just like they did when Jo-Jo worked her magic on me. The spider rune scars on my palms didn't itch and burn quite as bad as they had in the salon, mainly because the magic in the ointment wasn't as strong as Jo-Jo's raw, undiluted power. But it would do the job on Donovan Caine's bruised face.

I leaned forward and brought my anointed fingers near his face. Caine flinched and jerked back just before I touched him. What did he think I was going to do? Come up with a knife and slash his jugular? As if I would have made such a mess in my own apartment. As if I couldn't have killed him half a dozen times already tonight.

It was late, and I was tired. So I grabbed Donovan's chin, yanked his head down when he tried to pull away, and rubbed the ointment into his skin. After a few seconds, the healing, Air elemental magic started working on him. The bruises on his face yellowed and faded, while the cuts closed themselves up. Donovan felt his injuries easing and relaxed—as much as he could with his partner's killer within arm's reach.

"You have a very firm grip," Caine said. "Very hard. Very strong."

"Is that a compliment?"

He shrugged. "Just an observation."

I massaged ointment into the rest of his face, including his lips. The lower one had been split, and I swiped my thumb across the wound the way a lover might. Donovan stiffened at the intimate contact, but he didn't pull away. Instead, the detective studied me as I worked. His flat cop eyes took in everything from my posture to the circular motion of my hands to my breathing. Filing the information away for future use. When our truce was over, and he could come after me like he really wanted to—guns blazing.

"What's that on your hand?" he asked. "It looks like silver."

The rune. He must have seen one of the silverstone spider runes burned into my palms. The small circle surrounded by eight thin rays. Something else he didn't need to know about. I curled my fingers into a loose fist.

"It's nothing," I said. "Just an old scar. I've got lots of them."

"I bet you do," he murmured.

I finished with the ointment, stood up, and handed the detective a bottle of superstrength aspirin. "You might want to take a few of these too."

He took the bottle from my hands, careful not to touch my skin. His amber eyes caught and held my gray ones. I leaned against the sink, crossed my arms over my chest, and waited for him to say whatever he wanted to say.

"Thanks," Caine muttered. You'd think he was coughing up a lung the way he forced the word out between his clenched teeth. "For everything tonight. As weird and as wrong as it is, I wouldn't be sitting here now if it weren't for you."

"You're welcome."

He nodded, accepting my cool graciousness. "But don't think tonight changes anything between us. After we find the elemental, I'm bringing you in for Cliff Ingles's murder—whatever it takes, dead or alive. Don't forget that."

I turned on the hot water and washed my hands. "Don't worry, detective, I haven't forgotten about your vendetta. But you should remember what I did to those men in your cabin. Because I won't hesitate to do the same to you the second you get in my way. Understood?"

Donovan Caine watched smears of his blood drip off my hands and disappear down the sink. "Understood."

Caine swallowed a couple of aspirin and returned to the den. I screwed the top back on Jo-Jo's healing ointment and followed him. The detective seated himself on the sofa again. He might hate me, but at least he wasn't shy.

While we were in the bathroom, Finn had made himself a cup of chicory coffee. The rich, caffeine fumes drifted to my nose, and my stomach rumbled.

"Finn? Late-night snack?" I moved into the kitchen.

"Sandwich," he said, not even bothering to look up from the blue glow of his monitor. "But not turkey this time. Something else. Different bread too. Surprise me."

"Yes, master."

I grabbed a loaf of Sophia Deveraux's homemade sourdough bread I'd swiped from the Pork Pit, several bananas, and the peanut butter and sourwood honey out of the cabinets, along with some canned pumpkin. First,

I mixed the peanut butter and pumpkin together, producing a rich, creamy spread, which I slathered onto the bread. I topped the mixture with sliced bananas and drizzled honey over the fruit. As a finishing touch, I sprinkled some cinnamon on top of the whole thing, then topped it with another slice of bread.

I tore off a paper towel and handed it and the sandwich to Finn, who sank his teeth into the thick bread with obvious enthusiasm. Donovan Caine didn't move from the couch. I stared at him, wondering who'd be the first to end this Mexican standoff.

Caine looked at Finn's disappearing sandwich. "That looks good. Would you fix me one of those? Please?"

"Sure."

I made him a sandwich, then one for me, and a couple more for whoever got to them first. Donovan moved over to the table and sat next to Finn, while I got a gallon of milk out of the fridge and plucked some mugs out of the cabinet. I set the mugs on the table, then wrapped my hand around one of them and reached for my magic. Ice crystals frosted the container, guaranteeing that whatever was poured inside would stay cold. I repeated the process on the other two glasses.

Donovan stilled, and his hazel eyes narrowed at the small display of magic. "You're an elemental. An Ice."

I shrugged. "I have a little bit of magic, detective. That's all. Hardly worth mentioning."

Finn eyed me. He knew I had more than just a little magic, but for once he didn't contradict me.

I finished with the mugs and slid Caine's sandwich over to him. He picked it up but hesitated before biting down into it, as though just looking at the food I'd prepared was enough to make him keel over and start foaming at the mouth. He should have known by now that poison really wasn't my forte. A cheap, theatrical device, just like blackmail.

The detective chewed and swallowed. Surprise spread across his face. "This is really good."

"Better than the Cake Walk?" I asked.

He didn't look at me. "Not better, just different."

Finn elbowed the detective in the side. "I told you Gin makes the best sandwiches around."

Donovan didn't respond, but he took another bite and poured himself some milk.

I grabbed my own sandwich and milk, and joined the two men at the table. The peanut butter, pureed pumpkin, and banana wove a thick texture together, while the honey and cinnamon added a touch of tart sweetness to the mix. Perfect.

"Any new leads?" I asked Finn after I'd eaten half my sandwich.

He shook his head and wiped his fingers on one of the paper towels. "Not really. My contacts sent me some new intel on Halo Industries and the James sisters. I've scanned through it, but nothing's popped out at me yet. Maybe in the morning when I'm fresher."

My gray eyes flicked to the detective. "I think it's time you told us what you and Gordon Giles were talking about at the opera house."

Caine nodded. "Yeah, it probably is."

I was mildly surprised he was giving in so easily. Perhaps my sandwich really was that good. Or maybe the detective had finally realized working with us was his best option at this point. His only option, really.

Caine finished his sandwich, drained his milk, and started his story. "Gordon Giles contacted me about three months ago. Said he had information about a major embezzlement scandal at Halo Industries. Said he would give me all the information I needed to put several people away for a long time, if I would promise him protection."

"Why did he come to you?" Finn asked. "You're a homicide detective. White-collar crime isn't your specialty."

"Giles said it went beyond embezzling, that someone was using the money for some pretty nasty things. Bribes, payoffs." Caine's gaze shot to me. "Contract killings."

Nobody spoke for a moment.

"Giles said he'd been collecting information for months," Caine continued. "He was supposed to give me the info at the opera house, and I was supposed to set him up in a safe house."

"Let me guess. All the information was stored on a flash drive, the one the men at your cabin wanted you to give to them," I finished.

Caine nodded again.

"Did you tell anyone about Giles?" I asked. "Did anyone in the police department know you were meeting with him?"

"I told my captain, Wayne Stephenson, what Giles wanted a few weeks ago. He brought a few other guys into the loop. Depending on what Giles gave us, Stephenson said he might set up a task force to look into the embezzling."

Caine rubbed his hand over his head. But he didn't

protest once again that Wayne Stephenson had absolutely nothing to do with the Air elemental. Maybe he'd had time to think about it. Or maybe the shock of the betrayal was wearing off, and the anger was setting in. But Caine had come around on this point. Good. It would make things easier if he wasn't protesting Stephenson's innocence every step of the way.

So Stephenson had known about the meeting. Odds were the police captain had tipped-off the Air elemental to the fact that Gordon Giles was turning state's evidence. Maybe she'd bribed Stephenson to keep her informed. Maybe she had something on him. Either way, he'd blown the whistle. That's when the elemental had come up with her plan and decided on her radical course of action involving me, Finn, and Fletcher. Caine had probably been thrown in as a bonus, so he couldn't point the finger back at Stephenson.

I looked at Finn. He'd put it together too. He nodded, telling me he'd start digging into Wayne Stephenson.

"Did Giles say who was involved in the embezzling?" I asked.

"No," Caine said. "Although I suspected it might be Haley James. Giles mentioned her name several times. Like Finn said, this isn't my area of expertise. Giles fed me a few leads, teased me with some information, but that's it. That's all I know. Your turn."

Finn started. "Our turn? To share?"

"Try not to cry, Finn," I said. "Show him what we've got."

Finn spread out the IDs we'd taken off the dead guards and showed them to the detective. Caine didn't recognize any of the men, but he agreed the IDs were fake and probably wouldn't lead us anywhere. So Finn fished out the gold chain with the triangular tooth rune. The polished jet soaked up the soft kitchen light like a black sponge.

"Interesting," Caine murmured, studying the rune. "I've never seen this particular rune before, and I keep up with the symbols on all the gangs in town."

"I think our Air elemental constitutes a little more than a mere gang," Finn pointed out.

Caine grunted his agreement.

"We also have this." I slid over the business card. "You had two guys tailing you at lunch. One of them passed his card to some college girls. Finn's digging for info on him right now."

Caine picked it up. "Charles Carlyle? I thought I recognized him. He cleans up nicer than I remember."

"You know him?" I asked.

The detective's mouth tightened. "Unfortunately. Calls himself Chuck or Chuckie C. He's a small-time hood who likes to pretend he's bigger than he really is. Drifts from one crew to the next, always on the lookout for an easy score. A real slimeball. I ran into him a few times when I was working vice."

"Vice?" Finn asked. "Seems more like organized crime to me."

The detective shook his head. "You'd think so, but Chuckie likes the ladies. A new one every night, the younger the better. He's a vampire, you know. I think he gets off on the sex as much as he does the blood."

I nodded. Some vamps were like that. They all needed

blood, but lots of them also drew power from sex—or feeding off the emotions of others. Some vamps, especially the old ones who'd mastered their power long ago, were just as dangerous as elementals. Or more so.

"Where does Chuckie C. like to hang out?" Finn asked.

"Northern Aggression," Caine replied. "The nightclub in Northtown."

I frowned. That was the second time that name had come up. I flipped through Fletcher's file on Gordon Giles and scanned the contents. Yep, there it was, "Northern Aggression," written in the old man's tight, controlled handwriting. I tapped my finger on the paper. "Giles also liked to frequent Northern Aggression."

"So they worked and played together," Finn said.

Caine frowned. "What do you mean?"

"Charles Carlyle is currently an executive vice president at Halo Industries," I said.

The detective snorted. "That's got to be a mistake. Chuckie C. knows as much about business as I do. He's a hood, not a white-collar worker."

"No mistake, detective," Finn said. "Carlyle's financials show a regular paycheck deposited into his account every week from the company."

We sat there a minute, digesting the information.

"So what's our next move?" Caine asked.

"I'd like to see what's on Giles's flash drive," I said.

"It's been two days since the assassination attempt. The Air elemental and her men had to have searched Giles's office by now," Finn pointed out. "His house too."

"Yeah, but they haven't found it yet. Otherwise, they

wouldn't have been asking the detective about it." I looked at Donovan. "You have no idea where he might have stashed it?"

He shook his head. "Not a clue. Giles was holding on to it for leverage, until I could get the safe house set up for him."

I nodded. "All right. We'll forget the flash drive for now. We have Chuckie C., and we know where he likes to spend his free time. We'll hit the club tomorrow night and see what he's doing—and who he's doing it with."

Finn cleared his throat. "Northern Aggression is Roslyn's place. Might be good to clear it with her first."

I snorted. "I don't need Roslyn's permission to spy on a guy at her club."

Caine looked back and forth between us. "Who's Roslyn?"

"Roslyn Phillips," I replied. "The vampire who runs Northern Aggression. She's also one of Finn's good time girls, which is why he wants to go *clear things* with her first."

"Good time girl," Finn scoffed. "I resent that, Gin. Deeply. Roslyn and I happen to have a very loving relationship that's based on mutual concern and caring."

"You mean the two of you like to sleep together when you're both not with someone else."

Donovan stared at Finn, who grinned in return.

The detective shook his head, as though he was trying to banish the image of Finn doing the nasty from his mind. Something I was all too familiar with. In addition to needling me like a brother, Finn also treated me like a locker room buddy. Nothing more he loved to do than brag about his latest sexual conquest. It really was shocking that some jealous husband hadn't hired me to kill Finn years ago.

"So that's the plan?" Caine asked. "Squeeze Chuckie C. and see what pops out?"

"Do you have a better idea, detective?" I asked. "If so, please speak up."

Our eyes met, gray on gold. Each color hard, flat, unyielding. After a moment, Caine shook his head.

"I didn't think so," I said. "But don't worry, detective. I'll let you be the good cop. I'm so much better at being the bad guy anyway."

With nothing left to do for the night, we crashed. I took my bed, while Finn claimed the one in the spare room. Donovan Caine made himself comfortable on the pullout sofa in the den. I rummaged around in the closet next to the spare bathroom, pulling out some blankets and pillows for my unexpected houseguest. Hostess with the mostest, that was me.

I walked into the den and handed the bedding to the detective. "Knock yourself out."

"Thanks," he said.

Caine shook out the blue and green blankets and started making up the sleeper sofa. I drifted over to the front door and pretended I was double-checking the locks. I pressed my hand against the stone, listening to its faint murmur. Low and steady, just like always. Once more, I traced small, tight curls onto the surface of the stone—the symbol for protection. The runes shimmered silver before sinking into the wall and fading away. I sent a burst of magic through the rock to test my magical trip wire. A sharp note of alarm sounded back to me, rising to an ear-splitting shriek. If someone attempted to open the door and enter the apartment, that same sound would wake me.

It would also ring out if someone tried to leave. Donovan Caine and I might have an agreement, but our tenuous partnership might not keep him from sneaking out in the middle of the night. Or trying to. The detective wasn't going anywhere without me.

Caine put down one blanket and unfolded another. He wasn't an elemental, wasn't a Stone, so he couldn't sense or hear the vibration.

He fluffed out the last pillow and set it on top of the outstretched sofa. He turned to face me. I nodded a good night at him and headed for my bedroom.

"Sleep well." The detective's deep voice rumbled out and touched me, like a silk rope flicking against my spine. "If you can."

I glanced over my shoulder at him. "Why wouldn't I sleep well? Because my conscience is troubling me? Hardly."

"It should bother you."

"Because of tonight?" I shrugged. "I did what needed to be done to save your life, detective. Even you shouldn't fault me for that."

"Not because of tonight. Because of Cliff."

The old, predictable hatred flared in his hazel eyes, and his face tightened with determination. Caine was still counting down the minutes until he could come after me for his partner's murder.

For a moment, I considered telling the detective exactly what Cliff Ingles had been like. About the protection money he'd extorted from various pimps. About the vampire hookers he'd forced to give him freebies in the back of his city-issued sedan while he was on duty. About the thirteen-year-old girl he'd so brutally raped, beaten, and left for dead. The knowledge would wipe that self-righteous sneer off Donovan Caine's face. Burn it up like it had never existed.

But I held my tongue. That information was an ace up my sleeve, and I wasn't about to throw it down just for spite. Let the detective keep his illusions about his partner. I needed him focused on finding the Air elemental—not moping over how wrong he'd been about Cliff Ingles. Caine was so fucking idealistic. Still determined to believe in the good in everyone, despite all evidence to the contrary. It's going to get him killed one day.

I gave him a flat, cold stare. "I sleep like a rock, detective. Always have, always will."

I stepped inside my bedroom and shut the door behind me.

My sleep was dark, black, comforting, and free of any troubling dreams or flickering memories of Fletcher. Sunlight slanting in through the window warmed my face and crept in under my eyelids. I sighed, rolled over, and stared at the clock radio by the bed. Almost noon. Time to get on with things.

I crawled out of bed, opened the door, and padded into the den. Finn sat in front of his computer, a steaming cup of chicory coffee by his side. The familiar, comforting smell reminded me of Fletcher, and I felt the sharp pain of his loss. The image of his flayed body flashed in front of my eyes, but I pushed it aside and focused on my last memory of Fletcher—the old man drinking his own cup of coffee at the Pork Pit. I breathed in, letting the rich aroma coat my lungs, pretending Fletcher was warming the apartment with his ghostly presence. Pretending he was warming me.

Finn saw me step into the room. He waved at me, then pressed a finger to his lips and pointed at the sofa. I looked over the back of the furniture. A mound of blankets covered Donovan Caine like the thick layers of a burial shroud. I could just barely make out the top of his head through the fabric. For a moment, I wondered if the detective slept nude. Mmm. Wouldn't have minded a peek if he did.

Finn pointed to something beside the sofa. I leaned over. One of the detective's guns lay on the floor within easy reach. I frowned. Despite our truce, Donovan Caine still didn't trust me. What had he thought I was going to do? Slip out and murder him in the middle of the night in my own apartment? I was ruthless, not stupid.

I walked over to Finn. The mid-morning sunlight slipped through the curtains and highlighted his face, his strong features that were so similar to his father's. I leaned over and mussed his walnut-colored hair.

"What was that for?" Finn murmured, smoothing down his bed-head cowlick.

"Just because," I said, trying to hide the emotion that thickened my voice. "Late breakfast?"

"Omelets. Definitely omelets. Pancakes, too?" Finn asked.

I mussed his hair again, moved into the kitchen, and got to work. I pulled several eggs out of the refrigerator, along with cheese, milk, and butter. Packages of frozen strawberries waited in the freezer, and I plucked them out of the frosty depths. Flour, sugar, nonstick cooking spray, and pepper came out of the cabinets. Again, the steady process of cooking, of creating food, soothed me. I chopped tomatoes, onions, green peppers, and ham to put into my southwestern omelets. The berries went into the microwave to defrost. Buttermilk beaten with flour and just a hint of sugar formed the base of my pancakes.

The faint *clank* and *clatter* of dishes woke the detective. Donovan Caine let out a low groan and sat up. The blankets fell away, revealing the same jeans and T-shirt the detective had worn last night. So he didn't sleep in the buff. A shame, really.

Caine frowned, as though he didn't understand where he was. He caught sight of me, and the knowledge and memories of last night flared in his hazel gaze. His eyes cut to Finn, then back to me. He didn't relax.

"Morning," I said, flipping one of the strawberry pancakes.

The detective grunted something unintelligible. Caine rolled off the sofa and stumbled into the kitchen. He leaned on the counter and stared at the bubbling coffeepot like a teenage virgin would at a stripper.

"Mug?" he mumbled.

I opened a cabinet and passed him a white ceramic cup. Our hands brushed. Once again, that hot awareness of him coursed through me. My breasts tightened, and a pleasant ache pulsed between my thighs. But Donovan Caine was too caffeine-deprived to notice or respond in kind.

The detective sat at the table next to Finn and stared bleary-eyed into his mug. After a few minutes, the caffeine fumes worked their morning magic. The detective blinked and took a sip of his coffee.

"Gah!" He almost spit the steaming mouthful back out. "What the hell is this? Poison?"

"Nope, it's chicory coffee." Finn raised his own mug in salute. "It'll put hair on your chest."

Caine grimaced, but he kept drinking. The detective even poured himself a second cup.

When the pancakes were golden brown, I put them on a platter, along with several omelets. Plates, silverware, and napkins went onto the table, along with a pitcher of orange juice. Once again, I used my Ice magic to frost the container. Donovan Caine didn't say anything about my power, but his eyes stayed on me. Cool and calculating.

Everyone helped themselves to the food. Still suspicious, Caine didn't touch anything until after Finn and I had both swallowed several bites. But once he started, the detective ate more than the two of us put together.

"This is really good," Donovan Caine said, attacking his third strawberry pancake.

"You sound surprised," I said.

He shrugged. "I just didn't think an assassin would be able to cook like this."

"Well, I do get lots of practice with knives. You could say I'm multitasking."

The detective froze, his fork halfway to his mouth.

"I'm kidding. I enjoy cooking. It relaxes me."

"I'll bet," Caine muttered. But his unease didn't keep him from stuffing another bite of pancake into his mouth.

We ate in silence for several minutes.

"So what do you do when you're not assassinating people, Gin?" Donovan Caine finally asked.

I raised an eyebrow. "Why so curious, detective?"

He shrugged. "Just making conversation. Since we're stuck with each other for a while, I thought it might be polite to talk about something other than the fact we're going to commit a felony today."

"Only one?" I mocked. "You're selling us short, detective. The day is young."

Donovan's eyes narrowed. He realized he wasn't going to get anywhere with me, so he turned his gaze to Finn. "And you?"

"Oh, Finn isn't an assassin," I cut in. "He's much, much worse. He's a banker."

My snide comment took Finn by surprise, and he choked on his coffee. Donovan Caine let out a guffaw of laughter. It was the first time I'd heard the detective laugh without an undercurrent of angry sarcasm. A sharp sound, tinged here and there with bitterness, but not an unpleasant one. Rather like my laugh.

Caine smiled, his teeth flashing in his bronze face. The expression warmed his eyes to liquid gold. My breath caught in my throat. If the detective looked that good merely smiling, how would he look after a night of slow, sweaty sex? Mmm.

Donovan's smile faded under my intense gray gaze. "What are you staring at?"

"Nothing," I said. "Eat your breakfast. It's going to be a long day, and everyone needs to keep their strength up. Finn, what do your contacts say?"

Finn gave me a dirty look before answering. "Still no hits on the dead guys' fake IDs or any info on the tooth rune. Whoever the Air elemental is, she's running a tight ship. No leaks so far."

"Any news about me?" Donovan Caine asked. "Or the attack at my house?"

"Nothing on the morning news shows," Finn said. "The elemental must have cleaned up after herself. No talk of bodies, wind damage, nothing. However, according to my sources in the police department, your captain, Wayne Stephenson, is looking for you. He wants a word about your maverick investigation into the Gordon Giles case and the fact that you haven't reported in for duty today."

Caine grimaced, because his captain's interest in his whereabouts was more evidence Stephenson was involved with the elemental.

"Do you have anything on Stephenson yet?" I asked Finn.

He shook his head. "Nothing so far. At first glance, his financials look clean, and he's not dropping wads of cash on any vice or habit I can find. I'll keep digging."

We finished our breakfast in silence. I started to clear the dishes from the table, but Donovan Caine got to his feet and reached for the platter in my hands.

"Let me," he said. "I'm staying in your house, eating your food. It's the least I can do."

"My, my, my, handsome and polite," I drawled. "Your mama raised you right, detective."

His eyes sparked gold at the word *handsome,* as he took the platter and dumped it in the sink. I sat down, sipped my juice, and leered at the detective.

"What about Carlyle?" Finn asked, not sharing my fascination with Donovan Caine's ass. "We still going to brace him at Northern Aggression tonight?"

"Yeah. At this point, he's our best lead. Our only lead." I turned my gaze to Finn. "So call Roslyn and tell her we need to meet this afternoon."

"Last night you said you didn't need Roslyn's permission to storm her club," Finn said. "Why the change?"

I took another swig of juice. "Because she might know something else about Carlyle. You know how she likes to keep track of her guests' habits. And I want to know everything there is to know about the bastard before we confront him tonight."

✣ 18 ✣

Since we'd abandoned the SUV Finn had stolen yesterday, we were without transportation. So Finn had to boost another car from a parking garage four blocks away from my apartment. He stalked through one level of the garage, sneering and passing up several serviceable compact cars, before going down to the next level.

"What's he doing?" Donovan Caine asked as we walked along behind him. "This isn't the supermarket."

I snorted. "Tell that to Finn. He's a car guy. The more expensive and roomier it is, the happier it makes him."

Finn finally stopped in front of a late-model Lexus and nodded his head. "This will do for today. Tool please, Gin." He held out his hand to me.

"Didn't you bring your own?"

"Why carry the extra weight when you make such good disposable ones?" he countered.

I hated to admit it, but Finn had a point. I sighed and

reached for my Ice magic. Donovan Caine eyed the silver glow flickering over my palm, wondering what I was doing. A question I often asked myself when dealing with Finnegan Lane.

A few seconds later, I passed Finn a long, slender, wirelike rod. He took the cold, Ice wand and jammed it into the car window. The lock popped open, the rod shattered, and Finn wiped the remaining chunks of the wand off his impeccable jacket. Then he opened the door, sank down into the driver's seat, reached under the dash, and tugged on a couple of wires.

Thirty seconds later, the engine roared to life, and Finn gestured for us to get in. I took the passenger's seat, while Donovan Caine slid into the back. Finn steered the car out of the garage. A beautiful September day greeted us. Blue sky. Wispy clouds. Faint breeze. The sun gleamed like a gold coin, brightening even the grime and graffiti on the downtown streets and buildings.

"Where are we going?" I asked Finn. "Where have you tracked Roslyn to? The nightclub?"

Finn had made a call on one of my disposable cells and set up a meeting with Roslyn just before we'd left. "Nah, the club doesn't even open until eight. She's at home right now."

Despite the money generated by her nightclub, Roslyn Phillips didn't live in Northtown like the rest of the rich types. Instead, she made her home out in the suburbs just west of Southtown. Rolling hills cut through this part of Ashland like jagged teeth on a saw, although the scarlet, gold, and cinnamon color of the fall leaves helped to smudge the edges of the rough ridges. I rolled down my window and let the cool air rush into the car.

Thirty minutes later, Finn turned into a driveway lined with crimson maples. He drove up a steep hill before the trees receded, revealing a modest, two-story home made of gray brick. Black shutters and white flowerbeds framed the square windows, while a variety of colorful toys fought for space on the green lawn. Suburban bliss at its finest. All the house needed to complete the picture was a goofy golden retriever loping through the grass.

Finn parked the stolen Lexus, and the three of us got out of the car.

"Just let me do the talking, and everything will be fine." Finn smoothed down his suit jacket. He'd gone with a gray seersucker today, with a silver shirt that somehow made his eyes look even greener than they were.

"That was my plan," I replied. "You're the mouthpiece. Figured you'd use some of that storied charm you claim to have to pump Roslyn for information. Or were you planning to use a more persuasive technique today?"

Beside me, Donovan Caine snorted, but his mouth curved into a small smile.

"You're just jealous." Finn dug a canister of breath spray out of his pants pocket and squirted some into his mouth.

"Hardly. Been there, done you," I replied. "Adequate, but unremarkable."

Donovan Caine started at the revelation. He frowned, and something shimmered in his hazel eyes. But the detective masked the emotion before I could decipher what it was.

Finn clutched a hand over his heart. "Oh, Gin, how you wound me."

"I'm going to wound you a lot more if you can't sweet-talk Roslyn and smooth things over for us tonight," I snapped.

"Don't worry," Finn said. "Roslyn will shower us with cooperation, since you took care of her brother-in-law a few months ago. Or have you forgotten already?"

A man's face flashed in front of my eyes. Chocolate skin, curly hair, a dimpled smile, and black eyes that were even colder than mine. No, I hadn't forgotten Jeremy Lawson. My cheek twitched with a phantom ache. The half-giant had broken my jaw before I'd managed to cut him down.

Disgust tightened Donovan Caine's face. "You assassinated this woman's brother-in-law, and you think she's happy about that?"

I opened my mouth to respond, but Finn fixed the detective with a fierce look.

"Yeah," he snapped. "Bastard liked to beat on Roslyn's sister and her niece. Last time, they were both in the hospital for two weeks. The little girl is four, in case you were wondering."

The detective's gaze flicked to the toys in the yard, and the disgust drained out of his rugged face. "Why didn't she call the police?" Caine asked in a quieter voice.

"Roslyn did, but Jeremy had a couple of fishing buddies on the force and plenty of money to get everyone else to look the other way. The coppers wouldn't even file a domestic dispute report," Finn said. "So Roslyn decided to look for another, more permanent solution before he killed them."

Caine's gaze went to me again. Curiosity flared in his

hazel eyes, along with a flash of doubt. The detective had to be thinking about his partner, Cliff Ingles. Wondering if the other cop had done something like that. Wondering if that's why I'd killed him. I kept my face smooth as I stared back. After a moment, the detective dropped his eyes.

We reached the front door. A small plaque with a rune etched into it was embedded in the stone to the right. A heart with an arrow through it. Roslyn's symbol for her nightclub, Northern Aggression. Finn rang the doorbell. Cheery chimes echoed through the house.

After about twenty seconds, a shadow moved in front of the peephole. Somebody inside was studying us. Several locks clicked, and the door opened.

Roslyn Phillips was a beautiful woman, with eyes and skin the color of melted toffee. Her cropped, feathered black hair just brushed the edge of her strong jaw. Silver-frame glasses perched on the end of her pointed nose, and her face was free of the heavy makeup I'd always seen her wear. She looked younger without it, softer, and more vulnerable than I knew her to be.

A pair of black yoga pants covered her legs, while a matching shirt stretched over her chest. But the innocuous ensemble couldn't hide Roslyn's stack of full breasts, lush hips, and toned thighs that had most men wiping the drool off their chins after a few seconds. And Roslyn knew how to use her body to its full potential. She was one of the vamps who used sex to power up, along with drinking blood.

Roslyn's lips drew back into a wide smile, revealing her fangs. They were as pale as bleach. "Finnegan Lane. What a nice surprise." Her voice was a low, husky whisper.

"Roslyn, darling. So good of you to see me on such short notice." Finn leaned down and pressed a kiss to Roslyn's smooth cheek.

"Always a pleasure, Finn," Roslyn murmured. Her dark eyes drifted to the detective before resting on me. "And you've brought friends with you."

"The gent is Donovan Caine," Finn said. "And you know Gin, of course."

"Of course."

Roslyn stared at me, and I met her dark gaze with a neutral one of my own. I hadn't been there when she'd approached Finn about finding someone to kill her brother-in-law, since Finn was known as a man who could get all kinds of things done. But she'd seen me with Finn, knew I'd been chummy with Fletcher and worked at the Pork Pit. Finn had never told Roslyn he'd find someone to do the job, had never even admitted he knew anyone who would do that sort of thing. But three weeks after Roslyn had asked, her abusive brother-in-law had been found stabbed to death outside a Southtown strip club. I was sure the vampire had drawn her own conclusions—about a lot of things.

"Come in," Roslyn said. "We were just finishing up lunch."

She ushered us inside, then closed and locked the door behind us—with all three deadbolts. Roslyn Phillips didn't take chances with her safety. Smart woman.

Roslyn crooked her finger and led us through several rooms filled with heavy, wooden tables, Tiffany lamps, and old-fashioned settees lined with velvet. The antique furniture was in sharp contrast to the toys, books, and other childish doodads stacked on the tables, piled in the corners, and spread over the settees. Around me, the stone of the house alternated between low worry and carefree glee, given the varying emotions of its occupants.

We stepped onto a stone patio that overlooked a heart-shaped pool that had been covered up for the winter. A little girl who bore a striking resemblance to Roslyn sat in a princess-themed, pink castle planted in the backyard and pushed a blue dump truck through the grass. Every once in a while, she'd quit making *vroom-vroom* sounds long enough to nibble on the tomato sandwich clutched in her tiny fist.

Roslyn gestured at a table surrounded by wicker chairs with thick, flowered cushions. The remains of a Cobb salad littered a plate on the table, along with a frosted mug half-full of blood, a cup of chocolate milk, a pitcher of lemonade, and several glasses.

Finn sat in the chair opposite Roslyn's. Donovan Caine dropped into the seat beside him, while I took the last chair. I pulled it out from the table and angled it so I could see the little girl.

Roslyn held up the pitcher. Ice cubes clinked against the side of the glass. "Lemonade?"

Seems I wasn't the only gracious hostess around. We all accepted, and Roslyn dispensed the cold drink. I sipped the liquid. Tart and sweet at the same time, just the way I liked it. Mmm.

Roslyn fixed her eyes on Finn. "To what do I owe the pleasure, Finn? I thought we weren't supposed to meet until later this week at the benefit for the battered-women's shelter."

"Unfortunately, I'm probably not going to be able to make it to that," he said. "So I thought I'd see you today."

Roslyn tilted her head down and looked over the tops of her glasses at him. "Really? Is that why you came all the way out here? To tell me we aren't meeting later? I don't think so. You want something, Finn. Just tell me what it is. You know how much I hate it when someone bullshits me. It's bad enough when I have to do it to my clients."

He nodded. "All right. I'm interested in learning more about someone who frequents your nightclub and wanted to clear it with you first in case anything . . . unpleasant happens tonight when we have a little chat with him."

Roslyn's eyes cut to me before snapping back to Finn. "Who?"

Finn drew in a breath. "Charles Carlyle. Calls himself—"

"Chuckie C.," Roslyn finished in a flat voice. "I know him."

Roslyn didn't ask Finn any of the obvious questions, like why we were interested in Carlyle, what he'd done, or more importantly, what we were going to do to him. The vampire had been a Southtown hooker for a long time before she'd moved up into management. She knew asking questions was a quick way to get dead.

Donovan Caine leaned forward. "What can you tell us about him?"

Roslyn took a delicate sip of her blood and smiled. Her fangs were a crimson stain in her mouth. "My clients like their anonymity. My club wouldn't last long if I squealed to everybody who came knocking on my front door. Especially a cop like you. I know you used to work vice. I remember seeing you at Northern Aggression more than once."

Caine frowned and opened his mouth, but I cut in.

"He's with us," I said. "Detective Caine isn't going to bust you for anything. And if he ever dares to hassle you, I'll deal with him myself. Finn takes good care of his friends, Roslyn. You know that."

Roslyn took another sip of blood, then pushed her glass aside. "Fine, I'll play along, but only because it's Finn. What do you want to know about Carlyle?"

"Everything," Finn said. "What he likes, who he hangs out with, what the girls say about him."

Roslyn shrugged. "Not much to tell. He's a vamp who fancies himself to be a player and a great fuck, despite his tiny dick. Comes in almost every night and gets a private room in the back. Likes girls that look like they're twelve. Occasionally gets rougher than what we allow at the club. And he's always bragging to the girls about what a hotshot he is. How he's putting together his own crew and making his move in the underworld. Macho bullshit like that. A small fish, although he's been flashing a lot of cash lately. More drinks, more girls, a party for anybody he's friends with."

So Chuckie C. had cash to burn. More proof he was working for the Air elemental. She'd ponied up half my fee up front. Made sense she'd spread the embezzled wealth around to her underlings, too.

Finn reached into his jacket and fished out the head-shot of Gordon Giles from Fletcher's file. "What about this guy? Was he one of Carlyle's friends?"

Roslyn tapped a manicured nail on Giles's nose. "Gordon? Yeah, the two of them used to hang out a lot and party with the girls. Not so much recently."

Hmm. Sounded like Gordon Giles had dumped Carlyle around the same time he'd approached Donovan Caine about the embezzlement at Halo Industries. Maybe Giles had realized he was in over his head—or maybe he'd grown a conscience.

"So what do you really need?" Roslyn asked. "You said you wanted to talk to Carlyle at the club."

"Yeah," Finn said. "The private room he reserves . . . any way we could see and hear what's going on inside?"

Roslyn sat back in her chair and crossed her arms over her chest. "Perhaps. But like I said before, my clients enjoy their anonymity. They trust me with their secrets— *all* their secrets. I wouldn't last long if word got out I'd breached that trust."

Finn put on his most charming smile. "Surely you could make an exception just this once. For me."

Roslyn laughed, a light, pealing sound at odds with the hard set of her features. "You're a charmer, Finn, and I enjoy your company. You make me laugh, which is hard to do. But I'm not risking my business, my livelihood, so you can settle some vendetta with Carlyle."

Fletcher's ruined face flashed before my eyes. Vendetta? Oh no, this was much more than that. Since the vampire was going to be difficult about things, I decided to remind her exactly how good a friend Finn had been to her.

"Catherine's gotten so big since the last time I saw her," I said in a soft voice. "When you brought her home from the hospital after her surgery."

Roslyn's dark eyes went to the little girl playing in the castle, then snapped up to meet mine. Her gaze hardened, and her fangs poked out through her lips. Warning me to back the fuck off. Donovan Caine gave me a hard look, wondering what the hell I was doing. Finn just sighed.

"Looks like she's really enjoying that princess castle Finn gave her as a welcome home gift," I continued. "Tell me, how's Lisa, your sister? I haven't seen her in a while."

Vroom-vroom. Vroom-vroom. Catherine pushed her dump truck back and forth on the grass.

"She's fine," Roslyn said in a tight voice. "I keep Catherine during the day while Lisa goes to school. She's finishing up her business degree at Ashland Community College."

I gave her a soft, easy smile, like we were just two gals shooting the breeze. "Nice to hear they're doing so well—now."

Roslyn's mouth flattened into a thin line as she considered the meaning behind my casual words. Her fingers tapped on the table. After a few seconds, her hand stilled. "Yeah, they're doing much better—now."

The vampire stared at me. "There's a passageway that runs through the back of the club. Has eyes and ears in all the private rooms. We use it to look out for the girls and make sure they're being treated right. You could watch Carlyle from there. But he leaves the club in one piece—understand? I can't have people disappearing from the private rooms."

We could always grab Carlyle outside after we saw who he liked to party with. Easier that way anyhow. I nodded my acceptance to her terms. She relaxed the slightest bit.

"You're a peach, Roslyn." Finn leaned over and kissed her cheek. "A real peach."

Her face softened, and a genuine smile curved her lips. "You say that to all the girls."

"Maybe, but with you, I really mean it."

Roslyn patted Finn's cheek. He caught her hand and pressed a kiss to the inside of her palm. I cleared my throat before they could move on to other things.

Finn sighed. "Sorry, darling. Duty calls. We'll be at the club tonight. Perhaps we can meet later in the week after some of my present . . . difficulties resolve themselves."

"Of course. Call me when you get free."

And so business was concluded. I got to my feet. Donovan Caine rose as well. Finn sighed again, then did the same.

"Come on, Finn. I'm sure Roslyn wants to go see how Catherine's doing." I smiled at the vampire again. "Give our best to Lisa."

Her dark eyes met mine. "I will," she murmured. "I will."

❊ 19 ❊

Roslyn showed us out, then went back inside to put Catherine down for a nap. As soon as the vampire locked the door behind us, Donovan Caine turned to me.

"What the hell was that about? Threatening her niece like that?" His eyes blazed gold with anger. "The little girl was sitting right there."

"And was far too involved in her own imaginary world to pay attention to us," I replied. "It wasn't a threat. I was merely reminding Roslyn how Finn had taken care of something for her and that she owed him. It was business, nothing else, and Roslyn knew it. That's why she agreed to let us spy on Carlyle. Now she knows we're even again."

Caine kept his hard gaze on my face. "And if she hadn't agreed? What would you have done? Pulled one of your knives on the little girl?"

"Oh boy," Finn muttered and stepped back.

I tilted my head and approached the detective until I stood right in front of him. Donovan Caine didn't move away. More balls than common sense.

"I might be an assassin, detective, but I'm not a monster. I don't kill kids—ever. But if you ever dare to insult me like that again, I'll be more than happy to slit your throat." I palmed one of my knives, flashed it at him, brought it up to his throat, and tucked it back up my sleeve in one smooth, quick motion.

His face hardened with fury. "Just like you did Cliff Ingles?"

"Just like I did Cliff Ingles," I snapped. "But I'll give you the courtesy of leaving your balls attached to the rest of your body."

We stood there glaring at each other. Part of me wanted to punch Donovan Caine, smash my fist into his nose, and feel his hot blood spurt out onto my fingers. Another part of me wanted to pull him toward me, plant my lips on his, and melt the gold anger in his eyes into liquid passion.

Finn cleared his throat. "If you two are done with your little spat, we should go. Things to do and all that."

Donovan Caine glared at me a moment longer, then stalked over to the car, got in the back, and slammed the door shut. Finn and I followed him.

"By the way, good call on the castle, Gin," Finn said as he reached for the wires to start the car. "You were right. Much better than the stuffed dog I wanted to buy."

"You picked that out?" Caine asked. "That pink, plastic toy?"

I turned to look at him. "I happen to have been a little

girl, once upon a time, detective. I know what they like. Every little girl wants to be a princess."

A thoughtful frown overcame the angry tension on Caine's rugged face. "And what happens when they grow up?"

I thought of my mother and sisters and all the horrors that had happened the day they'd died. A bitter laugh escaped from my tight lips. "Then they just want to be little girls again."

Using all the usual precautions, we went back to my apartment. Finn headed to his computer to see if his contacts had found out anything more about Captain Wayne Stephenson. Donovan Caine sat on the sofa and turned on the television. The detective didn't speak to or look at me, and Finn was too engrossed in his e-mails to engage in substantial conversation. I took a nap, resting up for what was sure to be a long night.

Around seven, I got up, took a shower, and girded myself. Tight black jeans, leather jacket, boots, and a long-sleeved, black T-shirt with a pair of sequined cherries on the front. I grabbed my silverstone knives and even took the time to put on some makeup. My lipstick matched the scarlet color of the cherries.

I stepped into the den. Finn sat at his computer, sipping his fifteenth cup of chicory coffee of the day. He wore black pants with creases as sharp as my knives. A button-up shirt in a dark emerald covered his broad shoulders, while a black tie hung from his neck. Finn never dressed down.

"That's a rather dark outfit. Are you trying to imitate our Goth friend?" Finn asked, referring to Sophia Deveraux.

I shrugged. "She does have a certain style. Besides, I imagine things will get rather messy before the end of the evening. Hence, the black. Where's the detective?"

Finn jerked his head. "Just got out of the shower."

Donovan Caine naked, water droplets sliding down his lean body, his muscles clenching and relaxing as he washes himself. Mmm. Nice image. Despite our earlier confrontation, I still found the detective extremely sexy. He'd be even more attractive if he'd lose the righteous anger and the stick up his ass. But no man was perfect.

I strolled into the kitchen, grabbed a blackberry yogurt from the fridge, and dug a spoon into the creamy concoction. I was halfway done when the bathroom door opened, and Donovan Caine stepped into the den. He also wore a T-shirt and jeans, although his were baggy and frayed around the seams. A battered, brown leather jacket, not unlike my own, hung off his shoulders.

The detective stared at me, his hazel eyes fixed on my lips. I ran my tongue around the silver spoon and took another bite of yogurt. Gold desire shimmered in his gaze, followed by a flash of guilt. Looks like I wasn't the only one who'd been turned on before. Maybe I'd do something about that this evening.

Maybe I'd do a lot about it.

Finn boosted another car, a Cadillac with a spacious trunk, and we headed for the nightclub. Northern Aggression, of course, was located in Northtown. The building itself was nothing special—a large warehouse with an anonymous, glossy, officelike veneer as blank as a vampire hooker's face. Drive by it during the day, and you'd think it was another anonymous call center staffed by corporate drones.

But at night, it was a different story. A large rune hung over the entrance—a heart with an arrow through it. The neon sign flashed red, then yellow, then orange, highlighting the long line of people waiting behind a red velvet rope. Guys in suits, girls in next to nothing, and everyone in between, all sizes, shapes, and colors, all eager to get inside, get drunk or high, and indulge in their fantasies.

The nightclub catered to a wealthy crowd, and luxury sedans and SUVs packed the parking lot in front of the building and the two on either side. Finn parked our vehicle for the evening in one of the side lots, underneath the soft tendrils of a weeping willow.

"So what's the plan?" Donovan Caine asked.

"We wait for Carlyle to show, see what he's up to, and if anyone joins him. When he leaves, we grab him and take him back to his place for a private chat," I said. "A variety of things could happen after that, depending on how cooperative he is."

"Are you going to kill him?" the detective asked in a flat voice.

I turned to stare at him over the headrest. "Are you seriously asking me that question? Of course, I'm going to fucking kill him. Carlyle's working for the Air elemental. That means he's fair game as far as I'm concerned."

Donovan Caine shook his head. "I can't let you do

that, Gin, no matter how big a slimeball Chuckie C. is. I'm a cop. That means something to me, even if it doesn't to you."

I stared at the detective. His morals were going to get in the way the whole night unless I convinced him to ignore them—just this once. An idea came to me, one that turned my stomach, but it was something I had to do to get Caine to go along with us. "Finn, do you still have that photo on your cell phone? The one Goth girl sent you?"

He slowly nodded.

"Be a sweetheart and show that to Donovan, please."

Finn opened his phone and scrolled to the appropriate picture. He didn't look at the screen as he passed the device to the detective. Donovan took the phone. Shock and disgust and horror flashed in his eyes, one after another. I waited until I saw the emotion I wanted—sympathy. Sympathy for what Fletcher had endured. Sympathy I was going to twist to my advantage.

"Take a good, long look, detective. That's what the Air elemental did to my handler," I said in a soft voice. "And she didn't stop even when he was dead. She kept mutilating him. That's how I found him, lying in a pool of his own blood, his face and body almost unrecognizable from where she'd used her magic to flay him alive, to strip the skin from his body. The stench was . . . indescribable. She would have done the same thing to you, if I hadn't intervened. The exact same thing."

Donovan Caine didn't respond. He just kept staring at the photo of Fletcher's body.

"I promised you I wouldn't hurt any innocent people,

detective, and I won't. Like I told you before, I don't kill kids. Pets either," I said. "Even when I do kill, it's quick, fast, mostly painless. That, the image on that phone, is an abomination. The men at your house said Carlyle was with the elemental when she did that. He *helped* her do that to an old man that I loved. So yeah, I'm going to kill the bastard tonight. If you have a problem with that, you can leave. Right fucking now."

Donovan scrubbed a hand through his black hair, snapped the phone shut, and passed it back to Finn, who took it without a word. Donovan Caine closed his eyes. His jaw tightened. A muscle twitched in his cheek. A vein throbbed in his forehead. Finally, he opened his eyes and looked at me. Emotions flickered in his golden gaze. Shock. Anger. Disgust. Horror. Resignation.

"All right," he said in a thick voice. "You've made your point about Carlyle and the Air elemental. They're yours. But their mole in the police department, he's mine. I'll handle him, not you. Understood?"

I could live with those terms. "Understood. Now, let's go see if we can spot the bastard."

The three of us got out of the car and walked toward the front door.

Finn made sure his hair was smooth and sleek, his breath minty-fresh. He also straightened his tie until it was centered against his chest. "Just let me do the talking, and everything will be fine."

I rolled my eyes but let him step in front of me.

Finn strolled past the line of people waiting to get in,

ignoring the dirty looks and muttered curses that came his way. A seven-foot-tall giant holding a clipboard stood in front of the door, checking off names. Finn stopped in front of the giant and plastered a smile on his face.

"Xavier, my man. How are things tonight?" Finn held out a hand.

Xavier studied Finn with his oversize eyes. He turned his head to one side, and his neck cracked. The flashing heart rune made the giant's shaved head glitter like jet in the dark night. A knowing smile creased the giant's face as he took Finn's hand—and palmed the C-notes hidden there.

"Things are looking up," Xavier rumbled in a deep voice. "Roslyn said you were going to swing by. Enjoy your night, Finn."

Finn slipped him another hundred and winked. "Oh, we intend to."

Xavier unhooked his velvet rope and stepped to one side. And just like that, we were in like Finn.

The outside of Northern Aggression might have been faceless, but the inside had a distinct personality. One of delicious decadence. Crushed red velvet drapes covered the walls, the floor was an exquisite bamboo, and the bar itself was an elaborate sheet of Ice. Intricate runes had been cut into the surface of the bar, mostly suns and stars—symbolizing life and joy. Behind it, a man in a blue silk shirt mixed drinks. His eyes glowed blue-white in the semidarkness. The Ice elemental was responsible for tending bar and making sure his creation stayed in one piece until the end of the evening.

Men and women in various stages of form-fitting

undress roamed through the room, offering guests free champagne, chocolate-dipped strawberries, and fresh oysters. You had to pay for everything else on the menu, whether it was food, drink, sex, blood, or drugs. Most of the waitstaff were vampires, all were hookers. Every single one wore a necklace with a rune dangling on the end of it—a heart with an arrow through it—and a bright smile that hinted of the pleasures yet to come. All you had to do was ask—and be able to pay the price.

Some folks thrashed in time to the rocking beat on the dance floor. Others huddled close together in booths. Kissing, caressing, fondling, moaning. In some instances, the tables twitched and shook, as people fucked on the floor underneath. In other spots, red glows flashed, and smoke curled up to the ceiling from a variety of illegal substances. Everybody had a drink in hand. Every once in a while, a couple would head up the stairs at the back of the nightclub. The upstairs rooms were rented out by the half hour for those who wanted to be more comfortable doing the deed.

A second giant bouncer stood in front of another velvet rope off to one side of the warehouse. The entrance to the private rooms, reserved for Roslyn Phillips's special guests, who paid dearly for the privilege.

The three of us moved farther into the club, and I spotted Roslyn working the crowd. The black vampire roamed from booth to table to the dance floor and back again. Shaking hands, smiling, chatting up her clients, and encouraging everyone to indulge themselves in whatever way they liked. The vampire had traded in her yoga pants for a fitted silk suit in a bloody crimson shade. The suit jacket dipped into a deep V in the front, showing off her smooth cleavage, while the skirt stopped at mid-thigh. Tight, fitted boots with spiked heels reached up her knees.

More than one man and woman stopped Roslyn and whispered something into her ear. But the vampire smiled and politely declined the invitations. Her hooking days were over, and she wasn't on the menu anymore. Ah, the joys of management.

After a minute, Roslyn felt me staring at her. Her eyes narrowed, and she shook her head, telling me Carlyle wasn't here yet. I nudged Finn.

"There's your girl," I said over the din of the music. "Go keep her company. When she spots Chuckie C. and shows him to his private room, call me on my cell."

Finn nodded, already heading in Roslyn's direction.

"Now what?" Caine asked.

I jerked my head at the bar. "Let's go get a drink. Might as well make ourselves comfortable while we wait."

We threaded our way through the mob of people, skirted around the dance floor, and bellied up to the bar. Up close, the Ice sculpture was even more impressive and imbued with so much elemental magic it cast off a faint blue glow. Power trickled off the bartender, like water dripping from a faucet, as he held on to just enough of his magic to keep the bar from melting and in one piece. His control was impressive. My own weaker Ice magic stirred in response.

The bartender placed napkins down on the cold slab in front of us. "What can I get you?"

"I'll have a gin on the rocks," I said.

Donovan Caine raised an eyebrow. "Isn't that a little cliché? Gin ordering gin?"

I shrugged. "Maybe, but I like it. You?"

"Give me a Scotch, neat."

The bartender moved off to fill our orders. Donovan Caine swiveled his seat around so he could look out into the nightclub. I propped my chin on my elbow and studied him. Black hair, golden eyes, lean body. Not a particularly handsome man, in the classical sense, but it all added up to a rough, rugged package I found exceptionally appealing.

Donovan Caine might hate me, hate what I did, hate the ease with which I could kill. But the detective was attracted to me too. Wanted me like I wanted him. I'd seen it in his eyes that first night on the balcony at the opera house. Again in the Cake Walk. Earlier this evening when I'd been eating my yogurt. I glanced at my watch. Not even ten. We probably had a while to wait before Charles Carlyle made an appearance. And I had lots of ideas of how we could pass the time.

The bartender set our drinks in front of us. I slid a fifty across the icy bar to him. Caine tossed back his Scotch. I did the same to my gin. The cold liquor burned going down my throat, somehow transforming itself into sweet, comforting warmth when it hit my stomach.

I pushed my empty glass back across the bar and turned my attention to the detective. My gray eyes drank in the crook in his nose, the curve of his chin, the steady twitch of his pulse in his throat. Donovan felt my gaze, saw the hunger shimmering there. An answering heat sparked in his golden gaze, even as he tried to smother it.

"Why are you looking at me like that?" he asked.

I tilted my head and smiled. "I think you know."

"No, I don't. Why don't you tell me?"

My smile widened. "Why don't I show you instead?"

I leaned over, caught his face in my hands, and pressed my lips to his.

Not the sweetest or most romantic of kisses, but I enjoyed the sensation of the detective's lips on mine, even if he didn't. He tasted of the Scotch he'd just downed—hot, spicy, sweet, and salty all at the same time. His aroma filled my nose. Clean, like soap. It clung to him, as though embedded in his skin. Mmm.

I flicked my tongue against his lips. Caine stiffened. He didn't pull away, but he kept his mouth closed and his tongue inside. A shame, really.

"Come on, detective," I murmured against his tight lips. "Everybody else here is doing it. Why shouldn't we?"

"Do I really have to list the reasons?" he growled.

"No," I replied. "But I have just as many why we should. This is one of them."

I slid over onto his lap. Even though I'd given him no warning and very little to turn him on, Donovan's erection pressed into my ass, solid and straining. I kissed him again, lightly pressing my lips to his, then shifted my legs so I was straddling him. I rocked forward, then retreated, rubbing against his body, pressing my breasts to his chest, exploring this attraction that simmered between us. Mmm.

Donovan's hands clenched into fists on either side of me. All he could do to keep from touching me.

"Come on, detective," I murmured. "You want me, too.

I'm sitting on ample proof of that. After this is over, we'll go our separate ways. I've almost been killed too many times to count this week. So have you. Why shouldn't we work off some of that stress and have a little fun in the meantime?"

Donovan stared at me. Desire warmed his eyes, making them shine like twin suns. Still, he hesitated. I shifted my hips again, urging him on. The slight friction pushed him over the edge. The detective let out a low growl, wound his hand in my hair, and pulled my lips down to his.

There were no closed mouths this time. No light touches or hesitation. Our tongues thrashed against each other, driving deeper and deeper into each other's mouth. I splayed my hands on his chest, kneading his lean muscles, marveling at his coiled strength. He pulled me closer. His hands moved up to my breasts. I scraped my nails down his stomach. We both rocked, teasing the other with what we each had to offer.

After ten seconds, I was wet. After thirty, I ached for him. By the minute mark, I was ready to rip his jeans off and pull him down under the bar with me. But I wanted to be alone with Donovan Caine, wanted to forget about everything but him and how he made me feel.

"They have rooms upstairs," I whispered against his mouth.

More emotions flashed in his eyes. Desire. Guilt. Hesitation. Need.

Slowly, he nodded.

I grinned and leaned forward to kiss him again when I felt an odd, pulsing buzz on my leg. It took me a few seconds to figure out what it was.

My cell phone vibrating.

* 20 *

Finn was calling, which meant our prey for the evening had arrived. Damn and double damn Charles Carlyle. Because no matter how much I wanted Donovan Caine, no matter how much he wanted me, tracking the vampire came first. Finding out who his Air elemental boss was came first.

Avenging Fletcher came first.

I sighed. "Sorry, detective. Duty calls."

"I know," Donovan said in a husky voice. "I can feel your phone vibrating against my thigh."

Our gazes locked. Desire still brightened the detective's eyes, along with something else—relief. I wondered at the emotion. Relief about what? That he wouldn't betray his dead partner by fucking me? That his morals would remain intact for another night? Or that he wouldn't discover how good it would be between us and hunger for more?

My phone kept vibrating. I slid off the detective's lap,

pulled the cell out of my jeans pocket, and flipped it open.

"What is it, Finn?"

"Carlyle just walked in the front door, in case you were wondering," Finn said in a wry voice. "Or would you rather keep dry humping the good detective?"

My gaze cut to the front of the club. It took me a few seconds to pick out Charles Carlyle, aka Chuckie C., from the rest of the crowd. But once I did, it was easy enough to track him. The short, stocky vampire sported a black suit with wide, white pinstripes and white wing-tips. The black lights spread throughout the club made the stripes and shoes glow a bright fluorescent. Better than GPS. A black fedora covered Carlyle's bald spot. He also had two other accessories—a girl on either arm. The women sported the heart-and-arrow rune necklace of the club's workers. Chuckie C. was starting his tab off early.

Carlyle headed straight for the giant manning the entrance to the private VIP rooms. Carlyle said something to the giant. After a moment, the taller man stepped aside, and Carlyle and the girls entered the hallway.

"Where are you?" I asked Finn.

"Back past the VIP entrance in a booth with Roslyn."

I spotted the two of them, as close together as Donovan Caine and I had been a minute ago. "Stay there. We'll come to you."

I snapped the phone shut and turned to the detective. "Carlyle's here. Let's go."

*   *   *

We left the bar and slithered through the crowd until we reached Roslyn and Finn. One of the vampire's hands was out of sight under the table. Judging from the smile on Finn's face, Roslyn had been stroking more than his ego. At the sight of the detective and me, the vampire got to her feet and smoothed down her skirt. Roslyn stared at the sequined fruit glittering on my black T-shirt.

"Cherries. Cute," she said.

I grinned.

"Follow me." Roslyn headed toward a door in the very back wall of the club.

Donovan Caine fell in step behind her.

"Stay out here and keep an eye on things," I told Finn. "Carlyle might have friends coming to join him."

"Not a problem. I'm feeling a bit thirsty anyway." Finn winked, got to his feet, and wandered off toward the bar.

I caught up with Roslyn just as the vampire opened a door set into the red velvet that covered the walls. The opening led to a small hallway that stretched out in either direction before branching off at both ends. Roslyn closed the door behind us, lessening the rocking beat of the music.

"This way," she said and turned left.

We followed her down the passageway. A variety of rooms lay on either side of the hall. Offices with computers and printers, private bathrooms for the staff, a break room with vending machines and rows of metal lockers. The business side of the nightclub. The walls back here were covered with black velvet instead of red. It matched the carpet underfoot.

Roslyn made several more turns, leading us deeper

into this rabbit's warren. Each hallway was slightly narrower than the one before, until the final one we came to was just wide enough for one person to comfortably walk through. This passageway was constructed of dark paneling instead of velvet. A variety of narrow slits lined either side at eye level. Each one had a knob on the side so you could open and close it. Reminded me of something you'd find on the door of an old-fashioned speakeasy.

Roslyn stopped at the entrance to the hallway and fixed us with a flat stare. "Carlyle's in the third room on the right. You've got thirty minutes before I send one of the bouncers to check on the girls. Be gone by then."

I gave her a curt nod. The vampire stared at me a second before she turned on her boot heel and stalked back the way she'd come.

"C'mon," I said in a low voice. "Let's see what our friend Chuckie C. is up to."

Donovan counted the doors, and we stopped in front of the appropriate slit. The detective looked at me. I nodded, and he grabbed the knob and slowly, quietly, slid the panel to one side. The opening stretched out horizontally about two feet, but it was barely taller than an eye. There was enough room for both of us to stare inside.

Donovan Caine and I put our eyes close to the opening. The slit revealed a small room with a plush couch off to one side, along with a round table and a few chairs. The tops of several liquor bottles sat on a shelf just below us. A bar set against this wall hid the peephole. A mirror ball spun around overhead, splashing silver light everywhere.

Charles Carlyle hadn't wasted any time. One of the girls already had her head buried in the vampire's crotch. He had his hand up the other one's skirt, and his tongue down her throat. Smacking and sucking noises drifted out to us, along with a few moans from the ladies. The girls were pros. If I hadn't known better, I might have thought they were really enjoying themselves.

Donovan Caine shifted beside me, no doubt thinking about what had happened between us at the bar. A shame, really, that we'd been interrupted.

The scene went on for maybe three more minutes before Carlyle got his rocks off. The hooker who'd been on her knees wiped off her mouth, crawled up, and joined the other one on the couch beside Chuckie C. Both of them murmured nonsense about what a big, big man he was and how they only pretended with other guys, but with him, their pleasure was real. My lips twitched. Funniest damn thing I'd heard all night.

Carlyle fondled the two girls for a moment longer, then spanked them both on the ass—hard—and zipped his pants up. "Scram, girls," he said. "I've got company coming."

Company? That sounded promising.

Carlyle threw a couple of C-notes at the girls, which they tucked into their push-up bras, before blowing him kisses and leaving the room. Chuckie C. let out the sigh of a satisfied man, then got to his feet and hitched his pants back up into their proper position. I hoped the bastard had enjoyed that blow job. It was going to be the last one he ever got.

The vampire headed toward the wall where Donovan Caine and I stood peering at him. For a moment, I thought perhaps the stocky vampire had spied us spying on him. But he reached for a bottle and splashed some whiskey into a square glass. Getting himself a drink. He was so close to us I could have stuck one of my knives through the peephole and given him a shave. That moment would come soon enough.

Carlyle had just knocked back his first slug of whiskey, when the door on the far side of the room opened, and a man stepped inside. Carlyle blocked my view, but I could still see the other guy was a giant, with salt-and-pepper hair and a bulky frame that was slowly going to fat.

"About time you got here," Carlyle said.

"Sorry," the giant replied. "Some of us have been busy."

Donovan Caine stiffened beside me. Because the deep baritone of the second man belonged to his boss—police captain Wayne Stephenson.

"Whaddya want to drink?" Carlyle asked.

"Whiskey, and a lot of it."

Carlyle made a couple more drinks. Stephenson took a seat at the table, and Carlyle handed him one of the glasses and set the bottle on the table. Stephenson knocked back the amber liquid like it was water and poured himself another. Took a lot to get a giant drunk. Dwarves too. Humans and vamps were the only ones who couldn't hold their liquor.

"I told you on the phone, meeting was a bad idea," Stephenson muttered and downed his second drink. "Everybody's crawling all over my ass about the Giles murder. Did you know the bastard was a personal friend of the mayor? His college roommate or some such shit. Pompous moron's called me twice today."

Carlyle took a seat opposite the giant "And I told you she wanted an update. In person."

Stephenson's pale eyes flicked toward the door. "She's not coming here, is she? Bad enough I risk being seen with you. If she walks in the door—"

"Don't worry," Carlyle said. "This place is totally anonymous. Nobody cares what you do or who you do it with, as long as you don't skip out on your bill. As for the elemental, she had other fish to flay tonight and sent me instead. So your skin will stay right where it is—for now."

Stephenson drew a white handkerchief out of the breast pocket of his suit and mopped his forehead with it. I could smell the stench of his relief all the way across the room. "I wish I'd never gotten involved in this mess."

"You wouldn't be in this mess if you hadn't fucked all those ten-year-old girls on your daughter's soccer team," Carlyle's tone was light, conversational, like he was talking about whether it might rain tomorrow.

Donovan Caine let out a low, guttural growl. The sound a wolf might make before it ripped out your throat. His hands clenched into fists, and I heard his teeth grind together through his clenched jaw. So Stephenson was a pedophile. Would have been easy for the Air elemental to get her hooks into him. All she'd need would be a picture, just one, and the police captain would have been hers.

"What about the assassin?" Carlyle asked. "Anything on her?"

Stephenson snorted and poured himself a third drink.

"Bitch is a fucking ghost. None of my snitches know who she is or what she looks like. And none of the tips we've gotten have been worth a damn, I'm starting to think that sketch Caine gave us was total bullshit. I think she's gone. Out of town and out of the picture."

Carlyle digested the information. "What about the old man's son? The banker?"

Stephenson shrugged. "Finnegan Lane told his bank he was taking a vacation because he was so heartsick over his father's murder. I imagine he's on an island somewhere by now."

"What about Caine? Has the detective surfaced yet?"

Stephenson mopped more sweat from his forehead. "No, I can't find the fucker anywhere. He wasn't stupid enough to go back to his house. He hasn't reported in for work, and none of his buddies have seen him. He's gotta still be in Ashland, though. He doesn't have the resources to disappear like Lane does."

Carlyle leaned forward and speared the giant with a hard, flat stare. "You need to find the detective. Caine is a loose end that needs to be clipped off before he starts unraveling things. The elemental wants you to find him—ten minutes ago. I showed you the picture of the old man at the barbecue restaurant. You know what happens when she doesn't get her way."

Stephenson tossed back another drink. Some of the liquid courage must have finally kicked in because he glared back at the vampire. "I called Caine just like you wanted. If your crew had done its job and held on to him until the elemental got there, we wouldn't be wondering where the detective is and what he's up to. And I wouldn't be wondering when your boss is going to kill me. She'll kill you too, you know. As soon as she thinks she doesn't need you anymore. Bitch is crazy. Does she really think nobody will notice what she's doing? All the wiseguys she's hired? The fact she's building her own crew to take on Mab Monroe's organization? And that she's using money from Mab's own company to do it?"

"Nobody did notice the embezzling or anything else, until Gordon started digging around," Carlyle replied.

My eyes narrowed. So that's what this was all about. The Air elemental had been stealing money from Halo Industries to try to wrest control of the city away from Mab Monroe. To build a crew and fund a war against the Fire elemental. Gordon Giles had known about her embezzling and was going to blow the whistle on her to the cops. That's why he'd had to die. The Air elemental couldn't afford to let Mab get wind of her plans, not before she was ready to make her move. But since killing Giles outright herself would have drawn Mab's unwanted attention to Halo Industries, the Air elemental had hired me to take the fall—to come in and be Giles's conveniently dead killer.

But Stephenson was right. Bitch really was crazy if she thought she could take control of the city away from Mab Monroe. Because before the Air elemental could even get to Mab, she'd have to take out her flunkies first. The lawyer, Jonah McAllister, might not present much of a problem, although he had his own guards. But Mab's giant enforcer, Elliot Slater, he'd be a hard weed to mow down. And then there was Mab herself, the toughest task of all. David had had a better chance against Goliath than the Air elemental did of knocking off Mab Monroe.

But the revelation also told me something else—the Air elemental almost certainly had to be Haley or Alexis James. Nobody else was high enough up in the company to manage something like this. Carlyle was going to tell me later exactly which one of the sisters it was—no matter how bloody I had to get in the process.

Instead of arguing further with the giant, Carlyle sat back in his seat. He ran his finger around the lip of his glass, then gave Stephenson a sly look. Considering something.

"Perhaps you and I could come to an agreement," Carlyle said in a smooth tone. "Since you seem to be rather tired of working for the elemental."

Stephenson eyed him. "What kind of agreement?"

"We both agree it's only a matter of time before the elemental implodes," Carlyle said. "Who's to say after that happens you and I can't pick up the pieces?"

"What exactly are you proposing?"

Carlyle shrugged. "Nothing right now. Except you watch out for me, and I'll watch out for you until things settle down. After that, well, we'll just see what happens."

"What about the elemental?" Fear crept back into the giant's voice. "If she even thinks we're plotting—"

"Don't worry about the elemental." A smirk filled Carlyle's blocky face. "I've got a little insurance policy in place to keep her in line."

Insurance policy? There was only one thing Carlyle could have that the elemental wanted—Gordon Giles's secret flash drive with all of her dirty deeds on it. The vampire was going to be more useful than I'd anticipated.

Stephenson didn't respond to the other man's offer. But I could see the desperate hope in his eyes. The police captain would do anything to get out from under the elemental's thumb, even fall into bed with a hood like Carlyle. He didn't realize the vampire would treat him exactly the same, in the end.

"Just think about it," Carlyle said. "But not too long."

He finished his drink and jerked his head toward the door. "Now leave. I've got other things to do tonight before I see the elemental again."

Stephenson didn't need to be told twice. The giant mopped a final bit of sweat from his forehead, got to his feet, and walked out the door. Carlyle waited a few moments before putting the bottle of booze back in the bar and slapping his fedora on top of his head. He was leaving too.

Beside me, Donovan Caine pulled away from the peephole. I did the same and pulled the knob, covering the slit.

"That bastard," Caine muttered in a low voice. "That fucking bastard set me up."

The detective started to charge past me down the hallway, but I grabbed his arm.

"No," I said. "We're not here for your boss. We see what Carlyle has to say first, then you can go after Stephenson. That was our agreement, remember?"

Anger simmered in Caine's eyes, and the muscles in his arm bunched under my hand.

"You get Stephenson," I repeated. "You can deal with him any way you like—but not tonight. Carlyle's leaving. We need to grab him. I'm tired of running around and hiding in the shadows, detective. I want a fucking name. And Carlyle can give it to me. Now, are you coming with me? Or do I knock you out and leave you back here for Roslyn's giant bouncer to find?"

After a moment, Caine let out a tense breath. "All right. We'll do it your way."

I nodded. "Good. Let's go get the bastard before he leaves."

* 21 *

When we stepped back out on the main floor, I pulled out my cell phone and dialed Finn.

"Yeah?" he said over the din.

"Carlyle's leaving," I said.

"I know," Finn replied. "Stephenson's already out the front door. Chuckie C.'s settling up his tab for the evening with the giant next to the VIP entrance. Seems to be arguing about the price of something. While you two were eavesdropping, I took the liberty of wandering out to the parking lot to see if I could spot the vamp's car. Carlyle's driving a sweet little red BMW that's parked on the west side of the building. Three rows up from our car."

A hard smile curved my lips. "Perfect. Keep him in sight. The detective and I are heading for the Beamer."

We both hung up. I wove my way through the crowd, sliding from opening to opening. Donovan Caine was right on my heels. It took almost a minute for us to step outside Northern Aggression. The night air was a cool, welcome kiss on my face after the crush of bodies inside the nightclub.

"This way," I said.

The detective fell in step beside me. He'd dampened down his earlier anger at Stephenson, although his mouth was set into a hard, determined line. He reached behind him, drew his gun from the small of his back, and held the weapon down by his side. "How do you want to do this?"

"No need for a gun yet, detective. You and Finn hang back," I replied. "I'll approach Carlyle and subdue him. That way, he only sees me if something untoward should happen."

Donovan nodded. "All right."

The BMW was parked right where Finn said it would be. Hard to miss, really, since the vanity plate on the front read CHUCKEC. Donovan ducked down in the shadows behind a car a few feet over. I slid behind an SUV on the other side of the BMW and peered through the driver's side window.

Getting close to midnight now, and the air had taken on the sharp chill of fall. The music of the club pulsated outside, and I could hear the vibrations whispering in the concrete under my boots. Classic murmurs of sex, drugs, and rock and roll. A few smokers stood in a cluster two hundred feet away, puffing on who knew what. But other than that, the parking lot was deserted. Everybody was still inside, getting their groove on for the evening.

I palmed one of my knives, hilt out, and started counting off seconds in my head. Ten . . . twenty . . . forty-five . . .

Two minutes later, Charles Carlyle strolled around the side of the building. He walked with quick, purposeful steps. The confident stride of a man who thinks he's got everything figured out. That the world was his cherry to pop. Still, he cast a cursory look around, the way anyone would when walking through a dark area at night.

But he didn't see me. They never did, until it was too late. I smiled. Poor Chuck. I almost felt sorry for him. Until I thought about Fletcher.

I looked, but I didn't see Finn trailing the vampire. Finn could blend in with the shadows too, when he put his mind to it.

Carlyle walked closer, passing the car Donovan Caine crouched behind. The vampire whistled a soft tune and jingled his car keys in his fingers. He hit a button, and the lights on the BMW flashed once, disabling the alarm and unlocking the doors. Time for me to make my move.

I tiptoed out from behind the back of the SUV and approached Carlyle. The vampire had just hooked his fingers underneath the door handle to pull it open when I called out to him.

"Excuse me, sugar," I drawled in a soft voice. "Do you have a light? I seem to have misplaced mine. Can't put a damn thing in the pockets of this miniskirt."

Carlyle turned toward the sound of my voice, a smile already forming on his face. I quickened my steps, getting into position. I didn't look like he expected me to, and he frowned, suddenly suspicious.

"Who the hell are you—"

I might have been concerned, if I hadn't already used the hilt of my knife to coldcock him. The vampire blinked once before his eyes rolled up into the back of his head, and he pitched face-first onto the concrete. To my right, Donovan Caine stepped out from the shadows. Finn appeared from my left.

"Come on." I leaned down and grabbed the vampire under his arms. "Help me get this blood-sucking bastard into the trunk."

An hour later, I threw a pitcher of ice water onto Charles Carlyle's face. The cold shocked the vampire back into consciousness. So did the two hard slaps I laid across his cheeks. The stinging sensation in my palm felt good. Finally, I was *doing* something about Fletcher's murder, taking the initiative, instead of reacting to others.

"Wakey, wakey, Chuck," I said. "Time to rise and shine and spill your guts."

The vampire's eyes blinked several times in rapid succession before focusing on me and his surroundings. After loading Chuck into the trunk of our stolen car, we'd driven to the vampire's home in one of the suburbs on the edge of Northtown, the address Finn had found while digging for info. Nice place. Split-level ranch house, big yard, pool in the back. Being an executive vice president at Halo Industries, even in name only, paid better than I'd thought. So did being the Air elemental's right-hand man.

Finn, Donovan, and I had let ourselves into the house and dragged Carlyle along with us. Now the three of us stood in what passed for a game room—plasma television bolted to one wall, pool table in the corner, stacks of porn magazines and empty beer bottles everywhere. The only nice thing about the room was the stone fireplace that took up the back wall.

Donovan Caine had used his silverstone handcuffs to bind the vampire to a chair, which I'd dragged into the middle of the room.

Carlyle's eyes went to me, then to the two men looming behind me, then to the silverstone knife in my hand. "Fuck me," he muttered.

"Quick on the draw. I like that in a man."

I felt Donovan Caine's eyes on me, but I didn't turn to look at the rugged detective. Instead, I wandered around the room, twirling with my knife so the blade caught the light and flashed it back in Carlyle's eyes. Time to start playing the game.

"Nice place you have here, Chuck. Very nice. Did you pick it out yourself? Or did the Air elemental?"

The vampire gave me a guarded look. "What do you want?"

I smiled and held his gaze until I was sure he'd noticed just how cold and hard my gray eyes were. Carlyle might think himself to be a big man, but he knew when he was outmatched. His face had already tightened with panic, and the muscles of his arms and shoulders tensed underneath his suit as he discreetly tested the silverstone handcuffs that held him down. Bastard shouldn't have bothered. He wasn't going anywhere tonight except into the ground.

"In case you haven't figured it out, Chuck, let me tell you who I am. The Spider. The assassin you and your boss hired to kill Gordon Giles, then decided to double-cross. I'm sure you recognize my two associates."

Finn gave him a toothy grin that was almost as scary as my smile. The vamp realized there would be no sympathy there and turned his attention to Donovan Caine, trying to see if he had any kind of friend in the room. But the detective crossed his arms over his chest and put on his flat cop face.

"You've been busy, Chuck. Working for the Air elemental, framing me, having your men abduct and beat Finn, then doing the same to the detective. And I didn't really understand why—until I overheard you and Wayne Stephenson talking tonight at Northern Aggression." I clucked my tongue. "He's right, you know. Bitch is crazy if she thinks she's going to dethrone Mab Monroe as queen bee of Ashland."

Carlyle didn't say anything, but agreement flashed in his eyes.

"But you know that already, don't you, Chuck? You know this won't end well for her, and you've already taken steps to protect yourself."

The vampire's eyes narrowed. He'd overcome enough of his initial panic to realize I wasn't going to kill him— immediately. "What do you want?" he asked again in a stronger voice.

I put my hands on either side of him and leaned down until my cold eyes were level with his. "The flash drive. I want the flash drive. The one Gordon Giles made that contains the information on the embezzlement from Halo Industries. The one your Air elemental boss is so eager to get her hands on. That's your insurance policy, isn't it, Chuck? The elemental gets too wacko, and all you have to do is send the information to Mab Monroe. And she'll take care of the elemental for you."

Carlyle didn't respond, but the twitch in his cheek was all the confirmation I needed. The vampire really needed to work on his poker face.

"He's got the flash drive?" Donovan Caine asked behind me. "You're sure?"

"Oh, I'm positive," I replied, never taking my eyes off the vampire. "Tell me where it is, Chuck. Now."

Carlyle's eyes flicked off to the left, as if searching for an acceptable lie. His tongue darted out to wet his lips. "Say you're right. Say I . . . found the flash drive among Gordon's things when I was looking through them for the elemental. What's in it for me if I give it to you?"

"You get to die quickly, Chuck, instead of being tortured. That's all you get."

He let out a low snort. "Not much in it for me, then."

I shrugged. "Depends on how much you like pain."

I pulled back and brought the tip of my knife up where he could see it. Then I leaned forward again and drew the blade down his cheek, not deep enough to break his skin, but enough for him to feel the cold metal.

Carlyle let out a soft laugh. "You don't have the balls to—"

I cut him.

I carved a line from one side of his jaw, down his neck, and up to the other. The blade didn't sever his carotid artery, but the knife went in deep enough for him to really feel it. Blood oozed out of the wound and dropped like crimson tears onto the vampire's pinstripe suit. I'd just upped the ante in this poker game we were playing.

But Carlyle surprised me. He didn't start begging

or pleading or sobbing for mercy. Instead, the vampire clamped down a scream, his yellow fangs poking out through this lips, before his eyes shifted to the left again. I frowned, wondering why he was looking off to the side, instead of at me or the knife. Wasn't I scary enough for him? Few things could be more important at the moment to the vampire than the blade I'd just dug into his neck. Precious few. So I turned and followed his line of sight to the fireplace. Hmm.

I used the vampire's pant leg to clean the blood off my knife and stepped away from him. Relief flashed in Carlyle's eyes.

"Fuck," Donovan muttered, staring at the blood on the vampire's chest. "Did you have to cut him so deep? I thought you wanted answers out of him, not blood."

"I barely nicked him. He'll live. Watch him a minute," I told the detective.

Caine stared at me, then shook his head and took up a position in front of the vampire. Finn followed me back to the fireplace.

"What are you doing, Gin?" he asked in a low voice.

"Checking out a hunch."

I brushed my fingers against the stone fireplace. Behind me, Carlyle hissed with displeasure, but I tuned him out. Listening. Trying to sense any disturbance, anything out of the ordinary. There was a reason Carlyle kept glancing back here. I wanted to know what it was. But the stone's vibrations were low and muted. Like me, the vampire wasn't home enough to leave much of an impression in his house.

Still, I kept listening. And I realized there was something in the stone. A note of sly satisfaction. Anticipation. Pride. Eagerness. Centered in the fireplace and rippling outward.

Still listening to the stone, I trailed my fingers over the wall and walked closer to the center of the fireplace. It was beautifully constructed, made out of uneven slabs of blue and gray river rock fitted together to form an elegant arch, then the chimney itself. The construction was so perfect, so seamless, it could only have been achieved by magic, by another Stone elemental. It only took me a few seconds to spot the rune carved into one of the bottom corners. Two blocks side by side, with another sitting on top of them—a builder's rune. I made a note of the faint trickles of magic in the mortar that held the rocks together. Stones were the rarest of elementals, and it always surprised me to find another one, to see her work, to feel her power.

Then I concentrated, listening to stone, trying to find the exact source of the vibrations.

And I spotted one rock that was a little lighter, a little smoother, than the others, as if someone repeatedly touched it, rubbing it for good luck—or to open and close a secret compartment. The stone felt smooth and cool under my searching fingers. There. A small metal button on the underside. I pressed up on it. Something clicked, and the rock shot out, revealing a space about the size of a safety deposit box.

"Got something," I said.

"What?" Finn asked, trying to peer over my shoulder.

I looked inside the space. A blue folder embossed with the words *Halo Industries* sat inside, along with a small flash drive. There were also some pictures of Gordon Giles naked, posing in various intimate positions with a smorgasbord of hookers, many of whom sported the heart-and-arrow rune medallion of the Northern Aggression nightclub. Black, white, Hispanic, human, vampire. I flipped through the photos. Whips, leather, masks. Giles had been a little more serious about his prostitute predilection than Fletcher's file had let on. I turned one of the photos sideways. More flexible, too.

"What did you find?" Donovan Caine rumbled.

"The jackpot."

I plucked out the flash drive and showed it to Caine and Finn, then stuffed it inside my jeans pocket. I passed the folder to Finn, along with the pictures of Giles.

Finn rifled through them and let out a whistle. "Gordon was into some hard-core stuff. Take a look at this, detective."

Donovan Caine turned away from the vampire and stepped toward us. Behind him, something flashed in Carlyle's eyes. I felt a small bit of magic spark to life in the room.

And that's when the vampire made his move.

✳ 22 ✳

Metal. The vampire must have had a small, elemental talent for manipulating metal. That was the only way to explain the sudden surge of magic—and why his silverstone handcuffs popped off like they were plastic toys. I'd checked them myself. The chains had been as solid as my knives.

Carlyle leaped to his feet. Donovan Caine saw the motion too late. He'd just started to whip around and go for his gun when Carlyle put both hands onto the detective's back and shoved him. Vamps weren't as strong as giants and dwarves, but Carlyle had more than enough strength to lift Donovan off his feet and send him flying across the room. The detective's flailing arms caught Finn in the chest. Finn went down like a sack of potatoes and started coughing from the force of the blow. Donovan Caine didn't stop until he crashed into the stone fireplace.

Charles Carlyle bared his fangs at me and darted out of the room.

"Stay here!" I yelled, although I doubted Finn or Caine were paying any attention. "I'll get him!"

No time to check on either man. I leaped over Finn, who was still coughing, and sprinted through the house. Ahead of me, Carlyle's footsteps smacked on the floor, followed by the sound of the front door banging against the wall. The bastard was outside already. Fuck. I couldn't let him get away. The first thing Carlyle would do would be to call the Air elemental and tell her that Finn and I were still in town—and working with Donovan Caine. I didn't want that to happen. Not until I knew exactly what was on that flash drive—and which James sister moonlighted as a sadistic, magic-using bitch.

I ran out the front door, jumped over the steps, landed on the lawn, and hustled down to the street. My head snapped back and forth, and my eyes scanned everything in sight. Streetlights, parked cars, trees, shadows, other houses on the block. No sign of Carlyle anywhere. Which way had he gone?

Only one way to tell for sure. I dropped to one knee and put my free hand against the concrete sidewalk. The stone felt cool and porous under my fingers. Its murmurs whispered of the steady drone of traffic, the hum of lawn mowers, the laughter of the neighborhood kids. Typical suburban sounds. I concentrated, listening harder, going deeper, using my magic to sift through the vibrations. There. A fresh note of panic, starting here and scurrying to the right.

I tightened my grip on my knife and headed that way. I kept on the grass to the right of the sidewalk, not wanting the echo of my boots on the concrete to drift to Carlyle's ears and alert the vampire that I was still behind him. Let the bastard think he'd lost me. Let him slow down.

Because that's when I'd kill him.

The street split two ways, with one road continuing in a straight line in front of me and the other curving to the left before bending back to the right. Nobody ahead of me. My head whipped around, and I saw a glimmer of white before the darkness swallowed it up. I smiled. Those pinstripes in Carlyle's suit were better than road flares.

But I didn't run down the street after him. Instead, I sprinted forward, darted past some prickly holly bushes, and cut through someone's yard. I picked my way quickly, but carefully, through the lush grass, not wanting to trip and break my ankle on some stray toy that had been left on the lawn. Houses loomed two stories high on either side of me, their dark windows resembling giant, black eyes tracking my progress. I ducked under a clothesline and vaulted over a low picket fence into the next neighbor's yard. Getting in front of the vampire.

I repeated the process twice more, before the silver street glimmered in front of me. But instead of hurtling into the road, I slid behind a large rhododendron and peered at the area. My blood roared in my ears, and I drew in deep breaths, trying to slow my racing heart. The rush receded, and the sounds of the night washed over me. A whip-poor-will crying in a tree. Wind ruffling the grass and making a porch swing creak. A few bugs droning, despite the chill that had settled over the benign landscape—

Smack-smack. Smack-smack.

Footsteps off to the left coming my way, moving slower than before.

I palmed my other knife and moved forward. Several steps led from the house down into the yard, and I crouched on the far side of them, letting the concrete shield me from sight. Then I raised my head until I could just see over the lip of the steps. Ten . . . twenty . . . forty-five . . . The seconds slid by; a minute later, Charles Carlyle shuffled into view. The vampire might be strong, but his stocky body was built for short bursts of energy, not an extended run. He was already winded. Thanks to the streetlights, I could see the flush in his face, muddying his cheeks. Good. Tired men were easier to kill.

Every few steps, the vampire glanced back over his shoulder, but he never looked left or right or scanned the shadows around or in front of him. He wasn't expecting me to come from any other direction. Sloppy, sloppy, sloppy.

The next time the vamp turned his head, I darted forward. A four-foot-high fence butted up against the street, and I ducked down behind it. The gate lay to my right. Someone had forgotten to latch it, and the night breeze had pushed it open even more. Perfect.

The sound of the vampire's footsteps grew louder, and I realized Carlyle was talking to himself in a soft voice.

"Stupid, arrogant bitch," he muttered, passing the gate. "Thought she'd torture me. Hah. Old Chuckie C. showed her who was boss. Stupid bitch—"

My first knife slashed into his leg, severing his hamstring so the bastard couldn't run again. Carlyle had just started to scream when I popped up from behind the fence and used my other knife to cut his throat. A fountain of blood spewed out of the deep, lethal wound, spattering me and the fence.

Carlyle stumbled back, his wounded leg gave out, and he stumbled into a car before bouncing off and crumpling to the sidewalk. One hand clutched at his leg. The other tried to slow the blood gushing out of his neck.

I came around the fence and stood over him, a bloody knife in either hand. The vampire's eyes widened, and he tried to drag himself away. But he'd already lost too much blood. Carlyle managed to pull himself forward about two feet before his wet hand slipped off the wound in his neck. Arterial blood coated the sidewalk like black varnish.

I used the toe of my boot to turn the vampire over onto his back, then crouched down beside him. "Don't say I didn't keep my promise, Chuck. I'd told you that you'd die quick."

The vampire tried to gurgle something at me, but the effort was just too much for him. The sound snuffed out like a candle and died. A few seconds later, Carlyle did the same.

I waited until I was sure he was dead, then got to my feet. My eyes scanned the surrounding houses, but no lights snapped on. No curtains twitched. Nobody opened their front door. No one had heard the vamp die, but I still had to do something with his body. My gaze flicked to the fence. I didn't think the owner would appreciate finding blood spatters all over that in the morning.

So I pulled my cell phone out of my jeans pocket and hit one of the numbers stored in the speed dial. It rang three times before she picked it up.

"Hmph?" Sophia Deveraux answered with her usual greeting.

"It's Gin," I said. "Good news. I've changed my mind about not needing your services. How fast can you get over to Northtown?"

For once, luck smiled on me. Sophia Deveraux was in the area and arrived about ten minutes later, pulling up to the curb in her vintage black convertible. I eyed the car. With its long body, fins, enormous trunk, and creamy white interior, it looked more like a hearse than a classic car, especially this late at night. I showed the Goth dwarf the blood on the fence and the bush I'd dragged Charles Carlyle's body behind.

"Do you think you can clean this up before one of the neighbors wakes up and sees you?" I asked in a low voice. "Or do I need to stay and help you with the body?"

Sophia grunted and gave me a sharp look.

"Sorry. Just thought I'd ask."

While the dwarf got to work, I jogged back to Carlyle's house. The front door was still open. I stepped into the house, quietly shut it behind me, and headed toward the game room.

"Why isn't she back yet?" Donovan Caine's rough voice drifted down the hall to me.

"Because killing people takes time, detective," Finn replied. "She probably had to chase the bastard a few blocks before she caught up with him."

"And what if he caught up with her instead?" Donovan countered. "What if he got the drop on her? What if he killed her?"

Finn laughed. "Unlikely. Gin's been dissecting toads like Carlyle for years. Why the concern, detective?"

A pause. "Fuck if I know."

"Might it have something to do with the way the two of you were sucking face at Northern Aggression?"

Another pause. "You saw that?"

"Don't be embarrassed, detective. Those eyes, those lips, that firm body. She's a looker. And Gin seemed to be having a marvelous time on your lap."

Even though I wasn't in the room, I could imagine the smirk on Finn's face. I paused, wanting to hear the detective's answer.

"She's . . . something," Donovan admitted. "But I'm glad it stopped when it did."

A third pause, this time from Finn. "I never considered you a stupid man, detective, but when you say things like that, you make me wonder. You're glad you didn't fuck her?"

"She's an assassin, and she killed my partner," Caine snapped. "You don't fuck your partner's murderer."

"Oh, get off your high horse, detective," Finn replied in a sharp voice. "Cliff Ingles wasn't the saint you make him out to be. Quite the opposite. As for Gin being an assassin, well, we don't exactly live in Mayberry. She's done what she's had to in order to survive over the years. We all have, even you, I imagine."

"I've never killed people for money," Caine said in an acidic tone.

"Sure you have, detective. It's called your city paycheck."

Okay, time to stop this before the two men came to

blows. I tiptoed back down the hall, opened the door, and shut it again, hard enough so they could hear it. I made my footsteps loud and heavy.

"Finn? Donovan?" I called out.

"Still in the office," Finn replied.

I stepped into the room. Finn leaned on the edge of the pool table, rubbing his chest. Donovan Caine perched on the lip of the fireplace. A couple of shallow cuts decorated his hands, along with a bruise on the side of his face, but the detective didn't look like he'd been too damaged by getting tossed into the stone wall. Probably hurt his ego more than anything else.

"Where's Carlyle?" Donovan Caine asked.

"Feeding the worms," I replied.

The detective nodded. He didn't seem as broken up by Carlyle's death as I'd thought he would. Or maybe getting thrown across the room by the vampire had changed his perspective a bit.

"And the body?" Finn asked.

"Being taken care of by our mutual Goth friend."

Donovan stared at me, then Finn. "So now what?" he asked.

I pulled the flash drive out of my pocket and held it up. "Now we get out of here and go see what's on this— and why the Air elemental wants it back so badly."

✲ 23 ✲

Using all the usual precautions, we left Carlyle's house, dumped our stolen car in one of the downtown parking garages, and headed to my apartment.

Once we were inside, Finn opened his laptop and plugged in the flash drive. Donovan Caine dropped into a chair at the kitchen table and flipped through the matching folder we'd found in the fireplace hiding spot. I grabbed the photos of Giles and went through them. Injuries, bloody clothes, aches and pains, everything else was forgotten except for the information we'd found.

Finn was right. Gordon Giles had been into some kinky stuff. Leafing through the pictures, I saw much more of the middle-aged accountant than I'd ever wanted to. But I studied each image carefully. Hopefully, there was a reason Gordon Giles had kept these pictures, other than for his own private enjoyment. But nothing jumped out at me.

After about ten minutes of nonstop mouse clicking and the occasional burst of typing, Finn let out a low whistle and leaned back in his chair.

"You got something?" Donovan Caine asked. "Because I can't make heads or tails out of what's in this folder. It's just account numbers and file names and other gibberish that makes no sense to me."

"I'm not a forensic accountant and I'm usually more interested in hiding money than tracking it down, but it looks like Haley James has been skimming off the top of her own company," Finn said.

Not a surprise, but it was a welcome bit of confirmation instead of mere speculation.

"Are you sure it's her?" I asked.

Finn nodded. "If not, someone's framed her but good, because her password and log-in information are all over these files. Not exactly the kind of info you give out to just anybody, especially when you're the head of a company as large as Halo Industries."

"What do you mean by skimming off the top?" Donovan asked. "How is she doing it exactly?"

Finn shrugged. "Your usual embezzling. Padding expenses. Getting reimbursed for business trips she never took. Diverting company cash flow into offshore accounts. A couple hundred thousand dollars here, a few more there, you'd be surprised how quickly it adds up."

I frowned, thinking of the care that had been put into this whole operation, into framing me to take the fall for Giles's murder. "That sounds too easy, too obvious, too sloppy."

Finn shrugged again. "Keep in mind I've only been looking at these files for a few minutes. A company as large as Halo would generate hundreds, if not thousands, of files every single day. It's probably a very delicate operation, but we've got the exact, specific files you need to put it all together."

"Which is why Gordon Giles spent months collecting information," Donovan Caine said. "Which is also why he was going to be the state's star witness. Because he could understand how the money was being diverted and explain exactly where it was going."

"Do the files show where the money was going?" I asked. "What it was being used for?"

Finn clicked a few more times. "Looks like Haley James has hired several new executive vice presidents the past few months. Part of it went to pay their *salaries,* and I use that word loosely."

"Her crew, in other words," Donovan Caine chimed in. "The men she thought were going to help her take on Mab Monroe."

"I've also got several payments here made out to Carla Stephenson," Finn added. "Looks like ten payments of ten thousand dollars each. A hundred grand, total."

Donovan's face tightened. "Carla? That's Wayne Stephenson's daughter. She's ten."

"Probably not a donation to her college trust fund then, although that's what it's listed as here," Finn said. "Smart of him, putting it in her name. That's why it didn't immediately come up when I ran his financials earlier."

"Keep digging," I said. "I want to know everything there is to know about this scam."

We went back to work. Finn surfed files. Donovan squinted at the small print in the folder. And I picked up the stack of Gordon Giles's porn photos.

Thankfully, and to my slight surprise, not all of the pictures were of Giles doing vampire hookers every which way he knew how. There was a photo of an older lady I assumed was his mother, and several more of Giles in various locales holding up fish and beaming at the camera.

Although they were of a different sort than the previous pictures, they were still mementoes, small treasures the accountant had wanted to keep. Giles had probably put them all together so he could grab them at one time when Caine put him in witness protection. And then Charles Carlyle had stumbled across them and hidden them in his fireplace. Given the amount of porn I'd seen in the vampire's game room, I didn't have to guess why the hooker photos were on top—and covered with greasy fingerprints and other stains.

I was almost to the bottom of the stack when I came across a photo that didn't quite match the others. For one thing, there weren't any hookers in it. For another, it starred a very different person than Giles's dead mother.

Alexis James.

In the photo, Alexis James wore black Bermuda shorts, a tailored white shirt, and a floppy straw hat. She stood next to some sort of gray shark she'd speared with the gun in her hand. The poor creature hung upside down, its side slit open, guts hanging out for everyone to see. The shark's blood turned the dock a mottled brown, but Alexis was too busy smiling into the camera to notice it.

Classy. Gordon Giles stood off to one side. He was smiling too.

So Alexis had gone with Gordon on one of his fishing trips and speared herself a shark. Hell, maybe she'd even let the accountant spear her, and they'd had some sort of fishing trip fling.

I started to put the photo aside, when something caught my eye. A black blob in the middle of the picture. I scraped at it with my fingernail, wondering if it was just dirt that had somehow gotten on the print. But it didn't come off, and I realized it was part of the picture. What was that around Alexis James's neck? I held the photo up almost to my nose, but I couldn't quite make it out.

I got up and rummaged through one of the junk drawers in the kitchen until I came up with a magnifying glass. Then I sat back down and used it to go over the picture again.

Instead of the classic string of pearls I'd always seen her with, Alexis James wore a different sort of necklace in the photo. Oh, the slender white cord that encircled her throat still had pearls on it, but there was a large pendant set in the middle of necklace.

A tooth—a large, triangular-shaped tooth done in polished jet.

The tooth was the same as the jet symbol the guy at Finn's place had worn on a chain around his neck. The same symbol the man at Caine's cabin had tattooed on his wrist. The Air elemental's symbol. Her mark. Her calling card. I recognized the rune immediately—and what it really was.

"Son of a bitch," I said. "A shark's tooth. The rune is a fucking shark's tooth."

Haley James wasn't the Air elemental. Her sister was. Alexis was the one who'd tortured Fletcher, who'd been on her way to do the same thing to Donovan Caine. Alexis James was the one who'd been pulling the strings of Charles Carlyle and Wayne Stephenson. She was the bitch who'd set up this whole thing.

"What are you muttering about?" Finn asked. "Some of us are trying to concentrate."

I slapped the photo down on the table and tapped my finger on the necklace. "This—this is what I'm muttering about."

Both men leaned forward to stare at the picture. They spotted it at the same time.

"Is that—" Finn started.

"That looks like—" Donovan Caine chimed in.

"You bet it is," I snarled, cutting them both off. "That's the tooth. The Air elemental's precious rune. Alexis James is the one running the show, not her sister, Haley."

We sat there digesting the information. The cold knot of rage in my chest started beating like a clock, a slow, steady countdown to Alexis James's death. *Tick-fucking-tock.*

"But what about the files? The ones that implicate Haley James?" Donovan Caine asked.

We both looked at Finn.

"Alexis could be using her sister's log-in information," Finn said. "Wouldn't be hard for her to do."

"Or Haley could be handling the money, while Alexis does the dirty work," Donovan replied. "Alexis could even be making her steal, threatening her with magic."

"Doesn't matter to me either way," I said. "They're both going to die."

Donovan Caine shook his head. "No. You can't kill Haley James, not if she's innocent."

"Her sister's running around town using her magic to torture people. How innocent do you think Haley is?" I snapped.

The detective's eyes burned into mine. "Haley James could be as up to her neck in it as Finn is with you. Or she could be as innocent as that little girl playing in her princess castle while her madam of an aunt looked on. Until we know for sure, you can't touch her. Remember our agreement? No innocent people. This isn't negotiable, Gin. Not this time."

"Why? Because she's not a lowlife hood you've busted before?"

"Something like that."

The detective and I stared at each other. His eyes blazed gold with determination. Cold fury grayed mine out. Neither one of us looked away, and neither one of us was willing to give an inch. Still, despite myself, I liked sparring with the detective. Liked pushing him, liked him pushing back at me. Strength, conviction, and passion were traits I'd always admired, no matter how misguided they were in this case.

"There are other things to consider," Finn said in a cautious voice.

"Like what?" the detective asked, his eyes still locked on mine.

"Like that photo and bounty on Gin that's still float-ing around," Finn replied. "The fact the elemental wants you dead, detective. And your esteemed police captain, Wayne Stephenson."

"Stephenson's mine," Donovan Caine snapped, his gaze flicking to the other man. "I'll deal with him myself."

"How? By turning him in to internal affairs? That's the most crooked department on the whole force. He'll just bribe his way out of whatever charge they might bring against him," Finn replied.

Donovan's jaw tightened. "I don't know how yet, but I'll find a way."

I sighed. Bickering among ourselves wasn't getting us anywhere, but I knew from the tone of his voice Finn had something in mind. "What are you proposing?"

Finn smiled and put his arms behind his head. "Leverage."

"Leverage? How is that going to help us?" the detective asked.

Finn pulled the flash drive out of his laptop and held it up. "Because we've got this, and Alexis James doesn't. Now, Alexis might not be afraid of us, but there is one person she doesn't want to see this information. At least not yet. Not until she's finalized her coup de grâce."

"Mab Monroe," I said, picking up on his train of thought.

Finn nodded. "Mab Monroe."

"I still don't understand how that helps us," Donovan said.

"Blackmail," I replied. "We threaten to turn the information over to Mab unless Alexis James backs off and stops trying to kill us."

"We can also get her to withdraw the reward money

on you and convince Wayne Stephenson to take an early retirement," Finn said. "You have to admit, it's neat, all the way around."

He grinned, extremely pleased with himself. I rolled my eyes, but I couldn't disagree with him. Finn had occasional flashes of brilliance and coming up with this kind of compromise was one of them.

"Alexis James is still going to die for what she did to my handler. There will be no argument about that. No threats and no hunting me down after the fact," I said. "Can you live with that, detective? If so, I can live with the rest of what Finn's proposing. The bounty on me goes away, you bounce Stephenson out of the department, and we all get on with our lives."

Donovan Caine's hazel gaze darkened, and he stared into my gray eyes. After a moment, he nodded his head. "I can live with that. The question is how are we going to do it?"

"Easy," Finn said. "We sidle up to Alexis in a public place, drop the bomb on her, and wait for her to give in to our demands."

I shook my head. "Not Alexis, Haley. We go through Haley James."

Donovan frowned. "Why?"

"Because if she is involved, I get to add her to my list of things to do," I said. "And if she's not, well, she can start ducking for cover. That's what you let innocent people do, right?"

The detective didn't answer.

"So now all we have to do is find out where the sisters are going to be," Finn said.

"One step ahead of you." I pulled out my cell phone and hit another one of the speed dial numbers.

The phone rang four times before she picked it up.

"Do y'all know what time it is?" Jo-Jo Deveraux muttered in my ear, although her slow, syrupy drawl took some of the bite out of her words.

I glanced at the clock on the wall. "It's Gin, and it's 3:07. I need some information and possibly a couple of invitations. Think you can handle it?"

Jo-Jo laughed. "For you, darling? Anything."

❋24❋

At four o'clock the next afternoon, I found myself in the elegant confines of Five Oaks, the snobbiest, most exclusive, and most highfalutin country club in Ashland.

Jo-Jo Deveraux had called earlier in the day with the info I'd needed—the next event on the James sisters' social calendar. Haley and Alexis, along with five hundred other invited guests, were due to attend an afternoon fund-raiser for a battered-women's shelter that was being held at the country club. Jo-Jo had pulled a few of her drama mama strings and managed to secure invitations for Donovan Caine and me. Finn had already been invited, given the fact he moved money around for most of those in attendance.

Now I stood in the club's spacious main ballroom, watching the flow of people and waiting for the James sisters to arrive. Five Oaks was a massive complex of five circular buildings, and the ballroom was in keeping with the grand scale of things. The round room itself was several thousand feet wide and soared four stories into the air. A glass dome formed the ceiling, letting natural light stream down onto the club's members. Multiple sets of stairs led up to the upper levels, each of which featured a balcony that ringed the entire ballroom.

Floor-to-ceiling glass windows lined the curve of the back wall, along with two large doors that led out onto a wide stone patio. The impressive view showed off the club's smaller outbuildings, a series of acorn-shaped pools, tennis courts, and the smooth, green expanse, beige sand traps, and tall, colorful flags of the golf course.

People, clustered in small groups, talked, laughed, and sipped mint juleps on the main floor. Some had wandered up to have more private conversations on the second floor balcony. Others had taken their drinks and planted themselves at tables covered with pale peach linens. The country club's rune—an acorn—was stitched in gold thread in the center of each tablecloth. The event was going to feature a sit-down dinner later, but the booze and bullshit were already flowing.

I spotted several prominent vampires, elementals, dwarves, and giants in the crowd, each one doing their best to make their importance known to everyone else in attendance. But no one shone brighter than Mab Monroe. The Fire elemental looked polished and glamorous in a floor-length canary yellow gown. A fringed shawl covered her bare arms, and the ruby in her sunburst rune necklace flashed against her cleavage. Mab had planted herself in the exact center of the ballroom. People stood three deep around her, jockeying to get a moment of her attention. But Mab's giant guards for the evening kept the unwanted commoners from getting too close.

The other two members of the triangle of trouble were in attendance as well—Mab's lawyer, Jonah McAllister, and her enforcer, Elliot Slater. With his silver hair, snazzy suit, and capped teeth, McAllister looked every bit like the smooth talker he was. Slater's seven-foot figure loomed large over the crowd. A diamond bigger than an eye winked on the giant's pinkie.

I stood near the back wall, just on the fringes of a group of businessmen dressed in dark suits. A few of them shot me appreciative looks, but the frigid chill in my gray eyes kept them from approaching me. At least until they'd had a few more drinks.

To blend in with the rich folks, I'd donned a simple but elegant black wrap dress Jo-Jo had given me for Christmas last year. The garment was made of a loose-knit material and featured long, billowing sleeves that hid my knives. The material fell to my knees, allowing me to strap two more blades to my thighs. My purse held another knife. Black stilettos covered my feet, and I'd twisted my hair into a high ponytail, complete with two razor-sharp chopsticks.

My cell phone rang, and I plucked it out of my purse. One of the businessmen eyed me.

"My husband," I said in a pleasant voice. "The giant. Such a protective man. Likes to know where I am all the time—and who I'm with."

He gulped and turned his attention back to his drink. Evidently I didn't look fuckable enough to risk tangling with a jealous giant.

I stepped a few feet away from the group of men and opened my phone. "Any sign of them?"

"Not yet," Donovan Caine replied. "Although Finn seems to be enjoying himself at the bar."

I looked across the ballroom. After we'd entered the country club, we'd split up. Together, we were too noticeable, too much of a target. It was easier and safer to get lost in the crowd. Finnegan Lane had ensconced himself at the bar just inside the main entrance. Like every other man on the premises, he wore a tailored suit. The classic cut of the navy fabric highlighted Finn's broad shoulders, while the light filtering through the glass roof made his brown hair gleam. He was currently chatting up a dwarf dripping with diamonds. The woman had to be over four hundred by the looks of her wrinkled skin, rheumy eyes, and snow-white hair. Probably some client of his.

Finn saw me staring. He winked, raised his glass in salute, and went back to his conversation. Very little could distract him when he was working or entertaining a lady—no matter how old she was. Finn might not sleep with the old ones, but he enjoyed charming them as much as he did the young stuff.

"Finn always has a good time at these things," I murmured. "Sometimes I think he should have been born a woman so he could be a true debutante."

Donovan chuckled through the phone. A low sound that warmed me from the inside out.

My eyes drifted up to the second floor. Donovan Caine leaned over the balcony above my head, his phone against his ear. The detective wore one of Finn's suits in a blue color so pale it was almost silver. Caine's shoulders weren't quite as wide as Finn's, so the jacket didn't drape perfectly. But I'd felt the strength in his lean muscles at the nightclub. He'd forgone a tie in favor of undoing the top button of his white dress shirt, which let more of his bronze skin peek through. Classic, rugged, sexy. Donovan Caine looked good enough to eat. Mmm.

Our eyes met, gold on gray. Not for the first time, I fantasized about having my way with the detective. About feeling his mouth on mine, his hands on my body, the hard length of him moving inside me. Just the idea made me ache.

Donovan Caine stared down at me. His hazel eyes darkened to the color of smoked whiskey as his gaze went from my breasts to my legs and back up again. His gaze met mine, but this time he didn't look away. Emotions flashed in his eyes like lightning. Desire. Want. Need. Guilt. The detective was thinking about how much he wanted me. About how our time together was coming to an end, and soon he'd officially have to go back to hating me. Donovan was thinking about how much he'd like to take what he could get today and hate himself for it tomorrow.

Me too. In that moment, I made my decision. The detective was going to be mine.

Before the evening was through.

Something caught Donovan's attention, and he glanced down. "There's Haley James. Just coming into the ballroom."

I moved to my right, farther away from the business-men, so I could see Haley. She wore a short gold cocktail dress that set off her pale skin and blue-green eyes. The garment was a little risqué for this early in the day, cut almost to her belly button in the front, with her cleavage swelling on either side of the severe V. Her strawberry-blonde hair was swept up into a chignon, and large diamond studs winked in her ears.

Finn had spotted Haley James too. He turned more toward the dwarf he was talking to, presenting his back to the rest of the room, although he cocked his head to one side so he could still see Haley. Unless things got out of hand, Finn's job was to sit at the bar and keep an eye on the sisters. I wanted to know how Haley and Alexis reacted after I dropped the flash drive bomb on them.

"I see Haley," I told Donovan. "Where's Alexis?"

"Right behind her."

I looked past Haley to see Alexis James stepping into the ballroom. Like me, Alexis wore a little black dress with matching pumps. The usual strand of pearls circled her throat and wrist, although she'd added a couple more ropes around her neck. My free hand curled into a tight fist. I'd like to choke the bitch with her own pearls, but that would be too good for her. Too easy a way for her to die. I might kill people quickly on jobs, but this went beyond business—this was personal. Alexis James was going to suffer every bit as much as Fletcher had.

And then some.

But the James sisters weren't alone. Captain Wayne Stephenson shuffled in the door behind them. The pudgy giant wore a white suit that made him look even wider than he really was. Even though the room was air-conditioned, Stephenson dabbed at the sheen of sweat on his forehead with one of his white handkerchiefs. Just being within sight of Alexis probably made him nervous. Two more men wearing dark suits stepped inside the ballroom behind the giant. One of them was Charles Carlyle's friend from the Cake Walk. The other man had been with Alexis the night she'd gone to Donovan Caine's cabin. They both stuck close to Stephenson, like ducks waddling after their mother. More of Alexis James's flunkies. So now she was taking her entourage out in public with her. Interesting.

Stephenson and the two goons were unimportant at this point, so I stayed on the phone with Donovan and watched the women, waiting for my chance to get Haley alone. It took the sisters about five minutes to maneuver past the bottleneck of people in front of the entrance. But once they did, they split up. Alexis waved at someone and headed in that direction. Stephenson and the two men also drifted that way. Haley grabbed a mint julep from one of the passing waiters and moved to sit at an unoccupied table near the center of the room. Perfect.

"Here I go," I said, glancing up at Donovan Caine.

Caine nodded. "Good luck."

I smiled. "I don't need luck, detective. I have something better—leverage."

Cell phone in hand, I headed for Haley James. It took me the better part of two minutes to stalk across the ballroom carpet. My stilettos poked holes into the plush fabric, killing it one step at a time. Just like I was going to do to Alexis James in the near future. But I reached Haley without incident and dropped into the seat next to her. Alexis stood about fifty feet away, firmly entrenched in a group of people. She didn't notice me cozying up to her sister. Neither did Wayne Stephenson or the other two men, who stood behind Alexis. Good.

My sudden appearance startled Haley James, and she jerked back in her seat, almost knocking over her mint julep. Her wide blue-green eyes met my narrowed gray ones. The cold knot of rage twitched in my chest, and for a moment, my emotions threatened to overwhelm me. Anger, rage, disgust. Part of me wanted to palm one of my knives, stab Haley, and melt away in the bloody, screaming confusion. Let Alexis feel the loss of her sister as keenly as I did Fletcher's death, if the Air elemental bitch could feel anything besides glee at torturing people.

But I'd promised Donovan Caine that I'd give the other woman a chance to prove her innocence. And I didn't go back on my word. No matter how much I might want to.

So I laid my cell phone on the table and smiled at the other woman. "Hello, Haley."

She frowned. "Do I know you?"

I amped up my smile. "Well, sugar, we haven't officially met, but I'm sort of on your payroll. Your sister, Alexis, hired me to kill Gordon Giles."

It took a couple of seconds for my words to sink in. Haley frowned again, replaying what I'd said in her mind. An innocent woman, one who knew nothing about anything, would have vehemently denied the allegation. Been shocked and outraged by the accusation. Would have already been screaming bloody murder about sitting next to a self-proclaimed assassin. Instead, Haley's face shuttered, and her eyes narrowed to slits. Oh yeah, she was in this all right—up to her fucking neck.

"What the hell are you doing here?" she asked. "What do you want? Money?"

I laughed. The harsh, mocking sound made several people turn around and stare at me.

"Money," I sneered. "Do you think you can buy me off so easily? After what your sister's done? I don't think so."

Haley raised a sculpted eyebrow. "You were perfectly willing to take money to kill Gordon Giles."

I leaned forward. "That was before your sister decided to double-cross me. That was before Alexis tortured the old man at the barbecue joint. Before she had her goons beat my friend almost to death. Before she decided to kill the police detective to avoid any loose ends."

Since her offer of money had failed, Haley decided to try another tactic. She opened her eyes a little wider, as though her brave front was finally cracking. I had to give her credit, she changed direction smoothly. "This wasn't my idea, you have to believe me. Alexis is the one behind it all. She forced me to go along with her. To go along with everything."

"Nice act," I said. "Convenient too, to blame your sister for everything. But in case you haven't noticed, I ran out of mercy a long time ago. Guilt by association works just fine for me."

Haley let her lower lip quiver. "It's not an act. Alexis threatened me. Threatened to hurt me, kill me if I didn't do exactly what she wanted."

"Really?" I asked. "Is that why your log-in and password information are linked to the embezzled accounts? Because Alexis forced you to steal all that money from your own company?"

She nodded and swiped at the corner of her eye, as though brushing away a tear. Southern women might know a thing or two about melodrama, but Haley was laying it on thicker than frosting on a cake.

I snorted. "Sugar, you are a terrible liar. I've seen better acting from the vampire hookers on the Southtown streets."

Haley studied me a moment. Once she saw I wasn't buying her act, her face hardened once more. Back to playing the tough girl. Too bad I really was one.

"I know why you wanted Gordon Giles dead. He was going to go to the police about the embezzling, and you just couldn't have that. But there is one thing I am curious about," I said. "What's been the point of all this? Surely, you don't really think the two of you can dethrone Mab Monroe just by stealing a few million bucks?"

Haley shrugged. "That's Alexis's dream, not mine. She's the one who enjoys playing Mob queen with her Air elemental magic. Alexis thinks her magic makes her more powerful than it really does."

"So why?" I asked. "Why support her pipe dream?"

Haley's eyes flashed with hatred. "Because Mab Monroe stole our father's company, his pride and joy, bought up the stock right out from under him. But that wasn't enough for her. Daddy was fighting the takeover, fighting her, and she killed him. She told us she did and said if we wanted to keep on breathing, we'd better go along with her. That was two *years* ago. And now the bitch orders us around, tells us what to do, as if we don't know our own company better than she ever could. I'm just taking back what's mine. And if Alexis does manage to kill her, well, all the better. Maybe then our father can rest in peace."

The venom in her voice would have made most people drop dead. I imagine Mab Monroe would have only found it mildly irritating. So Alexis was the one with delusions of magical grandeur. Haley was just going along with her sister's plan so she could steal. Nice family.

"What the fuck do you want?" Haley snapped. "I assume there's a point to this meeting."

"I want you and your sister to walk away," I said. "Withdraw the reward money Halo Industries is offering for information about me. Get Alexis to call off her men, including Captain Wayne Stephenson. Finnegan Lane and Donovan Caine, the men your sister wants to torture and kill, they walk, too. We all walk away and keep breathing. And you can keep right on skimming millions off the top from your own company. I don't give a fuck about you stealing from Mab Monroe because you weren't smart enough to hang on to your own business."

She wouldn't be stealing that much longer, because I was going to put a knife in Haley's gut and cut Alexis every which way I knew how as soon as the sisters lowered their guard. I'd play the blackmail card now to get Finn and Donovan Caine free of this mess, but the bitches were going to die for what they'd done to Fletcher. Besides, they'd double-crossed me first. It was only fair.

Haley's face tightened at my insult, but she knew I wasn't finished. "Or else?"

I stared at her, my gray eyes as cold and hard as ice.

"Tell me, have you or Alexis heard from Charles Carlyle today?"

She didn't say anything.

I smiled. "I had the opportunity to speak with Chuck last night. He didn't say much, of course, but I did find something interesting in his possession—Gordon Giles's flash drive. Seems Chuck stumbled across it and decided to keep it for himself as insurance against Alexis turning on him. Of course, he won't be using it now, but he was nice enough to pass it on to me before he died."

For the first time, true panic sparked in Haley's bluegreen eyes.

"I read through the files. That's how I knew your login information was the one used to steal the money." I pointed across the ballroom to where Mab Monroe was still holding court. "Now, I could just go ahead and give the information to Mab. I'm sure she'd be *very* interested in learning more about your embezzlement, since she's your company's major stockholder. What do you think?"

The smallest gasp escaped from Haley's tight lips. Her face paled, and her forehead gleamed with the beginnings of a nervous sweat. Her control was starting to crack. "You—you can't tell Mab anything. She'll kill us, just like she did Daddy."

"I can do whatever the hell I want, Haley. I'm the one with the flash drive. Why, I could walk over to Mab Monroe this minute." I raised my arm as if to wave to the Fire elemental. "I'm sure I could get her attention—"

"No!" Haley grabbed my arm, trying to lower it.

Haley's shout echoed through the ballroom, overpowering the din of conversation. Several people turned to see what all the fuss was about, including Mab Monroe. The Fire elemental spotted me pointing at her and Haley clutching my arm. Mab frowned, but I just smiled and waggled my fingers at her, as though we were old friends. After a moment, Mab lifted her hand and waved back, even though she couldn't possibly know who the hell I was or why I was waving at her like a loon. Mab crooked her finger at Elliot Slater and whispered something in his ear. Slater snapped his fingers, and another one of Mab's giant guards walked over to them. Time to wrap this up.

"Think over my offer, Haley," I said. "I'm only going to make it this one time."

"You don't understand," she hissed. "Alexis is the one who wanted Gordon dead, not me. I wanted to pay him off, but she wouldn't hear of it. Said she wanted to teach him a lesson for turning on her. It was all I could do to convince her to hire an assassin, instead of doing it herself and getting caught. It would have been fine, if she'd just listened to me. But Alexis always complicates things. She had to get fancy and set you up, even though I told her it wasn't necessary, that it might backfire. But she didn't want Mab sniffing around us or the company. Not yet. Not before she's ready to make her move."

"And you're boring me with this because . . ."

"Because Alexis won't take what you're offering now," Haley replied in a shaky voice. "She won't back down, not from you, not from anybody. Before Daddy died, Alexis never threw her Air magic around. Nobody even knew she had any, except for the family. But after he died, she changed. Started using her magic for every-thing, started practicing with it so she could go after

Mab. Her magic . . . it's made her reckless, crazy. I can't reason with her anymore."

I gave her a cold look. "Then I suggest you try harder, Haley. Or you're the one who's going to be feeling Mab Monroe's wrath. I imagine she can torture you much longer than Alexis did the old man at the restaurant. Mab's had a lot more practice at that sort of thing. She could probably keep you alive for *days*."

Haley blanched, and her face took on a greenish hue, as though she wanted to vomit.

I plucked a business card out of my purse and held it out to her. The number for my cell phone was scribbled across it. "You have an hour to get Alexis on board, call me at this number, and agree to my demands. After that, well, who knows what will happen?"

Haley James snatched the card from my hand with trembling fingers and clutched it to her heaving chest. I gave her the hard stare another moment, then grabbed my cell phone, got to my feet, and strolled away.

✻ 25 ✻

I moved through the high-class crowd with ease, slinking my way past one group after another, and held the cell phone up to my ear.

"Did you hear all that, detective?"

"Yeah," Donovan Caine said in a grim tone. "I heard her."

I hadn't cut the connection with the detective because I'd wanted him to hear exactly what Haley James had to say for herself. That way, I couldn't be accused of putting words in her mouth—or compounding her guilt. Haley had made it abundantly clear she was okay with whatever Alexis wanted to do, as long as she got to keep stealing from her own company. The only time she'd shown any emotion other than haughtiness was when I'd told her I had the flash drive and that I was thinking about giving it to Mab Monroe.

Then she'd panicked. Nobody wanted to face the Fire elemental's wrath, not even someone as greedy as Haley James. She was probably running through the crowd right now, looking for Alexis, trying to think of some way to get her sister to meet my demands so she could save her own skin.

Haley wasn't the only one scurrying through the ballroom. So was one of Mab Monroe's guards.

Evidently I'd acted like too much of a loon before, and Mab wanted to know who I was—and why I'd been talking to Haley James. Her giant swept through the crowd after me like Sherman marching through Atlanta. I didn't dare turn around, but I heard the mutters of the people he bowled out of his way. I picked up my pace, darting around groups of people and shimmying around the waiters. I was quick, but the giant was bigger. It was only a matter of time before he caught up with me. Before his beefy hand clamped on my shoulder and he escorted me outside the ballroom for a little private chat—maybe even with Mab herself. A complication I didn't need right now.

"You've got a tail," Donovan's voice sounded in my ear.

"No shit," I said. "Where are you?"

"Same place as before. Middle of the second floor, leaning over the railing."

I glanced up. The detective was exactly where he'd said he was. He'd undone another button on his white dress shirt, and he looked sexy and rumpled in the afternoon light. Mmm. Too bad I didn't have time to enjoy the view.

"I see you," I said. "Find us someplace to hide from the giant. Empty room, supply closet, whatever. I'll be up there in a minute."

"Got it."

Caine turned and moved away from the balcony. My eyes swept over the crowd, looking for something I could use to slow down the giant. The mutters behind me grew louder. A minute, maybe less, before he'd catch me. My gaze landed on a waiter not so steadily carrying a full tray of mint juleps. Perfect.

I slowed my steps to get my timing just right. The waiter brushed past me, and I kicked his ankle as hard as I could with the point of my stiletto. He shrieked at the unexpected pain. I kept right on going, but the waiter went down like a dead man. His tray tipped over, and alcohol showered on everyone within a three-foot radius. A few icy drops spattered against my back.

For a moment there was horrified silence. In the next second, a mob of angry people converged on the guy, screaming and berating the poor man for being so clumsy. The throng was so tight, even the giant couldn't shoulder through it. While he tried to work his way around the tables and harridans shrieking about their alcohol-soaked dresses, I climbed up a set of stairs to the second floor and walked back the way I'd just come, weaving in and out of the clusters of people on this level. Below me, Mab Monroe looked at the crush of guests and frowned. She knew something had gone wrong. She just didn't know what yet.

I lowered my head, moved away from the balcony, and kept walking, not so fast as to call attention to myself, but not dawdling either. I held the phone back up to my ear. "Where are you?"

"Supply closet. Hang a left at the end of the hallway. Second door on your right."

I made the appropriate turn. This hallway was deserted, so I opened the door, stepped inside, and shut it behind me. Caine waited inside, leaning on a metal rack full of toilet paper. I leaned against the wood and let out a long breath.

"That was close."

"Too close," Caine agreed.

"What about Haley?" I asked the detective. "What did she do after I confronted her?"

"Nothing much," Caine said. "She sat there for a moment, looking at your back; then she got up and scurried off into the crowd."

Going to find Alexis, just like I'd thought she would.

"Now what?" Caine asked.

"Now we stay in here until Mab and her guard lose interest in me and Haley James calls," I said. "Neither one should take too long."

I moved past the detective. Besides the metal rack he leaned against, there wasn't much in the closet. A mop and a bucket. Several boxes of plastic gloves. A ratty love seat that had been salvaged from one of the club's salons. I dialed Finn on my cell phone. He answered on the second ring.

"You really should have stuck around," he said. "That waiter you tripped is still getting screamed at. Sounds like a flock of crows cawing to each other."

"Where are you?" I asked.

"Still at the bar," Finn replied. "Talking to Grace."

Finn must have winked at her, because through the phone, I heard a woman laugh. The sort of high, squawking sound the wicked witch always made in fairy-tale movies. Must be the old, wizened dwarf I'd seen him with before.

"Grace says hello," Finn replied.

"Good for Grace," I snapped. "Want to tell me what's going on down there?"

Finn sighed. "Can't you ever just relax and enjoy the show?"

"No. Now tell me what happened after I left Haley. The detective said she got up and ran off into the crowd."

"Straight to Alexis," Finn said. "Haley pulled her sister outside onto the patio. The two of them are talking right now. Alexis does not look pleased. Stephenson's with them too. Poor bastard looks faint. Keeps mopping his forehead with his handkerchief."

I smiled. Good. About time the bitch realized who she was dealing with. "Keep an eye on them, but don't let them see you. If they start to leave, call me. Don't follow them."

"Yes, master," Finn sniped. "And don't worry. Grace will keep me company."

Finn hung up, and I did the same. I set my cell phone on the metal rack, right next to the toilet paper. Then I went over to the love seat and plopped down on it. The cushions squawked under my weight, and a loose spring poked me in the ass. I shifted, but I couldn't get away from the offensive metal.

Donovan Caine pushed away from the rack and paced

back and forth, taking five quick steps from one side of the closet to the other. His shoes squeaked on the floor, and I felt the beginnings of a headache stir behind my eyes.

"Are you going to pace for the next hour?" I said. "Because it's already gotten on my last nerve."

The detective didn't say anything; he just kept pacing. His quick, controlled movements caught my gaze, and my eyes traced over his shoulders. His clean, soapy scent filled the closet, overpowering the burning smell of disinfectant. I remembered the last time we'd been in such close proximity—last night at Northern Aggression. How hard Donovan Caine had felt against me. How much I'd wanted to finish what we started. And there was the promise I'd made to myself. To take what I could today before the detective and I said good-bye tomorrow.

I checked the watch on my wrist. Fifty minutes. Plenty of time. Finn was downstairs keeping watch and schmoozing the elderly dwarf, and we were safe enough up here. Haley and Alexis James should be scrambling, trying to figure out what to do, how to answer my demands. That had been the whole point of blindsiding them in public. They weren't a threat to us right now. As for the giant, it would take him hours to search the country club, if he even bothered. Mab Monroe had probably called him back to her side already, considering the mess I'd made getting away from him.

Donovan Caine and I had fifty long minutes all to ourselves. My eyes slid down the detective's body. I couldn't think of a more pleasurable way to pass the time.

I cleared my throat. Donovan stopped his pacing to look at me.

"You know if the James sisters agree to our demands, this is over. Tomorrow, we'll all go back to our regularly scheduled lives," I said. "Finn. You. Me."

Donovan nodded. "I know."

He stared at me, emotions sliding over his face. Desire. Want. Need. Guilt. His hazel eyes devoured me, moving from my lips to my breasts and legs and back up again. But he made no move to come toward me. No move to take what he so clearly wanted. Up to me, then.

I got to my feet and slowly approached him. My stilettos clacked on the floor. Donovan flinched at the sound, but he didn't look away from me. He couldn't, any more than I could stop coming at him.

I stopped about a foot in front of the detective. My gray gaze drifted over his body, as his had done to mine a moment before. Lean shoulders, solid chest, coiled strength. I liked what I saw.

"You're an attractive man, detective," I said. "I'm an attractive woman. And here we are, all alone. Together."

He didn't say anything. Didn't take the opening. So I continued.

"Yesterday, when we were at the nightclub, when I was sitting on your lap, I didn't want to stop. I wanted to tear your jeans off, wanted to feel you inside me, going deeper and deeper until we were both screaming. Didn't you?"

A muscle in his cheek twitched. Still, Donovan didn't move.

"Despite our differences, I'm attracted to you, detective. Something about you fascinates me. I want you like I haven't wanted anybody in a long time. I think you feel the same way about me."

For a moment, I thought he wouldn't answer. But he did. "I do want you."

His voice was low, tight, strained. The confession cost him. It was all he could do to keep from reaching for me. Good thing I had no qualms about making the first move.

I stepped into his arms and put my hands on his shoulders. Then I raised my head and gazed into his hazel eyes. "So, why don't we do something about it?"

✶26✶

Caine stared at me. "Not a good idea, Gin. We're here for a reason, remember? To get the James sisters to back off. Nothing else. They could be looking for us."

Wild desperation colored his eyes. Caine was trying to save himself, but I wasn't going to let him.

"A poor excuse. Haley and Alexis are too busy arguing about what to do right now. Even if they weren't, they wouldn't find us. They probably think we left the club already to go somewhere and wait for their call. Until then, we've got nothing but time."

I leaned up and put my mouth beside his ear. Caine's shoulders jerked underneath my hands. He was on the edge.

"If you're worried about protection, well, I take my little white pills, so there won't be any unwanted consequences. And I assume you have a condom or two in your wallet like most men." I drew in a deep breath. "As for the issues between us, I don't care that we'll be on opposite sides again tomorrow. After everything that's happened, I want what I can have today. I want you, detective. Right here, right now."

I pressed my lips to his.

It was like I'd shocked him with a live wire. He just—exploded. Donovan Caine let out a growl and yanked me to him. He turned me around and backed me against the wall, his hands bunching up the soft fabric of my dress. The detective crushed his lips against mine. This time, I didn't have to tease his mouth open. His tongue was already thrusting against mine. I welcomed the sensation.

His smell—that intoxicating, sharp scent of soap—filled my nose. Shredding my own control. My hands were everywhere. His face, neck, chest. Kneading, clutching, wanting more. Wanting to feel every inch of him at once. Trying to hang on to something that would be gone the second we left this room.

Once he had my dress out of the way, Donovan Caine reached for my panties. He ripped them off in one motion and plunged two fingers inside me. I moaned, already wet and aching for him. I hooked one leg around his waist, giving him better access. Caine pumped his fingers inside me in a quick, steady rhythm, going deeper every time. He groaned with me.

"I've wanted to do that since the first moment I saw you on that balcony," he whispered against my lips. "Wanted to feel you."

"Then don't stop." My voice was husky with desire. "Don't stop."

Our mouths and tongues came together again, even as Donovan stroked me.

There was too much tension, too much feeling, too much need, between us to wait any longer. Donovan's free hand fumbled with his pants, getting his wallet out of them before the fabric whispered to the floor. I tried to push down his boxers, but the black silk snagged on his jutting erection. Frustrated, I ripped open the flap, freeing him, while he tore open the foil packet with his teeth and covered himself with the condom.

"Now," I rasped. "*Now*."

Caine picked me up, and I wrapped my legs around his waist. He pushed me back against the wall and slammed his cock into me, thrusting into me as hard and fast as he could. In a frenzy now. We both were.

I moaned again at the slick feel of him moving deeper and deeper inside me. My nails dug into his shoulders. Every time, he thrust in, I clenched myself around him, tighter every time, getting closer to the orgasm I so desperately craved. To that sweet release. Caine buried his head against my neck. The metal rack next to us shook and rattled with our movements.

It all felt so damn good it hurt.

But it was over too quick. Less then a minute later, Caine jerked a final time and shuddered against me, finding his release. I felt him deflate and slip out. So much for stamina. I'd pushed him too hard, too fast. He was done, but I still ached with hot, throbbing need. And it wasn't going to go unfulfilled.

"I'm—I'm sorry." Caine lowered me to the floor and stepped back. "That was too rough."

"It wasn't too rough," I said. "But we're not finished yet."

I put my hands on Caine's shoulders and maneuvered

him over to the love seat. His knees hit the back of it, and he plopped down on the spring-filled cushions. I straddled him, getting rid of the used condom and then taking his thick length in my hands. His breath quickened against my neck.

"Come on, detective. Rise back to the occasion." I teased his wet tip with the sharp point of my fingernail.

"Is that a challenge?" His voice was thick and husky with sex. His hands moved to my waist, drawing me closer.

I got up on my knees and rubbed his cock against my core. "More like an incentive."

It didn't take long for the detective to spring back to life and produce another condom from his wallet. This time, it was my turn to be on top. I set the pace, riding him long and slow, going up, then grinding down on him, a little deeper, a little quicker every time until he was muttering my name over and over. *Gin, Gin, Gin.* Like it was some sort of prayer—or a curse. Sexiest damn thing I'd ever heard.

Caine groaned. His hands went to my breasts, massaging them through the fabric of my dress and bra, making me ache that much more. His lips were against my neck, and he teased me with quick nips of his teeth. I braced my hands on his shoulders, urging him on. The lean, ropy muscles there bunched and coiled just like he did inside me. My own muscles clenched and quickened in response. The pressure inside me built and built.

I threw back my head and let the orgasm rip me away from myself.

*   *   *

After we finished, we sat there on the love seat. Shoulders touching, one of my bare legs just on top of his. Not entwined exactly, but not distant from each other either. I would have liked to put my head on his shoulder, close my eyes, and relax. Let myself fully enjoy this brief moment of peaceful pleasure. But I couldn't do that. The sex had been personal enough already. We hadn't made love, but we hadn't just fucked either. The beginning of a warm softness for the detective had blossomed in my chest. But I didn't want to think too much about that right now.

I'd been right about one thing, though. Donovan Caine was an excellent lover. I felt more sated than I had in a long time. There was something to be said about the experience of an older man, rather than the college boys I usually slept with. The young ones were just grateful they were getting laid—they weren't too interested in doing anything to scare me off. Like fucking me hard and fast the way Donovan had. Or letting me do the same to them.

The detective started laughing. Sharp chortles of laughter tumbled from his lips until the force of it bent him over double, his chest touching his knees.

"What's so funny?" I asked.

"This. Us. You. Me. Together."

I arched an eyebrow. "I didn't think it was so much funny as satisfying. Was I wrong?"

Caine wiped tears of hysterical mirth from his flushed face. "Oh, no. It was definitely satisfying. But you're an assassin, you kill people, you killed my partner. I'm a detective, a cop, supposedly one of the good guys, and I just fucked you. Twice."

"So what's the problem?"

Donovan Caine eyed me. "You really are cold, aren't you? With nothing but ice in your veins and a slab of stone for a heart."

Cliché alert. But the detective's well-worn words described me—more than he'd ever realize.

"Don't you understand what I've done?" Caine asked. "I've gone against everything I believe in. And for what? You?"

He was pulling away from me. I'd known it was coming, but it still pricked me like a needle. I willed the softness in my chest to harden, and my cold mask settled over my face once more.

"You don't believe in fucking women?" I kept my tone light, trying to salvage something from this. A little bit of happiness I could remember later.

He ran his hand through his short, black hair, rumpling it even further. "That's not the point. I should be arresting you, turning you in for your crimes, not wondering if I have enough juice left in me for round three."

I shrugged. "We both had a good time. Why are you bringing morals into it? Because there was nothing very saintly and upstanding about the way you were moaning my name five minutes ago."

Caine stiffened, but he couldn't argue with the truth. Still, the aching need, the hot pleasure, the sweet release, was wearing off, and the old doubts were filling his eyes, along with one emotion he just couldn't quite shake— guilt about fucking his partner's killer. The detective wasn't going to get over it. Not today, maybe not ever.

I suppose I could have told him about Cliff Ingles and

how dirty the other cop had been. But I didn't know that it would change things between us. Donovan's partner would still be dead, and I would still be the one who'd killed him.

All of which meant that the honeymoon was over already. A shame, really.

I swung my leg off his and got to my feet.

"What are you doing?" Donovan asked, his eyes fixed on my bare legs.

"Getting dressed," I said in a cold voice. "It's almost time for the sisters to call. I suggest you do the same."

I shoved my ripped panties into my purse and pulled my dress back down into the appropriate position. Beside me, Donovan Caine zipped up his pants. We didn't speak to each other. I grabbed my cell phone and slid it back into my purse. Then I cautiously opened the door to the supply closet. Nobody lingered in the hall. Mab must have called her giant back to her side. Good.

We left the cramped closet, walked around the second-floor balcony, and took a different set of stairs down to the ballroom floor. The crowd had grown during the better part of the hour we'd been gone, and now the people and conversation buzzed like horseflies. It took me a moment, but I spotted Finn still sitting at the bar. His companion had changed, though. Instead of the old dwarf, a young, attractive Asian woman smiled and let him ply her with drinks. I jerked my head at Finn. Donovan nodded, and we headed that way.

"Do you see the sisters?" Donovan Caine murmured.

I glanced at him. A hard mask had settled over the detective's face, pushing the guilt from his eyes. The detective was putting aside his conflicting feelings long enough to get the job done. What a professional.

I started to say no, when a flash of gold caught my eye. Haley James. The petite woman's eyes were fixed on the ballroom exit. Her mouth hung open as though she was gasping for breath as she power-walked in that direction. She was moving so fast I didn't see how she was keeping her feet in her strappy sandals. Her actions made it seem almost like someone was chasing her. One moment she was there, the next, she had disappeared. I scanned the crowd looking for Alexis.

There the bitch was, about a hundred feet behind her sister and closing fast. Tight mouth. Narrowed eyes. Hard features. Alexis was storming after her sister. I wouldn't want to be Haley when she caught up. Captain Wayne Stephenson was right behind Alexis. So were the two goons. The four of them approached the ballroom exit—

"Finn! Finnegan Lane!" a sultry voice called out.

Damn and double damn.

I was a couple hundred feet and several dozen people away from the bar, but I still heard her yell his name. So did Alexis James. The Air elemental stopped right where she was, as if she'd been struck by lightning. Stephenson had to pull up to keep from slamming into her. The goons hit his broad back and bounced off like Ping-Pong balls. They managed to stay upright.

Roslyn Phillips smiled, murmured an apology, and stepped around Alexis James. The vampire's eyes focused on Finn, and she was oblivious to the Air elemental's sudden interest in her. Alexis followed Roslyn's gaze. Her mouth curved up into a grim smile as she spotted Finn, who'd half-raised his hand in greeting to Roslyn. Grabbing Roslyn's arm, Alexis yanked her back, then barked a command at Stephenson. He grabbed Roslyn around the waist and started carrying her out of the ballroom. The two goons flanked him. A few people gave the group curious stares, but nobody moved to intervene. The folks might be richer in Northtown, but they didn't like to get involved in other people's problems any more than those in Southtown did.

Roslyn didn't know what the hell was going on, but she started struggling. A giant dragging you anywhere was never a good thing. The vampire sank her fangs into Stephenson's forearm before he got her out of the room. Finn bolted out of his seat after them.

Oh, *fuck*.

I'd started moving as soon as I'd heard Roslyn call Finn's name. So had Donovan Caine. Our footsteps pounded into the carpet as we ran for the exit. But there were too many people for us to move in a straight line. Zigzag, zigzag, zigzag. That was all we were able to do.

I'd just spotted some daylight, a hole through the crowd, when someone stepped in front of me, blocking my path. I glanced up. The giant Mab had sent after me before.

"There you are," he rumbled. "Ms. Monroe wants a word with you."

No time to be subtle. I drove my knee into his groin. He yelped and bent over. I'd already palmed one of my silverstone knives, so I popped him in the windpipe with the hilt of it. Choking, he stumbled back. The giant's ass hit a table, and it flipped over. Drinks and food spilled everywhere. Shouts and curses rose up, but I was already on my way out the door.

It was a straight shot from the ballroom to the front entrance of the country club, but I didn't see Alexis James, Stephenson, or Finn in the hallway. They had to be outside already. Getting past the giant had cost me precious seconds.

I ran down the hall toward the front door. Donovan Caine's footsteps scuffed the carpet behind me. The outside door was open, letting the afternoon sun stream in through the entrance. But it didn't warm me. Not one damn bit.

I raced outside. My head swiveled left, then right. There. A limo sat at the curb halfway down the steep hill that led up to the front of the club. Wayne Stephenson smashed his fist into Finn's chest. His body immediately sagged. Unconscious. Stephenson shoved him in the back of the limo, then got in after him. Alexis James, Roslyn Phillips, and the other two goons must have already been inside because there was no sign of them.

"Finn!" I screamed, running in that direction. "Finn!"

Too late.

The door slammed shut. Tires screeching, the limo pulled away from the curb and disappeared into the afternoon sun.

❖ 27 ❖

For a moment, I just stood there, not quite believing what had happened. That Alexis James had Finn and Roslyn Phillips. Luck, that capricious bitch, had really fucked me over today.

Donovan Caine ran up behind me. Sometime during the commotion, the detective had drawn the gun from his ankle holster.

Then Fletcher's training took over, as it so often did. My eyes flicked back and forth. Several limo drivers had gotten out of their cars, wondering what all the drama was about. The tuxedo-clad valets by the front door stared at me with open-mouthed shock. Once he got his breath back, Mab Monroe's giant wouldn't be far behind.

"We need to get out of here. Now," I said in a low voice.

I stalked into the parking lot. Donovan Caine holstered his weapon and followed me.

Since we didn't want to run the risk of handing a stolen car to a valet, Finn had decided against boosting another car and had instead driven his own Benz to the country club—and he still had the keys. Time to get another ride.

I hurried through several rows of vehicles until I was out of sight of the curious limo drivers and valets. After about two minutes of searching, I found a BMW that was several years old—prealarm, in other words. I used the hilt of my knife to smash the window, then hotwired the vehicle. Finn wasn't the only one who could liberate cars, although he did it with much more panache and far less mess.

I slid in behind the wheel. Donovan Caine got into the passenger's seat.

Neither one of us said a word as I hit the gas and the car roared away from the country club.

I drove about two miles, pulled into the far corner of the first gas station I saw, and stopped the car. Then I grabbed my cell phone out of my purse.

"What are you doing?" Donovan asked.

"Calling Finn."

The phone rang once. Twice. Three times. Four—

"Hello?" Instead of Finn, Roslyn's voice whispered over the line.

"It's Gin."

"I'm so sorry, Gin. I didn't realize—"

"It's okay, Roslyn," I said, trying to soothe her, keep her calm. "It's not your fault. It's mine, for being sloppy.

Everything's going to be all right. You'll be back home with Catherine real soon. Now, put Alexis James on the line."

I hit a button, activating the speaker phone, and held the cell out toward Donovan Caine so he could hear the conversation too.

"Who is this?" a woman's voice came on the line. Cold, hard, smug.

"Hello, Alexis," I said.

Alexis James's laughter echoed out of the speaker. "So you know my voice. Good. It will make this easier."

"Where's your sister?" I asked. "Where's Haley?"

I'd much rather deal with Haley James. She'd seemed somewhat amenable to my proposal to walk away. But more than that, she was afraid of what I'd do if she didn't give in to my demands. Haley was afraid I'd turn the information over to Mab Monroe and let the Fire elemental deal with her and her sister. Haley didn't want to die at the Fire elemental's hands like her father, Lawrence, had.

But Alexis James wasn't like Haley. She was too power-hungry to be sensible, to be afraid of Mab. An undercurrent of insanity colored her voice, a small peal I could hear among the smugness. Alexis was high on her own magic, and she never wanted to come down from it. No wonder she thought she could take out Mab Monroe. She probably thought she was Wonder Woman too.

And now, Alexis had something I wanted, something I cared about—Finn. This was not going to end well. For any of us.

"Haley's gone," Alexis said.

My gray eyes narrowed. "What do you mean gone?"

"The bitch decided to run for it," Alexis sneered. "Told me about your so-called demands. She said things were getting too complicated and she left."

That would explain why Haley had scurried out of the country club before her sister.

"And you didn't go after her?"

Alexis laughed. Again, the delicate note of madness colored her voice. Beside me, Donovan Caine cocked his head. He'd heard it too.

"Why would I? Haley's just been holding me back, always telling me to be cautious and sensible. Let her run and hide from you and Mab Monroe and all the other scary people out there. I'm better off without her." Bitterness crept into her voice. "I'm the one you're dealing with now, not her."

I didn't say anything. Faint rumbles and muffles could be heard in the background. A car horn beeped in the distance. They were still in the limo, getting farther and farther away from the country club with every second. And I had no idea what direction they'd taken, no way of tracking or following them.

"And who am I speaking with?" Alexis asked.

"You know exactly who this is. You and your boys have been hunting for me for days now."

"I want to hear you say it."

I drew in a breath. "I'm the Spider, the assassin you hired, then double-crossed."

Donovan Caine flinched at the words *the Spider*. They reminded him once again of who and what I was, even if he'd let himself forget for an hour. His face hardened, and the guilt flickered in his eyes. Caine was thinking about Cliff Ingles, his partner, and how he'd just betrayed him by fucking me—and enjoying the hell out of it. The detective's lips, the ones that had been so hot and open against mine, pressed into a tight, closed line. Damn and double damn. Now was not the time for Caine to start hating me again and vowing to bring me to justice no matter what.

"What do you want, Alexis?" I asked.

"The flash drive and any copies you might have made of it," she said.

"In return?"

"You get your friends—in more or less one piece."

A series of *slap-slap-slaps* sounded, followed by a low groan. Finn, getting the shit beat out of him for the second time in less than a week, probably by Captain Wayne Stephenson. A painful, dubious achievement. A final *slap* rang out, followed by a high-pitched, stifled scream. Roslyn. The giant had hit Roslyn hard enough for the vamp to feel it.

My free hand clenched into a tight fist. "Listen up, bitch. I don't pay for damaged goods. You tell Stephenson to quit beating up my man right fucking now. And if he or your other two goons even *think* about touching the woman in any way, I'll hand-deliver the flash drive to Mab Monroe myself and let her track you down. Hell, she'll probably have the mayor give me a medal for bringing you to her attention."

Silence. A calculated gamble. Alexis James might not be afraid of Mab Monroe's magic, but she had to realize getting the other woman involved would only make matters worse for her. That's why Alexis had hired and double-crossed me in the first place—to smooth her path to usurping glory. Alexis still needed the flash drive to disappear, hopefully more than she wanted to hurt Finn and Roslyn or call my bluff. But I wasn't bluffing. I'd do exactly what I promised—except I'd find a way to get to Alexis James long before Mab Monroe did.

"Agreed." A reluctant promise, wrapped in uncertainty.

"Where do you want to make the exchange?" I asked.

"The old rock quarry on the outskirts of town. Do you know it?"

I closed my eyes. Memories and images flashed through my mind. Playing there with Bria as a child. Cowering underneath the rocky outcroppings after the Fire elemental had murdered my family. Jo-Jo sitting with me among the rocks, showing me how to master my elemental magic. Fletcher hunched on a seatlike slab of stone reading a book while I ran lap after lap around the quarry, circling my way from the bottom to the top and back down again.

"I know it."

"Two hours. Be there with the flash drive, or your friends die. Slowly."

Alexis hung up. I hit a button, doing the same, then stared at Donovan Caine. The detective looked back at me, his hard cop stare tightening the planes of his face.

I sighed. "Go ahead and say it."

"This is your fault. Alexis James has hostages because

of you." His eyes frosted over. "Because you were too busy fucking me to watch her."

"There was no way of knowing Roslyn would call out to Finn, and that Alexis would grab them both," I said. "I'll admit leaving Finn at the bar was a miscalculation on my part."

Disgust filled Donovan's amber eyes. "A miscalculation?"

His disgust, his anger, knifed into me, piercing my heart. But I pushed the feeling aside. Now was not the time for emotion. Now was the time to be as cold and hard as the Ice and Stone magic that flowed through my veins.

"You're not angry about Finn and Roslyn. You know that was a fluke, something that would only happen one time out of a hundred," I snapped. "No, you're angry because you didn't push me away in that closet. Face it. You were a willing participant, detective, and you thoroughly enjoyed yourself. So don't place all the blame for this mishap on me."

Caine's hands clenched into fists. He looked like he wanted to punch something—me.

"You can blame me and hate me and call me all the nasty names you want—later," I said. "Finn and Roslyn are in danger. You saw that photo of my handler, what Alexis James did to him. She'll torture the two of them exactly the same way. You can help me save them, or you can stay the hell out of my way. Your choice, detective."

Donovan Caine stared at me, hate and disgust shimmering like gold fire in his eyes. "I'll help you—for Roslyn's sake. Because she has a niece she loves. Because she's the type of person I've sworn to protect. But I'm not doing this for Finn and sure as hell not for you. I couldn't care *less* about *you*. Are we clear?"

His words ripped into me, but I kept my face neutral. Impassive. Hard. Cold.

"Crystal," I replied. "Now let's move."

Using a circuitous route, I drove the car back to my apartment. I glanced in the rearview mirror, but no one appeared to be following us. One less thing to deal with. Then again, Alexis James had no reason to follow me now. She already had her leverage.

Donovan Caine stared straight ahead, eyes fixed, body tense. He didn't say anything on the drive over, but I could feel the self-loathing and rage seething off him. If he got any hotter under the collar, he'd spontaneously combust.

Fifteen minutes later, we hit the downtown district. I parked the car in a garage three blocks away from my apartment building. We walked the rest of the way. I got out of the elevator before the detective and went to my apartment door. While I fiddled with the key, I let my fingers touch the stone. The same low, steady murmur sounded back to me. Finn hadn't given up the location of my apartment. I smiled. Good for him. Too bad for Alexis James. Because part of me had wanted someone to be waiting inside. I would have enjoyed taking the edge off my anger by killing some of Alexis James's minions.

I opened the door and went into my bedroom, not

bothering to wait for Donovan Caine to follow me inside. I stripped off my dress and stilettos, and put on my usual assassin clothes. Black pants, long-sleeved T-shirt, socks, boots. I crumpled up the fancy cocktail dress and ripped panties and threw them in the trash can beside the bed. They both smelled like Donovan, and I didn't need any distractions right now.

Not with Finn and Roslyn's lives hanging in the balance.

I went over to my dresser and opened the top drawer. A thin vest lay inside, not unlike the ones I usually wore on assignments. I put it on, then opened the second drawer down. A row of knives encased in black foam glinted up at me. I stuffed two in my boots. Two more went up my sleeves. A fifth knife got tucked against the small of my back. I was already wearing the silver watch with the garrote wire inside, so I double-checked it, making sure the wire could be easily pulled out of the timepiece. I could do more damage with the knives, but if the opportunity presented itself, I'd strangle Alexis James with the wire.

Oh, I wanted her to suffer for what she'd done to Fletcher, for how her men had beaten Finn and Donovan Caine, for daring to frame me in the first place. But the most important thing now was rescuing Finn and Roslyn. I had a better chance of doing that if I killed Alexis the first chance I got. Dead was dead. As long as everyone else was still breathing and she wasn't in the end, well, I'd just have to be happy with that. Fletcher would understand. He'd rather Finn be alive than his murderer tortured.

Because Alexis James wouldn't be content to trade

Finn and Roslyn for the flash drive. No, she'd see this as an opportunity to take care of us once and for all. She'd double-crossed me before, and she'd do it again without hesitating. But this time, I knew it was coming and I was planning accordingly.

When I was ready, I went back out into the den, where Donovan Caine was gearing up. The detective had taken off the suit he'd borrowed from Finn. Now he wore jeans, hiking boots, a black T-shirt, and a leather jacket. Caine bent over and clipped a holster and a snub-nosed revolver to his ankle. When that was done, the detective straightened. He took a gun from the small of his back, ejected the clip, and checked it. Satisfied everything was working, he pushed the clip back into the gun.

But he didn't put it away. Instead, Caine lowered the weapon to his side, his finger not quite on the trigger. He didn't look in my direction, but I knew what he was thinking. That I'd caused him enough problems. That he should just kill me now. Avenge the murder of his partner. Go after Finn, Roslyn, and Alexis James by himself. And end this attraction he felt for me. Several birds, one stone, as Finn would say.

"Are you going to shoot me, detective?" I asked in a soft voice. My fingers rubbed the hilt of the knife I'd already palmed. Nothing was going to keep me from getting to Finn. Not even Donovan Caine and what I felt for him.

The detective stared at the gun in his hand. He didn't meet my gaze. "Part of me wants to," he admitted. "For everything you've done. For all the people you've killed. You deserve to die."

"Probably," I said. "But if you kill me, Roslyn Phillips dies too. Alexis James will flay you alive with her magic before you even get close to saving the vampire. Her blood will be on your hands. Finn's too."

"That's what you say."

"That's what I know," I said. "Those guns of yours might be nice, but you don't have any magic, detective."

His eyes narrowed. "And you have so much? I've seen your Ice magic. It's not that impressive."

"No, it's not."

I didn't mention the fact I could control another element, Stone, far better. That Jo-Jo Deveraux had always told me I had more raw power than anyone she'd ever seen. That sometimes the knowledge of what I could do with my Stone magic, what I had done with it, even scared me.

"But I'm not worried with morals the way you are. I don't care what's right and wrong. I'd be perfectly happy to stab Alexis James in the back the first chance I got."

Donovan Caine didn't disagree with me.

"Just . . . just tell me this. Why did you do it?" he asked in a rough voice. "Why did you kill Cliff Ingles? Who hired you?"

Ah, there it was. The question he wanted an answer to. The one I knew he'd ask me sooner or later. The one that those left behind always asked. The only one that could maybe ease his guilt over fucking me.

"You don't want to know."

"Tell me," he demanded. "I need to know. I have to know."

For all his toughness, for all the things he'd seen in

his life, Donovan Caine was still very idealistic. Still hoping, still wanting to believe in the inherent good in people.

Because of that, because of this softness I felt for him, I didn't want to tell him how perverted his precious partner had been. Didn't want to tell him about the little girl's brutal rape and beating. Knowing what Cliff Ingles had done would shatter any remaining illusions Donovan Caine had about his partner. And probably people in general. If you can't trust the guy you're riding with in the squad car, then who can you trust? The knowledge would harden something inside of him, the way my family's murder had done to me seventeen years ago.

"Somebody wanted Ingles dead, so I made him that way. I don't kill and tell, detective. Not now, not ever," I said. "I know you think your partner was a saint, but Ingles had his secrets, just like the rest of us. You want to know why I killed him, figure it out for yourself."

Donovan's face tightened. He didn't like my stonewalling him, but I didn't give him time to think about it.

"Now are you going to put that gun away and help me? Or are you going to do something stupid and die on my floor?"

Caine sucked in a breath, then let it out. His eyes flashed gold, and his hand clenched around the gun. For a moment, I thought he'd made the wrong choice. A fatal choice. But the detective raised the weapon and stuck the gun against the small of his back.

"I'll help you," he said. "I owe you that much for saving me that night in my cabin. And I can't leave people to die, no matter who they are."

Caine didn't say what he would do afterward. I didn't ask. "Good," I said. "We've got less than an hour. Let's move."

We got back into the car I'd stolen, and I checked the clock on the dashboard. Forty-five minutes and counting. An icy hand crept into my chest and wrapped around my heart, holding it tight as a lover, whispering of all the bad things that could happen. There was no fear for myself or the fact I might die tonight. A very real possibility of that. Alexis James was an Air elemental who enjoyed using her power to kill. She was every bit as dangerous and deadly as I was. Even worse, she was high on her magic, coming apart at the seams, like a rag doll slowly losing her stuffing, one puffy piece of fabric at a time.

No, my fear wasn't for myself. It was for the others. Fear for Finn, even Roslyn. And what the elemental might have already done to them—or would do. Despite her promise, Alexis James might decide to have a little fun with her food. And I wondered whether or not they could survive it until I got there.

Carved out of one of the taller mountains in the area, the Ashland Rock Quarry squatted like a leper on the edge of town. At one time the quarry had been one of the focal industries in the city, employing thousands of folks. But whatever rock or ore or gemstones had been hidden under the earth had long been exhausted, and now the quarry stood empty, with only the murmur of the stones to break the silence. The only people who came here these days were dwarves who tapped into the sheer walls of the quarry with their small pickaxes, looking for something sparkly to take back home to the kids.

We arrived at the rock quarry fifteen minutes before our time was up. I approached the area from the south, taking a little-used access road I remembered running across more than once as a kid. The same access road Bria and I used to hopscotch down as children.

"Have you been here before?" Caine asked. The first words he'd spoken to me since we'd left the apartment. "Not many people know about this road."

"When I was a kid, I used to come out here and play sometimes."

The detective gave me a strange look, but he didn't pry. I didn't offer any more information, like the fact I'd also come to the quarry to listen to the stones talk to me. To attune myself to the different vibrations they gave off. To practice my magic. To find a bit of peace in a world that had been turned upside down.

"What about you?" I asked.

He shrugged. "Just for the occasional body dump. It was a popular site a few years ago. We still come out here several times a year. In the spring, Cliff and I—"

I never learned what Cliff and he did in the spring. Caine shut up and stared out the window. Brooding. About me, about us, about the fact I'd hadn't told him why I'd murdered his partner. And that maybe, just maybe, Cliff Ingles had gotten exactly what he'd deserved.

A few minutes later, I slid the car into a stand of maple trees about a mile out from the quarry, parked it, and got out. So did Donovan Caine, who turned to face me across the hood.

"Why are you stopping?" Caine asked. "We're not that close to the quarry."

"Because you're not coming in with me."

"Why not?"

"Alexis James is an Air elemental," I said. "You won't stand a chance against her."

"And you will?"

I nodded. "Like it or not, I can do things you won't let yourself, detective. Besides, Alexis is expecting me to come alone. She won't like the company. It will make her twitchier than she already is. I'm going to get her attention, have her focus on me. Your job is to circle around behind her and get Finn and Roslyn out of there—no matter what. Alexis is sure to have Stephenson with her and probably those two goons from the country club. You need to take them out if we have any chance of surviving this. Can you do that?"

The detective nodded.

"Good. Let's get this over with."

Donovan Caine looked at me a final time, and our eyes met. Gold on gray. I knew what he was thinking. The same thing I was. Two hours ago, we'd been buried inside each other. Now we were both probably on our way to our own deaths. Irony. Another fucking bitch.

Once more I felt that spark of softness in my chest, but I was careful not to let it show in my eyes or face. If he sensed it, if he was kind to me now, I wouldn't be able to focus. Wouldn't be able to do what needed to be done. A luxury I couldn't afford. Not now, not ever.

Caine nodded his head at me. His way of saying good luck. Or good-bye. I was surprised he bothered with the nicety, given the near meltdown he'd had in my apartment. But the detective had bucked back up on the ride to the quarry. He knew he had to work with me a little while longer if he wanted to save Finn and Roslyn. Then—then he could turn on me.

Donovan Caine stepped away and melted into the shadows, heading toward the back side of the quarry. I waited until I couldn't see him anymore, then squared my shoulders and started walking down an embankment to the front of the massive hole. As I strode along, I touched the various knives hidden on my body. One in either sleeve. Two more in my boots. One against the small of my back. The cold silverstone metal of the weapons comforted me, the way it always did. Alexis James might kill me, but I wasn't going down easy.

I walked about half a mile before I saw the entrance to the quarry. The city had long ago given up keeping out the bums and wayward kids, and a rusty sign read *Enter at your own risk*. The remains of a tall iron gate ringed the entrance, but I stepped through a gap where someone had pried the bars loose, and headed inside.

The quarry was shaped like a deep, wide bowl that was over a mile wide. The walls of the quarry rose several hundred feet above my head. Bits of quartz flashed in the gray twilight, reminding me of cameras at a sporting event. For a moment, I felt like I was in some sort of ancient Roman coliseum. A gladiator forced to fight tigers and lions and other men just so I could see another sunrise. In a way, I supposed I'd been a gladiator since I was thirteen, always fighting to survive, and distancing myself from the ugly things I had to do in the process.

I never realized how fucking tired I was of it until right now.

I didn't have to touch the stones to hear their vibrations. With so much of the raw element around me, the sound rang in my head, a low, steady drum, punctuated here and there by sudden beats of unease and anticipation. The stones knew something was wrong, that something had disturbed their slumber and the slow wear of the weather and years beyond the usual deer and squirrels and stupid, drunken kids who slipped from the high banks and fell to their deaths.

A milky white glow arched out beyond a curve in the rock. I'd seen that light before, when Alexis had flipped out at Donovan Caine's cabin. She'd grabbed on tight to her magic already. The only way to make her let go was to kill her. I hoped I was strong enough to do it—for Fletcher.

I rounded the bend, and there she was.

Alexis James.

The Air elemental stood in the open about five hundred feet farther in the quarry, where the stone walls rose to their highest peak. The milky white light flickering on her palms bathed the bitch in an angelic glow she didn't deserve.

Alexis's elegant cocktail dress was gone. Or at least covered up. Now she was wearing the same black cloak she'd sported outside Donovan Caine's cabin the night she'd come to torture and kill him. I wondered if she'd worn the same thing when she'd murdered Fletcher. If my mentor's blood was trapped in the fabric. The billowing material made Alexis look like some wannabe wizard out of a Harry Potter book. It didn't really go with the pearls that ringed her neck—or the large jet tooth that hung in the middle of the gleaming strand. The same necklace she'd worn in the fishing photo Gordon Giles had hidden away.

I eyed the rune. Power. Strength. Prosperity. The tooth was as big as my palm and polished to a high gloss. The rune was even bigger than the ruby sunburst Mab Monroe was so fond of wearing. Alexis James was showing off for me.

And she wasn't alone.

My eyes went to Finn and Roslyn. They stood side by side, their hands tied behind their backs with silverstone cuffs. Finn sported a series of fresh cuts and bruises on his face. One of Roslyn's cheeks was red and puffy. Their clothes were torn and bloody, but other than that, they looked no worse for wear. Better than I'd expected. Alexis had kept her word about one thing, at least.

Three men with guns flanked Finn and Roslyn, forming a potential triangle of death around them. The same three men who'd gotten into the limo at the country club. Captain Wayne Stephenson. Charles Carlyle's friend from the Cake Walk. The third anonymous flunkie. They must be all the men she had left. Otherwise, she would have brought them all here to kill me. Good to know I'd dispatched the rest of her troops already. That meant there'd be no one to talk after the fact.

I wondered if Donovan Caine had circled around behind the three of them yet. If he could see his senior officer pointing a gun at Roslyn's head.

Finn nodded and gave me an encouraging smile. Roslyn pressed against him. Her fangs poked out of her lips. The vampire was ready to bite anyone who gave her the opportunity. Good for her.

"Assassin, so good of you to finally join us," Alexis James said, throwing back the hood of her cloak.

❊ 28 ❊

"So you're the mysterious Spider." Alexis James's blue-green eyes flicked over me. "I thought you'd be taller."

I returned her cold stare with one of my own. "And I thought you'd have more taste than to wear that clichéd witch's cloak. What are you? Twelve?"

"Ouch," she said. "Killer insult."

I didn't respond.

"You've caused me quite a bit of trouble, you know," Alexis said.

I shrugged. "Trouble has a habit of finding me. And I have a habit of dealing with it."

Her eyes narrowed. "As do I."

We stared at each other. Magic flickered like lightning in Alexis's gaze, brightening her eyes until they were almost pure white. A similar glow outlined her palms. She was focusing on her power, ready to use it on me the instant I stepped out of line. I could feel her Air elemental magic snapping around her like a dog at its master's feet. The sensation of the opposing element made my skin crawl. Or perhaps that was just because I'd seen what Alexis liked to do with her magic. How she liked to flay people alive with it.

"So tell me," I said, trying to give Donovan Caine as much time as possible to come in behind them. "Of all the assassins out there, why did you pick me to double-cross?"

"Because you were the easiest to identify."

"How?"

"What's the old saying? Loose lips sink ships? Or in your case, get your photo on the six o'clock news." Alexis chuckled at her seeming cleverness. "You might not know it, but my old friend Gordon Giles liked to visit hookers. Seems he needed a little help getting it up and was embarrassed by more traditional relationships."

I'd seen exactly what kinds of relationships Gordon liked to have in his photo stash—ones that involved costumes.

"When I realized Gordon was suspicious about where so much of the company's money was going and was poking around, I made Stephenson follow him and pick up the women he was with to see what he'd told them, if anything," Alexis continued. "Gordon was smart enough to keep his mouth shut to the whores, but Stephenson got some interesting information out of one of them. Information about an assassin called the Spider."

So that's how they'd found us. No good deed goes unpunished. Fucking pro bono work.

"It turned out you'd done some work for the hooker. Killed a cop for her. It took some legwork, but I managed to identify your handler and contact him. The rest was easy." Alexis smiled.

I flashed back to the file Fletcher had compiled on Gordon Giles. Fletcher had noted Giles's tendency to visit hookers. Not to mention all the kinky pictures I'd found along with the flash drive. So Giles had visited the woman whose daughter had been raped. The one who'd contacted Fletcher and asked me to kill Cliff Ingles. We'd come full circle with the irony and bad luck tonight.

Finn stared at Alexis. Hate flashed in his green eyes, making them burn even brighter than hers did. A muscle twitched in his puffy cheek, but he held himself still. Finn knew better than to make any sudden moves. He knew I'd take care of Alexis—or die trying.

"The old man was easy enough to find at the barbecue joint," Alexis continued. "But you, we never could spot you."

Of course they couldn't. I took great pains to make sure no one ever followed me from the Pork Pit back to my apartment. Besides, I was just another lowly restaurant worker. As Evelyn Edwards, the asylum shrink had said, someone like me couldn't possibly have been moonlighting as someone like the Spider in my spare time.

"So that's why you brought Brutus in," I said. "To take me out at the opera house. Since you couldn't find me to do it yourself after the fact."

"Brains too. Aren't you the complete package?" Alexis smiled again. "But enough talk. Let's get down to business. Do you have the flash drive?"

I slowly reached into my jeans pocket and pulled it out. "I do."

"That's it?" she said. "That's the only drive? You haven't made any other copies?"

"I couldn't copy the drive. Gordon Giles encrypted it with some kind of weird software. You look at it the wrong way, and all the data gets erased."

An easy lie. Just before I'd left the apartment, I'd used my laptop to send out a timed e-mail with all the information on it. At exactly six o'clock tomorrow morning, the e-mail would be sent to officials at the police department, the *Ashland Trumpet* newspaper, and Mab Monroe. Unless I was alive to stop it. Just a bit of added insurance. I might die tonight, but Alexis James's days would be numbered as soon as Mab got the e-mail. I'd feel that satisfaction even in death.

"What about Donovan Caine?" Wayne Stephenson spoke up.

Alexis turned to him. "What about Caine?"

The captain stared at her. "She had to be the one who saved him from those men you sent after him. They've got to be working together. So where is he? Why isn't he here? You said it yourself. He's a loose end that needs to be tied off."

Alexis dismissed his concerns with an airy wave of her hand. "We'll find the detective later. He can't hide forever. The assassin's here, and she's got the flash drive. You know what to do. Kill her. Now."

Stephenson didn't hesitate. He raised his gun and fired at me.

The bullet slammed into my chest, spun me around, and knocked me to the ground. The flash drive flew out of my hand and landed somewhere on the rocky floor of the quarry. Stephenson might have been a crooked cop, but his aim was true. The bullet hit my heart dead on. It would have been a lethal shot—if I hadn't been wearing my vest.

I usually wore some sort of vest when I worked, especially when I knew I was going into a meeting that wasn't going to end well. Made it easier to carry certain supplies, like fake IDs and cash. But this particular vest was special because it was embedded with silverstone. The metal was tougher than Kevlar and would stop anything short of a missile. It would even absorb a fair amount of elemental magic before it started to soften and melt. Funny, how it had come in handy already.

But the force of the bullet still hurt, like I'd been beaned in the chest with a ninety-mile-an-hour fastball. But I gritted my teeth and lay perfectly still, waiting for the inevitable.

The echo of the gunshot reverberated through the rock quarry, booming like thunder off the walls. It slowly faded away, replaced by an eerie quiet. The stone under my cheek muttered uneasily at the sharp retort, but I blocked out the noise. Ten . . . twenty . . . forty-five . . .

I hadn't even counted to a minute when I heard the words I'd expected from Alexis James.

"Get the flash drive," she said. "And put a couple more in her head, just to be sure."

I had to admire her thoroughness, if nothing else. Footsteps crunched on the rocky ground behind me. The tread was slow and even, and I couldn't tell which one of the three men she'd sent over. My hand curled around the knife I'd palmed. Didn't much matter.

A hand settled on my shoulder and turned me over. I looked up into the man's face. Carlyle's friend from the Cake Walk. His eyes widened in surprise, and his lips pulled back, revealing a pair of yellow fangs.

"She's not—"

Last words he ever said.

I rammed my knife into his heart. The man stumbled back, and I used his momentum to pull myself up. The move surprised the others, and they stood there, not quite sure what had happened.

"Run!" I screamed at Finn and Roslyn. "Now!"

Finn slammed his shoulder into the second man, who stumbled back. Roslyn darted past him and sprinted away. Finn fell in step behind her, and the two of them ran as best they could with their hands cuffed behind their backs. They disappeared around an outcropping of rock. Stephenson and the other guy didn't know what to do—shoot Finn and Roslyn or come after me.

They chose me.

I threw the dead man aside and dived to my right. Three more bullets zipped over my head. I rolled up, grabbed one of the knives in my boots, and threw it. The weapon caught the second man in the stomach. He screamed and dropped his gun. The man yanked the knife out of his gut, his hand black and shiny with his own blood. Stupid of him. He took a step forward and crumpled to the ground. He'd bleed out in a minute or so.

That left Stephenson and Alexis James. I grabbed the knife out of my other boot so that I had one in both hands. But the police captain was quicker than I was. He got off another shot. This one went into my vest too. I couldn't keep myself from staggering back. He put another round in my vest, and I went down on the ground. One of the knives slid from my grasp and clattered on the rock.

"I'll deal with her!" Alexis screamed. "You get the other two. Now!"

Stephenson turned and started running. But the giant was out of shape, and his pace was plodding and slow. I hoped Finn and Roslyn had enough of a head start to elude him until Donovan Caine could help them.

That left me and Alexis alone in the quarry. I scrambled up, getting ready to throw both of my knives at her. I needed to kill her—now. Before she reached for her magic.

Too late.

Even as I came up on one knee, Alexis James's eyes turned completely white as she fully embraced her power. The milky glow on her fingertips turned into magical flames, licking at her skin. In less than a second, the flames coalesced into a large ball of pure power, burning like a beacon between her fingers.

"Go to hell, bitch!" Alexis hissed and threw the magic at me.

✳ 29 ✳

Jo-Jo Deveraux had been right. My knives weren't going to help me this time. Only one thing could save me now—my magic.

I closed my eyes and reached for the elemental power flowing through my veins. The stone mumbled under my feet, sensing my rising magic. I concentrated on that stone, on its vibration, and let it feed my own magic, forcing my power through my veins onto my skin, hair, eyes, clothes. Making them as hard and unyielding as the rubble on the ground and the jagged stone walls that surrounded me—

The ball of Air magic slammed into my chest, right where my heart would be. Alexis James wasn't messing around with me the way she had with Fletcher. She'd gone for the kill shot first.

It was like being hit by a fierce tornado, but worse. The force of the blast knocked me back on my ass and tore my knives from my hand, even as the wind screamed in my ears. The Air elemental magic slammed into me, trying to break through my Stone magic. Trying to overpower me and strip off my skin in one fatal blow.

Stone and Air didn't mix, any more than Fire and Ice did. Opposing elementals never meshed, and I could feel Alexis's power reacting to my own. The wind howled and thrashed against my body even louder than before. But I concentrated on my own magic, listening to the murmurs of the rocks underneath my body, drawing my strength from them. They were still here, despite being mined and blasted and dug into. Despite the passage of time and the harshness of the elements. Despite everything. They'd survived, and so could I.

I gritted my teeth and pushed back against the Air magic, against the wind battering my body and pricking my skin like cold needles. The silverstone metal in my vest also reacted to the surge of power, absorbing some, but not all, of Alexis's magic. There was too much of it for that. The garment grew hot and heavy on my chest. I reached for more of my own Stone magic, using my power to drive the Air magic away, to push it back, to squeeze the life, the energy out of it.

It worked.

The wind, the ball of magic battering at my torso, dimmed and died, puffing away into nothingness. But I didn't let go of my magic, my power. Slowly, I got to my feet, concentrating on my magic, my element, letting it make me as hard as I needed to be to survive this.

Alexis's eyes narrowed. "I hit you square in the chest.

Why aren't you dead? Why isn't your skin, your body, nothing more than a pile of mush?"

I didn't answer. Let the bitch figure it out for herself. Alexis reared back and threw more of her Air magic at me. The blast of wind hit me in the chest again. Nothing wrong with her aim.

I didn't fall this time, but my feet slid back on the rocks, as though they were made of ice. I pushed back with my Stone magic, waited until the wind died down, then started forward once more.

But Alexis wasn't giving up. Since her Air magic wasn't immediately working the way she thought it would, she reached into her cloak and pulled out a gun. She fired off three shots. One rattled off into the twilight. One of the bullets caught in my vest, adding to the heat on my chest. The sharp, painful blow was enough to make me lose my grip on my Stone magic, just for a second. But that was plenty of time for the third bullet to slam into my left shoulder, instead of bouncing off my rock-hard skin, like it would have if I'd been properly focused. Pain exploded in my body, and I could feel the hot blood spurting out of the wound and staining my shirt. But I shut it all out and grabbed my magic once more. Nothing mattered now but killing Alexis.

Alexis lowered the smoking gun. I was closer to her now, close enough for her to finally notice the silver magic burning in my eyes and the gray, chiseled tinge to my skin.

Alexis hissed. "You're a fucking elemental."

"Just like you, bitch."

I started running and threw myself at her. Alexis wasn't

expecting the move, and she wasn't able to get another shot off before I slammed into her. Her concentration broke, and the gun slipped from her fingers. She fell to the floor of the quarry with me on top of her. Kicking, punching, clawing. I might have been skilled, but Alexis's magic and frustration had put her into a frenzy. She absorbed my sharp punches like I hadn't even hit her and roared back with several of her own.

Kick. Slap. Punch. Punch.

We rolled round and round exchanging blows, when we weren't throwing our magic at each other. Alex pummeled me with the wind. I shoved back with my Stone magic, blocking her vicious attacks.

After ten seconds, I was starting to get tired. Thirty seconds in, I was sucking wind. By the minute mark, it was all I could do to keep going. Using so much of my magic was quickly draining me. The bullet and the fire it caused in my shoulder weren't helping matters.

Then Alexis got in a lucky, unexpected punch, and my head slammed back against the rock. For a second, the world went black. My Stone magic flickered and started to slip away, like water being swallowed up by arid sand. I struggled to hold onto my magic, my power, to focus on it and nothing else. If I let go of my magic, I'd get dead. Her Air power would wash over me and flay me alive, forcibly rip and tear the skin and muscle and bone from my body until I was nothing but a pile of ruined flesh.

Alexis saw me weakening. She positioned herself on top of me and hit me in the face again and again. The blows further dazed me, and my Stone magic weakened that much more. I could feel the Air magic now, lashing against my skin like a whip. Blisters started to form on my face, neck, and hands as the magic and the oxygen it contained forced its way underneath my flesh.

Alexis raised her hand, and her fingers flashed to life. Once again, her Air magic made them burn like a welder's torch. She brought her hand up, positioning her fingers above my eyes. She was going to use her magic to put them out and tear the skin off my face.

Just like she'd done to Fletcher.

Her hand dipped downward, but I caught it with my own and shoved it back. I'd held onto enough of my magic so that her Air magic didn't immediately rend my skin, but it was just a matter of time. A minute. Two, tops.

Back and forth, our hands seesawed, her burning fingers coming closer and closer to my face every single time until all I could see was their milky white glow. More blisters swelled up on my skin, threatening to burst. That was agony enough. I couldn't imagine what the pain would be like when they ruptured. I wasn't going to last much longer. Not like this.

Fletcher, I thought desperately. What would Fletcher do? *Kill the bitch any way you can.* I could almost hear his gruff voice murmuring in my ear.

"Give it up, assassin," Alexis crowed. "My magic is stronger than yours. You can't win. Air trumps Stone, in this case."

And that's when it hit me. That's when I finally realized I'd been going about this the wrong way. I never would have done a hit by confronting someone head-on. Frontal assaults rarely worked in my line of business. Fletcher had taught me that. I was the Spider. The woman who hid in the shadows. Sneak attacks were what I did best. Outthinking people, outmaneuvering them, that's what I excelled at. That was my real strength.

Time to go back to it.

I had enough juice left in me for one final burst of magic. Maybe two. So far, I'd been on the defensive, trying to block Alexis's magic. I'd never liked being on the defensive. I needed to end this. Now.

So I threw my right hand out to the side, as far away as I could from her body and the Air magic howling around her like an invisible wolf. Alexis thought I was weakening that much more. She paused a moment to allow herself a triumphant chuckle.

That luxury cost the bitch her life.

With my outstretched hand, I reached for my other magic—my Ice magic. That element had always been far weaker than my Stone magic. All I could really do with it was make Ice crystals and cubes and other small shapes.

But it was enough.

The spider rune scar on my hand iced over. My fingers closed around the edge of the jagged icicle I'd created in my palm. Cold comfort. I snapped up my wrist and slammed the crude weapon into Alexis James's heart.

The milky white flames on her fingertips snuffed out, like a candle doused by a stiff wind. The icicle broke off in her chest, so I threw my hand out to the side and made another one. This time, the cold weapon went into her neck. I turned my head to the side. Her blood spattered onto my left cheek, stinging it like hot wax. The pressure made some of the blisters on my face burst. I gritted my teeth against the searing pain.

Alexis James's eyes widened, and she clawed at the cold cylinder in her neck. But I didn't wait for her to pull it out. I formed another icicle and cut her throat with it.

She gurgled and put both hands over her windpipe.

Too little, too late.

I'd severed her jugular. Alexis might have been able to recover from it, if she'd known how to use her Air magic to heal instead of kill. But she didn't. And a cut artery was one thing all her power, all her precious Air magic, couldn't help her with. Alexis had been right. My magic hadn't been stronger than hers. I'd just used it better.

Alexis pitched forward, and her blood soaked into my clothes, hair, skin. The last dregs of her magic erupted from her body, pummeling me a final time. The silverstone vest pressed down on my chest like a scalding rock. The metal had absorbed all the magic it could and had liquefied. It sloshed around like water and leaked out of the shell of the vest. I just lay there under Alexis, focusing on my own magic, using enough of the Stone power to shield myself from the screaming wind and superheated metal.

After about a minute, Alexis's blood slowed to a trickle, and the wind whistled away. It always amazed me how quickly life, warmth, could turn dead and cold. I gathered up enough strength to roll the elemental off me and take off my melted vest. I threw the ruined material to one side. More silverstone leaked out of the fabric and pooled on the ground like a pale river.

I turned my attention to Alexis James. She'd flopped onto her back, staring up at the stars that had already started to populate the darkening sky. She coughed once, and more of her blood spattered on the rock around her. The stone under her body took on a harsh mutter.

I staggered to my feet, watching her die. I leaned down just before Alexis James slipped away and stared at her. The Air elemental's pained gaze flicked to me.

"I don't know where you're going," I said. "But if you see Fletcher Lane, tell him Gin says hello."

❄ 30 ❄

The milky white magic in the Air elemental's gaze dimmed, dulled, and leaked out of her eyes. But I didn't move until I was sure Alexis James was dead. I idly wondered if I should get her gun and put three in her head just to be sure—

Click.

I was so focused on Alexis that I didn't hear the gun until it was too late. Something that was happening a lot lately. I turned.

Wayne Stephenson stood behind me, his weapon level with my chest. The giant was less than twenty feet away. He wouldn't miss. Not at this distance. I was too exhausted to reach for my Stone magic again, to try and harden my skin with it, and my silverstone vest lay in a crumpled, melted heap at my feet.

At least I'd killed Alexis James first. Finn and Roslyn would be safe now, assuming Stephenson hadn't already shot them. The pudgy police captain didn't look so good. His breath came out in ragged gasps, and sweat rolled down his forehead like he was standing in the shower.

The giant looked at me, then at Alexis's still body. He pulled a white handkerchief from the breast pocket of his suit and mopped some of the nervous moisture off his beefy face.

"I can't believe you killed her. You did me a favor, you know?" he said. "I wish I'd never gotten involved with that psychotic bitch. But she had pictures of me with a girl. I couldn't say no to her, to any of it."

More confirmation Alexis had been blackmailing Stephenson and further affirming my opinion that blackmail was the lowest form of arm-twisting.

"And then she promised me more. More money, more girls, anything I wanted. And all I had to do was find you, kill you . . ."

He was babbling, but I didn't say anything. The longer he kept talking was the longer I kept breathing. My eyes flicked to the ground. One of my knives lay about two feet off to my right. I might be able to lunge for it and throw it at Stephenson before he shot me. I tensed. Only chance I had.

But Stephenson wasn't completely gone. He saw I wasn't paying attention to his ramblings. His eyes sharpened.

"But this will fix it," he said. "This will fix everything. I'll say you killed Alexis, and I killed you. It'll work. I can make it work."

Stephenson raised his gun—

I dived forward, going for my knife and trying to get out of the path of the bullet—

A shot rang out, then five more in rapid succession—

My head snapped up. Stephenson towered over me. He teetered to one side, then toppled to the ground like a mighty oak that had been felled by a lightning strike. I saw three small, neat wounds in back of the police captain's skull. The same place Brutus had wanted to shoot me a few days ago. Three more holes leaked blood in the giant's back: two in his kidneys, one in his heart. I raised my eyes to the man who'd been standing behind the giant. The one who still had his gun raised.

Donovan Caine.

He walked over to Stephenson's body and stared down at his dead captain. His hazel eyes darkened, his face drooped, and his whole body just sagged. Once again, the detective reminded me of Atlas, bearing so much on his lean shoulders.

I sat up, too tired and bloody to do anything else. I'd carried my share of the load tonight too.

Donovan's hazel eyes flicked to me, then to Alexis James's body. He moved toward me, gun still clenched in his hand. I reached down and palmed my knife. I wasn't going to let the detective kill me. Not because of Cliff Ingles. Not because of anything.

Survival no matter what. The very first lesson Fletcher had taught me. One I'd learned even before I'd met the old man.

Even if killing Donovan Caine would extinguish whatever light might still be left inside me.

Caine stopped about three feet away from me. "You killed her. You killed Alexis."

I didn't say anything.

"How did you do it?" he asked. "I saw her magic. She was lighting up the whole quarry with it. And the wind . . . you could hear the wind screaming. How did you avoid it?"

"I got lucky." My voice was weak and raspy.

"Alexis is dead. Stephenson's dead. Which means our truce is officially over."

Donovan Caine raised his gun, pointing it at my forehead. My hand tightened around the hilt of the knife.

"You killed my partner."

I didn't say anything. If he started to pull the trigger, it was over. I'd stab him and leave his body here with the others. I'd deal with Finn and Roslyn and the cops and the consequences later, along with my emotions.

"You're an assassin, everything that's wrong with this city, everything I hate." The detective tightened his grip on the gun. "I should kill you right here, right now. Do the city, the world, a favor."

I wondered if he thought killing me would be a public service. If the mayor would give him a medal for it. My chapped, blistered lips twitched, and I wanted to laugh. Funniest damn thought I'd had all day. Hell, all week.

The silence stretched out between us. Seconds that felt like a lifetime.

Caine lowered his gun. "But I can't. I can't kill you. I feel something for you. Lust, gratitude, curiosity, I don't know what the fuck it is, but it won't let me kill you, no matter what you've done. So what does that make me?"

"A good man," I said in a soft voice.

Caine shook his head. "No. It just makes me stupid."

He threw down his gun and walked away.

*   *   *

I sat there, wondering at my reprieve and trying to muster up the strength to move, when a car drove into the bottom of the quarry. The same car I'd stolen from the country club earlier this evening. The vehicle slid to a stop a few feet away, kicking up dust and blood. Finn bounded out of the driver's seat and ran over to me. Roslyn Phillips also got out of the car and followed him at a slower pace.

Finn stopped in front of me, his green eyes sweeping over my clothes, body, face. Once he realized I was more or less in one piece, he relaxed.

"What happened?" I croaked. "How did you get away from Stephenson?"

Finn jerked his head at Caine, who stood a few feet away brooding over the giant's body. "Roslyn and I ran into the detective. He exchanged a couple of shots with the good captain, who turned and ran like a scared little girl."

I nodded. So Caine had come back after Stephenson, not to save me. Not surprising, except for the disappointment that fluttered in my chest.

Finn kept staring at me. After a moment, he smiled. Amusement filled his green gaze.

"What's so funny?" I asked.

"Oh, nothing. But tell me, whose face do you think looks like shit now?"

I touched my cheek and winced as pain shot through me. Alexis James had been stronger than she'd looked. She'd gotten in some solid whacks, not to mention the ugly, puffy blisters her Air magic had raised on my skin. Every part of me felt sore and raw and chapped from the intense magic I'd survived, and the bullet throbbed in my shoulder. "Mine."

"Yours," he agreed.

Finn held out a hand, and I let him pull me to my feet and into a tight hug. His arms closed around me, and hot tears stung my eyes.

"I thought I'd lost you too," he whispered in my ear.

I pulled back gave him a crooked smile. "You should know better than that."

Roslyn Phillips stood off to one side. The vampire looked mussed and tired. Her dark gaze focused on the blood leaking out of Stephenson's back. Her fangs gleamed like pearls in the twilight.

"Thirsty?" I asked.

Roslyn snorted. "For that giant shit? I don't think so. I'm just sorry I didn't get to tear the bastard's neck out myself."

I grinned at her. After a moment, she smiled back.

Donovan Caine cleared his throat. I turned so I could see the detective.

"You and Finn need to leave. Now," he said. "Roslyn, you're staying with me."

"Why?" I asked in a soft voice.

Caine swept his hand over the bodies that littered the quarry floor. "Here's what happened. I went off the grid to investigate the Gordon Giles case. Men came to my house to kill me, but I escaped from them. I've been hiding low the last few days tracking down leads, one of which was Roslyn. Thanks to her, I discovered Gordon's files, but

Alexis James found us. She brought us out here to kill us, but I managed to turn the tables on her instead."

"What about Stephenson?" Finn asked.

Caine shrugged. "He was pretending to work for Alexis to bring her down. He came to the rescue, but was killed in the crossfire."

"You know Stephenson was working for Alexis, that he liked to abuse young girls. Why are you protecting him?" I asked.

"Because he has a wife and a daughter who'll need his pension. Because they shouldn't suffer for what he did." Caine's eyes flashed with amber fire, daring me to contradict him.

I didn't. "And the mysterious woman at the opera house?"

"Mistaken identity," Caine said. "Alexis picked her out to frame her. A composite sketch of a person who never really existed. I'll think of something."

"I'm sure you will," I murmured.

"Where do I come in?" Roslyn asked. "Why do you need me to stick around?"

Caine looked at her. "Because people saw Stephenson drag you out of the country club. And I need somebody to back me up."

I stared at Roslyn. "Are you okay with being a star witness to all of this?"

The vampire shrugged, but I saw something flicker in her eyes. Guilt. Hmm. Something to think about later.

"Think you can sell it?" Donovan asked her.

Roslyn laughed. The delicate, pealing sound reminded me of wind chimes. "Oh honey, selling myself was what

I did for years. So yeah, I think I can manage it. You just tell me what you want me to say. By the time I'm done, the angels will be crying."

I believed her. Donovan did too, because he nodded his head.

"Well, it's nice and tidy all the way around," I said. "You think your superiors will believe that bizarre fairy tale?"

Caine shrugged. "Don't know, don't fucking care. That's the story I'm sticking with. Plus, I have this."

He held up the flash drive. The detective must have picked it up off the quarry floor while I was having my reunion with Finn.

"It's all the proof I need," Caine said. "I already used my cell phone to call it in. The first units will be here in ten minutes."

I grimaced. "Time for us to go, then."

"Time for you to go, then," he agreed.

Finn looked back and forth between the two of us. "I'll get the car."

He trotted over to the vehicle. Roslyn followed him. I swayed back and forth for a moment before finding my balance once more. My eyes met Donovan Caine's. Gray on gold.

"I suppose this is good-bye, then," I said.

"It is. Don't let me catch you again," he said in a harsh tone. "I won't be so generous next time."

There was that confidence again. One of many things I found so appealing about the detective. I tipped my head. "Don't worry, detective. I'm the Spider. I know how to stay hidden in the shadows, remember?"

Guilt and a touch of regret flashed in the detective's eyes, although he kept his face hard and remote. I did the same, even though a knife of emotion twisted into my heart.

Finn and Roslyn said their good-byes, and the vampire went to stand by the detective. Finn pulled the stolen car over to me. Somehow, I stumbled forward and picked up my various knives and the remains of my ruined vest. Then I yanked open the car door. I fell into the cushioned seat and flopped around like a rag doll, all the strength gone from my body.

Finn stared at me. "Gin—"

"Not tonight, Finn. Not tonight. Drive," I said. "Just drive."

I put my head back against the seat and closed my eyes.

❖ 31 ❖

Finn drove me straight to Jo-Jo's. This time he had to help me up to the porch while he banged the cloud-shaped rune knocker against the door.

The familiar, heavy footsteps sounded, and a moment later, Jo-Jo Deveraux threw open the door. Her eyes widened at the sight of my battered, blistered face.

"Ding-dong," I said. "The bitch is dead."

Jo-Jo just smiled.

"Are you sure you couldn't have killed her sooner, Gin?" Finn asked. "Before she made your skin look like you had the worst case of chicken pox and poison ivy ever?"

"I don't know," I sniped. "Why don't we rewind time and see how you would have fared against Alexis James's Air magic?"

Finn cocked an eyebrow. Jo-Jo sat in front of me, but I glared over her head at him.

"Shush," Jo-Jo said. The dwarf's eyes glowed white with magic. "It's harder to concentrate while you two are having one of your spats."

Jo-Jo had spent the last hour pouring her magic into me. Unlike Finn's previous wounds, most of mine had been caused by elemental magic, which meant they were harder to heal, despite Jo-Jo's own strength and expertise. Magic was always harder to undo than it was to create in the first place.

The dwarf using so much of her magic on me at one time also hurt like hell. Even though I knew Jo-Jo would never harm me, my body felt like it was still back in the rock quarry being thrashed with Alexis James's Air magic. Which is why Sofia Deveraux stood behind me, pinning my arms to my sides so I wouldn't move or try to get up out of the padded chair before Jo-Jo was finished with me.

She sent another surge of her Air magic into my left arm, working on the bullet that was still lodged in there. I gritted my teeth and looked for something to focus on besides the way Jo-Jo's power made the spider rune scars on my palms itch and burn—along with the rest of my body. My eyes latched onto Sophia's hands. Despite the Goth dwarf's love affair with black, pale, little-girl-pink polish covered her short fingernails.

"Nice color," I said.

Sophia grunted her agreement and tightened her grip on me. I bit back a groan. I could have been pinned under a Mack truck, and it wouldn't have felt as strong and solid as Sophia's hands. No wonder she could throw dead bodies around like they were plastic dolls.

While Jo-Jo worked, Finn filled the dwarven sisters in on everything that had happened the past few days.

"So Alexis James actually thought she was going to dethrone Mab Monroe?" Jo-Jo asked. "She's not the first one to think that way. Poor girl was really touched in the head, wasn't she?"

"Stupid," Sophia agreed in her raspy voice.

I thought of the pure, raw power Alexis James had possessed. Her desire to take on Mab for control of Ashland didn't sound as far-fetched to me as it once had. But Alexis was dead now, and that was all that mattered.

After Jo-Jo fixed the damage, Sophia let go of my arms, and she and Finn moved into the kitchen to get something to eat. Jo-Jo got up, went over to the sink, and washed my blood off her hands. I stayed where I was in the padded chair, relaxing.

"You were wrong," I said.

Jo-Jo wiped her hands off on a paper towel. "About what?"

"About nothing being able to penetrate my Stone magic. Alexis James's Air power did."

The dwarf shrugged. "You said yourself your concentration broke. Next time, you'll know what to expect. Besides, you're still young, Gin. You're just now fully coming into your power."

"But Alexis was stronger than I was," I protested. "Her magic was stronger. I felt it. You saw what she did to me with it."

Jo-Jo gave me a sly look. "If she was so strong, how

come she's rotting out in the quarry and you're sitting here in my chair?"

I didn't have an answer to that.

The dwarf chuckled. "Pure strength is one thing, darling, whether it's magical or natural. It'll only get you so far. But how you use what you've been given—that's what really matters. When you figure that out, ain't nobody going to be able to touch you. Not even me or Mab Monroe."

Jo-Jo threw her paper towel away and started puttering around the salon. While she worked, I just sat there in the chair pondering her words—and the cold fear they raised in me.

The Alexis James story played out for the next week. To say it was a circus would have been to underestimate the rabid appetite of the Ashland media. Story after story flooded the airwaves and newspapers about James and the trail of bodies in her wake. Donovan Caine must have been a better liar than I'd given him credit for, because the detective placed the blame for everything on Alexis, and nobody seemed willing to contradict him.

Haley James might have, if she'd been able to. But her home burned to the ground with her in it the night after the incident at the rock quarry. Only the house's stone foundation survived the blaze, along with a few of Haley's teeth. Everything else was totally obliterated by the heat. The fire was ruled an accident, and the coroner said Haley probably died from smoke inhalation, since he didn't actually have her body to autopsy. But I had no doubt Mab Monroe had paid Haley a visit for hiding Alexis's activities from her. So the very thing Haley had feared came true after all. Irony. What a bitch.

Finn made his own discreet inquiries into the matter, reaching out to his various contacts. He wanted to know if Haley had spilled her guts to Mab, if she'd said anything to the Fire elemental about Fletcher, Finn, or me. About what we did or what the James sisters had hired us to do. But evidently, Haley had never gotten the chance. Rumor had it that Mab had been so enraged at Haley's part in the embezzlement scheme that the Fire elemental had fried her on the spot. No questions asked. And with Alexis and the rest of her men dead, there was no one else to tell the tale. Which meant that Finn and I were safe from anyone else nosing around or blowing our cover to Mab.

A week after the incident at the rock quarry, we buried Fletcher in Blue Ridge Cemetery. Me, Finn, Jo-Jo, Sophia, the waitstaff and cooks from the Pork Pit, some of Fletcher's buddies, who were as gnarled and old and grumpy as he'd been. Roslyn Phillips also showed up for the service, although the vampire stood off to one side by herself.

It was another gorgeous fall day. Cerulean blue sky, bright sun, clouds that were smoother than marshmallow creme. The cemetery stood on a plateau on top of one of the mountains that ringed Ashland and offered a spectacular view of the sprawling city and countryside below. The grass gleamed like gold underfoot, while the burnt sienna and scarlet leaves painted the landscape with even more color. The mountaintops around us were smoky blue smudges against the sky.

We ringed a plain wooden casket burnished to a high gloss. Fletcher hadn't wanted anything fancy, he hadn't been that kind of man, and Finn had respected his father's wishes. The preacher had just started the graveside service, and people were already weepy. Several of the waitstaff and cooks snuffled into tissues. The old men dabbed their eyes with white handkerchiefs. Finn did the same. Jo-Jo Deveraux bawled like a baby, unashamed of her many tears, even though they were ruining her makeup. Sophia stood over her older sister, patting her back. The younger dwarf was dry-eyed, just like me. I'd cried my tears the night I'd found Fletcher's body. Now, I just felt . . . empty. Hollow. Another piece of my heart was gone, and it was never coming back. Just like all the other bits I'd lost over the years.

As the preacher spoke the traditional words of comfort, my mind drifted back to the day Fletcher had taken me in . . .

My family had been gone nine weeks now. Maybe ten. Time had little meaning to me anymore. All that mattered was finding enough food for one more day and someplace that wasn't too cold to sleep at night. Something that was getting more difficult as winter approached. My favorite spot was next to this barbecue restaurant called the Pork Pit. A crack in the alley across from the back of the restaurant was just big enough for me to squeeze into. I liked the small, tight space and the muted contentment of the stones in the surrounding buildings. Both of them made me feel safe, even though I knew it was only an illusion.

Then there was the tall guy who ran the restaurant. Barbecue Man. That's what I called him. He knew I hung around out back, but he didn't yell or chase me away like the folks at the Italian and Chinese restaurants did. He even let me do odd jobs for him, like sweep out the stockroom. Last week I'd helped him defrost the freezers and clean these weird pink stains out of them.

He'd given me fifty bucks for a day's work. I'd used the money to buy a black fleece jacket, a turtleneck, and the thickest pair of gloves they had at the Goodwill store. Barbecue Man was a lot nicer than the nuns over at the soup kitchen. They wanted to save your soul before they offered you so much as a glass of water. Hypocrites.

Barbecue Man had given me a hamburger a little over an hour ago for cleaning the gum off the tables in the front of the restaurant. I licked the last of the crumbs from my fingers, trying to make every single bite last. But Barbecue Man didn't skimp with the meat, and this was one night I wouldn't go hungry—one of a very few. The sandwich made me sleepy, and I curled into a tight ball and dozed off in my little crack, having survived another day on the streets of Ashland.

Sometime later, the stones woke me, their murmurs rising to a low, steady wail, thanks to the protection curls I'd set into the brick. My own sort of alarm, to keep me safe from the drugged-out bums, vampire prostitutes, and pimps. Something I'd seen one of the street elementals do, although she'd used fireballs to trigger her alarm instead of something else. Fire elementals had it so easy. They could use their magic to keep warm at night, and if somebody messed with them, they would get a face full of flames. Not for the first time, I wished I'd been born a Fire instead of a Stone.

I rubbed my eyes and sat up, clutching the loose brick in my lap. I'd used my magic to pry it out of one of the alley walls a few days ago. A pitiful weapon, but it was better than nothing. It only took me a moment to find the source of the alarm. A man stood in the shadows to my left. I stilled, hoping he wouldn't see me. I was very good at staying still and quiet. Being invisible was a necessary skill I'd perfected these past few weeks.

The back door of the restaurant opened, and Barbecue Man came out, carrying the last of the day's garbage. He whistled a cheery tune as he slung the refuse in the Dumpster.

The man stepped out of the shadows. He raised a gun and pointed it at Barbecue Man's back. And I realized he was going to kill him. He was going to shoot Barbecue Man.

"Watch out!" I screamed.

Barbecue Man turned. He saw the gun and jerked to one side. The shot went wide. Barbecue Man threw himself on top of the other guy, and they fell to the alley floor. Kicking, punching, cursing. The man with the gun crawled on top of Barbecue Man and wrapped his hands around his throat. Strangling him. He was going to kill Barbecue Man.

Unless I did something to stop it.

I'd seen plenty of horrible things on the street. People shot, stabbed, beaten. Bums strung out on drugs and jonesing for more. Elementals driven crazy by their own magic. Vampire hookers sucking the life out of folks who didn't pay their tab. I'd learned not to get involved in anyone *else's problems. That was a quick way to die. But Barbecue Man had been nice to me when no one else had. He didn't deserve to get robbed behind his own restaurant. Besides, if he died, I'd have to move on to somewhere else. And I didn't want to do that.*

So I reached for my magic. I let the Stone power fill my veins, and I stared at the back of the Pork Pit, focusing my attention on the rust-colored bricks. One brick that was already loose began to move and vibrate, working itself free of the wall. The men continued to struggle. I sat there, holding my magic, waiting for my chance.

Barbecue Man clawed at the other guy's eyes, and the stranger pulled back, putting some space between them. All the opportunity I needed. I focused, and the vibrating brick flew out of the wall. The heavy stone struck the man in the temple, and his neck snapped to one side. I heard the crack all the way across the alley. A sound I'd heard before. The one that made me want to throw up. I'd broken his neck. I'd used my magic to kill yet again. What kind of monster was I?

Barbecue Man gasped in a deep breath. Then he shoved the other man off him and stood up. I huddled in my crack, wondering if Barbecue Man would call the cops. If he did, I'd use another brick. But just to stun him. I wasn't going to kill Barbecue Man. Not him.

Barbecue Man reached down and picked up the loose brick. He stared at me a moment, then turned and knelt beside the other man. Barbecue Man smashed the brick against the stranger's head three more times. Blood spurted everywhere. I clapped my hands over my mouth to keep from screaming.

"*Fucking clients,*" *Barbecue Man muttered.* "*Always wanting to double-cross you just so they can save a little money.*"

He dropped the brick and wiped his bloody hands on his blue apron, further staining the greasy material. Then he turned and walked over to me. I shrank back into my crack, my hands tightening around the brick in my lap.

Barbecue Man leaned down until his eyes were level with mine. Not for the first time, I noticed how bright and green his gaze was. Like the lights on a Christmas tree. It would be Christmas soon, but I wouldn't have a tree this year. No presents, no family, nothing. All of it gone, burned to ash by the Fire elemental.

"*Thanks, kid,*" *Barbecue Man said.* "*You helped me out of a tight spot there. What's your name?*"

Barbecue Man wasn't doing anything threatening, but I could still sense the strength in his body. He was a dangerous man. I didn't want to do anything to upset him.

"*Gen . . . Gen . . .*" *It was all I could get out. My full name was too much to say right now.*

"*Gin?*" *he asked.* "*Like the liquor?*"

I nodded, too afraid to do anything else. Barbecue Man studied me, taking in my ripped jeans and the too-big shoes I'd dug out of the trash.

"*Where's your family?*" *he asked in a not-unkind voice, considering the blood on his hands and apron.*

"*Dead,*" *I whispered.* "*Everyone's dead and gone.*"

Barbecue Man studied me for a moment longer, then nodded, as if he'd decided something. "*You look hungry, Gin. Would you like to come inside and get something else to eat? Maybe clean up a bit? It's warm inside the restaurant.*"

Oh, to be warm, if only for a little while. But I wasn't stupid. I didn't trust Barbecue Man. Not after what I'd just seen him do. But I had my magic and my will to survive. If he tried anything, well, I supposed one more death on my conscience didn't much matter at this point. How much hotter could they make hell?

I nodded. "Yes, sir."

Barbecue Man straightened and held out his hand. I took it, and he pulled me to my feet, leading me inside . . .

"Gin?"

A pair of fingers snapped in front of my face, breaking through my memories. I jerked back and looked at Finn.

"Are you still with us?" Finn asked.

I shook away the rest of the old memory. "I'm sorry, what did you say?"

He nodded his head at the casket. "I was asking if you wanted to throw your flower in now. Before they start covering up the casket."

Sometime during my trip down memory lane, the preacher had finished speaking, and the service had ended. A couple of guys in dirt-stained coveralls leaned on shovels in the distance, impatient to get on with their grungy work.

"Of course," I murmured.

I stepped forward. Finn had already tossed his flower in, and a white rose rested on top of the golden wood. So did two others, a pink rose from Jo-Jo and a black one from Sophia. I clutched my red rose. The thorns dug into the spider rune scar on my right palm, pricking my skin, drawing my blood, but I didn't care. I let out a deep breath and threw my rose on top of the others.

The petals spread out when they hit the surface of the casket, kissing it like I had the old man's face just before they'd shut the lid on him.

"Good-bye, Fletcher," I whispered.

* 32 *

One by one, the other mourners came over to Finn to pay him their respects and tell him how sorry they were about the old man. A few offered me their condolences as well, but most of the attention focused on Fletcher's son, not the stray girl he'd taken in off the streets. As it should be, I supposed.

During a lull, I wandered over to Roslyn Phillips. The vampire wore a somber black suit, but the subdued fabric did little to disguise the lush curves of her body. A matching pillbox hat perched on top of her head, and a faint breeze made the lacy veil flutter against her cheeks. I moved to stand beside her, and we both watched Finn talk to a dwarf bent double with rheumatism, arthritis, and old age.

"Good of you to come," I said in a soft voice. "I know it means a lot to Finn."

Roslyn nodded. "I wanted to be here for him. The least I could do."

"You mean since you inadvertently got his father killed?"

The vampire stiffened like I'd just stabbed her with one of my knives. Her shocked eyes met mine. "How did you—"

"How did I figure it out?" I shrugged. "I'll admit it took me awhile. The whole time Alexis James was chasing me, I couldn't figure out why she'd picked me to set up or even how she'd found Fletcher in the first place. But she told me that night in the rock quarry. You heard her. She got the information from one of Gordon Giles's hooker friends, the one whose daughter was raped, the one I killed Cliff Ingles for."

I stared at Roslyn. "Gordon had a whole stack of photos of himself with prostitutes, most of whom wore the heart-and-arrow necklace that's the signature for your club. The hooker Alexis squeezed for information, she was one of your girls, wasn't she?"

After a moment, Roslyn jerked her head in confirmation. No use denying it now.

"I imagine the hooker came to you, wanting time off to take care of her daughter, who'd been so brutally raped and beaten. You told her about Fletcher and Finn. That they could arrange certain . . . accidents for people. When Alexis James had Stephenson pick her up, the hooker had to give them something to save her own skin—and she picked Fletcher and Finn."

"I thought I was doing her a favor. I never dreamed this would happen. If I'd known how it was going to turn out—" Roslyn started.

"Save it," I snapped. "It's done now. There's no changing it."

We stood there, side by side, and watched another mourner come up to Finn. Tension radiated off Roslyn's body like cold did mine.

"Are you going to tell Finn?" she finally asked.

I waited a few seconds, letting her sweat. "No. There's no reason for him to know, and it would only sour things between the two of you."

"I really do care for him," Roslyn murmured.

I stared at her with my cold, gray eyes. "I know you do. And he cares for you, which is why I'm letting you live. That, and Catherine."

Roslyn frowned. "Catherine?"

"She needs you. I know what it's like to be without your family. That little girl deserves better." I turned so Roslyn felt the full force of my hard stare. "But if you ever mention what Finn and I do to anyone else, I will slice you up and burn the leftovers. And anything, *anything,* Finn or I need that you can provide, you will from now on until I say otherwise. No questions asked. Understood?"

After a moment, Roslyn slowly nodded. Relief shimmered in her eyes. She knew she'd made a mistake—and that I was letting her off easy.

"Good," I snapped. "Now go pay your respects to Finn, before I change my fucking mind."

I drifted away from the crowd and headed toward the very top of the cemetery. Fletcher Lane wasn't the only person buried here that I'd known.

A series of five graves lay atop the ridge, shaded by

a massive maple that seemed to pierce the sky with its arcing limbs. A stone statue had been mounted above the five plots, marking them. Even though thick curls of kudzu covered the stone and the rest of it had been pitted by the rain and wind, the shape was unmistakable. A giant snowflake. The rune of the Snow family, my murdered family.

My eyes drifted down from the statue to the graves themselves. My father, Tristan's, tombstone was the most weather-worn. He'd died when I'd been a child. I barely recalled his gray eyes, much less what he'd been like. But the others—I remembered them in vivid detail. Eira, my mother. Annabella, my older sister. And Bria, the baby of the family. Runes marked their tombstones. A snowflake, an ivy vine, and a primrose, just like the three drawings I'd done.

I walked past their graves until I came to the fifth one on the end of the row.

Genevieve Snow. Beloved Daughter and Sister. That's what the tombstone said, along with the dates of my birth and supposed death. A rune had also been carved into the stone. A small circle with eight thin rays radiating out of it.

A spider rune—identical to the scars on my palms.

I'd thought I'd feel something staring at my own tombstone, my own cold grave, but I didn't. Just . . . emptiness at everything I'd lost. First my family, now Fletcher. Not much left for me to hold on to.

"A friend of yours?" a low voice called out behind me.

I turned to stare at Donovan Caine.

The detective stood a few feet away. He wore a black funeral suit that outlined the lean strength of his body. Caine moved to stand beside me. As always, he walked with that loose, easy confidence I found so attractive. But the detective looked a little thinner than I remembered. A little more haggard, and the lines on his face cut a little deeper into his bronze skin, as though something was haunting him. Something he just couldn't quite shake. I wondered if it was me. I'd certainly thought about him often enough in the week since the incident at the rock quarry.

Donovan's eyes met mine. Emotions flashed in the hazel depths, the way they always did. Weariness, resolve, curiosity. Caine's gaze slid down my body, taking in my black pants suit and low pumps, before flicking back to my hair. A chocolate brown color now, with caramel highlights. As close as Jo-Jo had been able to dye it to my natural color. Letting that grow in would take time. It always did. Like so many other things.

His golden gaze read the tombstone. "A friend? Or was this someone you killed?"

I thought of the happy, innocent little girl I'd been and the night everything had changed. The night my mother and sister had been murdered. "You might say that. What are you doing here?"

Donovan jerked his chin at the mourners below. "I came to pay my respects."

"How did you find out about Fletcher?" I asked.

He shrugged. "People are a lot more willing to do me favors these days. I asked one of the rookies to pull all the deaths that happened the night Gordon Giles died. There was only one that matched the cell phone picture you showed me."

"I see."

Donovan hesitated. "I'm—I'm sorry about him, Gin. I know he was Finn's father, that he was important to you."

I gave him a wry smile. "Thank you, detective."

We stood on the hill watching people drift away to their cars. Respects had been paid, and the appropriate words had been said. Now it was time to go back to the land of the living. Something Fletcher wasn't a part of anymore.

"I saw you on television the other day," I said. "Nice medal the mayor gave you for solving the Gordon Giles case. Very big and shiny."

Donovan shifted on his feet. "It's going into a drawer, with all the rest of them."

More silence.

"Why did you really come here, detective?" I asked. "Last time we saw each other, you came within a hair's breadth of trying to kill me for murdering your partner."

He rubbed his hand through his short, black hair and barked out a laugh. "Fuck if I know."

"Maybe it's because of this."

I grabbed his tie, pulled him close, and kissed him. Donovan stiffened, momentarily shocked by my boldness. But then, the heat flared between us, as bright and strong as ever. A flame, a fire that wouldn't die. Donovan growled, wound his hand in my hair, and pulled me closer, until I was flush against him. I breathed in, letting his sharp, clean scent fill my nose. His tongue met mine, and we melted into each other, pouring our feelings, our frustrations, our desires, into one perfect kiss.

All too soon it ended.

I dropped my hands from the detective's tie. Donovan Caine backed away. Our gazes met, gray on gold. Then the detective turned on his heel and walked away. I waited a minute before following him at a slower pace.

Donovan Caine went over and said something to Finn, who looked surprised by the detective's sudden appearance. Finn hesitated a moment, and the two of them shook hands. Then Caine left, walking past Fletcher's casket. He didn't look back.

I strolled over to Finn, who was staring at the detective's retreating form with a confused look on his face.

"I never thought he'd show up here," Finn said.

"Well, he did. But he's gone now. I don't think we'll be seeing the detective for a while."

Not until Donovan Caine could come to terms with whatever he felt for me. Not until he could reconcile wanting me, the woman who'd killed his partner, with the guilt he felt about not avenging Ingles's death. Not until he could accept all the dark things I'd done, all the people I'd killed—if he ever could.

There was nothing I could do to change how the detective felt or hurry him along. But I was the Spider. I was patient enough to wait him out.

I reached into my purse, pulled out a pair of black sunglasses, and slid them over my eyes. "I'll see you in two weeks. Try not to get into too much trouble while I'm gone. I'd hate to have to interrupt my vacation to bail your ass out of a jam."

"Where are you going?" Finn asked.

"Key West," I replied. "I hear the cabana boys are particularly oily this time of year."

✶ 33 ✶

I got on a plane that afternoon. By midnight, I was listening to the sound of the ocean from the balcony of my hotel room. The wind whipped my hair around my face and blew the tang of salt up to me. The moon overhead painted everything a dull silver.

I raised my latest round of gin to the frothy ocean waves. Ice tinkled against the side of the glass. "Here's to you, Fletcher."

Only the ocean waves answered me, so I knocked back the liquor, closed the balcony door, and stumbled off to bed.

Over the next few days, I did all the things a tourist would normally do in Key West. Watched the sun set over Mallory Square. Visited Hemingway's home. Stared at the cats with too many toes. Took a couple of scuba diving tours. Bought myself some cheap shell jewelry and some real key limes. Drank tropical drinks until I never wanted to look at another pineapple or mango again.

Once I'd exhausted the tourist traps, I lounged by the ocean, reading books and admiring the hard bodies of the lifeguards and cabana boys. Fletcher was right. There were lots to choose from. I struck up a conversation with one of them, Renaldo, who was putting himself through school by working at my hotel. Renaldo made it clear he was more than willing to engage in a few hours of hot, sweaty, meaningless sex—and that he wouldn't even expect a tip afterward.

But his eyes were brown, not gold, and I sent him away.

I also spent a lot of time staring out at the horizon, sipping boat drinks, and thinking about what I wanted to do when I returned to Ashland. Because I didn't want to go back to being an assassin. I knew my strengths, my skills, my weaknesses. As the Spider, there was nothing left to prove to myself or anyone else. And it just wouldn't be the same without Fletcher. No one would be waiting at the Pork Pit late at night for me. No one would ask if I'd been hurt or how things had gone.

No one would care.

More importantly, the old man had wanted me to retire. That had been his final wish, and I was going to honor it, even though I had no clue what I was going to do with myself. But it was time to use my skills for something else. What that something else was, I didn't know yet.

But I found myself strangely eager to find out.

*   *   *

I returned to Ashland two weeks later, feeling refreshed, rejuvenated, and still slightly sunburned and hung over from all the fruity boat drinks I'd had. I went straight to the Pork Pit, where the others had decided to wait to welcome me home.

It was late, and night had already fallen over Ashland. Blackness cloaked the street, except for the neon pig gleaming its bright blues and pinks over the front door of the Pork Pit. I stood outside in the inky shadows and looked in through the window. Finn, Jo-Jo, and Sophia had already gathered inside the storefront. Finn sipped a cup of chicory coffee at the counter. I could smell the warm, comforting fumes even out here on the street. Sophia pushed a mop back and forth across the floor. Jo-Jo fluttered back and forth, refilling Finn's cup, wiping down tables, checking on her sister.

Not the family I'd originally started out with, but a family nonetheless. One that I'd do anything to protect. I pulled open the front door. The bell chimed, and I walked through.

Everyone's head swiveled in my direction, and a moment later, I was bombarded with hugs, back slaps, and questions about my trip. Sophia, in particular, hugged me so hard she cracked my back. Felt good, though.

While the others chattered at me, my eyes swept over the interior of the restaurant. The door, the cash register, the stools. Everything that had been broken the night Fletcher died had been replaced. A dim shape beside the cash register caught my eye, and I realized what it was—the old man's copy of *Where the Red Fern Grows*. Sophia must have rescued it from the mess. Still, the Pit felt smaller without Fletcher here, emptier than it had been before, despite the others' presence. I wondered if it would always feel this way to me now.

But this was not the time to be melancholy, so I pushed my dark thoughts away and told the others all about my long-awaited vacation. Jo-Jo, in particular, was interested in my tales of oily cabana boys. Eventually, the four of us settled around one of the tables in the middle of the restaurant.

"I brought you all something," I said, reaching into the cheap straw tote bag I'd picked up in Key West.

Finn's green eyes lit up. He loved presents. "What is it? Money? Expensive liquor? Long-lost pirate treasure? Doubloons?"

I dumped a plastic bag of key limes onto his lap. Finn's face fell faster than a lopsided cake.

"Cheer up," I said. "If you're a good boy, I'll make you a key lime pie."

"I'd rather have some margaritas," he whined.

"You're getting a pie, so suck it up."

Finn stuck his lip out in a mock pout.

I reached back into my bag and pulled out a small glass bottle shaped like a seashell. "And for you, Jo-Jo, I have this fine bottle of perfume."

She pulled off the stopper and sniffed. "Smells fresh and salty, like the ocean. I like it."

"And finally, for Sophia, there's this lovely item."

I pulled a pale pink leather collar out of the bottom of the bag. Tiny, mother-of-pearl sand dollars dangled from it. The dwarf took it from me. She stared at it a moment, then shook it once. The sand dollars clacked together like wind chimes. Sophia's lips curved up into a small smile. Happiest I'd ever seen her.

"And there you have it," I said. "The sum total of my vacation."

I didn't tell them that I was permanently on vacation from being an assassin. That I'd retired from being the Spider. There would be time enough to do that later.

Finn pushed his bag of limes to one side of the table. "Well, I've got something for you too. Several things, actually."

I raised an eyebrow. "Like what?"

Finn cleared his throat. "Dad's estate was settled today. The will was read. Besides a boatload of cash, he left you something else."

"Really? What?"

Finn opened his hands wide and smiled. "Ta-da."

I wasn't easily surprised, but my mouth dropped open. All thought fled. It took me a moment to form coherent words. "Fletcher left me the Pork Pit? Why would he do that? It's not like I need the money—or the headache."

"Because he knew how much you love the restaurant," Jo-Jo said.

"Love it," Sophia rasped her agreement.

My eyes traced over the booths, the tables, the cash register, the bloody book sitting beside it. I did love the restaurant, just as much as I'd loved the old man. They'd always been one and the same in my mind. And now it was mine. A comforting warmth filled my chest that I hadn't felt since before the night Fletcher died.

"Dad also wanted you to have this." Finn handed me a small envelope.

Gin. My name was scrawled across the front in Fletcher's tight, controlled handwriting. Fletcher. I missed the old man.

But that didn't keep me from tearing open the envelope. An index card lay inside. On the front was a note that read: *Don't ever think it was your fault. Whatever it was, however it happened, you couldn't have stopped it. Do us both a favor and don't stay in the business too long. Live in the daylight, kid. Love, Fletcher.*

My eyes misted over just a bit, but I turned the card over and read the rest of the writing. It took a moment for the words to register, but when they did, I shook my head and smiled.

"Cumin. That's the secret ingredient in his barbecue sauce. Of course. Cumin." I waved the index card at Finn. "Fletcher finally told me his secret ingredient. After he died. The old bastard."

Finn smiled and raised his coffee in a silent toast to his father. The bright green of his eyes reminded me of the old man.

"Are you sure you're okay with this?" I asked. "Me taking over the restaurant? Fletcher should have left it to you. He was your father."

"Are you kidding?" Finn asked. "Barbecue stains are hell on silk shirts. Believe me, I'm okay with you having the restaurant. Besides, he was your father, too."

Once again, I thought of the night Fletcher had taken me in. How he'd saved me from selling my body on the streets. How he'd taught me to be strong and to always survive. Fletcher Lane might be gone, but I'd never forget what he'd given me.

"Yeah," I said. "I guess he was."

The party broke up soon after that. But right before she left, Jo-Jo Deveraux pulled me aside and handed me a thick manila folder.

"Here," she said. "Fletcher wanted you to have this too. It was something he'd been working on for a long time. What you do with it is completely up to you."

I hefted the folder. It was heavy, with at least an inch of paper stuffed inside it. "What's this?"

"You'll see," the dwarf said. "We'll talk about it later, when you're ready."

I frowned at her mysterious tone, but Jo-Jo smiled at me.

"Now tell me again which hotel you stayed at," the dwarf said. "I want to get me a good look at those cabana boys when I take my vacation in the spring."

By the time I said my good-byes it was almost midnight. I left the Pork Pit, but I didn't go straight home. I was retired, not stupid. I walked three blocks, cut through twice as many alleys, and doubled back before I even thought about heading to my building. Before I entered my apartment, I pressed my fingers against the stone that outlined the door. The vibrations were low and steady just like always. No visitors since I'd been gone. Good.

I stepped inside the apartment and flicked on the light. Everything looked the same as I'd left it—including the three rune drawings on the mantel. I wandered over to the pictures. A snowflake, an ivy vine, and a primrose. The symbols for my dead family.

But now one was missing, one I needed to add. I was going to do another drawing, I decided. One of Fletcher, or maybe the Pork Pit. Didn't much matter either way. They were one and the same to me.

Although I wanted to take a shower and fall into bed, I plopped on the sofa and opened the thick envelope Jo-Jo Deveraux had given me. Might as well see what secrets it contained, what Fletcher had been working on before he'd died that merited so much paper. Curiosity. I really needed to learn to control that.

I undid the clasp, pulled out the thick sheaf of paper, and started to read. It was a report written in mannish cursive. *Sept. 21, fire reported at 7:13 a.m. Residence fully engulfed in flames on arrival. Multiple casualties feared . . .*

It took a few seconds for me to realize I wasn't reading about some strange fire. That I'd been there, that I'd felt the flames tongue my skin like an eager, sloppy lover. I looked at the next page. A glossy photo showed the charred remains of a human body, arms outstretched as if begging for help—or mercy. My stomach clenched, but I kept going.

Autopsy results, photos, police reports, newspaper clippings. It was all here. Everything that had ever been written, photographed, gossiped, and speculated about the fiery murder of my mother and two sisters seventeen years ago.

Fletcher.

The old man had known exactly who I was, why I'd been living on the streets, what had happened to my family. Somehow, I'd let it slip, or he'd put it together himself. It must have taken him years to compile this information. But he had.

And he'd left it with Jo-Jo to give to me.

Why? I wondered. Why? What was the point of this? My mother and older sister, Annabella, were dead. I'd seen them die with my own eyes. Reduced to ash. They weren't coming back. And Bria, my baby sister, had been buried alive, pulverized, by the collapsing rubble of our house. All that had been left of her had been some blood-stains. She was gone too.

So why had Fletcher left me the information? What had the old man expected me to do with it? Track down the Fire elemental who'd killed my family? Take my revenge on the bitch? I'd been blindfolded when she'd been torturing me. I had no idea who she was, much less if she was even still alive. Or had the old man wanted me to do something else entirely with the information?

My hands started shaking, and I threw the papers down on the coffee table before I scattered them everywhere. But I wasn't quite quick enough. A loose sheet of paper and a photo slid out of the stack and landed facedown on the floor. I stared at them. A second ticked by. Then five, then ten more. A minute later, I was still staring at them.

Finally, I sighed. Fucking, fucking curiosity. The one thing I wish the old man hadn't taught me.

I picked up the paper first. It was blank, except for a solitary name written in Fletcher's handwriting. *Mab Monroe*. The Fire elemental's name was underlined twice, but that was it. There was nothing else on the paper. Why would the old man have written her name down and stuck it in this file? Was she the elemental who'd killed my family? Did she know who did? Fletcher had always longed to see her die. Was it because of me? And what she might have done to my family? Or did the old man have some other vendetta against her? Something I'd never known about?

My head pounded, and I rubbed my temple. After a moment, I looked away from the name. I was too shocked to puzzle out the old man's motives tonight, so I set the sheet aside and reached for the photo. It had landed facedown on the floor. I stared at it a few seconds before my hands felt steady enough to pick it up. There was a date on the back written in Fletcher's tight hand. August of this year. Only a few weeks ago. I turned the photo over—

And my heart stopped.

Because the woman smiling out of the picture looked like my mother. Long, blond hair, cornflower blue eyes, rosy skin. But it wasn't my mother. Her nose was a touch too long, her mouth a bit wide, her eyes harder than I remembered. But I still recognized her face, even though I'd only been thirteen the last time I'd seen her and she had just been eight. Seventeen years had passed since then. The terrible night I'd thought she'd died along with our mother and older sister.

My eyes latched on to the necklace she wore. A silver-stone pendant rested in the hollow of her throat. A rune, shaped like a primrose. The symbol for beauty. The same rune I had up on my mantel.

"Bria," I whispered. "Bria."

My baby sister was alive.

Turn the page for a sneak peek at the next book
in the Elemental Assassin series,

Web of Lies

Jennifer Estep

Coming soon from Pocket Books

"Freeze! Nobody move! This is a robbery!"

Wow. Three clichés in a row. Somebody was seriously lacking in the imagination department.

But the shouted threats scared someone, who squeaked out a small scream. I sighed. Screams were always bad for business. Which meant I couldn't ignore the trouble that had just walked into my restaurant—or deal with it the quick, violent way I would have preferred. A silverstone knife through the heart is enough to stop most trouble in its tracks. Permanently.

So I pulled my gray gaze up from the paperback copy of *The Odyssey* that I'd been reading to see what all the fuss was about.

Two twentysomething men stood in the middle of the Pork Pit, looking out of place among the restaurant's blue and pink vinyl booths. The dynamic duo sported black trench coats that covered their thin T-shirts and flapped against their ripped, rock star jeans. Neither one wore a hat or gloves, and the fall chill had painted their ears and fingers a bright, cherry red. I wondered how long they'd stood outside, gathering up the courage to come in and yell out their trite demands.

Water dripped off their boots and spread across the faded blue and pink pig tracks that covered the restaurant floor. I eyed the men's footwear. Expensive black leather, thick enough to keep out the November cold. No holes, no cracks, no missing bootlaces. These two weren't your typical, desperate junkies looking for a quick cash score. No, they had their own money—lots of it, from the looks of their pricey shoes, vintage T-shirts, and designer jeans. These two rich punks were robbing my barbecue restaurant just for the thrill of it.

Worst fucking decision they'd ever made.

"Freeze!" the first guy repeated, as if we all hadn't heard him before.

He was a beefy man with spiky blond hair held up by some sort of shiny, hair-care product. Probably a little giant blood in his family tree somewhere, judging from his six-foot-six frame and large hands. Despite his twentysomething years, baby fat still puffed out his face like a warm, oozing marshmallow. The guy's brown eyes flicked around the restaurant, taking in everything from the baked beans bubbling on the stove behind me to the hissing French fryer to the battered, bloody copy of *Where the Red Fern Grows* mounted on the wall beside the cash register.

Then, Beefcake turned his attention to the people inside the Pork Pit to make sure we were all following his demands. Not many folks to look at. Mondays could be slow, made even more so today by the cold bluster of wind and rain outside. The only other people in the restaurant besides me and the would-be robbers were my dwarven cook, Sophia Deveraux, and a couple of customers—two college-age women wearing skinny jeans and tight T-shirts not unlike those the robbers sported.

The women sat shocked and frozen, eyes wide, barbecue beef sandwiches halfway to their lips. Sophia stood next to the stove, her black eyes flat and disinterested as she watched the beans bubble. She grunted once and gave them a stir with a metal spoon. Nothing much ever bothered Sophia.

The first guy raised his hand. A small knife glinted in his red, chapped fingers. A hard, thin smiled curved my lips. I liked knives.

"Chill out, Jake," the second guy muttered. "There's no need to scream."

I looked at him. Where his buddy was blond and beefy, robber number two was short and bone-thin. His wispy hair stuck up due to uncontrollable cowlicks, instead of an overabundance of product. The locks were a bright red that had probably earned him the nickname Carrot, at some point. Carrot shoved his hands into his holey pockets, shifted on his feet, and stared at the floor, clearly wanting to be somewhere other than here. A reluctant sidekick at best. Probably tried to talk his buddy out of this nonsense. He should have tried harder.

"No names, *Lance*. Remember?" Jake snarled and glared at his friend.

Lance's bony body jerked at the sound of his own name, like someone had zapped him with a cattle prod. His mouth dropped open, but he didn't say anything.

I used one of the day's credit card receipts to mark my place in *The Odyssey*. Then, I closed my book, straightened, slid off my stool, and stepped around the long counter that ran along the back wall of the Pork Pit. Time to take out the trash.

The first guy, Jake, saw me move out of the corner of his eye. But instead of charging at me like I'd expected, the half-giant moved to his left and jerked one of the girls up and out of her booth—a Hispanic girl with a pixie haircut. She let out another squeaky scream. Her thick, beef sandwich flew out of her hand and spattered against one of the storefront windows. The barbecue sauce looked like blood running down the smooth, shiny glass.

"Leave her alone, you bastard!" the other woman shouted.

She jumped to her feet and charged at Jake, who backhanded her. He might have been only a half-giant, but there was still enough strength in his blow to lift the woman off her feet and sent her careening into a table. She flipped over the top and hit the floor—hard. A low groan sounded.

By this point, Sophia Deveraux had become a little more interested in things. The dwarf moved to stand beside me. The silver skulls hanging from the black leather collar around her neck tinkled together like wind chimes. The skulls matched the ones on her black T-shirt.

"You take right," I murmured. "I've got left."

Sophia grunted and moved to the other end of the counter, where the second woman had been thrown.

"Lance!" Jake jerked his head at the injured woman and Sophia. "Watch those bitches!"

Lance wet his lips. Pure, uncomfortable misery filled his pale face, but he trotted over to the injured woman, who had pushed herself up to her hands and knees. She shoved her wild tangle of blue-black hair out of her face. Her pale blue eyes burned with immediate hate. A fighter, that one.

But Lance didn't see her venomous look. He was too busy staring at Sophia. Most people did. The dwarf had been Goth before Goth was cool—a hundred years ago or so. In addition to her skull collar and matching T-shirt, Sophia Deveraux sported black jeans and boots. Pink lipstick covered her lips, contrasting with the black glitter eye shadow on her eyelids and the natural pallor of her face. Today, the color motif extended up to her hair. Pale pink streaks shimmered among her cropped black locks.

But Jake wasn't so dumbstruck. He pulled the first woman even closer, turned her around, held her in front of him, and raised the knife to her throat. Now, he had a human shield. Terrific.

But that wasn't the worst part. A bit of red sparked in the depths of his brown eyes, like a match flaring to life. Magic surged like a hot, summer wind through the restaurant, pricking my skin with power and making the scars on my palms itch. Flames spewed out from between Jake's clenched fingers, traveling up and settling on the knife. The blade glowed red-orange from the sudden burst of heat.

Well, well, well, Jake the robber was just full of surprises. Because in addition to being a petty thief, Jake the half-giant was also an elemental—someone who could control one of the four elements. Fire, in his case.

My smile grew a little harder, a little tighter. Jake wasn't the only one here who was an elemental—or very, very dangerous. I cocked my head, reaching out with my Stone magic. All around me, the battered brick of the Pork Pit murmured with unease, sensing the emotional upheaval that had already taken place inside and my dark intentions now.

"I said, *nobody fucking move.*"

Jake's earlier scream dropped to a hoarse whisper. His eyes were completely red now, as though someone had set two flickering rubies into his baby-fat face. A rivulet of sweat dripped down his temple, and his head bobbed in time to some music only he could hear. Jake was high on something—alcohol, drugs, blood, his own magic, maybe all of the above. Didn't much matter. He was going to be dead in another minute. Two, tops.

The red glow in Jake's eyes brightened as he reached for his magic again. The flames flashing on the silver blade flared hotter and higher, until they licked at the girl's neck, threatening to burn her. Tears streamed down her heart-shaped face, and her breath came in short, choked sobs, but she didn't move. Smart girl.

My eyes narrowed. It was one thing to try to rob the Pork Pit, my barbecue restaurant, my gin joint. Down-on-their-luck elementals, vampire hookers, and other bums strung out on their own magic and jonesing for more could be excused that stupidity. But nobody—*nobody*—threatened my paying customers. I was going to enjoy taking care of this lowlife. As soon as I got him away from the girl.

So I held up my hands in a placating gesture and kept the cold, calm violence out of my gray eyes as best I could. "I'm the owner. Gin Blanco. I don't want any trouble. Let the girl go, and I'll open the cash register for you. I won't even call the police after you leave."

Mainly because it wouldn't do me any good. The cops in the southern metropolis of Ashland were as crooked as forks of lightning. The esteemed members of the po-po barely bothered to respond to robberies, especially in this borderline Southtown neighborhood, much less do something useful, like catch the perps after the fact.

Jake snorted. "Go ahead. The police can't touch me, bitch. Do you know who my father is?"

In addition to being a Fire elemental, Jake was also a name-dropping prima donna. A wonder he'd survived this long.

"Don't tell them *that*!" Lance hissed.

Jake snorted and turned his red eyes to his buddy.

"I'll tell them whatever I want. So shut your sniveling mouth."

"Just let the girl go, and I'll open the cash register," I repeated in a firm voice, hoping my words would penetrate Jake's magic high and sink into his thick skull.

His red eyes narrowed to slits. "You'll open the cash register, or the girl dies—and you along with her."

He jerked the girl back against him, and the flames coating the knife burned even brighter, taking on an orange-yellow hue. The silverstone scars on my palms—the ones shaped like spider runes—itched at the influx of magic. I tensed, afraid he was going to do the girl right here, right now. I could kill him—easily—but probably not before he hurt the girl with his magic. I didn't want that to happen. It wasn't going to happen. Not in my restaurant. Not now, not again.

"Jake, calm down," Lance pleaded with his friend. "No one's making any trouble. It's going just like you said it would. Quick and easy. Let's just get the money and go."

Jake stared at me, the flames dancing in his red eyes matching the movement of the ones on the knife blade. Pure, malicious glee filled his crimson gaze. Even if I hadn't been good at reading people, that emotion alone would have told me that Jake enjoyed using his magic, loved the power it gave him, the feeling of being invincible. And that he wasn't going to be satisfied with just stealing my money. No, Jake was going to use his Fire power to kill everyone in the restaurant just because he could, because he wanted to show off his magic and prove he was a real badass. Unless I did something to stop him.

"Jake? The money?" Lance asked again.

After a moment, the fire dimmed in Jake's eyes. He lowered the glowing blade a few inches, giving the girl some much-needed air. "Money. Now."

I opened the register, grabbed all the wrinkled bills inside, and held them out. All Jake had to do was let go of the girl long enough to step forward and grab the cash, and I'd have him. *Come on, you bastard. Come and play with Gin.*

But some sense of self-preservation must have kicked in, because the beefy half-giant jerked his head. Lance left his post by the injured woman, tiptoed forward, snatched the money out of my hand, and stepped back. I didn't bother grabbing him and using him as a hostage. Guys like Jake weren't above leaving their friends twisting in the wind—or stuck on the edge of my blade.

Jake licked his thick, chapped lips. "How much? How much is there?"

Lance rifled through the green bills. "A little more than two hundred."

"That's it? You're holding out on me, bitch," Jake snarled.

I shrugged. "Monday's a slow day. And not many people like to get out in this kind of cold weather, not even for barbecue."

The Fire elemental glared at me, debating my words and what he could do about them. I smiled back. He didn't know what he'd gotten himself into—or who he was messing with.

"Let's just go, Jake," Lance pleaded. "Some cops could come along any second."

Jake tightened his grip on his flaming knife. "No. Not until this bitch tells me what she did with the rest of the money. This is the most popular restaurant in the neighborhood. There had to be more than two hundred dollars in that cash register. So where did you hide it, bitch? You wearing a money belt underneath that greasy blue apron?"

I shrugged. "Why don't you come and find out, you pathetic fuck?"

His eyes grew darker, redder, angrier, until I thought the sparking flames flickering inside might actually shoot out of his magic-tinted irises. Jake let out a furious growl. He shoved the girl away and charged at me, the knife held straight out.

My smile widened. Finally. Time to play.

I waited until he got in range, then stepped forward and turned my body into his. I slammed my elbow into his solar plexus and swept his feet out from under him. Jake coughed, stumbled, and did a header onto the floor. His temple clipped the side of one of the tables as he went down, and a resulting bit of blood spattered onto my jeans. The sharp blow was enough to make Jake lose his grip on his Fire magic. The prickling power washing off him vanished, and the flames snuffed out on the knife in his hand. The hot metal hissed and smoked as it came into contact with the cool floor.

I looked to my right. The woman Jake had thrown across the room scrambled to her feet and prepared to launch herself at Lance. But Sophia grabbed the girl's waist and pulled her back. The woman started to struggle, but the Goth dwarf shook her head and stepped forward, putting herself in front of the customer. Lance swallowed once and backed up, ready to turn and run. But Sophia was quicker. The dwarf punched him once in the stomach. Lance went down like an anvil had been dropped on him. He crumpled to the floor and didn't move.

One down, one to go.

I turned my attention back to Jake, who'd rolled over onto his side. Blood dripped down the side of his head where he'd cut himself on the corner of the table. The half-giant saw me standing over him, curled halfway up, and slashed at me with his cooling knife. Idiot. He didn't even come close to nicking me. After Jake made another flailing pass with the blade, I crouched down and grabbed his wrist, bending it back so he couldn't move it. I eyed the weapon in his locked hand.

"Fuck," I said. "Get a real knife. You couldn't even peel potatoes with that thing."

Then, I plucked the blade from his chapped fingers and snapped his thick wrist.

Jake howled in pain, but the noise didn't bother me. Hadn't in years. I shoved him down onto his back, then straddled him, a knee on either side of his beefy chest, squeezing in and putting pressure on his ribs. Giants, even half-giants like Jake, hated it when they had trouble breathing. Most people did.

I adjusted and tightened my grip on the knife, ready

to drive it into his heart. A flimsy weapon, but it would do the job. Just about anything would, if you had enough strength and determination to put behind it. I had plenty of both.

A small, choked sob sounded, drawing my attention away from Jake and his high-pitched, keening howls. My gray eyes flicked up. The girl huddled underneath a table a few feet away, her knees pulled up to her chest, her eyes as big as quarters in her face, tears sliding down her flushed cheeks.

A position I'd been in, once upon a time.

A couple of months ago, the girl and her tears wouldn't have bothered me. I would have killed Jake and his friend, washed the blood off my hands, and asked Sophia to get rid of the bodies before I closed up the Pork Pit for the night.

That's what assassins did.

And I was the Spider, one of the very best.

But I'd had an epiphany of sorts two months ago, when my mentor had been brutally tortured and murdered inside the Pork Pit—in the very spot Jake and I were in right now. The old man, Fletcher Lane, had wanted me to retire, to take a different path in life, to live in the daylight a little, as he was so fond of saying. I'd followed Fletcher's advice and quit the assassin business after I'd killed Alexis James, the Air elemental who'd murdered him.

"Hmph."

Behind me, Sophia grunted. I looked over my shoulder at the dwarf, who still had hold of the other woman.

The girl was unsuccessfully trying to pry the dwarf's stubby fingers off her waist. Good luck with that. Sophia had a grip like death. Once she had you, she didn't let go—ever. My gray eyes locked with Sophia's black ones. Regret flashed in her dark gaze, and the dwarf shook her head just the tiniest bit. *No*, she was saying. Not in front of two witnesses.

Sophia was right. Witnesses were bad. I couldn't gut Jake with the two girls watching and get rid of the body afterward. Not in my own restaurant. Not without blowing my cover as Gin Blanco and leaving everything behind. And I wasn't going to do that. Not for a piece of trash like the Fire elemental. But that didn't mean I couldn't let Jake know exactly who he was dealing with.

I waited until there was a lull in Jake's howls, then tipped his head up with the knifepoint and gazed into his eyes. They'd lost all hint of their red, fiery magic. Now, his brown irises were wide and glossy with panic, fear, pain.

"You ever come to my restaurant and fuck with me or my customers again, and I'll carve you up like a Thanksgiving turkey."

I slashed down with the knife, breaking the skin on his beefy neck. Jake yelped at the sting and clawed at the slight wound with his sausage-thick fingers. I slapped his hand away and nicked him again. The smell of warm, coppery blood filled my nose. Something else that hadn't bothered me in a long, long time.

"Every time you move, I'm going to cut you again. Deeper and deeper. Nod your head if you understand."

Hatred flared in his gaze, taking the edge off the pain and panic, but he nodded.

"Good."

I clipped his temple with the knife hilt. Jake's head snapped to one side and fell onto the floor. Unconscious. Just like his friend Lance.

I stood up, wiped my fingerprints off the knife, and dropped the weapon on the floor. The half-giant didn't stir. Then, I got to my feet and headed for the girl, still crouched underneath the table.

She shrank back against the legs of a chair at my approach, like she wanted to melt into the metal. Her pulse fluttered like a mad butterfly against her temple. I put my friendliest, most trustworthy, charming, southern smile on my face and crouched down until I was eye-level with her.

"Come on, sweetheart," I said, holding out my hand. "It's over. Those men aren't going to hurt you now."

Her chocolate eyes darted to Jake lying on the floor. Her gaze flicked back to me, and she chewed her lip, her teeth white against her toffee skin.

"I'm not going to hurt you, either," I said in a soft voice. "Come on, now. I'm sure your friend wants to see how you are."

"Cassidy!" the other woman called out since Sophia still wasn't letting her go. "Are you all right?"

Her friend's voice penetrated Cassidy's fearful daze. She sighed and nodded her head. The girl reached out, and I grabbed her trembling hand. Cassidy's fingers felt like thin, fragile icicles against the thick scar embedded in my palm. I tugged the girl to her feet. She eyed me with understandable caution, so I kept my movements slow and small, not wanting to startle her.

"I'm fine, Eva," Cassidy said in a low voice. "Just a little shook up is all."

Sophia let go of the other woman, and I stepped back. Eva rushed forward and caught her friend in a tight hug. Cassidy wrapped her arms around the other women, and the two of them rocked back and forth in the middle of the restaurant.

I walked over to Sophia, who was watching the two women with a flat expression on her pale face.

"Friendship. Ain't it a beautiful thing?" I quipped.

"Hmph." Sophia grunted again.

But the corner of the Goth dwarf's lips turned up into a tiny smile.

The two girls hugged a minute longer before Eva pulled a cell phone out of her jeans.

"You call the cops," Eva told her friend. "I need to let Owen know I'm okay. You know how he is. He'll freak when he finds out about this."

Cassidy nodded her head in sympathetic agreement and pulled her own phone out of her jeans. The two women started dialing numbers, instead of asking me, the restaurant owner, to do it for them. Not surprising. If you wanted the cops, you called them yourself. You certainly didn't depend on the kindness of strangers to do it. Not in Ashland.

I frowned. Cops. Just what I needed. Some of Ashland's finest getting an eyeful of me, the former assassin, a Goth dwarf who liked to dispose of dead bodies in her spare time, and the two guys we'd so easily dispatched. Not the kind of attention I wanted to draw to myself, even if I was retired now. Nothing I could do about it now, though.

Sophia went back to the stove to check on her baked beans. Eva spoke in a low voice to someone on her phone. Cassidy finished her 911 call and sank into the nearest chair.

The girl stared at Jake on the floor, then her brown eyes flicked to the bloody knife. Her lower lip quivered, her eyes grew glossy, and her hands trembled. Trying to hold back the tears. Something else I'd had to do, once upon a time.

I walked over to the counter and picked up a glass cake plate filled with the black forest cookies I'd baked this morning.

"Here." I took the top off and held the plate out to her. "Have a cookie. They've got plenty of sugar and butter and chocolate in them. They'll help with the shakes."

Cassidy gave me a wan smile, took one of the chocolate treats, and bit into the concoction. The bittersweet chocolate melted in her mouth, and her eyes brightened with pleasure instead of worry.

Eva finished her call and sat down next to her friend. Her hands didn't tremble as she snapped her phone shut, and she looked at Jake with a thoughtful expression. The only sign anything had happened to Eva was a red welt on her cheek, where her face had smacked into the floor. The girl had a level head on her shoulders and a firm grip on her emotions. But that didn't mean she wouldn't crash later.

I held the plate out to her. "You, too."

Eva took a cookie, broke it in two, and stuffed half of it into her mouth. Not shy, either.

I also plucked one of the chocolate treats off the stack. Not because I had shaky nerves, but because they were damn good cookies. After a month of trying, I'd finally perfected the recipe.

I looked at the two unconscious men on the floor. Lance lay spread-eagle next to one of the booths where Sophia had dropped him. Blood continued to drip from the cuts on Jake's throat and temple, staining the floor a rusty brown.

I grabbed another cookie off the plate and watched him bleed.

Bestselling Urban Fantasy
from Pocket Books

BENEATH THE SKIN
BOOK THREE OF THE MAKER'S SONG
Adrian Phoenix
Chaos controls his future.
One mortal woman could be his
salvation. The countdown to
annihilation will begin with his choice.

THE BETTER PART OF DARKNESS
Kelly Gay
The city is alive tonight… and it's her job
to keep it that way.

BITTER NIGHT
A HORNGATE WITCHES BOOK
Diana Pharaoh Francis
In the fight to save humanity, she's the
weapon of choice.

DARKER ANGELS
BOOK TWO OF THE BLACK SUN'S DAUGHTER
M.L.N. Hanover
In the battle between good and evil
there's no such thing as a fair fight.

Available wherever books are sold or at
www.simonandschuster.com